Henry W. Bellows

The Old World in its new Face

Vol. I

SALZWASSER
VERLAG

Henry W. Bellows

The Old World in its new Face

Vol. I

Reprint of the original, first published in 1868.

1st Edition 2022 | ISBN: 978-3-37501-421-6

Verlag (Publisher): Salzwasser Verlag GmbH, Zeilweg 44, 60439 Frankfurt, Deutschland
Vertretungsberechtigt (Authorized to represent): E. Roepke, Zeilweg 44, 60439 Frankfurt, Deutschland
Druck (Print): Books on Demand GmbH, In de Tarpen 42, 22848 Norderstedt, Deutschland

THE OLD WORLD IN ITS NEW FACE.

IMPRESSIONS OF EUROPE IN 1867–1868.

BY

HENRY W. BELLOWS.

VOL. I.

NEW YORK:

HARPER & BROTHERS, PUBLISHERS,

FRANKLIN SQUARE.

1868.

These Letters, written for my Parishioners, are affectionately inscribed to the Members of the First Congregational Church in the City of New York, by their Friend and Minister,

HENRY W. BELLOWS.

CONTENTS TO VOLUME I.

THE OLD WORLD IN ITS NEW FACE.

I.

ON THE OCEAN.

AT SEA, STEAMSHIP VILLE DE PARIS,
230 Miles due West of Brest,
Monday, May 27, 1867.

NINE days total abstinence from the pen is such an exception in my paper-scratching existence, that nothing but severe illness on land, or that perpetual sickness called "the sea," could account for it. Yet this is the first drop of ink I have shed since the 18th inst., when, at just 3 P.M., I heard the ship-gun bid our adieus to friends and *terra firma*, and walked down into the low dining-saloon of this capital steamship to look at the lovely basket of flowers, arrayed in their own beauty and innocency—chiefly white buds—which my Sunday-school children had sent to speak their fragrant and dewy good-bye to their minister. "Nothing to do." That is the miracle that astonishes me, as I walk up and down the deck and peer into the various cubby-holes of this little world. Ville de Paris! Yes! It is Paris in miniature already here! French out of every mouth, French hours, French dishes, French "garçons," French taste, furniture, decorations, every thing except a French bottom and engine, which happily are Scotch, from the Clyde.

Our travels in foreign countries are begun from the start,

and when the first morning that breaks at sea is Sunday, and we find the whole day as secular as the necessary arrangements for sorting and seating the passengers make it, and not one sign of American Sabbath-decorum about it, we feel that we have indeed been turned loose into another world. And what a world it is! In this narrow, long, and slender vessel, three hundred and fifty feet long and not more than forty-five wide, smooth as a snake, and with a sting in its tail from which it seems fleeing in terror, are crowded over five hundred souls—three hundred and fourteen passengers and over two hundred hands. Although French largely predominates, there are Spaniards from Mexico and Cuba ; Germans from California and the West ; two Catholic bishops and thirteen priests on their way to the Convention called at Rome for the 29th June ; Jews and Infidels ; at least five-and-twenty passengers from the Pacific coast who lost connection at the Isthmus with the direct line via the West Indies to Europe, and were forced to come round and take the same company's steamer at New York. We have perhaps fifty American passengers, most of whom try to talk a little French, judging by myself, with indifferent success, even in the opinion of the waiters paid not to laugh at our jargon. It is a most orderly and respectable company of people ; too many for thorough sociableness, and on too short a voyage to develop the resources of the passengers. Madame Ristori and her troupe excite little curiosity. She is a better actress than sailor, and lies most of the time wrapped up in furs and hood, either on deck or in the saloon, resting from the fatigues of her eight months' campaign in America. A most motherly head of her dramatic family she seems to be. They flock respectfully but dependently about her, and receive her counsel or consolation or sympathy as that of a supreme authority. She has evidently great practical judgment and force of character.

Not a bit of theatrical nonsense in her manners, no painful
self-consciousness, no airs of importance, no attention to
pleasing effects ! She is simply independent, strong, patient,
and commanding, and nobody would for an instant imagine
her to be the idol of a flattering public, carrying home the
gold and frankincense of her triumphant progress. She has
made, it is said, two hundred and four thousand dollars by
her eight months' playing in America for herself alone, not to
speak of supporting and paying her large company, and putting seventy-five thousand dollars into Mr. Grau's pocket.
This is doubtless more than any dead or living actress or
actor ever made in the same period of time by force of individual genius. It is, perhaps, not to be wondered at that
Ristori (who must feel her personal charms to be on the
wane) returns in September to New York to put a fresh
sickle into this golden harvest. So swift a repetition of her
performances seems to me a doubtful experiment on a public
ninety-nine hundredths of whom understand not a word she
utters. American curiosity has been satisfied ; how much
interest there is in these performances beyond that, the next
season will test.

Among our passengers are some French officers returning
from Mexico. One of them has spent his three months' *leave*
in a rapid tour through the United States, and pronounces
the liberal opinion that fifty years will make America the
greatest country in the world.

Our voyage, now nine days long, and with probably only
one day between us and Brest, has been monotonous in the
extreme. We have had neither calm nor storm ; neither summer nor winter. Are not all seasons much alike on that
great leveler, the ocean? Not a whale has spouted for the
children's amusement, and the seldom lacking porpoises have
almost withdrawn their gambols from our track. Icebergs

have not disputed a foot of the way. An infrequent sail has
called every body to the deck, and the only excitement, besides passing the steamship Etna, has been the anxious inquiry by signal from a Prussian vessel returning from a long
cruise whether France and Prussia had declared war. The
cuisine of the Ville de Paris is excellent enough to furnish a
pastime of several hours a day to such of the passengers as
have succeeded in keeping any appetite for food. But a large
percentage have, from the very start, been unable to appear
at table except in the calmest weather, which has not been
two days out of the nine. No inconsiderable number of both
men and women have not yet left their berths. The crowded
passenger-list makes a double service of meals necessary, and
the *salon* is never accessible except early in the morning or
late in the evening, as a withdrawing-room. The ladies' cabin
is overflowed when a dozen women, with their dozen children,
are in it, and a darker and more dismal retreat can not be
conceived of. The smoking-room is small, and suits only
those to whom tobacco fumes have become a "native air."
In short the deck, which is swept by cold Marchy winds, or
the state-room, which is steeped in the inevitable odors of the
ship, is the alternative of the passengers, when not at their
meals—the cheerful part of their sea life. The funnel is a
great resource, standing between the passengers and freezing.
We gather round it and sit upon its hot flange until we can
decide whether it is better to perish with heat or cold, for any
intermediate state seems denied us. The calendar says it is
the last week in May ; our blood declares it to be November.
It is probable that any attempt to heat the cabin would be
only adding to our misery ; but let nobody fail to provide
every kind of wrap who crosses the Atlantic in any season.
A lazier life than ours is inconceivable, and I confess to a
dull enjoyment of this enforced idleness, even accompanied

by a general good-for-nothingness of feeling. The absence of all care and all necessity for exertion of will, intellect, heart, has been a negative pleasure.

The sea appears to paralyze the conscience for at least ten days. I feel no reproach in an idleness which on shore would drive me into bitter remorse. Nonsense or listlessness seem innocent and appropriate occupations. No reading is too trashy to be welcome. Even the tawdry melodramatic rags of Miss Muhlbach's historical (?) novels (a kind of red and yellow bull-fighting interest it is) are supportable, despite the terrible low level in moral tone, or artistic merit, in those tricky, popular, but short-lived stories, in which the historic facts are exaggerated and the fictitious quality is spoiled by an undigested and unconscientious habit in the author. I have not even had the comfort of being seasick. I have only been sick of the sea. Whether my poor stomach had not spirit enough left in its debilitated state for an insurrection, or whether my successive voyages have conquered the peculiar sensibility which produces nausea, I can not tell ; only certain it is that with my whole family miserably sick with *la maladie de la mer*, I have been wholly free from it even in the most agitated conditions of the ocean. My recollections of the sufferings of that horrible seasickness have all been revived by the spectacle around me. I half wonder at the courage that dares invoke that awful fiend, after repeated experiences of his malignity. Here is a man who lies helpless in his berth from American pier to European dock, and who has done it now for the twenty-fifth time. Here is a charming lady, with three lovely boys, who can not keep a mouthful down, and her nurse is sick, and her lusty baby cries by the ship bells from watch to watch. No wonder what a witty wag said of this spasmodic horror, " that the first day he feared he should *die*, and the second he feared he *should not."* No wonder ·that other more militant sufferer wanted to live only to thrash the unfeeling ·rogue who wrote " A life on the ocean wave, a home on the rolling deep."

Our steamer is a screw, and she has wriggled us into screws too. She rolls like a revolving auger, boring an endless gimlet-hole in the eastern horizon. What keeps her this side up, when, so far as the effect on the feelings are concerned, she might as well turn over and have done with it, is an ever-returning mystery. Down, down she goes, as if with the firmest purpose of sinking her bulwarks under the water ; and just as you are reconciled to the inevitable destruction, up, up she springs as lively as a grasshopper, to courtesy just as provokingly on the other side. Amid this " roly-poly," "gammon and spinach " have a poor chance with most ; but I am a lucky exception for this once. Our ship is a stanch vessel, no cracking and snapping of timbers or joints. She glides through the water like a bird through the air, without jerk and without pause, and her rate is rarely under three hundred miles a day. There is a good deal of discussion as to the water merits of side-wheels and screws. Doubtless, the side-wheeler is steadier, but the screw is safer and more economical, and will finally drive the side-wheels off the course. As to the question whether " pitching" or " rolling" is the less miserable, it must probably be settled by saying that the form not immediately present is the more tolerable of the two. The Ville de Paris would, doubtless, have carried us to Brest in nine days, but for the loss of part of one of the flanges of her screw, broken upon her last voyage. The captain reckoned the loss in speed at one hour per day. The French government exacts two hundred francs fine for every hour over ten days this line occupies in delivering the mail at Brest, but allows any hours gained within ten days by the swifter vessels, to be credited to the account of the slower steamers or the unfortunate passages. The waiters are compelled to report· all the *buono mano* given them by the passengers to .the owners, who, after deducting for breakages through carelessness of the *garçons*, divides the residue among all the ship's company. The steward of our part of the ship reported having paid in one hundred francs, of which he received only six and a half back !

We are now, 8 P.M., within one hundred and twenty miles of Brest, and are meeting numerous sailing vessels. The passengers are full of pleasant excitement in view of the end of the voyage. About half go ashore at Brest in the morning. Their trunks, in awful array, are already piled on the bow-deck. The Ristori company, it is said, (twenty-eight in number), have one hundred and four trunks, many of gigantic size. The residue of us keep on to Havre. The passage by rail to Paris, by Brest, is seventeen hours, and our friends who leave us expect to reach there by Wednesday morning at dawn. We hope to reach Havre about that time, and thence to take the cars for Rouen, about two hours' ride, and, spending one day there, to be in Paris on Thursday morning. We shall all go to bed to-night with the delicious expectation of opening our eyes upon a green coast and *terra firma* in the morning. Our voyage will then be really accomplished, although seventeen hours of coast-sail, passing, we hope, between Guernsey and Jersey, will remain to be done to-morrow. Meanwhile, let us thank God that the ocean is over-past in safety and essential comfort.

Spite of twenty clergymen on board, there has been no public service or worship on the ship, although two Sundays have passed. The majority are, doubtless, Catholics ; and, though invited to preach, we have preferred hearing the litany of the waves, and watching the altar-lamps of the stars, to leading so promiscuous a company in a verbal service which could be intelligible only to few, and grateful to a still smaller number. It is very different with our Christian brethren at Boston now, and I have talked over with our friend Staples, of Milwaukee, the anniversary week that begins to-day there. We were with them in spirit.

II.

FIRST VIEWS OF PARIS.

Paris, Sunday, June 3, 1867.
Grand Hotel de Castile,
101 Rue Richelieu.

WE arrived in Paris from Rouen by rail on Thursday, 5 P.M., May 30; found a clerk of Bowles, Drevet & Co. waiting for us, and were soon conveyed to our lodgings, on the third floor of an old palace in the very heart of Paris, within a stone's throw of all its busiest and most brilliant life. Here we have an establishment complete within itself—drawing-room, dining-room, two elegant chambers, and three or four pretty ones. We could set up housekeeping to-morrow if we liked. Instead of that, we go down stairs to the admirable restaurant of the Hotel Castile and take our meals when it is convenient.

Three days, during which we have not thrown off our sea-sickness, or become wonted to *terra firma*, do not afford much experience of French life. But it is time enough to leave a general impression, which may only lose vividness by familiarity. The general aspect of an external civilization, splendid and finished beyond our utmost conceptions, is undeniable. Paris, over whose principal streets and parks we have been continually wandering since we arrived, is one great spectacle of architectural vastness, splendor, taste and finish, where magnitude, costliness, arrangement, and effect combine to surprise and delight the eye. The city is laid out with scenic art. It seems the work of one mind, in which all the parts are subordinate to the whole, and every private interest or convenience is subservient to a public result. Whereas in England or America you feel that the public has what is left after private interests and convenience have all been satisfied, you feel here that the public helps itself *first* and flings the crumbs to the private citizen.   Paris, therefore, imperial and spectacular as it is, is to a wonderful extent cosmopolitan and universal, and, therefore, spite of Emperor and police, popular and democratic.   For what can be so enriching and satisfying to the humble and poor as the feeling that while they have little or no private property, they are actual share-holders in immense public wealth and conveniences and splendor, to the common use of which they are freely invited !   When I saw a poor woman sitting on the grass in the Tuileries, within stone's throw of the palace, with her day's work of sewing lying round her, and her baby playing near, apparently in full enjoyment of the public protection and of the beauty of the noble garden, I understood how despotism might be rendered very tolerable by an enlightened policy, and how France and Paris — with their glory and strength and beauty—stand in the place of private possessions to millions of her people.   They walk and stroll in her boulevards and parks, gratified and dazzled with the variety and elegance and charm that everywhere greets them, without those feelings of discontent which we might expect from not being able to appropriate more to strictly private use.

Every body is *at home* in Paris, in one sense, and in another every body is out of doors.   The people live in the streets and *cafés*.   The sidewalks are thronged, and you would think the whole population had agreed to take tea or coffee, wine or *eau de vie* together on the Boulevard des Italiens between 8 and 10 P.M. !   Such a perpetual picnic on pavements was never seen.   But then the pavements are so broad and smooth, and the streets so clean and free from dust, that it is almost as comfortable as and far more lively than eating and drinking at home. Homes of some sort these well-dressed, genteel people must have; but where are they? All the streets, little and big, seem given up to shops. Private doors, with names and numbers, are not seen. No porch or portico welcomes you to Mr. Smith's or Mr. Jones's residence! You find after awhile that all except the selectest few live in apartments; three or four rooms on a floor—and that you approach them usually through a court opening into an interior square, from which, by a common staircase, you ascend to your *entresol*, your first story, two flights up, your second, three, and so on. Paris doesn't mind climbing, and such a getting up stairs was never anywhere else so indispensable. Broadway has hitherto seemed to me to present a tolerable example of denseness in the population of a street; but almost any considerable street in Paris beats it outright. Could you have seen the Boulevard des Italiens yesterday, when the Emperor of Russia entered Paris, you would have supposed the whole world paved with French hats. We looked down on a mile of solid Frenchmen, who stood waiting quietly enough the coming of the *cortège* filling the middle of the street, and seemingly about as thick as they could stand; the murmur of their voices was positively sublime, a low roar as of Niagara heard at a short distance. Suddenly the police darted at this crowd, and with batons swinging like an orchestra leader's at the final score, drove them back on to the sidewalks, while a company of horsemen pressed upon them at a fast trot, and then, at once flashed by the two Emperors in a close state carriage (of a single pair) surrounded by a troop of silver lancers, and followed by a dozen other gala carriages with their reception suites, and some plainer ones, probably containing the ministers or diplomatic corps. It passed like a meteor, only a few seconds in view, and the crowd, which had been hours assembling, dispersed in a few minutes to allow the usual festive air of the street to resume its sway. The wife of one of the ministers told me that the newspapers having announced, without authority, that the diplomatic corps would go to welcome the Russian Emperor, Louis Napoleon had ordered them out—most reluctantly to themselves—as it would not do to allow any public announcement of so· much importance to seem to be made without imperial authority. Perhaps the papers were not called to serious account for their impertinence !

The crowd of carriages, generally shabby *voitures*, of one horse, with a leather-stove-pipe-hatted driver, is inconceivable. We saw regular horse-meat butcher shops in Rouen, and doubtless they exist in Paris ; but most of the horses we have seen would hardly serve to feed the crows. A more forlorn set of skeletons could hardly rise from a battle-field of cavalry, to greet Napoleon's spectral review. And indeed, these poor Paris cabs appear to have a worse than dog's life of it. With ten or fifteen thousand of them in the service, they are so cheap (say thirty cents for a drive of three miles, or sixty cents per hour) that they are in incessant use and even difficult to obtain at certain hours of the day. Their speed is not that of royalty, which it seems always drives furiously, and increases pace according to rank. The Emperor alone may drive six horses. The private equipages on the Champs Elysées and in the Bois de Boulogne are many of them elegant, and some very sumptuous, with postillions in blue or red silk doublets, and parti-colored leggings ; but the carriages of all sorts seemed clumsy compared with our own. Amid all the kaleidoscope variety and confusion and noise of Paris, in which coachmen's cries of " *a la bas,*" or out of the way, and a furious cracking of whips—in the air—for the horses seem inaccessible to the lash—and notwithstand-

ing the vast shifting crowd—there is an air of leisure and
festivity which makes you feel as if the real Frenchman's
business was enjoyment. The general expression of countenance is a good-natured raillery. The earnestness and
anxiety of the American face is totally lacking. A kind of
refined Celt—with a turned-up nose, irregular features, a ban-
tering look and a carefully-disposed dress — a fancy shirt-
bosom and a bright-colored neck-tie, light gloves and nice
boots :—the Frenchman twirls his cane as the Spanish woman
flutters her fan, and seems at perfect ease, and with unlimited
time at his disposal. He sits down to his *eau-de-vie* and his
cup of coffee, in the open street, as if he never intended
to get up. He fumbles his *Figaro*, or evening newspaper, as
if all that concerned him in the world were in his grasp.
Perhaps his wife and daughter are with him, as easy and
contented as himself, but more likely, under forty, he has no
such encumbrances (if not in humble life). He lights like a
butterfly in the sun, and is quiet and comfortable. He came,
you know as little whence ; he goes, you know as little whither.
In the evening you will find him, perhaps, at the open-air concert *a la Musard*, where one hundred and fifty of the best
orchestral performers render the best and the newest music
to perfection, and where, amid the mild radiance of countless
moons of gas, and in the shelter of beautiful trees, you sit with
five thousand decorous " *Parley-vous* " for an hour, to mingle
music and tobacco-smoke, *eau-sucré*, or something stronger.
A little later, you may see him at the Jardin Mabille or Des
Fleurs, where the *demi-monde*, in most hypocritical decorum,
set the fashions for the rest of the world, while all sorts of
strangers and natives dance in a somewhat free manner, and
foreign virtue and piety improve their opportunities for seeing
how gay and elegant folly can be made, and how discreetly
self-abandonment can carry herself before company. The

B

theatres and operas will probably have the attention of a few thousand more ; although the Frenchman is never fully at home in any kind of house.

The streets and shops are a perpetual " exposition," much more attractive and seeable than any set exhibition of wares can be. You pass through narrow passages (connecting streets together by a sort of *inland navigation*) which glitter with jewelry and small wares, and in which even vegetables and meats are so arranged as to make a part of the artistic display ; for in France, they have carried the art of exhibition to perfection. Every grocer's, fruiterer's, dry-goods, butcher's shop is a study of neatness, picturesque display and appeal to admiration. The windows are each studies done in some one of the different styles—now with fruits, then with clothes ; here with confectionery and there with jewelry ; in this quarter with shawls, in that with boots and shoes ; on this side with bread and cakes, on the other with bottles and glass-ware. The gas is double refined and in double quantity. The night is as light as the day. All the cabs must carry lanterns after dark, and this gives the view as you look down, say from the Arc de Triomphe upon the Champs Élysées, a look as if the long broad road were buzzing with myriads of gigantic glow-worms.

But, after all, there is a cozy *inside* to Paris as well as a brilliant outside. The courts, around which so many of the larger houses are built, furnish cool and quiet retreats from the noise and rush of the streets. It is charming to experience how sudden and unexpected the change is. And then, Paris is full of passages, a kind of covered way, which we have tried to imitate in a few American cities in what we call arcades—but which here furnish in bad weather admirable opportunities for shopping in all its varieties and within the most compendious space.

Doubtless there is the same kind of privacy here, to those who know how to find it, that we enjoy at home, only it is harder to understand. Indeed, strangers must live a long time in any foreign city or country, to begin to do justice to its *best* side. I feel just now, in spite of all this show and splendor, perfectly satiated, and half-nauseated with Paris— simply because it presents to me so exclusively its outside, its nationality and worldliness. I feel a steady tendency to demoralization in its atmosphere. But this is owing to ignorance of the customs, imperfect acquaintance with the language, and the complete removal of customary foundations and points of departure. Just now, the quantity of things crying to be seen is discouraging and overwhelming. One feels like running away from the excess, and resisting this exhaustion of the powers of admiration. But it will not do to throw away such costly opportunities, and so I shall hold my reluctant attention to the grindstone of this revolving Paris, and let the sparks fly as they will, in hopes of getting some new edge from the painful process.

I have seen the magnificent Place de la Concorde with its glorious fountains, doubtless the finest and most imposing square in the world. Every guide-book describes it, and I will not. The Bois de Boulogne is a wonderful piece of un-French nature, left in a simplicity truly refreshing after all the artificial stateliness that leads to it. It is said to contain two thousand acres, and furnishes an endless drive, which may be perpetually varied.

It is not too late here to speak of the beauty of the country between Havre and Rouen, which is up to the best English cultivation, and possesses a natural variety of surface not easily found in England. It is as if some of the more picturesque counties of Massachusetts had received the last touch of the most exquisite gardening. After the sea, this sudden introduction to summer wealth and spring freshness, with all the finer vegetables — tomatoes, cauliflowers, artichokes, peas and beans, and all the small fruits in perfection, strawberries, cherries and apricots—with poplars looking for the first time handsome in their native fields, slender and lady-like, not ragged and stiff — was refreshing beyond description. The disgusting nuisance of the Custom House, where *nothing* was done with great patience and thoroughness, could not make our entrance into France, by the pleasant gate of Havre, any thing but charming. The city itself is pretty and most picturesque in its surroundings. Its docks shame our piers, and the shipping moored safely almost in the heart of the town gives a half-Venetian air to the streets. Rouen, which we reached the noon of our first day ashore, gave us a day's enjoyment such as we can hardly hope to find exceeded by any later day's experience. Apart from its sublime Cathedral and equally celebrated Church of St. Ouen—by many authorities deemed the best extant specimen of pure Gothic—Rouen contains such relics of the Middle Ages in its domestic and street architecture and in its usages, that every step in every direction was a surprise and a gratification, a lesson and a delight. We fairly reveled in its strangeness and quaintness — its glorious churches and its happy and prosperous people. But more than enough for the present.

III.

THE REVIEW AND EXPOSITION.

PARIS, June 7, 1867.

YESTERDAY we went with all the world to the great review on the Longchamps, or race-course, in the Bois de Boulogne. This magnificent park seems large enough to rusticate all Paris in. Its breadth appears equal to its length, and its thorough simplicity and naturalness, its amplitude of open space, and its abundance of trees and shade, fit it for public displays and private enjoyment.

The field of the review could not have been less than a plain of a mile square. Around the square were gathered the sight-seeing Parisians in dense masses. Every point of advantage was crowded with a special swarm of people. The trees were hanging with human fruit, producing the oddest effect in the distance. On one side of a small portion of the square (the usual stand of the judges and favored spectators at the races) some thousand fortunate persons enjoyed the privilege of a raised seat, in the immediate vicinity of the Empress and her ladies, and in direct front of the Emperor's position as he reviewed the troops. In different parts of the field were posted what seemed about forty thousand infantry, fifteen thousand cavalry, and five thousand artillerymen. There may not have been as many, or there may have been more. But it took the troops an hour and twenty minutes (part of the time at double-quick, and with the cavalry on the full trot) to pass the point we occupied. Promptly, at the

moment announced, the Emperor's *cortège*—all mounted—
appeared at the most distant corner of the field.   It was
welcomed by a blast of trumpets, which, taken up by a hundred bands, echoed round the vast plain.   The three monarchs, the Emperor of the French on the right, next the Emperor of Russia, and next to him the King of Prussia, rode in
front, followed by a long *cortège* of brilliantly-uniformed officers (perhaps a hundred), their respective staffs, and other distinguished functionaries.   Gortschakof and Bismarck were
said to be among them.   A special troop of cavalry (the Emperor's guard), very splendid in equipments, followed the Imperial train.   At a brisk trot, this gold-and-silver-burnished
company rode round the whole field, inspecting the general
appearance of the troops at rest.   They were greeted with
"Vive l'Empereur" in moderate transports.   Passing near
our stand, the general appearance of the Emperors was distinctly made out by the aid of a good opera-glass.   Louis Napoleon, who rode a pretty sorrel horse, had on a blue sash
and fewer orders than his companions.   His hair was lighter
than I had expected ; his face is heavy and cold, without a
trace of the beauty of his family, yet not without the mould
of his house.   He is thick-set, but rides well and bows gracefully.   The Emperor of Russia, who rode a black horse (his
own, brought from St. Petersburg for the occasion, and without that square-cut English tail which is now adopted in
France), is tall, only fairly good-looking, with dark beard, and
without any of the commanding air of his father.   The French
Emperor talked much with the Russian, and little, seemingly,
with the Prussian monarch.   The King of Prussia has little
that is distinguished in his appearance at a distance, but is
represented, by those personally acquainted with him, as fascinating in his manners ; specially to ladies.   At a certain
moment the monarchs rode out of the field into the enclosure

just before the Empress's stand, and made their salute to her and her court. Then, having taken their post perhaps thirty rods off, fronting the stand occupied by favored spectators, the troops passed before them in review.

First, the infantry, in battalions of about five hundred men, sixty men in line, mostly in the usual red-breeched, white gaitered, low-capped uniform of the French infantry, but varied by regiments in blue and yellow, by zouaves and chasseurs with all sorts of head-pieces, and in all colors, and all varieties of equipment. They marched well. Their bands were admirable. The drum-major of the first column twirled his staff before and behind his head, threw it twenty feet in the air, catching it as it fell, and went through a quite wonderful but ridiculous exhibition of his skill, which was greeted with shouts of derisive admiration. The successive bands, as they approached the stand, filed out of the procession and played for the troops to pass the imperial review under the stimulus and correction of the loudest and most emphatic music. Its influence on the marching was very obvious, for that almost instantly degenerated after passing the imperial eye and getting beyond the distinctest sound of the music. The artillery was beautifully displayed. In great force, drawn by strong and admirably trained horses, and moving with the precision of infantry, it passed by, leaving an impression of prodigious power. The legs of the horses spouted like water broken over a dam, as each line threw itself forward in perfect regularity, while their even-clipped tails flowed like a row of fountains behind. The cavalry followed, with almost equal effect, but it was not until they formed a line of half a mile long in the field, and advanced by line at full gallop, for about a quarter of a mile, bringing up suddenly in unbroken front within a few rods of the imperial party, that the most majestic effect was produced. The approach of this vast body of

horse presented an image of animal irresistibleness not easily
to be surpassed. The utter wiping out of the imperial company seemed involved in its possible advance a few rods farther—a catastrophe which would have seriously modified the
map of Europe and the fortunes of humanity!

After the review—which finished with the promptness
with which it began—the royal company and *cortége* dis-
mounted and joined the Empress and her party within the
tribune or stand. At a distance of perhaps a dozen yards, I
saw the introductions and hand-shakings of monarchs and
queens and princesses going on. The Empress was marked
by a dress purely white with a green parasol. I could not
see the expression of her face. Those who did described it
as worn and changed. The Imperial Prince, although just
recovering from an abscess (which, it is said, would have got
well in a short time if he had not been treated by an anxious
court physician and treated as heir to the throne), is not, I
am informed on excellent authority, of an invalid constitution,
but on the contrary, a well-made, firmly-knit boy, usually enjoying excellent health, and promising to perpetuate his
father's line. The Prince of Prussia was pointed out. His
wife, Victoria, eldest daughter of the English Queen, is represented as a woman of fine intelligence, humane feeling, and
excellent practical wisdom. She led the Prussian ladies in
the benevolent ministrations of the late war. She lately spent
an hour or more among Dr. Evans's collections of sanitary
memorials and illustrations in the Exposition, and displayed a
most lively and intelligent interest in the operation of the Sanitary Commission. The Emperor and Empress have separately visited this collection. Just over the way, in the sanitary collection of other nations (under the auspices of the
" *Comité Internationale* "), the Empress expressed a desire to
examine the contents of a knapsack, and in taking out the

articles one by one, finally spilled from a tin box a considerable quantity of matches, which she at once began to pick up, and persisted in collecting to the last match, with all the humility and inherent neatness of her sex. The Emperor in his turn applied his royal thumb and finger to removing a cigar which one of the attendants had carelessly left burning upon some part of the material, accompanying the act with a quizzical look and word. The Emperor has the credit of combining a lively interest in details with a command of general principles. He is said to be intimately acquainted with the expenses of his privy purse, and to watch it with care. He mends his own fire, and watches his own thermometer, and does not forget the advantages of his early adversities.

This peaceful meeting of great monarchs in Paris, especially of those either lately confronted in actual war, or in the imminent danger of it, is regarded with profound interest here, in its bearings on the future. Perhaps the opportunities of meeting afforded such men as Gortschakof and Bismarck and Raouher are even more significant and fruitful than those enjoyed by their masters. It is said that the bases of many important international arrangements have been agreed upon. Happily in our day, wars are not as they were once, the caprices of monarchs and ministers, but the gravitations and necessities of States; and I can not attribute, therefore, as much importance to the gatherings of kings and their ministers, as most men. These gentlemen may hobnob ever so affectionately to-day, and be compelled to face each other in angry correspondence or in arms next month, if the interests or sensibilities of their respective countries are threatened. Far more important in its bearings on the future peace of the world is the " Universal Exposition," gathering together in one vast museum, not only samples of the natural products and industrial and artistic fabrics of all countries, but calling together such immense popular representations of all the great nationalities.   The mutual dependence of countries on each other, the grounds of mutual respect, and the infinitely suggestive lessons of the Exposition will do much to educate the public opinion of the world.   The small space occupied by weapons of war in the collection, compared with that taken up by the products of peace, is of itself instructive ; and it is noticeable how little attention is paid by the people at large to any thing but the purely industrial display.

Of the Exposition itself, I suppose by this time the public must be fully informed, so far as definite description is concerned.   The catalogue itself is a duodecimo of over two thousand finely-printed pages.   The area covered must be a half-mile square.   Within this square, filled to its utmost capacity with countless edifices outside the main building, to show in their architecture and to exhibit in their contents the characteristics of all nations, is built the Palace of Industry, a marvel of strength, arrangement and adaptation.   Running round an open garden, beautifully laid out in flowers and fountains, circles a promenade next to which is the Museum of the History of Labor, and then in concentric circles ten immense galleries (on one level) each devoted to one grand class of objects.   The *first* gallery or "circuit" is devoted to a most extensive display of the works of art of all nations. The *second* to the materials of the liberal arts—such as books and paper, materials for the painter and designer, instruments of music, medical appliances, every thing connected with photography ; mathematical and scientific instruments, maps, plans, etc.   The *third* gallery to furniture, and all objects destined for dwellings—such as sideboards, tables, bedsteads, chairs, billiard-tables, carpets, curtains, glass and china, wall-paper, cutlery, bronzes, and tin and copper ware, clocks and watches, lamps and chandeliers, perfumery, trinkets, etc. The *fourth* gallery to clothing in the largest sense, and other objects carried about the person—such as threads and yarns and silk, and all their products, shawls, laces and broideries, bonnets and under-clothing, corsets, cravats, gloves; made-up goods, caps and wigs, shoes and boots, children's clothes; jewelry in the most astonishing splendor, arms that are portable, trunks, valises, travelers' bags, tents and exploring or traveling necessaries, toys and games. The *fifth* gallery is devoted to the natural and manufactured products of the mine, the forest, the sea, the non-alimentary agricultural products—fibres and textiles, tobaccos, tans and tinctures, oils, rosin, wax, etc.; to chemical and pharmaceutic products — acids and alkalis, salts, gutta percha and India rubber, mineral waters, medicines, bleaching processes, dyeing, stamping and transferring, leather and furs. The *sixth* gallery to machines, instruments, tools and processes connected with the useful arts, mining machinery, and methods of working metals; agricultural tools and processes, manures and fertilizers; woods; weapons or instruments used in hunting and fishing; all tools used in drainage, cheese and buttermaking; bread, chocolate, ices, materials of chemical art, of pharmacy and tanning; generators of steam, stoves, heaters, with all plans for rendering them safe; forcing pumps and engines, dredges and earth-excavators, chimney and smoke-pipes and jacks; apparatus for fountains, machines and apparatus for general mechanical purposes—weighers and measurers, regulators and governors, counters and registers, lifters and elevators, hydraulic machines, mill-wheels, motors of air, of gas, or electro-magnetic; balloons; planing, mortising, punching, compressing machines; flax and cordage and their manufacture, webs of weaving and spinning; clothing and all processes of manufacturing hats, shoes and garments; furniture and its manufacture; paper, paints and printing; carriages of all descriptions; materials connected with railways—rails and other fixtures, rolling-stock, repairing-shops, locomotives, cars, plans of stations, etc.; telegraphing in all its processes; materials and processes of public works and architecture—bridges, aqueducts, viaducts, canals, light-houses, monuments, hotels, workmen's houses, gas-pipes and water-pipes; materials used in navigation—models of ships and boats, docks and basins, piers and dykes, sails and signals, buoys, submarine machines, diving-bells, means of safety in case of fire and shipwreck, yachts. The *seventh* circle is devoted to foods in all their different states of preparation, cereals in seeds and flowers, grains ground and otherwise, farinaceous preparations from potatoes, rice, beans, tapioca, sago, arrow-root, macaroni and vermicelli; substitutes for bread; nuts and extracts of meats; bread in all forms, and pastry; spiced and easily-preserved cakes; fats and oils; milk, natural and preserved; eggs, flesh and fish in all their preserved forms; vegetables and fruits, condiments and stimulants, sugars and confectionery, fermented drinks, alcoholic and malt liquors, wines and beers. The *eighth* circle is devoted to living products and specimens of agricultural skill—farmhouses, barns and stables, distilleries, refineries; wine, oil and cider presses; living animals—horses, beeves, sheep, camels, mules, pigs, rabbits, birds, dogs; useful insects—bees and silk-worms; fish, aquaria and artificial fish-producers. The *ninth* circle is devoted to horticulture—forcing-rooms, hedges, watering-apparatus, flowers and flowering shrubs, fruit-trees. The *tenth* circle is devoted to materials and methods for ameliorating the physical and moral condition of the people—plans and models of school-houses, apparatus and elementary methods, maps and models, libraries and school-books, almanacs, time-tables, aids to memory, furniture, clothing, and food of all kinds, distinguished for combined cheapness and utility; specimens of the popular costumes of different countries, with a view to exhibiting which is best adapted to climate, occupation, and is most in harmony with national traditions; specimens of dwellings for the people, both cheap and wholesome and convenient; products of all kinds manufactured by distinguished workmen at any trade. It is necessary to bring this long and dull list of the classification of the Exposition before the reader, if only by its weariness to produce something of the effect of vastness and variety, which in a thousand-fold degree is produced upon its beholder by the Exposition itself. "The Exposition" is a magnificent success in all particulars. What the early critics of the building or the arrangements for showing the treasures in it, meant by their complaints and disparagements, it is now difficult to conceive. I can not imagine any plan better adapted to its purpose, nor more thoroughly carried out. Instead of a temporary edifice, it has immense strength; the vast and beautiful supports and braces of iron, and its complete security, give it the appearance of a permanent structure. A raised promenade of great beauty and size runs about midway from the centre to the circumference round the whole interior, giving a bird's-eye view of the whole display. The outer circle of the main building is devoted to the restaurants of all nations, where every people may find their national dishes served by native hands in the costume of their own country. The French, however, have so impressed the excellence of their *cuisine* upon all travelers, that the basis of all cooking is now Gallic.

Nobody will be disposed to wonder or regret that France leads the world in an Exposition upon her own soil and in her own capital. In London or New York it would be different. The astonishing pains all the great nations have taken to be well represented must be most gratifying to Louis Napoleon, and shows a truly enlightened sense of the importance and usefulness of the occasion. The United States is not discreditably displayed. A fair show of its industry is offered. It attracts great attention, and there is little or nothing in it which is not of practical importance. The private enterprise shown in erecting costly buildings in this enclosure, shows a full sense of the value of advertisement. It is almost inconceivable that these temples and pagodas and light-houses and stables and cottages should ever be pulled down and removed. But I suppose they will be. For here in France they do the most astonishing things in the way of putting up and pulling down things, which would make even American enterprise shudder to contemplate. The city of Paris has just expended a fabulous sum in a *fête* for the Emperors. Last night Louis Napoleon gave in the Tuileries another, which can not have cost less than a quarter of a million of dollars — in the illumination, which was of the brightness of day, and in the temporary staircases which united the front of the palace with the gardens, and in the immense floral decorations. Who pays for these extravagances? The people, in the end. It is a wonder they do not see it more clearly. We have little conception in America, with all our alleged excesses, of the extravagance in the aristocracies of Europe.

IV.

ASPECTS OF FRENCH LIFE.

PARIS, June 8, 1867.

LAST evening the Prefect of the Seine (the Mayor of Paris) gave a great ball at the Hotel de Ville, to the imperial guests. The splendid palace was illuminated outside with gas, which is now so arranged along the chief lines of all the public buildings as to make an immense and universal illumination very easy, however expensive it may be. Inside, thousands of wax candles shed a full mild light on the gilded and curtained walls of this gorgeous edifice. About six thousand guests were present. There was neither announcement nor introduction, but on delivering his ticket of invitation, the guest was passed up the long staircases, by lackeys in red plush breeches and gold-laced coats, or between the Emperor's guards with muskets in their rigid hands, looking like lifeless statues. Arriving at the top, he was passed from room to room amid flowers and fountains, until he arrived at the chief saloon. Here the principal ball-room was railed off and made accessible only to the diplomatic corps or other official functionaries. Raised seats surrounded the dancing floor, and from an outside gallery a few hundred fortunate guests could look down upon the scene. This gallery was itself the most beautiful part of the scene. Broad and colonnaded, several hundred feet long, and wide enough for a large promenade, it was completely covered with a gilded, temporary lattice-work which was overrun, ceiling and sides,

by a delicate vine of living green, converting it into a vast
arbor more elegant and graceful than any species of decoration I had ever seen.   The guests were all in knee-breeches
or tights, with silk stockings, and more than half in uniform
or court dresses. . A kind of Quaker-cut coat, embroidered in
gold, or silver, or parti-colored silks and satins, with lace
cravats, and orders of all devices and varieties, formed the
ordinary costume ; others appeared in black, with the inevitable breeches, pumps and white gloves.   The ladies, with the
exception of more jewels, were not dressed otherwise than in
our own American ball-rooms ; they were more plump and
large than our women, but had little of their pure and brilliant complexion or regularity of features.   They looked,
however, in better health, and had most charming manners.
There was no pushing or rudeness in the vast crowd, and
although the floor showed the tags of torn dresses and scraps
of muslin, on the whole the ladies carried their trains through
the crowd with unexpected safety and success.   At 10½ P.M.
a blast from the band, breaking into the Russian Hymn, announced the arrival of the Emperors and their suites. . The
streets, for a mile approaching the Hotel de Ville, had from
an early hour been lined with people to watch the royal carriages, which are so lighted as to show their interior and passengers.   A great curiosity to get a view of the guests instantly showed itself, and was restrained only by general
courtesy from becoming a rush.   I could not push, nor did
I know enough of the premises to find a point of observation,
and it was at least two hours before I got any sight of the
imperial party.   There could not have been more than two
sets of dancers, and these I never got near enough to see.
At about 11½ P.M. the royal company made a tour of the
rooms, and even then I had only a glimpse of their heads.
But about midnight, by a lucky chance, I found myself

jammed with a friend into a narrow passage, through which
the Emperor passed, and in spite of a dozen officials with
silver chains round their necks who tried to crowd us out of
the way, we could not disappear, there being no place to disappear in, and accordingly standing stock-still we had a view
almost at fingers' ends of the whole brilliant company. First
came the Emperor of Russia with the Empress Eugenie; he
was firm and sober, looking a little as if a Polish assassin
might be lurking even in that guarded company; she gracious
and affable, but faded, and not commanding in beauty or
bearing, and dressed much like any other lady. Then came
the King of Prussia, with some unknown princess; then the
Emperor of France, with the Princess Mathilde. Louis Napoleon, born 1808, has a poor walk and an uninteresting
presence. He looks care-worn and cold, anxious and reserved. His complexion is pallid and his expression depre-
catory. His hair is fast turning grey. There is nothing to
excite enthusiasm in his look or manner. In private, he is
reported as mild-spoken, amiable, and of quick intelligence;
but his face is both impassive and unpromising. All the
portraits flatter him. The Princess of Russia, a general favorite, followed. Bismarck, a noble, tall, full-faced man, clad
in a white uniform, with an air of power and victory, was in
the procession, and interested me more than any body. A
poorer-looking set of men, generally speaking, it would be
difficult to collect. Many were very short and crooked;
many insignificant in face and carriage, and their elaborate
dresses only added to their indifferent aspect. The value
set on ribbons and orders, on titles and family names, is past
all belief to an American; and the intense curiosity to see,
and the deference shown to these crowned heads, by their
own subjects, is wonderful, to use no other adjective.

Supper was served through the evening at various counters,

behind which stood numerous liveried waiters. It was ample
and dainty, without foolish profusion.   Unintoxicating drinks,
and ices, and sherbet, with punch and lemonade and *no* wines,
so far as I saw.   There was great moderation and decorum
shown about the tables.   Nothing can exceed the general
courtesy marking the ordinary intercourse of average-con-
ditioned foreigners.   Americans have something to learn
from them in this direction.

Sunday, June 9, we attended military mass at the Hotel
des Invalides.   The old soldiers, who really are venerable
and decayed in appearance, occupied the broad aisle, standing with their lances in hand.   While the ordinary mass went
on at the altar, a band of music played, with delicious skill
and taste, airs and marches selected from the operas, adapting
them artfully, if such a thing can seem possible, to the solemn
service.   The incompatibility is so complete to an American
Protestant, that it was bewildering to observe no sense of in-
congruity in the minds and manners of the Catholic and
French congregations, with which the large church was filled.
Either the thing done is so sacred that no associations can
desecrate it, and music, secular or sacred, makes no difference, or else custom has failed to create the sense of unfitness, in their minds, in which we have been educated.   The
morals and the *religion* of all countries must be studied much
more independently of each other than has hitherto been
common.   It is not safe to argue from one to the other.   The
duties owed to God of worship and supplication, do not appear to rest on any moral basis among Catholics generally.
They are of the nature of allegiance to the rightful sovereign
—who may be good or bad, but who, nevertheless, is on the
throne, and whom it is treason not to serve.   Catholics, therefore, show themselves very religious so far as punctilious attention to external forms is concerned, and no inference can

be drawn from this, either for or against moral character. The immoral may be just as punctilious as the moral, and certainly, taking a whole people together, Catholic nations are technically more *religious* than Protestant ones. The *moral* quality of peoples must be looked for in other directions. It depends more on general education, domestic training, and the self-respect which accompanies the possession of *liberty* and the responsibilities of a career. There are certain excellent moral rules and customs which are not moral in our modern sense of coming from the conscience. They are like the honor among thieves, which is so reliable and yet so purely *im*moral in its origin. It is important to recognize the advantages of those prudential and social virtues, which are the products of experience and necessity, but which do not necessarily imply moral life or moral elevation. It is on this principle alone than we can understand the conventional virtues which distinguish French society, and which flourish independently of the vices 'which equally mark it. In respect to veracity and honesty in dealing, a great dependence might be placed on those who would think very little of chastity. On the other hand, it would be grossly unfair to argue either irreligion or immorality from the different notions prevailing in France and Catholic countries generally in respect to the uses of Sunday, or the commingling of holidays and holydays. The most moral and religious minds and hearts see nothing, feel nothing incompatible in a sacred service in the morning, and a *fête* in the afternoon, and it is doubtful whether all the wisdom on this subject is on the Protestant side.

Yesterday afternoon, for instance, from ten to fifteen thousand people went from Paris to Versailles (twelve miles out), men, women and children, to pass a summer half-day in the exquisite walks and woods of that paradise of fountains and arbors, and vistas and statues, and allegory and history, and romantic associations. A more refreshing, innocent, and decorous relaxation could not be imagined. Not one sign of drunkenness, not one act of indecorum, marked the occasion. Very little eating or drinking, even of the most harmless kind, prevailed. Most of the company went out in second-class cars, with return tickets, at two francs a head, and no doubt it was to most a novelty which they perhaps allow themselves only once in the season. The vastness of the expense involved in the endless multiplication of fountains—all fed with water pumped into vast reservoirs from the Seine—is almost enough to supply Paris itself with water. Considered purely as a piece of monarchical splendor and self-indulgence, the scene is an aggravating example of the way in which the people were once sacrificed to the ambitious caprices and luxurious whims of princes. Happily, what for generations was confined to the eyes of monarchs and courts, is now opened freely to the people ; and it is the peculiar and auspicious feature of the government of Paris and France, since Napoleon's days, that the national accumulation of pictures and statues and ground is put, in the largest way, at the service of the public. This, indeed, does even a dangerous amount of propitiation. It works to uphold, by the charms of a life of so many festive opportunities, a system of government essentially repressive and tyrannical over thought and speech. Like the cathedrals and the showy ritual which, as the common property of the people, make every Catholic feel as if his own personal pride was involved in maintaining so grand a display, so the large and brilliant out-door life, passed amid objects of taste and beauty and splendor, which belong to most Europeans, but specially to Frenchmen and Parisians, reconciles the people to a Parliament in which no real power resides, a press without freedom, little home-life, and a general reaction on the principles of self-government which were making progress here before Paris was made the spectacular city it has become. Democratic, France doubtless is, in its tastes and customs; but its democracy is social rather than political, in contradistinction to our own land, where it is political rather than social. I venture to say that less jealousy exists between rich and poor, high and low, in France than in America, and that people care even less for the status of those they associate with. They ride in second-class cars, they drive in shabby hacks, they meet freely in public places, and there is a jovial and kindly intercourse between them. Moreover, waiters, drivers and common folks are intelligent and sharp-witted within their own sphere of life. The French head is characteristically well-developed, and the face expressive.

It is surprising, however, how little interest in political or other general news the people seem to take. The newspapers are very poor and scanty as compared with ours. The interest in universal concerns is small. America is of much account only in the eye of far-looking economists and statesmen. Improved as our reputation is, the ignorance about us is still gross, and the indifference still more so. They know that somehow we are getting away millions of European people, although few of the emigrants are French—who have no taste and little skill in colonial work (witness Algeria, which it takes about as many troops to keep in order as it has population). They know we are growing rich and powerful, but they have no notion of our civilization, or superiority in substantial respects. They have no conception of the relative higher kind of civilization, greater independence, intelligence, earnestness and dignity which marks our whole life. An American can afford to smile at their splendor and accumulated riches, their equipages and spectacles, their titles and orders, and feel that the real progress of civilization is now going on upon the other side of the great ocean.

The great ball at the Tuileries on Monday last is said to have exceeded even that at the Hotel de Ville in costliness and splendor. The illumination in the garden was visible at several miles distance. Great temporary staircases were made from the drawing-rooms direct into the gardens, and the company found the grounds so prepared that white satin slippers received no stain from walking upon them. Baron Hausmann is the conjuror who extemporizes the magnificent *fêtes* of the Emperor. He it is who has carried out his will in the transformation of the streets of Paris, where mighty masses of buildings have been cut through, as if they had been made of cheese. France, so far as its exterior, its monuments, its churches, its quays and its roads are concerned, has been set in wondrous order by Louis Napoleon, who will be long remembered as the Renovator of the public magnificence of Paris and all the other chief cities of the Empire. This is the age of improvements in France, not the age of inventions. Indeed, external splendor and comfort, order and peace, rule far more than ideas in this great country at this hour. It is not the day of great men, or of noble women.

V.

CHARITY AND RELIGION.

PARIS, June 21, 1867.

THE public institutions of charity and instruction in Paris are on a scale corresponding with the grandeur of the public works in general. They are of course less visited and less known by travelers, who are apt to confine themselves to what is merely pleasing or wholly novel. But no one can obtain any proper conception of the largeness and splendor of the French nation and government who does not acquaint himself with the schools, the hospitals, the asylums—at least to a sufficient degree to understand their immense scale, and the liberality and thoroughness with which they are sustained and administered. The most I have been able to do in this hurried journey, is to visit a very few, selecting those most celebrated, and on the oldest or the largest foundations. To begin with charities, let me give a brief account of the "Salpêtrière," a sort of almshouse and hospital, where, for more than two hundred years, succor and shelter, food and medicine have been freely furnished to aged women, beyond the years or without the ability to support themselves. There are here within the city boundaries and in an enclosure, one side of which is a mile long, forty-five separate buildings devoted to this purpose. A beautiful park and flower-garden, a large church, ample and cleanly dormitories, bakeries, kitchens, a washing department, wards for the bedridden, for the insane, for the incurable, as well as comfortable accommodations for merely outworn and feeble old women, present an affecting evidence of the care the government has for utterly helpless and superannuated poverty and misfortune. Excellent ventilation, good arrangements for heating, various and agreeable food, ample space for exercise and relaxation in the open air, mark the establishment. A spirit of humanity, exemption from needless discipline, freedom of ingress and egress, with due attention to the taste for what is beautiful, are other delightful characteristics of this vast refuge for infirmity. The only punishment for disorderly behavior is expulsion from the advantages of the hospital, for a longer or shorter period. The size of the grounds may be inferred from the fact that sixty thousand visitors were expected to participate in the *Fête Dieu* (Corpus Christi) which the inmates were preparing, by the erection of floral altars, to celebrate on the next Sunday. There are beds for six thousand women in this grand hospital, which boasts of being the largest in the world.

From this magnificent infirmary, one of the oldest in France, I went to one of the newest, founded within a dozen years by the Countess of Roy, who bequeathed 3,000,000 francs to establish a model hospital for the acutely ill, called after her maiden name the "Bossoniere." This hospital, which has over six hundred beds, is built upon the most approved pavilion model. There are twelve pavilions, of three stories each, and in each story beds for thirty-four persons. The wards are perfectly distinct and widely separated ; the grounds spacious and beautiful. The administration is conducted in the corner buildings of the great square around which the hospital is erected. The wards are lofty, ceiled with a hard, painted and polished substance which prevents the absorption of malarious moisture, and the ventilation is secured by suitable entrances for pure air, and exits for foul.

The windows are large and frequent. The beds are all curtained with white dimity, which seems a strange departure from the most modern lessons of hygiene, but they are clean and often changed. The lavatories and closets are excellent, sweet and convenient. Each bed has a shelf over the top and within reach of the patient. The beds of wool, packed over once a year, rest upon a sacking which is lifted on open springs of nearly a foot in height, allowing the air the freest circulation *under* the bedding. A room for the preparation of medicines or special diet is connected with each ward, a very unusual and admirable addition. In this hospital the heating is all done by hot water. Half the building is ventilated by an expensive steam-apparatus, which sucks the air down from the belfry of the church, where it is pure and fresh, and forces it up, either heated or not, into the dormitories. The apparatus works admirably, and is a perfect success as to the result of supplying at all times the needed amount of fresh air. But it is costly, requires much steady attention and frequent repairs, and it is feared will not be copied on account of its expensiveness. The other half of the hospital is supplied with air by the ordinary laws of gravitation, but with great attention to proper openings for the circulation. I regretted not being able to learn, in the absence of the head of the institution, what the ratio of mortality was on the two sides of the building, where these two methods of ventilation were so immediately contrasted. This hospital seemed to be in the hands of Sisters of Charity, who looked well fitted to their charge.

My next call was in a distant part of Paris, at the Foundling Hospital, formerly styled the Hospital for " Enfants trouvés," but now changed to " Enfants assistés." For many generations, and until quite recently, any infant, the child of sin or shame, of misfortune or want, could be left at the turnstile of this hospital, without questions asked or identification. The ring of the bell by the person bringing the child, caused the attendant, always waiting inside, to turn the softly-lined box outward, to receive the little stranger, who, by another turn, was brought within the reach of a warm and abiding protection. This refuge for the fruits of shame has fitly enough been deemed of late a dangerous encouragement to sin; and now its mother, or some near friend, is required to present every child brought to the asylum, and to furnish its name and history. Since the privilege of a secret asylum was lost, infanticide is said to have increased in Paris, where, however, it is less common than in New York, if some recent statements may be believed. It would, of course, be likely to be less frequent in a city like Paris, where, marriage being difficult, other relations between the sexes are common, and accompanied by less sense of shame and sin.

Nothing could be more affecting than the sight of the wards of this asylum. Long rows of little cribs curtained with white, each containing a sleeping babe, with a little medal round its neck—its sole connection with the home it was never to know—presented a picture of mingled innocence and sin, of helplessness and efficient protection, which could not be thoughtfully contemplated without contending emotions. Two "infants of days" were brought in while I was in the hospital. They were carried at once to the baby-ward, and the name, age, and other required facts sewed to the child's cap; a medal (the duplicate of which was given to the parent) was tied about its neck, and the little one, duly washed and clothed, was put to the breast of one of the wet nurses, and then laid in its little fairy-like crib. After a few weeks these children are sent into the country for the benefit of pure air. I could not find out how the country home was related to the city one; whether the children were scattered among families, or went into another public asylum. But it is certain that the children are subject to the authority of the hospital until they are twenty-one. They are bound out at proper ages to trades, and disposed of in many careful ways. There were children here of all ages, from a month old to seventeen, and very many of them were at play in the lovely garden. There has been in all the public institutions I have visited, something *un*official in the manner of the keepers and assistants which, considering the rigidity of method that characterizes the whole of French life, is a remarkable testimony to the essential *bonhommie* and kindly nature of the people. Little distinguished for depth of feeling, they are free from hardness, ferocity, and vindictiveness, and their almost uniform courtesy of manners appears even among the commonest of them, and throws a kindliness over the police and over all custodians and officials, which is not wanting even in almshouses and prisons. The thoroughness, airiness, cleanliness, and spaciousness of the Foundling Hospital repeated the surprise which every fresh visit to any French public institution perpetually provokes. How has it happened, is the continual question, that, in an old, crowded country like this, such ample room has been secured for all public purposes? that churches, charities, streets, parks, schools, are never crowded into corners, or jammed in between incongruous buildings? In the newest and least crowded of countries—America—*space*, either because it is so common, or because its charm is not appreciated, is the last thing which is provided for about public buildings, churches, schools or residences.

Anxious to see the common schools of Paris, I obtained, not without difficulty, a special permit, and visited one boys' and one girls' school. The boys' school contained only about 60 children from 6 to 14 years of age. Two Catholic priests had it in charge. It was in two rooms—with a large open shed attached, where nearly half the boys were seated in the open air, learning their lessons from monitors—who repeated, out of a religious book, certain sentences wholly beyond any suggestion of meaning to children of such tender age, but which they learned by rote. In the older class-room, the walls were hung with admirable illustrations of all weights and measures, and with provisions for object-teaching. The excellent French method of *dictation* was here in full operation. The teacher dictates a sentence of some length to the whole class, who write it out in their copy-books. Here is a combined exercise in attention, memory, spelling, grammar, writing, composition, and style. What preliminary attention is given to writing, and whether our pot-hook system is pursued, I could not find out, but it is certain that these children (and all French children who go to school at all) write a freer, handsomer, and more useful hand at an earlier period than any other children in any country. I examined some twenty copy-books, and was astonished at the general correctness of the boys' writing. The ordinary elements of popular education were all thoroughly taught. But the schoolbooks seemed wholly in the interest of Catholic superstition. It is not because the authority of the Roman Church was applied in them, or the precepts of their faith reiterated, that I complain ; nobody could properly object to that ; but that a mass of puerile superstitions, legends and false miracles was emptied into the memories of these children in place of interesting facts and truths either of natural or universal history, or any thing instructive in ethics or science. It is said that an association of ladies exists in Paris, whose object is to reform the evils of this system, by preparing proper schoolbooks for the common schools. But while the Catholic religion is at the bottom of the policy of the French government, and is upheld as a means of governing the masses, there is little hope of any success in this direction. An examination of the " Annuaire de l'Instruction Publique pour l'annee, 1867," shows that an immense machinery controls the system, in which the Church has a very weighty finger. There is a minister of public instruction, who is a Secretary of State, and member of the Imperial Cabinet (M. Duruy). Carnot, Cousin, Guizot, Cuvier, have held this important position in former years. Under various departments, 1st, of registration and of archives and administration generally; 2d, of the administration of colleges and higher schools; 3d, of schools of a second class ; 4th, primary schools ; 5th, learned societies and libraries ; 6th, financial accounts ; under these various heads comes every thing connected with the examination, selection and support of teachers and professors ; with the building and furnishing of school-houses ; with the ordering of courses of instruction ; with pensioning worn-out instructors and even their widows. All medical and law schools, as well as schools of theology, are included. As to the higher education, the arrangements are admirable, the teaching is free and accessible ; as to the lower, it is still formal, not designed to stimulate intelligence, but to create serviceable and pliable subjects. There is an imperial council of public instruction, in which it is pleasant to find the names of Troplong, Milne, Edwards, Michel Chevalier, Le Verrier and Giraud. But the ominous presence in the same council of Mons. Darboy, Archbishop of Paris, of Dubreuil, Landriot, Meignan, Lavigerie, all archbishops of other French provinces, indicates the intention of giving the Church a large hand in the popular education. It is pleasant, however, to find Archbishop Darboy at the head of the Central Committee of Patronage for Asylums of Charity —under the patronage of the Empress, and to find in the

official record the names of thirty noble and distinguished
ladies, charged with the duty (how purely honorary I can not
tell) of visiting these asylums. The names of 6000 teachers
of public instruction are furnished in the " Annuàire." The
names of distinguished pupils are published in a roll of honor.
Great attention is given to perpetuating all literary distinctions and services, and of regulating all decorations and
titles. After all, the budget of national instruction is only
about twenty millions of francs—which I suppose is less than
the cost of instruction in the single State, I might almost say
City, of New York. It must not be forgotten, however, that
there are three sources of support for education, that of the
Nation, that of the *Departments,* and that of the *Communes;*
and that altogether it is estimated that at least seventy millions of francs are expended on popular education — which
would perhaps be about two-fifths of what is expended in
America. I learn, only since writing the above, that there is
to be allowed henceforth a great liberty in the choice and
use of books in schools, and that they are not to be ruled out
by ecclesiastics.

Of religious education there is a great show, and immense
pains taken by the priests to keep the paysans and common
people in the love of the Church by *fêtes,* and by appeals to
the senses through music, forms and method. The prestige
of the Church is of course prodigious, and it is backed by all
the splendor of architecture and pictorial art, of old associations and saintly memory, not to speak of the excellent and
indefatigable works of mercy done by Sisters of Mercy and
priests. A simple-hearted, sincere and disinterested class
they are ; their faces marked by purity, self-control and unworldliness. It was curious to see a party of six of these
holy women, in their white, elephant-eared bonnets, examining the laces and jewelry of the Exposition, without cupidity

or envy in their countenances, and as if satisfied with their own choice of an unworldly life, without being censorious to those who had chosen otherwise. Dogmas are rather implied than taught, the modern Catholics being, as M. Laboulaye observed, much like their very opposites, the Quakers, in saying very little about doctrine, but seeking to recommend their system by good works. The Church has still a prodigious hold upon the common people, while the middle class are rather apathetic than opposed to it, and the fashion of. the cultivated class (when not influenced by political considerations) is sceptical, materialistic, atheistic, especially with young men. Protestantism makes next to no headway. Never popular in France, it seems to find no soil for its modern growth. That inconsiderable Protestant communion which shares the support of the government, makes, it is said, no progress. It is now torn by a violent internal controversy. The Coquerel party is very nearly as large as the so-called Orthodox party, and is likely enough at the next elections to prove itself in the majority. Should it do so, doubtless the Orthodox party, of whom M. Guizot may be considered the leader, would secede and insist on a separation. At present the Orthodox party is slightly in the ascendant, and is striving to force the Unitarian or liberal party (they dislike and avoid the name Unitarian) to secede without carrying any portion of the government support with them. This they are, properly enough, too wary to do. What the government will do in case the Coquerel party proves itself the majority, it is difficult to imagine. They have never recognized, and on the contrary have refused to recognize, a Unitarian Church in France ; and yet if Protestantism in any form is to make head, it must be under some new phase of the Unitarian movement. I fully believe that an avowed American Unitarian Church would flourish in

Paris. At present there are two chapels here of American origin; one, the American Chapel so-called, founded partly by Unitarians and considerably supported by them, but under the protection and direction of the Evangelical Alliance, and on a strictly Trinitarian platform. It has just paid off the debt upon the pretty chapel in the Rue de Berri, where the Rev. Dr. Eldredge (formerly of Detroit) ministers morning and evening. The congregation is respectable in numbers, and a body of excellent intelligence. In the morning a modification of the Episcopal service is read, to conciliate the Episcopalians, and in the evening the ordinary Congregational service is observed, to content the less formal portion of the worshipers. Dr. Eldredge very kindly urged me to preach, and although, to save him embarrassment, I at first declined, yet, on a hearty renewal of the invitation, I accepted, on the score of not neglecting to meet any overtures in the direction of Christian toleration and fellowship. It was Trinity Sunday, a fortunate day to inaugurate a policy of charity toward Unitarian Christians; and after the stated pastor had read the service, including the special collection in honor of the Trinity, I preached a serious sermon, without denominational ear-marks upon it, such as I am in the habit of preaching in my own pulpit, and without a word of special adaptation either to the place or time. It was cordially received, and I have much reason to praise the courage and courtesy which the minister showed in departing from the antecedent usages of the American Chapel. Dr. Peabody was asked to preach while here, but unexpectedly left too early to accept the invitation.

The Episcopal Church, under Rev. Mr. Lawson, is succeeding fairly, and now has, what I believe has not happened before, the support of the resident Minister, Gen. Dix. Till this time our national Ministers have attended, it is said, the

American Chapel. I have seen such crowds of Americans and of Unitarians in Paris that I wonder an independent movement is not made here for a strictly Unitarian Church. I believe it would succeed by' aid of English and American support, and even win some French followers.

At a meeting to which I was specially invited, at the chapel erected by the Society for Evangelical Missions, in the grounds of the Exposition, the subject of the keeping of the Sabbath, or the " Sanctification de Dimanche," was discussed with earnestness by several of the leading ministers of the French Protestant Church. The Rev. Pasteur D'Hombres and Rev. Mr. Fiesch were the chief speakers. They were earnest men of the Orthodox school, and prayed and spoke with the usual positiveness and narrowness of their tribe, and in a way as little likely to produce any effect on ordinary French feeling as though they had attempted to overthrow the light-house near by, by pelting it with paper pellets. Some laymen spoke more to the point in showing the economical advantages of a cessation of labor on Sunday, and it is by that door, if any, that Sunday will become a day of rest in France. Nothing can be more idle than to attempt to saddle France with a Scotch or a New England Sabbath. The truly religious people in France (for there are some) are just as much opposed to a Puritanical Sabbath as the most worldly and careless. It behooves us to understand the working of this business at home, and the amount of lazy and self-indulgent neglect of religion under a demure exterior, before we throw too many stones at French impiety. It would be a glorious work to revive faith and piety in France (and at home!), but the Sunday can only be changed here by a total change in the feelings and customs of the people. It will be an effect and not a cause.

There have been many interesting meetings of gentlemen

from all countries held in committees at the Exposition. The amount of hard work thus done is prodigious. I have been delighted with the business-like precision, order and attention of these meetings—prompt, short, to the point, and always leaving the business advanced. The presiding officer in all cases has been true to his name, and has kept out irrelevant topics. No meeting of more importance has occurred to my knowledge than that on weights, measures and coins, the object of which is to universalize a common standard. Progress is certainly making, and there is a reasonable hope that France, Great Britain and the United States may agree to make their five-franc piece, dollar and sovereign exactly interchangeable (the sovereign standing for twenty-five francs). I met Senator Sherman, President Barnard and Hon. S. B. Ruggles at the *séance* of about a hundred gentlemen at the Salon d'Empereur, in the old Palace of Industry (Champs Elysées). They had all good hope of some very important results from this series of meetings, which touches one of the most immediate questions in the commerce and peace, and in the exchanges of ideas and advantages of all countries.

The meetings of some of the representatives of the nations who were parties to the Genevan Congress, touching the neutrality of battle-fields and the application of more humane principles to armies, have of course had more of my time and heart. I find a noble ardor animating those representatives. They are men of high position at home, and they bring very generous and humane feelings, as well as clear and systematic intelligence, to the treatment of their subject. It is most encouraging to find how rapid is the progress of true Christian feeling on the subject of the treatment of the sick and wounded in time of war. The late war between Prussia and Austria illustrated the working of the principles of the Genevan Congress admirably. Dr. Evans has written a book in which the facts are carefully set forth, and he is circulating it extensively in Europe, where it can not fail to do vast good. The Princess of Prussia, who is warmly American in her feelings, and a thorough friend of the Sanitary Commission, is earnestly advocating the participation of women in works of mercy and self-improvement. The Queen of Prussia, a learned and admirable woman, is also devoted to this work. I am proud to say that the example of the United States Sanitary Commission has had an unexpected effect on thinking people in Europe. It is spoken of everywhere with a sort of enthusiasm, mingled with astonishment, as a sample of what free institutions can do to develop the sympathetic life and humane affections of a people. M. Chevalier, Senator of France and leading practical economist (the French Cobden), told me that the Grand Jury (the final authority of the Exposition) had awarded three " prizes of honor."—the highest distinction conferred, and of which, perhaps, five-and-twenty may be accorded in all—to the United States : 1, one to the Atlantic Telegraph, and specially to C. W. Field; 2, one to House for his Printing Telegraph; 3, one to the United States Sanitary Commission. I hope this intelligence may not prove premature, and that what is true now may experience no reversal before the day of distribution, early in July.

I leave Paris to-morrow, after twenty-four days' busy observation, for Belgium and Holland. I ought not to omit saying that I have enjoyed special interviews with Chevalier and Laboulaye, from which I have derived great pleasure and instruction.

VI.

THE MIND OF FRANCE.

PARIS, June 23, 1867.

THE last pleasure we had in Paris, and among the greatest, was to hear Laboulaye, in the closing lecture of his course, at the College of France. He came into the lecture-room—a plain hall, with benches narrow and uncomfortable for the hearers—at precisely the moment he was due, 12½ P.M., and there found perhaps three hundred men, mostly of middle age, or above it, assembled to hear him. Thirty ladies were seated nearer the Professor in an enclosure separated from the rest of the room by a low railing.

M. Laboulaye is fifty-six years old, stoutly built, and of about the medium height ; he has a broad forehead, with thin hair, black like his eyes. He reminded me by turns of Washington Irving, Professor Agassiz, and Dr. Dewey. He was buttoned up to the throat, showing the decoration of the Legion of Honor in his button-hole. He came in, took his seat amid the plaudits of the audience, and instantly began his lecture. It was extempore, but varied by frequent quotations from book or manuscript. His style was as exact, compact and finished as if he had been reading ; without hurry, repetition, lapse or flaw. It was as if he spoke from memory, except that none of the effort and none of the dead and second-hand quality of a memorized speech were observable. He gave facts and dates, even hours and minutes, in describing the events attending the conflicts of Parliament and the King, in the reign of Louis XVI., without once referring to his notes, or a single pause or strain of recollection. Remaining seated, his manner was narrative, and his tone hardly above a colloquial one, yet with such animation of style, voice and gesture, that perfect attention and perfect audibleness were the rewards of his skillful delivery. For the first ten minutes his gestures were all with his left hand, of which all the fingers spoke, and I began to think him left-handed ; but later, I found him using either hand with equal grace and significance, and occasionally both. His utterance and manner seemed to me the perfection of professional oratory. Natural, animated and various, it was yet dignified, didactic and measured. His general theme was French Revolutions, and his immediate lecture involved too much that touched the present passions of the Liberals in France not to require the utmost delicacy of handling to make it a safe utterance. The Professor made the facts speak for themselves, and only by looks or tones indicated his own sympathies. A delightful humor, delicate as Irving's, ran through his discourse, which, reduced in his countenance to a latent smile, broadened in the audience into free laughter and cheers. The faintest shadow of his inner meaning, suggested only by a particle or a tone, was converted by his hearers into full and solid meaning. Evidently, a perfect understanding subsisted between Laboulaye and his audience, and if he had talked Republicanism outright, he could not have spoken in a manner more thoroughly liberal. He concluded his lecture, just an hour long, with an exordium in which he intimated the difficulties under which his treatment of a theme so delicate had been conducted, and made a noble plea for liberty of speech, education and action, which was as temperate and wise as it was inspiring and eloquent. Amid an enthusiastic burst of sympathy from the audience, M. Laboulaye rose, bowed and retired.

There is in M. Laboulaye a moral earnestness, and an insight into the springs of true human worth and true social growth, which places him in a most dignified and valuable position. He seems a man incapable of being tempted by ambition or seduced by political office. His sympathies are broadly human, and, on human grounds, intensely American. His acquaintance with our history and affairs was that of a native citizen. He knew things, I found, not only in gross but in detail. I found his table covered with American books, papers and cards. He was in regular receipt even of our Unitarian monthly, which he had too kindly attributed to my care. I asked him when he was coming to America; but he gave no encouragement to the hope I expressed that it might be soon, and even doubted whether it could be at all. Happily, no man needs less to come for the perfecting of his knowledge of us; and no man less, to make himself known to Americans; yet to whom should we give a heartier or more respectful and affectionate welcome?

I called, by his own appointment, a few days ago, on Michel Chevalier, who, as the most brilliant political economist of France and one possessing a statesman's opportunities, had a lively interest for me, and especially as, in some sort, Cobden's ally in the treaty of commerce between France and England; and also as the heir in part of De Tocqueville's influence. He is a Senator of the Empire, and that is to be in a certain degree hampered and compromised; but all his positive influence is enlightened and modern, and is sustained by the most extensive reading and study. He has a brilliant way of putting statistics which gives a great charm to his writings. His conversation is less striking, answering more to his appearance, which promises little vigor or *esprit*. He is not thought to have been very favorable to our cause in the late war. I found him less buoyant about our prospects than I should have liked ; but perhaps as much so as an advocate of retrenchment and an enemy of the wastefulness of war could be expected to be. He was warm in his expression of satisfaction that the war had terminated so favorably. I found in his son-in-law, M. Le Play, a son of the distinguished historian of the Industry of France, a book of immense method and fullness, of which the Astor Library has a copy, to which I have owed many valuable suggestions in past times.

It is impossible to leave Paris or France without an increased sense of the material majesty of the nation and country. The American idea of France is derived too much from English prejudices to be correct, and we look at it too much in our generation through the feelings we have for its immediate government, to do justice to the permanent character which belongs to the people, and to appreciate the immense liberties and privileges which have been slowly wrested from the successive dynasties, and which no régime dares to invade. The industry of the country is so various, its ingenuity and taste so pre-eminent, and its resources so rich and self-contained, that its wealth is easily accounted for, and can not be readily diminished by bad government. But what is most impressive is the union of longevity with youth. Ages have stored up their accumulations of riches in architecture, arts, and public works. The country is teeming with agricultural labor and experience. Its wines and silks and laces supply the world. Its importations are light, its exportations enormous. Its people are sober, industrious and saving.

Life is reduced in all its economies to a finished system. Waste or superabundance is unknown, and the people bear the marks of general health, due to the wisdom of their personal habits, the mixture of labor and leisure, their aptness for recreation and their knowledge how innocently to mingle in social relaxations. A universal pride in their country and a devotion to its glory sustain the government in constant improvements, and the people find their freedom and happiness largely in the provisions made for their daily enjoyment of out-of-door life in the midst of public gardens, abundant light, and cheap music.

The great cities are everywhere marked with evidences of the care of the government to gratify the national pride in monuments and public works. It is no wonder that the Frenchman is of all men the least disposed to emigrate, and thinks himself the citizen of the foremost nation. The government is not slow to encourage his self-complacency. The very "Exposition" now in progress is only one of the means it takes to show its people that France can beat other nations in every form of industry and art, and can fill half the whole space allotted to the world with her own manufactures and products. She has made her capital the pleasure-ground of the civilized human race. The superfluous wealth of all countries sets toward her beautiful boulevards. A perpetual stream of gold obeys the superlative attraction of her exquisite civilization, and flows steadily into her unreturning hand. She visits no other country, but entertains all. And she is entitled to her privilege ; for it is difficult to believe that the world has ever seen in any period of its history a city so deserving of wonder and admiration as the City of Paris. Of the strength of the existing government there can be little doubt. Louis Napoleon has known how to surround himself with able administrators, and has devoted himself to the glory of France. His character does not inspire moral enthusiasm nor personal respect, but it does awaken the sentiment of admiration for ability, courage, persistency and power.

He has made the army his ally, by a steady regard to its self-complacency, and has placed France so much at its mercy, not only by the fortifications of Paris, but by the whole military discipline of the nation, that it is hard to see how any Revolution can occur without its aid, or how its aid could be won away from the dynasty he has established. And perhaps the liberties of France are as likely to flourish under his natural successors as under any other masters of a more popular sort. France is a democratic Empire. There is a passion for personal rule and imperial display, united with a craving for a large possession of popular independence. This independence is hardly political, and is only poorly representative. Neither the parliament nor the press are free ; nor is there any sufficient right of assembling together for the consideration of public questions or the manufacture of public opinion. But the government concedes largely, and with an even freer hand, what the people would vote to themselves if they had the chance. She takes away the appetite for political action by granting the fruits of it in advance. Interference, either by the police or by any other authorities, with individual rights, is small. Life and property are wonderfully safe. The idealists and political philosophers are, of course, intensely dissatisfied with a state of things which does not recognize any of the great precepts of political liberty. They feel the thraldom of the press and of the assembly to be an intense humiliation ; but I doubt much if the people commonly enough share their sentiments to make the prospects of any change for the better very encouraging.

I doubt even if the death of the Emperor would be attended by the changes which are commonly predicted in England and America. But France is a dangerous country to prophesy in or about, and I will not pretend to have any adequate materials for a valuable judgment about its political future. But certainly my respect for the nation and the government has increased with a nearer view of it.

VII.

AMSTERDAM.

●

AMSTERDAM, June 30, 1867.

WE attended divine service this morning at the West Kerk of the Dutch Reformed Church. It is a venerable and large building, formerly a Catholic church, stripped naked of all its former magnificence excepting a showy organ of white marble columns and much gilded tracery, and so adapted to Protestant worship. Over the preacher's head is an immense sounding-board, and over each of four other elders' seats are also sounding-boards. The minister was clad in gown and bands; his clerk, perhaps the precentor, who sat just below him, was in bands also. As many as six functionaries, elders perhaps, in solemn black and bands, and black gloves, carried round bags attached to long poles, and collected money. They seemed to carry the bag twice to each person. Then the beadles or pew-openers, in white jackets and velvet caps, wanted money also. The congregation was large and attentive. The men put on and off their hats, and stood up or sat down at pleasure, but it was all done with a decorous air. The seats were hard enough to make standing a great relief, and in cold weather these stoveless churches must make a hat a necessary protection. The preacher was grave, earnest, graceful, and of a full and pleasing voice. His gestures were singularly pertinent and expressive, but he used gesture even in his extemporaneous prayers. I could not have believed that Dutch could be

made so pleasant to the ear. The singing was congregational, the music being printed and permanently adapted to
all the psalms and hymns, and the numbers of the psalms
and hymns were placarded on the pillars of the church.
Every body had a large Bible, bound in red Russia, with
clasps, open before him.   These Bibles, I noticed, were all of
an authorized version, countersigned in autograph by a person appointed to avouch each copy.

· Not knowing the language, we mistook an harangue of
fifteen minutes long for the sermon, and wondered that the
money-collectors should be so busy during the whole of it ;
but we found this was followed by a much longer address,
after a Psalm, which was doubtless the sermon proper. It
was pleasant to see the origin of the Dutch Reformed
churches at home, and to feel how little the stream had
changed its quality by flowing under the sea all the way to
America.   It seems more like Sunday here in Amsterdam
than in any place we have been since leaving home.   The
people look solid, grave, and attentive to their religious
duties, and Sunday is observed with as much strictness as
it can be in a city where sixty thousand Jews and fifty thousand Catholics are said to live.   It is not possible to be in a
Protestant part of Europe without feeling how immensely
great the change is in the moral and intellectual elevation of
the people, and how great the decline in taste, picturesqueness of life and beauty of worship.

Amsterdam is picturesque in a certain sense. Its old
gables, jutting forward and breaking the horizon with their
scolloped fronts ; the circular shape of the streets ; the mixture
of land and water ; the gleaming canals ; the dark brick houses
with their polished green doors, their large windows and their
heavy-ironed stoops ; the trees in the streets ; the arching
bridges ; the charity-girls, on various foundations, all in their ·

several distinctive uniforms ; the lumbering wagons, the occasional sledge—a carriage-body on runners drawn by a horse driven by a man on foot, who drops a greased rag now and then before the runners to lubricate their passage over the pavement ; the peasants in their gilded head-ornaments and snowy caps ; the sober citizens, unsmiling but gracious and formally polite—all give an air of much interest and novelty to the city.

Before visiting the museums we took an afternoon drive to the chief curiosity of the neighborhood, the little village of Broek. It is about six miles off, after crossing the ferry, and the road to it gives an opportunity of seeing the very careful system of dykes by which Amsterdam is defended from the ever-threatening sea. Naturally enough, Holland is skillful in hydraulics, as she owes her wealth and security to the success with which she keeps out of the water and the activity she displays upon it. The level of the canals inside her dams is only 1½ feet above low tide, and she can only open the gates that exclude the tide during the short period when the sea is lower than this level, or for a short period longer to effect a circulation in the water. The greatest nicety of management is studied in this whole business, the metre indicating the hundredth part of an inch in the height of the water. The dams are very broad at their bases, and built solidly in stone, sloped and rounded at what would else be angles, to avoid needless friction with ice or tide. It seemed as if dyke within dyke had been built, to make disaster less possible. We noticed recent repairs on minor dykes of earth, where withes of osiers, laden with gravel, were sunk to form a strong embankment. The road to Broek seems to be upon one of these dykes. It is smooth, narrow, and somewhat circuitous, but in parts runs through very narrow passages and over very narrow bridges. In the

canal by its side—as we supposed, the main artery in the rear
of the city—we saw many narrow but good-sized screw steam
ers full of passengers, going out of Amsterdam at a rate perhaps of eight miles per hour. They did not seem to agitate
the water or tear the banks as I should have expected.
Broek, which I remembered with interest from a former visit,
has a great reputation for cleanliness. It is a kind of miniature village, where the streets and houses are all on a baby-
house scale, where, no horses passing, no dust is kicked up,
and where abundance of water and a pavement of brick between the rows of houses make it very easy to keep every
thing clean. There is really nothing very remarkable about
it, and one is amazed at the sheep-like procession of travelers
that now for thirty years have followed each other into it.
There is nothing half as well worth seeing as in any one of
the small towns or villages in Holland, which travelers rush
by without notice. But it is the fashion to see Broek, and
we saw it.

There are several charming collections of pictures here
of the Dutch school, old and new, and it is pleasant to see
that the modern genius is not unworthy its origin. Mr.
Foder's collection is an admirable evidence of how much
talent for painting still exists in Holland.

One room in the king's palace here (originally built as a
town-house) is worthy special notice. It is thought by many
to be the finest room in Europe. It is a hundred feet high,
and lined with Carrara marble to the very ceiling. Many
other rooms in the palace are similarly enriched. There is
a remarkable degree of purpose in all the decorations of the
old palace, which dates back nearly three hundred years. It
is built on fifty thousand piles.

The more one studies Amsterdam the more sensible he
becomes how great a triumph over difficulties the whole city

is. Resting on a bog, it has the solid majesty of a city founded on a rock. It has created great public buildings; a fine botanic garden—distinguished for the beauty and healthiness of the wild beasts collected in it; a public park; and streets on streets of most substantial houses, full of elegance and comfort. Its great banking is done in little quiet, out-of-the-way cubby-holes, where no sign exists of what is going on within. We mistook Mr. Hope's office for a ticket-office, and applied for tickets to a neighboring picture gallery. It took a half-hour to find another banker's, who seemed hiding away from customers. Holland, in spite of its marshy foundations, is a most solid place. The people are grave, earnest, self-respectful, and you experience at every turn evidences that they are even better than they look—worthy descendants of a noble ancestry.

VIII.

PRUSSIA AND THE RHINE.

BINGEN ON THE RHINE, July 8, 1867.

THE railroad took us from Amsterdam to Düsseldorf in about four hours and a half. Passing from Holland into Prussia we found ourselves, the moment we crossed the frontier, in a military country, and felt at once the change from a nation at rest and in the ordinary condition of things to a nation aroused and thrilled through and through with new life and ambition. The depots seemed almost American in the activity and crowded appearance they presented. Soldiers were almost as thick as civilians, and they looked like men with business on hand, and not mere frames for uniforms. The country, too, though old and uninteresting in itself, presented an appearance of rapid improvement, and looked new with its new life. The farther we have gone into Prussia, the more the awaking of the nation has struck us. The recent war has put this country into a striking sympathy with the United States in the revival of all its energies, the consciousness of power, and the prevalence of the sentiment of nationality. The mighty and successful effort it lately made against Austria, so far from exhausting its strength or ambition, has only nerved it for greater things, and aroused every drop of military feeling in a people who have not forgotten Frederick the Great. It will be fortunate if this rising tide of public life is safely directed into economical channels.

The Luxembourg question was settled not without much resistance from the popular feeling, which would have enjoyed an opportunity of measuring swords with France. How long the itch for a chance to pay off old scores with their natural enemy, as Prussia holds France to be, will be controlled by prudent statesmanship remains to be seen. But we saw daily evidences that among the people at large, and specially the army, war with France would bring every Prussian to the front, and render almost any amount of personal sacrifice easy. It is to be hoped that the magnificent series of military displays France has lately made for the entertainment of her royal visitors will do something to arrest the recent perilous disposition to underrate the power and spirit of the French. Earnest and vigorous as Prussia is, and great as the late increase of her warlike power, she is not a match for France, and would engage in a rash undertaking to presume upon her victory over Austria, and try conclusions with Louis Napoleon. We are too warm lovers of the new German Empire—for that is the manifest destiny of things here—to wish to see it risked by a war with France. Meanwhile, let us confess the strength of the favorable impression all the Prussian officers have made upon us. A handsomer, more intelligent, or more spirited set of soldiers we have never met. They certainly wholly outshine the French officers in mere exterior promise. Tall, well-made, soldier-like in bearing, they have the manners of educated gentlemen, and look as fit for peace as for war.

The King of Prussia, a man of seventy, it will be recollected succeeded his brother only five years ago, although owing to the paralytic condition of the late King he had been regent for ten years before he came to the throne. A great stickler for military etiquette and discipline, and a determined upholder of his prerogative, he has never been popular with the

D

liberal party, nor indeed with the people generally, until since the late war. Two years ago he shared with Count Bismarck the odium of dissolving the Parliament because it would not vote supplies for an increase of the army. The wisdom of the policy they had steadily pursued, of increasing and every way strengthening the military power of the country, has now been revealed by the results of the struggle with Austria and the consolidation of North Germany with Prussia; and the popularity of King William and his Prime Minister has suddenly become quite overwhelming. Even the liberals begin to believe the government friendly to their hopes. The King himself, whom I saw at Paris, and again at Ems, looks like a sensible, serious and simple-minded man. He rode last Saturday into Ems, which was decked out in charming holiday attire to receive him, with a simplicity quite extraordinary. A single outrider preceded him. His carriage was unaccompanied by others. He had one officer on the seat with him—and two mounted men followed. He wore a rather plain uniform, and the fatigue-cap of Prussian officers. Nothing could be less pretentious. The country people from the neighborhood had assembled to greet their new king. The streets were gay with triumphal arches and flags and garlands. Thousands of small trees had been brought from the forest and stuck into the pavements, to wear for a day or two the appearance of growth and permanency—the most expensive and elaborate form of festive decoration I ever saw undertaken, and wonderfully successful. The King spent two or three days in the little watering-place, and moved about with almost the freedom of a private person, exhibiting no distrust of his subjects, and meeting everywhere with hearty and affectionate respect. Count Bismarck was not with him. He is, however, very popular, and not insensible to his laurels. I heard this story from a good source at

Paris: Some one said to the Count, "Was not your excellency afraid that the people at Paris, instead of shouting 'Vive le Roi,' would cry 'Vive Bismarck?'" "No," said the Count; "I knew exactly what they would say, and it was far more gratifying than any thing else they could have said. First '*Vive* le Roi,' and then '*Voila* Bismarck.'" And certainly "Voila Bismarck," on every occasion when he moved in any public procession, was the general exclamation. Every body was curious to see him, and eager to point him out to his neighbor.

Düsseldorf is a model German town, solid, dull, devoted to art and music, with a fine park and capital accommodations for the first necessity of the Germans, a place for gathering over their wine and beer with their wives and children, and spending at least two evenings in the week in the open air, with orchestral music and pleasant chat. The night I passed in town happened to be the anniversary of the battle of Königgrätz, and from 5 to 10 P.M. the best portion of the citizens were in the tea-garden, adjoining the town-hall, enjoying the rational amusement of excellent music from two bands, one of strings and the other of brass, who alternated with each other. Had a member of the Total Abstinence Society entered that assembly and seen a hundred tables covered with bottles half empty, of every shape and color, mingled with mugs of beer and cups of tea and coffee, and men, women and children seated about them, and all partaking of the various drinks, he would have been in despair at the complete sway of wine-bibbing among the people of Düsseldorf. The first ladies and gentlemen, the ministers of religion, the young women, the old men, the innocent children, all would have been in one condemnation—a wine-bibbing generation. And yet a careful survey of the garden would have failed to show one single person excited to indiscretion or the loss of self-control—one single noisy or tipsy man. And here for four or five hours are whole families in the open air, engaged in domestic and social chat, enjoying music and the sympathy of their fellow-creatures instead of being scattered and divided as with us—the old here, the young there, the men in one place, the women in another. As I looked upon the cheerfulness and moderation, the cordial intercourse, the absence of carking cares or of haste and self-condemnation in this German tea-garden, I felt that Germany understood social life far better than any portion of America. As to the attempt to abolish drunkenness in America by a general assault upon the use of all things that can intoxicate, it is well meant, and has its excellent effects. But it is greatly to be feared that it is not enough in accordance with natural laws to be a permanent influence. We must improve family life, and specially must we cultivate the participation of men and women, old and young, in common pleasures, before we can hope to exorcise the demon of excess and sensuality from American society.

It is much to be regretted that the friends of temperance have of late been trying to unsettle the opinion that drunkenness is rare in the vine-growing countries. It is so patent in France and in Germany that intemperance in the form of drunkenness is a most exceptional vice that only willful blindness or partisanship could deny it. I do not recollect to have seen one tipsy man since I left Paris, and only one in Paris, and I have diligently sought the places where, in our country, they would be found. The truth is, wine is one of the most common and one of the most beautiful gifts of Providence ; an article joined with corn in the praises of saints. The countries which possess it understand its use, and are just as little subject to excess in using wine as in using corn. Excess is found everywhere, and all Heaven's gifts are liable

·to abuse ; but to expect France and Germany to give up wine or beer is absurd, nor would any thing but harm come from the attempt to enforce their disuse by legislation. Special efforts must be made in northern climates to resist the tendency to strong drinks, which is aggravated by cold and by the necessity of harder work to live, not to add gloominess of weather, short days and much darkness.

However, I was somewhat horrified to find, later, in common use among field-laborers, both women and men, in certain districts aside from the Rhine, a fiery alcoholic drink called potato-whisky—strong, intoxicating, and full of fusil oil. It is a part of the daily ration of field-laborers in the region about Frankfort—a half-pint per day. And in harvest-time even this does not satisfy them. They expend a certain portion of the extra pay of this season in adding to their whisky ration, and many of them then drink, I am told, to drunkenness. This is a proper deduction to be made from the universal temperance observed among the better classes, and should give some pause to the inquirer's verdict upon the sobriety of wine-making countries. Unhappily the whisky is only twenty-three cents per gallon, and wine is many times dearer. It is, however, universally conceded that drunkenness is more and more rare even among this field class, and that it is wholly confined to it, with rare individual exceptions. I shall press the investigation wherever I find opportunity, and report results without fear or favor, be they in accordance with theories or expectations or no.

It was pleasant in Düsseldorf to see one or two familiar specimens of Leutze's genius, losing nothing by the neighborhood of pictures from the hands of the best living artists. Several of the pictures which so long hung in the Düsseldorf Gallery in New York greeted us like friends from the walls of the Permanent Exhibitions of Modern Pictures in their native home. It is difficult to overestimate the influence of that old gallery upon American taste for art. It was for fifteen years the best collection of pictures Americans had access to, and gave thousands their first idea of good painting. I went to Düsseldorf more out of gratitude to that gallery than for any other reason, and I can truly say that I found I had seen more of the place in New York than was to be seen in Düsseldorf itself. With the exception of two or three pictures of the two Achenbachs, and one or two of Sohn's, I saw nothing in the way of art which paid me for a day's delay in the town.

It is an hour's journey by rail from Düsseldorf to Cologne. The cathedral occupies the horizon five miles before reaching the city, and seems longer in the distance than close at hand. Two hundred workmen are still busy in renewing the crumbled glories of this magnificent church. It will take a quarter of a century, even at the brisk rate the repairs are now going on, to put it in good condition, and a quarter more to finish its towers. Then it will, indeed, be the St. Peter's of Gothic architecture. The churches of Cologne are all interesting from their antiquity and the remains of the Roman style, which prevails over the Gothic. The famous shrine of the voices of the eleven thousand virgins who suffered with St. Ursula in the fourth century (?) is still the centre of curiosity for travelers. A most curious collection it is. The good faith in which the pious sacristan exhibits it, was the most interesting part of the exhibition. His face, simple and devout, glowed with holy confidence, as he looked with an interest that years of familiarity had not weakened, upon a splinter of the true cross and one of the original vessels that held the water that in Cana was changed to wine, the missing fragment of which he was good enough to assure us was in Notre Dame at Paris! The credulity of devout Catholics is only equaled by the incredulity of undevout Protestants, and is on the whole the more interesting extreme. Cologne is reviving in trade and importance, and is losing its world-renowned celebrity for being the filthiest city on the Continent. At least twenty original Jean Maria Farinas keep up the manufacture of the most popular perfume that ever refreshed the nostrils of fainting women. It is natural that the worst smelling place in Christendom should have invented the best artificial odor. Parents, surnamed Farina, baptize their children Jean Maria, to entitle them to use the name in the manufacture of Cologne water, a foresight which our American enterprise has not yet attained to. It illustrates the stability and continuity of European usages.

We were fortunate enough to approach the Rhine from the flats of Holland, with senses hungering for variety in the scenery, and prepared to enjoy every elevation on the landscape. Nineteen years ago we had reversed the journey and come to the Rhine from Switzerland, to belittle its hills with the memory of the snow-crowned mountains we had just left. I could hardly have believed that the effect would have been so different. The Rhine, which in prospect had affected our imagination and excited our expectations more than any part of Europe, grievously disappointed us on our first visit. We returned to it, therefore, with very moderate hopes, and were now carried away in the most unexpected manner by its beauties, which it seemed as if nobody had duly extolled. From Coblentz to Bingen it is one delicious succession of landscapes, ever varying, and presenting the most vivid contrasts : dark and overhanging precipices on one side ; open and cultivated fields on the other ; hills beginning in the most soft and verdant garden-culture and ending in craggy and inaccessible peaks. The terraces of the vine, mighty stairs for giants to climb, are opposed by smiling fields checkered with harvests of all the grains just ready for the reaper. The suddenness of the changes, the depth of the ravines, the jaggedness of the rocks, the richness of the colors of earth and stones, the beauty of the ruins of castles, growing from rocks and looking as old as nature itself, spring from every crag. The splendor of the associations brought to mind by the names of the villages that make almost a continuous tour of the banks ; the curious long boats that pole their slow way up, or are dragged by horses or by men and women on the banks ; the churches that lift their solid towers from every cluster of houses ; the landscape, changing under clouds and passing showers, or slowly fading in the long twilight or brightening with the setting sun ; the stream itself so rapid and so full—copious, swift, and laden with memories of Alps and glaciers ; the lowly valleys opening at the Lahn, the Moselle, the Nahe, and fifty other points, each different and all beautiful—all this combines to make the Rhine the most picturesque and haunting river in the world.

Some Americans aboard our steamboat tried to persuade us that the Hudson was more beautiful. We admired their patriotism more than their taste. The Tennessee river about Chattanooga has more resemblance to the Rhine than the Hudson. There is nothing on the Rhine equal to the view of the Catskill Mountains from near Hudson, but that is the only exception in its favor. In all other respects the Hudson is inferior, in vivid contrasts, variety, ruggedness and softness, richness of color and picturesqueness of effects.

IX.

HOMBURG AND GAMING.

HOMBURG, near Frankfort,
Germany, July 20, 1867.

BADEN-BADEN, Homburg, Wiesbaden, Ems, are among the chief watering-places of this bath-loving, mineral-water-drinking, Continental people. Pretty much all the water drank on the Continent is mineral water, wine and beer superseding water in its ordinary use as a beverage. There is a mania among physicians in France and Germany for this kind of cure. Drugs and lotions are out of fashion. Nature is installed as the great apothecary. She has a prescription already made up in her great subterranean dispensary for every malady. Her chief pharmacy is the region of Nassau, where the petty princes of Germany are custodians of her concoctions, ranged along in sparkling or cloudy vials, hot, lukewarm and cold, and sold to suit the wants of all sorts of invalids, to the great benefit of their needy exchequers. Salt, soda, iron, magnesia, sulphur, and all their various compounds, at every temperature, and in all proportions, are distributed along the footholds of these petty ranges of mountains, and hither in July and August flock the ailing and the feeble, the sick and the not well, to try the virtues of these natural medicines. With the really ill, the gouty, the rheumatic, the consumptive, and the halt and blind, come the countless hosts of dyspeptics, and the victims of luxury, self-indulgence and sloth, the high livers and the bad livers, to recruit their wasted powers and strengthen their feeble digestion. And following in their train the whole flock of pleasure-seekers and fashion-mongers. What the precise connection between mineral-springs and gambling-tables is I will not undertake to say, but certain it is that their juxtaposition is close and constant in most countries, and most of all in this. What costume and equipage, balls and drives, flirtations and champagne, or what are called "American drinks," are to Saratoga and the Sulphur Springs, gambling is to the baths of Germany—the steady accompaniment and attraction, the chief talk and excitement.

Here in Homburg, nature and art have combined to form a lovely summer resort. It is situated on the flank of the Taunus range (an humbler sort of Catskills) six hundred feet above the sea level, with pleasant woods on one side, full of game, and on the other smiling fields, in lovely swells, checkered with grains. A mountain range, colored with purple hues and attracting clouds in every form, to crown their castled summits with aerial architecture, lies in the southern direction ; and to the north the spires of Frankfort and the numerous villages that people the wide plains between the Main and the Rhine. A cleanly town of six thousand inhabitants, with well-paved and well-built streets, and presided over by a venerable schloss or castle, the home of the reigning family for four or five hundred years past,—it is only perhaps within twenty years that Homburg has taken on such prominence as a watering-place. But immense enterprise has marked the administration of its interests during this period. The centre of interest is the *Kursaal* or cure saloon, theoretically and originally the house over the chief spring, where invalids assembled to bathe and drink the waters ; but now only the public temple of pleasure, the centre of festivity, the sheltered promenade, the restaurant, opera-house, music saloon, and above all, gambling hall ! The Kursaal at Homburg is said to be the most costly in Europe. It is over five hundred feet long, built around three sides of a hollow square, two stories high, and substantial and elegant within and without. The chief saloon or music hall is lined with colored marbles. The gambling-rooms are rooms of pro-digious size and height, painted in the most gorgeous hues, and decorated with marble and gilding. Elegance, luxury and splendor characterize the whole building. Liveried lackeys, of most commanding mien, patrol the apartments and preside in the passages. Decorum and order every-where prevail. Carelessness of dress, negligence of manners, absence of strict courtesy, would be instantly corrected by the officials. The people of the town and the soldiers (whose name is legion all over Europe) are not allowed to enter this place. But it is as open as the grave for all others.

And here is the grand exchange of all the visitors. Beau-tiful grounds, on which the rear of the Kursaal opens, invite to exercise in shady walks and to repose on comfortable seats. A charming band of forty performers plays an hour at the springs (a half-mile from the Kursaal) between seven and eight in the morning, and then on the grounds of the Kursaal between three and four and seven and nine in the evening. There are twenty good hotels in the town, where most visitors dine and breakfast, and where casual comers find beds. But visitors staying for a week or two commonly take lodgings in the town, which may be said to be wholly given up in all its comfortable buildings to this temporary purpose. The owners build their own homes with reference to this thrifty use ; and in three months expect to reap a harvest which will go far to support them through the year. Meanwhile, they themselves retreat into little cottages built in their own yards, leaving their nice homes to the liberal strangers, who pay only fair prices for excellent accommodations. We have, for instance, on the second floor, three large, lofty and well-furnished apartments, as quiet as though in the depth of the country, commanding a superb view, and not five minutes' walk to the Kursaal, for which we pay forty guldens per week (about sixteen dollars). We have our breakfast (a separate charge) at our lodgings, and go to " The Victoria," or " The Four Seasons," or some other hotel for our dinner, which is furnished for about seventy-five cents per head. This is certainly very moderate living for a centre of European pleasure-seekers. At $7\frac{1}{2}$ in the morning all the visitors (if the weather serves) are found at the springs. Here a mile square of walks, beautifully adorned with flowers and shrubs, and kept, chiefly by the hands of women, in excellent order, invites to gentle exercise. There are four chief springs, but supereminent among them, as our Congress Spring at Saratoga, is the " Elizabethan," so named after an English princess, wife of a favorite reigning duke of this little duchy. It is far from pleasant in its flavor, having seventy per cent. of common salt in its composition ; but it is found an active aperient, and as such is immensely popular with those who bring torpid livers and weak digestive functions to Homburg. The " Kaiser Brunnen" is more of a tonic, charged with iron and sulphur, but agrees very well with the " Elizabethan," so that my morning dram is two tumblers of the first and one of the last, taken under strict medical advice and with certain qualifications of diet, especially the avoidance of fruits and salads.

After an hour and a quarter spent in gentle exercise and social chat, and in imbibing the water at proper intervals, the visitors go to their breakfasts, usually with an improved appetite, but how much due to air and exercise, and how much to the waters, I will not undertake to say. There is little activity in the public life of Homburg between 8 and 11

A.M. A few seek the reading-room, but most are quiet in their lodgings. But at 11 A.M. occurs one of the great events of the day! The gambling-tables are opened with much ceremony! The officers or administrators of the *bank* come in with the money, about £30,000, which is to be played for that day; and it is counted with much formality and placed on the table in full public view. Even that portion of it which is in 1000-franc bills and is kept in a little box on the table, has an indicator in the shape of a gold coin for every 1000-franc note, kept upon the cover, and changed as the fortunes of the bank change. The bank is pledged to lose no more than the fixed sum thus publicly counted out on the morning of each day. It must play every day till 11 o'clock P.M., or until it is broken. Of course this seldom occurs; but it does occur occasionally, possibly two or three times each season. There is a set of hired clerks who play for the bank — four at the *Rouge-et-noir* tables, six at the *Roulette*. The tables, of which there are five, accommodate each, perhaps, twenty persons sitting and as many standing —called technically *la galerie*. Around them there are commonly as many looking on curiously as there are players. Perhaps there are not a hundred persons in the whole three or four thousand visitors who come exclusively to play, or who are seen regularly at the tables. But probably a quarter of all the visitors make an occasional stake for excitement and amusement. Deep playing is sure to attract a crowd of spectators, and commonly at any given time there will be only one person at each table who is playing for a stake of five Napoleons—about $20—for each "coup," that is, each deal of cards or turn of the roulette. Most of the players pledge a two-florin piece (eighty cents) on every *coup*. Even at this rate, as the deal occurs once in a minute or two, much money may be lost or won in a half-hour; and for the heavier players, who begin with five Napoleons and double their stake every time, it is plain that several thousand francs may be changed from the private pocket to the bank, or from the bank to the private pocket, in ten or fifteen minutes. I have seen men and women both going away minus two or three thousand francs after a half-dozen *coups*, and some others carrying away as much after ten minutes' successful playing. Usually, however, large players are too fond of the excitement to leave because they are fortunate. They stay more commonly to shift their fortunes and leave their winnings with the bank. If every gamester left the table when the chances were in his favor, the bank would soon be out of capital. But it reckons too surely upon the appetite which success stimulates. No doubt it looks with gratification upon the good fortune which often attends the risks of novices, for it expects to reap its final harvests from their deluding passion for the game. Every body understands that the chances are by a small per cent. in favor of the bank; but it is equally understood that beyond this avowed advantage the game is conducted with entire fairness. The bank has in its favor, besides about 18½ per cent., only the advantage of its capital, said to be two million pounds, owned by a joint stock company in shares of £25, and, it is said, distributed among widows, orphans, and all sorts of people in the place. It is said that a bold player of large capital, by continually doubling his stake, would be sure to save himself so long as his capital held out, and many play upon this principle, not to make, but not to lose, and at the same time enjoy the excitement of the game. But, after all, few have any considerable capital to fall back on, and the bank has this great advantage over ninety-nine hundredths of all its competitors.

I have tried to analyze the fascination of this game by watching the faces and the play of those engaged in it. A more serious company it is hard to conceive of than the one gathered around these tables. Silence, gravity, unsmiling attention, absorption in the business in hand, a strained composure and fixed expression, neither moved by success, nor disturbed by ill-luck, are the prevailing characteristics. You look in vain for the nervous, impassioned, suicidal expressions of countenance you are taught to expect. Most of the company at play look beautifully unconscious of any thing unusual, disgraceful or sinful in their occupation. They are simply intent upon the game, each man watching his stake with unfeigned interest, but with a practiced knowledge of the risks, and a feeling that he may gain at the next turn what he lost in the last. The possibility of success is always before the player, and he sees success attending his neighbor. The fact that in one minute, by sinking a florin, you may make it two or twenty, presents an excitement which to those without moral scruples on the subject must be very fascinating. Nothing but a well-considered and established conviction of the public and private demoralization and peril of gambling could prevent persons from dipping into its deceitful waters here, where a sort of exceptional license covers gambling from reprobation ; where all its concomitants are decorous ; where drinking and carousing and the more common forms of dissipation are suppressed ; where people of excellent social position and general respectability—lords and barons, bankers and countesses, gentlemen and ladies of fixed standing—are found amusing themselves at the gambling-table, and where it is open and legalized and conducted with unquestioned fairness. Then it is doubtful whether the lookers-on are not really participants to the extent of lending the countenance of their presence to the immoral game. Curiosity and a desire to study human nature under a powerful passion has drawn me very often into the saloon ; but I confess I never felt quite innocent even in watching this beguiling and perilous fountain of ruin and corruption. The chief evil is not done here at Homburg, or at other public tables. It is the passion which is first awakened under the comparatively innocent circumstances of these public and honestly-conducted gambling-rooms which leads thousands of young men, and old ones too, to private play, until it becomes the business of their lives or the ruin of their fortunes and bodies and souls. The more habitual players here seem to be old men and women. Byron calls "avarice a good old-gentlemanly vice." Certainly the love of the excitement of gambling seems to survive most other passions. No form of gambler has appeared so truly disgusting, however, as that of the old woman. A young countess, lovely in person, and dignified and self-possessed, whom I saw now losing, now winning, considerable sums, did not lose quite all her charms in the atmosphere of the gambling-table ; but several old hags in lace and jewels, who sat hour after hour at the board, seemed made up to disgrace their sex and their age.

The superstitions of the players are a singular exhibition of the credulity of those who have generally ceased to have any faith in God or man. No groveling worshiper of an imaginary toe-nail of an imaginary saint ever exceeded in superstition the mass of the men and women who sit at these gambling-tables, solemnly pricking holes in their card-gospels, from which they read their guidance and through which they peep into the future fortunes which await them. Victims to absurd mysticisms about lucky numbers and false inferences from the abused law of averages, they go religiously on, trusting in their stars and tied to their dotage. One very pious gambler who believes in our glorious liturgy, but not in preaching, hurries from his Sunday prayers to try his luck at *Roulette*, upon the 24-10 (chap. and verse) of the text the minister announces! Another turns his Bible to see what psalm opens, or what page cuts, and hastens to try his luck under such blessed guidance! Now it is the Nine which the divinities of the gambler's table have consecrated, and the next day Seven or Twenty-three. If Maximilian is shot by seven men on the 19th June, 7 and 19 would be the secret talisman of the first gamester that heard the news, if he were not warned by the fate of the noble gambler in thrones, who staked his life and lost it upon the throw! Were there 31 words in Napoleon's letter to M. Rouher, offering him the diamond cross of the Legion of Honor, it would be ground enough for a bare-headed Frenchman here, who carries his velvet cap in his hand in rain and shine, to play all day on that number, confident of coming out winner by 11 P.M., at which time the tables close! Failure to-day would do as little to cure the folly of such a hope as the empty results of ignorant and fanatical expectations do usually to correct superstitions. It is not the fruit of the superstition, but the superstition itself which is precious! Religion, even in its falsest form, is more disinterested than defamers of human nature suspect. But enough of this hateful but fascinating theme.

Dinner is important to idlers, and we dignify it daily with an hour and a half's attention. We have tried the *table-d'hôtes* of a half-dozen hotels, to see if one German dinner were possibly any less bad than another. By diligent attention to every course (skipping the intolerable ones, where grease and vinegar contend for victory), one may satisfy the absolute cravings of hunger, which eight hours after a very modest breakfast are sure not to be without importunity. But the courses are individually so meagre in quantity, that there are none too many of them to make up what, eaten together, will be, in the language of California, " a good square meal." It may be an idiosyncrasy, but none of my party like vinegar in their poached eggs ; nor tarragon in every stew, nor salad and sweetmeats flanking roast mutton, nor fish and pudding half-way through dinner. Nor are we content with a dozen dishes of meat and one of vegetable, carefully saved (probably stringed beans), and served separately after the meats are gone. But then, *our* customs are very hateful to Germans, and we must try and like to sleep on inclined planes, too short by six inches for our proportions, and not to smother under their down beds, used as blankets, and to endure their terrible cuisine, where too sour and too sweet are always sickening our palates, and where tasteless butter and often sour bread vex our daily patience.

I wish I had time to tell you about a Roman camp (the finest extant perhaps) which is traceable within two miles of this place, where urns are found full of undisturbed dust, with the tear bottles lying near by; or of my visit to one of the great German wine cellars at Frankfort, where some famous wine, forty-five years old, tastes like very poor old cider, though very precious and wholesome. But enough for Homburg. We shall stay here another week, to give the waters a full chance, and then away for Heidelberg and Switzerland. There are three hundred Americans here, it is said. I find several valued parishioners among them. Where are they not?

X.

GERMAN LIFE.

HOMBURG LES BAINS, July 22, 1867.

IGNORANCE of the languages is a terrible obstacle to any clear and satisfactory intercourse with the natives of European countries. Those who *speak* French and German (to read them is of little service) are seldom competent observers, or sufficiently interested in important inquiries to improve their opportunities; while among the few travelers who thirst for a true acquaintance with the political, social and economic life of these great countries, it is rare to find one who possesses a practical familiarity with the tongues that can alone unlock their secrets.

It is of the utmost importance, therefore, that our colleges and schools should use new diligence in drilling their pupils in the effective knowledge of spoken French and German. If educated visitors to Europe possessed the fluent use of these two tongues, we should in a single generation derive untold and invaluable information from their comparison between American and European life. At present, we seldom draw much reliable instruction from their reports and observations. Americans associate abroad almost exclusively with each other, and are essentially blind and deaf to the inner life or usages and experiences of the peoples they visit. They return home with erroneous impressions, superficial views, and the prejudices they brought with them. I speak from a humiliating experience, and feel that all I venture to say upon

what interests me more than any thing else, the moral life of
the countries I am journeying in, is subject to the deduction
of a very limited range and a very shallow depth of observation.

I was fortunate enough yesterday to visit a German gentleman of wealth, intelligence, and a ripe experience, who had
lived, twenty years ago, long enough in America to acquire a
thorough knowledge of our language, institutions, manners
and feelings, and who had·been long enough back in his native country to have all the familiarity with its present life
and all the German feeling essential to a proper account of
the existing condition of Germany.   In company with a late
Governor of Rhode Island, with Mr. Wells, the Commissioner of Revenue, and our excellent and devoted American
Consul-General at Frankfort, Mr. Murphy, I had the valuable
opportunity of an hour or two of conversation with Herr G.
There were four of us pelting him with inquiries, note-book
in hand, and a more ready, competent and unfailing witness
and furnisher of precise and valuable information I never yet
saw under the process of cross-questioning.   He is one of
those men the whole business of whose remaining life should
be to answer intelligent questions concerning the economic
and social life of Germany.   I never happened to meet his
superior in quick apprehension and explicit and full information, in the sphere of every-day observation.   The village in
which Herr G. lives is half-way between Homburg and Frankfort, on the banks of the little river Neider.   There he has a
large farm, which he carries on under his own eye for a part
of the year, living in the winter in Frankfort.   He raises
pretty much every thing that is grown in the Middle States of
America.   He sends milk to market, and his cattle are all
stall-fed.   His cows continue perfectly healthy, although they
never leave their stable.   A cow is worth about forty dollars,

a farm-horse about sixty. Common field-laborers are hired at about twenty-four dollars a year wages, with their board, which is estimated to cost about sixty dollars a head more.

Women receive only about sixteen dollars a year, and are allowed the same quantity of food. Their daily ration is two pounds of bread, about a quarter of a pound of cheese, sufficient potatoes, with butter or lard to cook them with, on four days of the week, and every other day a half-pound of meat, beef, mutton or veal. Cabbages, which are sold at a dollar the hundred head, are considered an article of luxury, and do not enter into the common food of the laboring class. The farm-hands are not furnished from the village; they come from Bavaria and the Fulda country, where they have little patches of land and cottages to which they return in the winter. The villagers have usually, in this Rhine region and about the Main, a little farm of perhaps ten, fifteen, twenty acres, which they work themselves, and from which they draw their living. These little strips of farm-land are worth from $500 to $800 per acre. They are dreadfully embarrassed by regulations about the time and method of their tillage, made necessary by the way in which they lie, tier behind tier, away from roads, the soil being too costly to allow the space which would be necessary for an open way left fallow. These fields are divided into three classes, the summer fields, the winter fields, and the Branch. The summer fields must all be planted by the 15th May, after which no right of way is allowed to the owner to visit his land with cart or horse, or to carry over his neighbor's field any thing likely to injure the crop. The winter fields must be sowed to wheat or other winter crop by the 15th October, for the same reason. The Branch, or the fields in which potatoes and other crops are raised, requiring frequent visits at short intervals, are by themselves, and a road, half on one man's land and half on his neighbor's, must be left open at all seasons. Of course, the character of the crops planted in the other fields must be confined to these conditions. A special officer is appointed in each village to see these strict laws enforced. These necessary but burdensome regulations must be considered as of the nature of a tax on labor and production, and would in any close competition spoil the chances of a market for people thus tied up and burdened. In Germany, as in France, the laws partition out the landed estate of a deceased proprietor among his children, and this has already gone on so far that the right of way in certain districts to these fractional lots exceeds the value of the land. Special legislation is called for in France, and will soon be needful in Germany, upon this point.

There is no considerable chance for labor-saving implements of agriculture in a country where labor is so cheap. Still, improved ploughs are gradually creeping in. Mr. G. introduced a new American plough into his fields a few years ago, and an interdict was immediately put upon it by the council of the village. He was obliged to apply to the highest authority in his country for a reversal of this restraining process. It was granted, and he put his plough to work. The next season the whole potato crop in the neighborhood failed, with the exception of Mr. G.'s. This put the farmers on inquiry, and it was discovered that a few inches deeper ploughing with the new implement had carried the roots beyond the source of the rot, and the farmers at once adopted quite generally the American plough. It is in this way that improvements are slowly but surely creeping into the costly and wasteful methods of this German gardening which is here called farming.

Farm-labor is not intelligent. It is chiefly Catholic in its origin, and comes from regions that are not enterprising or forehanded enough to emigrate to America. The emigration to our country is usually from districts the most advanced in comfort and mental activity, and it is the best and not the worst part of the laboring population that goes to America. A certain kind of elementary education is compulsory in Prussia and over Germany generally. The government furnishes the teachers, but the parents of the children pay their wages. If any are too poor to do this, the expense falls upon the village. The cost of roads and bridges and their maintenance is a tax on the village. Each village has its burgomaster and its council. The chief officer, or mayor, is paid a small salary of from fifty to one hundred florins (forty cents is a florin). The council, elected by the villagers, has authority to lay taxes and collect them. These villagers are often intelligent, and very commonly take a weekly newspaper. Their houses, huddled too much together, and with none of the charms of our American village-homes, are yet comfortable, and the streets are usually cleanly; but the appearance is gloomy and monotonous. The villagers, however, meet after their day's work, to talk over local and personal matters and to discuss politics over their beer and pipe, and are not without enlightened views of their interests.

Just now, of course, the great topic of conversation is the gain and loss of the forced union of so many lately independent States with Prussia. Prussia carries matters with a pretty high hand, and has not been very careful to propitiate the regions she has annexed. No process could render such a change acceptable. But the tender point, after all, is the question of taxation. Some abatement has been made of the tax on land, which is of course popular. But a considerable increase has been enforced in the income-tax, so called, by which it is extended to a class that hitherto escaped. The common laborer now pays, say two per cent. on his year's earnings. All who have an income over a thousand rix dollars, pay three per cent. The taxes are not high on the whole, but they are collected monthly, and in a somewhat vexatious manner. First, two assessors from without the immediate district go from house to house, determining the taxable property of each citizen. His house-rent is regarded as the basis of the estimate, and it is assumed that his income is five times the amount of his actual or estimated house-rent. He may protest, but then he must submit to a sworn and very detailed examination of his actual resources, and in case of falsification, he must pay three times the amount of his tax. In the city and larger towns a fixed day in each month is publicly advertised, on which each citizen must pay in his monthly tax. In the villages the circuit tax-gatherer comes in, it may be unexpectedly, and rings his bell, like a town-crier, up and down the streets, and every taxable citizen must hurry out and settle his account with the government. The amount of time and the amount of soreness involved in this frequent operation strikes an American with wonder. A tooth pulled a little once a week till it was slowly dragged out would be its most natural parallel. I saw this operation going on in the little picturesque town of Friedberg, in Hesse-Darmstadt, and it seems general in Germany.

Mechanics' wages are about fifty cents per day. In Frankfort an income of $4000 enables a man to live handsomely, and keep his carriage and horses, a thing not justifiable on less than three or four times that amount in any commercial city in America.

There are considerable woolen factories, and indeed factories of all kinds, in this region. German rivers are commonly small and with little fall of water, and where a feeble water-power, which might answer four months out of the year, exists, it is not economical on the whole to use it. All the mills, therefore, are run by steam.   I met yesterday the hands from a mill returning two or three miles to the village where they lived from their daily work.   It is plain that the science and the cheap labor of the Continent, especially in Belgium and Germany, are going to give England a very serious rivalry in textile and iron manufactures.   Coal and iron by the existing railroad systems are now brought very closely together, and it is found more economical to carry them both to the labor, than to bring labor to them.   Some English capitalists are erecting iron works in Germany to save themselves from the ruinous competition of her cheap labor. There is one thing about English manufacturing capital which deserves special commendation.   It depends upon increase of skill and adaptation to circumstances to secure its returns, and does not expect that the government will fly to its rescue with an extravagant tariff the moment it discovers a miscalculation in its plan.   In America every petty local interest or private manufacture, the moment it finds its ill-chosen business incapable of contending with the competition of countries favored by cheaper labor and better skill, hurries to Congress and demands a protection which costs the nation perhaps a million or two of dollars in enhanced prices for the encouragement of a branch of manufactures which may not have a half-million of capital engaged in it in the whole country.   This is most unjust and oppressive, and ought to be frowned on by the common sense of the people. If we can not practice an economy and a skill such as all other countries have to use in sustaining a fair competition with their neighbors, our manufacturing interests will suffer and ought to suffer when they undertake branches of business to which our climate and our circumstances are wholly unadapted.   This seems specially true of all silk manufactures and of many other.   Any general objections to protec-

E

tion, founded on theories of free trade, may well be withstood, but we ought not to protect feeble branches which never can be inoculated into our system, and which are purely for the interest of a few individuals at a great expense to the body-politic.   Americans have a great natural aptitude for ingenious machinery, for skillful labor, for economy in production, and for intelligent industry.   We ought to encourage and to depend far more than we do upon this resource, but our recent legislation is positively discouraging this quality, and foreign industry looks with a smiling self-congratulation upon the folly which is undermining our progress and improvement, by accustoming our manufactures to artificial protection, while it debilitates skill, prudence and economy in production.

American government stocks are in large and increasing demand in Germany, and they are purchased not on speculation but for investment.   The area over which they are rapidly spreading is already very large.   Orders come in to the Frankfort Bourse every day, not only from all parts of Germany and Switzerland, but from Austria, Hungary, and even Moldavia.   In short, they seem the favorite security at this time.   The general estimate of the Frankfort bankers of the amount of these stocks now held on the Continent, is not less than five hundred millions.   So scarce are they, that a demand for two hundred thousand in a day would raise the market price of them.   Probably if they should rise to ninety per cent. some would be sent back to America.   The amount of them is pretty accurately known by the number of coupons sent to Frankfort, the moneyed centre of American securities, for collection.   Baron Rothschild (of Paris) is now here with two of his brothers.   Their great house, it is said, does not deal in American Bonds.   The Baron (the eldest brother, for they are all Barons, I believe) is a man of eighty, but in excellent preservation, and commonly to be seen at the spring early in the morning, looking as cheerful, unpretending and simple as if neither age, nor vast affairs, nor honors and emoluments were resting on his shoulders. He dresses rather young, has a light and un-Jewish complexion, and is specially gallant and disengaged in his manners. His intercourse with his grandchildren (young ladies) is particularly charming. Indeed, the manners of the people in all classes in Germany are most easy and attractive, and in somewhat painful contrast with our home brusqueness and slovenliness.

XI.

RELIGION IN GERMANY.

HOMBURG LES BAINS,
Near Frankfort-on-the Main,
Germany, July 28, 1867.

IT is Sunday morning. I am sitting on the outskirts of this little town, on the flank of the Taunus range ; with fair meadows before me green as May ; scattered trees, tall and thickly leaved, and each with an individual character, waving their Sabbath worship ; the mountains, with their forests, crowned with old towers, are in near view ; all the houses are covered with red tiles and are themselves of a yellowish grey ; the white roads, high and straight, contrast beautifully with the varied colors of the checkered harvest-fields. It is still and sober as a New England Sunday. Within fifty rods of us—though wholly out of sight and hearing—a thousand summer visitors are filling the grounds of the public promenade and lounging and chatting in the Kursaal of this most popular of German watering-places and public gambling rendezvous. All day long four great gambling-tables will be surrounded by eager players, and cards and *roulette* will be psalm and gospel, prayer and hymn for men and women brought up in Christian countries. A band of gay military music will fill the Sabbath air from time to time. " There is no God, there is no immortality, there is no judgment to come," will be the litany of the general service, the collect for the day. Within a few hours' journey of us are Worms, and Erfurt, and Eisenach, and the Wartburg— the scenes of Luther's life and labors and the birthplaces

of the Reformation. We are in the places where Protestantism has achieved its greatest triumphs under the flag of
Prussia, the most Protestant of German countries. Even
the peasantry are emancipated from Catholic superstitions
here, and nowhere in Europe have I seen as yet so few
priests, or so little of the old faith. There is a German
Lutheran church here, and an English missionary chapel,
and this evening at 7 I shall go, as I did last Sunday, to
join in the public worship of the Scotch Church, which sends
excellent preachers all the way from Glasgow to keep an
altar of the old Kirk warm here in Homburg, during the
period when English and Scotch visitors throng these baths.
Last Sunday a Rev. Mr. Lang preached, extempore, an impressive and appropriate sermon, which, with the service generally, was edifying and in a most liberal spirit. He asked
me to unite with him in the pulpit service, but I declined.

In spite of these small indications of zeal, the general
impression here and in all other parts of Continental Europe through which I have passed, is one of painful decay in
the faith and spirituality of the people. Roman Catholicism prevails as a powerful political system and a still mighty
superstition over great regions ; but where it has died out
nothing vigorous has shot up in its place. The people, escaped from superstition, and brought into contact with a
free, secular life, have settled into an easy self-satisfied
materialism, chastened by music and the love of order and
decorum, but without aspiration, devoutness, or faith in the invisible. Protestantism, as it appears here, is a chilled, repulsive, ungrowing thing, entering very little into the national or
the social and domestic life, and apparently not destined in
any of its present forms to animate the passions or win and
shape the hearts and lives of the middle classes. Religion
preserves in the splendid old churches, ruined monasteries

and bishops' castles, such instructive mementoes of its old tyr-
anny and costliness, that it is almost universally associated
with a dreaded political past and a deceased childhood of
reason and common sense.   Out of the present elements of
faith and worship in Germany I see no prospects of any
healthy and contagious religious life arising.   On the contrary, the science, political tendencies and social experience of
the country seem to me all fitted to extinguish what little
Protestant life there is, and to leave more and more bare the
secular basis of existence.   This is all the more probable because life without faith or piety is so agreeable, decent and
moderate here—social experience and the love of order and
pleasure acting as substitutes of religious principle, and producing so largely what were long considered its earthly fruits.
Never have I seen a people in whom the desire to make the
most of life had taken on so systematic a method and such
general and well-understood rules of economy in the use of
appetites and passions.   There is neither suspicion, shame
nor self-accusation apparent in a life whose recognized object
is enjoyment.   The instincts for God and immortality which
animate so many in our country to self-denying and self-sac-
rificing lives, and which are strong enough to rebuke the
conscious worldliness that does not admit their sway, appear
here to be taking a very long and deep sleep.   It is not
here the just emancipated working class, as in England,
which shakes off faith in God and Church with submission to
the ruling class ; it is not the young professionals who cultivate scepticism as a distinction (as in France) ; it is not the
gay and dissolute who slip the bonds of faith, the better to
enjoy the freedom of their passions, as with us in America ;
but here it is all classes—the most industrious, educated and
respectable not excepted—who seem to have discarded the
religious view of life and to have settled unostentatiously,

I might almost say unconsciously, into a prudent, orderly worldliness, which asks of human nature very little except a decent regard to propriety and an enlightened use of its opportunities of present satisfaction. Of course it would be presumptuous on so short an acquaintance to pass a final judgment of this sort upon a whole people, and I shall keep my mind open to the correction of a larger and longer study. But my present painful impression is a very strong one ; and on the whole it is what would be expected from a state of society in which the public religion has for so many centuries been a superstition, an oppression and a splendid monopoly. It is very plain that the Catholic Church is counting much and acting vigorously upon the manifest incompetency of any Continental type of Protestantism to gain the affections or govern the wills of the people. This it is which makes kings and princes lean so much that way, and encourages the Pope and his mighty council of bishops so strenuously to foretell the revival of the Roman Catholic sway. But I can not see any reason in these predictions. For some time yet, perhaps for a generation or two more, Christian faith and worship will probably be undergoing a natural decay on the Continent. Life will grow more and more secular, and the people will try out to the bottom what purely socialistic elements can do to satisfy their desires for happiness. It is encouraging to see at least a wholesome reality and positiveness in this, modern life. The world and its solid contents, and the immediate capacities of personal and social enjoyment, are at least unquestioned realities. There is no hypocrisy, sentimentalism or idle asceticism, no priestcraft or bigotry likely to be associated with their use, and religion has so long abused and maligned the world that it will take a good many generations to give its claims their rightful place in the regards of men. When it revives with power, it will produce a more real and more reasonable faith, and give Christianity a deeper and more complete hold than it ever yet has had upon society. Nobody acquainted with the permanent needs and capacities of human nature need fear that religion will die out, or can doubt that the present lull in its influence will be followed by a mighty sweep of its holy breath when the common air of the world has been exhausted of vitality, and the noble sentiments begin to gasp for life. There must soon develop itself, I think, a great general discontent with this level life of regulated and systematic worldliness. But at present it is satisfying and victorious.

There is, of course, a religious body in Germany, and it is in the main soundly orthodox in its theology. In Berlin and other great cities you find Protestant churches well attended, especially by women, where the preaching, if a little sentimental and vague, is still earnest and evangelical, and where the prayers and hymns are very thorough in their orthodoxy. The general participation in the singing gives much warmth to the worship. This is true also of the German Catholic worship, where, unlike other Catholic churches, the people universally sing, and seem really interested in and to be helping on the worship. There, however, it is only the humbler class that attends. But these manifestations are exceptional. This kind of faith is against the grain and spirit of the time. Evangelicism is maintained in the Protestant Church by prodigious effort on the part of a few anxious and faithful souls, alarmed at the general tendencies of thought and life, and willing to shut their own eyes and the eyes of others if only so the old confidence and the old piety can be upheld or brought back. Meanwhile the intelligence, the political aspiration, the science and philosophy, the experience and courage of the community are all leaning the other way. The universities, as a rule, are favoring the secular and nonreligious view and feeling. The savans and metaphysicians are mostly openly or covertly sceptics and positivists. A few months ago, at one of the universities, the birthday of one of the most venerable and popular of the professors was celebrated with literary and social festivities, and after dinner, it is said, in an address to the company, he openly boasted of his atheism. Hegelianism seems to be the prevailing philosophy, and while its right wing is cautiously respectful to Christian faith, its left is, less dangerously perhaps, denunciatory of it. The labors of Strauss have produced more effect than we are aware of among the educated minds of Germany. The authenticity and genuineness of the Gospels, it seems very largely assumed, have been finally discredited. Miracles, few scholarly men, not tied to official necessities, have the courage to treat with the least respect. It seems settled, at least for the time, by the physicists of England and the savans and metaphysicians of France and Germany, that whatever else may be true about Christianity, there is no need of considering any farther the possibility of events like the resurrection. Is it possible for Christianity, as an institution or a religion, to survive the prevalence of opinions so radically destructive as this?

And yet, those who know most and think most seriously and candidly, are forced to acknowledge that the Straussians and the savans have as yet the best of the argument and the weight of scholarship and learning with them, and that the weapons with which they are to be conquered are not yet forged. It is evident that in the deep instinct which makes profoundly religious natures cling, even against the evidence of unanswerable arguments, to the supernatural authority of the Gospel faith, there is now a disposition to turn from the purely literary testimony of authentic Gospels to the evidence —always so much valued in the Catholic world—offered by the living witness of the Church. Allow that the Gospels (if it must be so) were not written as early as has been affirmed by learned Christians—nay, that they did not exist until the early part of the second century—certainly the Church had existed for a century before! Is it not difficult, except on the theory of the essential truth of the supernatural facts in the Gospels, to account for their origin and their reception as they are presented in the Gospels, at a period when the memory of men was so little removed from the alleged time and place of their happening? and is it not even more difficult, if the Gospels did not exist, to account for the faith which had originated the Church, and for the supernatural character of that faith on any hypothesis but that of a miraculous source? We do not get rid of Christianity by getting rid of the New Testament! We have to account for the existence of the Church and the Gospel which it taught and believed, whether the New Testament is authentic or no. Whether any philosophy of human nature, or any tendencies to the love of the marvelous, will furnish as credible a key to the origin of the Church and its early supernaturalism as the hypothesis of the reality of the facts which it claimed to begin from, remains to be seen. Hostility to the Roman Catholic theory of a living witness in the Church has doubtless blinded Protestants to the importance of this branch, or rather root, of testimony. The Bibliolatry of Protestant orthodoxy has weakened confidence in the self-evidencing truth of a living Church. But there is evidence of a reviving sense of the indispensable importance of this witness, and if the question of this generation, touching the authenticity and genuineness of the Gospels, is answered negatively, there will still remain the deeper question of the origin of the Christian Church and the faith of that Church.

It does not appear that the liberal element in the Protestantism of Germany, I mean that branch of its Protestantism which we should consider most in sympathy with Unitarianism, is very earnest or creative. It seems still rather a negation of orthodoxy, than an affirmation of the positive truths of Christianity. A large part of it, I should say, from all I can learn, is much in the condition of the Arminianism and Arianism which, before the positive secession of the Unitarian party in Massachusetts, beat with feeble pulse and in a sort of conscious trance within the breasts of the majority of the clergy of the old Bay State. The liberal pulpit does not affirm its faith positively ; it simply does not affirm the old faith more than it can help doing, and maintains the institutions of religion in a perfunctory way. Forced to take positive ground, I fear that a large part of this extensive body would be compelled to abandon Christian territory altogether. In short, here, as to a less but still a large degree in America and England, the educated and emancipated mind of the country is so much more in love with liberty than with truth, and so much more interested in general truth than in religious truth, that Christian faith and Christian institutions concern them only so far as they can be made a part of general culture, and they are always ready to drop from the Christian tree, on to the ground of universal philosophy, if it is seriously shaken.

With such tendencies and with such pioneers, liberal Christianity has feeble chances in this or in any other country. Probably, until the supernatural authority of the Gospel is substantiated by its old friends—until orthodoxy has made firm ground for a positive faith in revealed religion, liberal Christianity on the Continent will not advance as an organization. It has not earnestness and faith enough to make its own ground of travel. It is not the less true because it is lost in the contemplation of its own liberty. It is not the less alive because it has no shell to live in, but it is incapacitated for locomotion and self-propagation. It is curious to see how dependent on each other orthodoxy and liberal Christianity just now are. Take away the spirit of liberal Christianity from orthodoxy, and it would rust in its hinges and fall into dust and ashes. Take away the form of orthodoxy from liberal Christianity, and it evaporates like an essence out of its vial. But this can not always be so. Orthodoxy has one great service to render the Church and humanity before she finally retires. She still has the prestige and the organization, the numbers and the wealth of the Christian world with her. She has the piety and mystic faith and flavor of the holy past—the habit of belief and the custody of the vessels and ordinances of the Church. What Catholicism did and is still in part doing for Protestantism, keeping up her connection with the holy places and the first beginnings of the Christian faith, orthodoxy will for a time have to do for the reformed Protestant faith, which is to be some richer and more embodied form of that liberal Christianity which it has been the privilege and pain, the glory and the crucifixion of a handful of people to maintain in a crude shape for one generation.

There is a certain expectation of a coming Church in the air of even cultivated and sceptical Germany. Meanwhile scholars and savans are rather desirous that their wives and daughters should profess and enjoy any form of Christian faith that will interest them.

No class of persons in Germany has touched me so much as the class just above the peasants and just below the proprietors—the lowest stratum of the middle class. Serious, modest, intelligent, humble, industrious, self-respectful, there is, especially among the women, a certain promise of spiritual life, an unworldliness guaranteed by their inability to participate in the pleasures of those above them and their distaste for the habits of those below them, which seems to say that from them is likely to spring a new generation of souls, unspoiled by empty metaphysical subtleties and uncorrupted by worldliness, who, when a larger freedom has broken their chains of toil and aroused their hopes of a career, and in a better day, when God is no longer lost in Pantheistic clouds, or drowned in his own universe, and Christ has escaped from the critics' nails and spear—worse than his crucifiers—may revive Christian faith and worship, and bring back the tender aspiration, the sweet comfort and the solemn obligations that flow from faith in a living, personal God—*extra mundis*—and in a risen and ascended Saviour, and the immortal life that awaits his disciples.

I am aware that I have given a somewhat dark view of German religion, and shall be glad to correct it by brighter impressions hereafter. Some scholarly friends assure me that in the highest circles of German learning and thought positive Christianity has won the victory intellectually as well as spiritually over Hegelianism.

XII.

NUREMBERG.

NUREMBERG, Bavaria,
August 4, 1867.

WE left Homburg after three weeks' stay, with great regret. Our pleasant lodgings had acquired almost the charm of a home. To the lovely landscape on which we had looked for so many tranquil hours we bade farewell with sadness, and to our faithful hosts, who had become our friends, we could not say good-bye, with the feeling that we were never to meet again, without some moistening of the eyes.

Convinced that we had better see the Tyrolean Alps before visiting Switzerland, we resisted the strong inclination to follow the Rhine to Schaffhausen and so enter that most attractive region, and struck off from Frankfort toward Nuremberg, on the way to Munich and Innsbrück. The daily, we had almost said hourly, showers of the last month have had one compensation ; they have kept the country clothed in its spring vesture. Early May could not present a tenderer green in the grass, and this is now seen in all our journey, in lovely juxtaposition with yellow harvest-fields. We had not been prepared to find so picturesque and charming a country between Frankfort and Nuremberg. But the railroad following the streams, and specially the Main, presents a constant succession of picturesque views which will not permit the foreign traveler to take his eyes off the landscape. We noticed that our German fellow-travelers had no difficulty in sleeping through it all. The immense density of the population in this heart of Germany has produced its necessary effects upon the tillage and the internal improvements of the country. The drainage, the embankments, the terracing of the hill-sides, the careful stoning of the banks of the rivers, and the costly improvements of the navigation of the Main, with the thorough care of the land—all indicate the worth of the soil, the difficulty of making it meet the wants of so many people, and the economy of protecting every foot of it from possible waste by flood, and of reclaiming every inch of even the most sterile declivity. Men, women, children, cows, dogs, all must be made productive in a region where mouths are so many and land so scarce and dear.

The stoning up with solid masonry of many of the steep hill-sides to secure an uncertain harvest of grapes, gives an American such a painful sense of the relation between labor and land in this crowded country, that he only wonders that still more of the Germans do not make their way to America, which, in respect of space, must seem to them a parradise. We do not half realize as yet the cardinal advantage we have over the Old World in our public lands. Abundant room has more to do with the success of American institutions than any one feature in our national condition. Along the little stream from Aschaffenburg to Würzburg, the tillage and drainage and the management of the brook all gave it the appearance of a kind of baby-house or miniature exhibition, in which the object might have been to illustrate in a pretty model how perfect this kind of economy could be made. But when we found it extending for twenty miles in the same fashion we gave up our theory. The railroads in Germany are beautifully ordered; the embankments solid, the bridges firm, the depots elegant, the service punctual. At every station-house, as the express train passes, an official clothed in a red coat, or in the uniform of the line, stands out conspicuously, in military posture, his hand to his cap, to salute the engine-driver, and give assurance of a clear track. The rate of travel is moderate, but the time-table is sacredly kept, and the feeling of an almost absolute security is quite delightful and thoroughly justified by the almost total exemption for years from any fatal accidents. The cars, even the second class, in which we always travel, are most comfortable and free from every objection, except that of smoking, which in Germany is so universal a custom that nobody seems to take any exception to it. There are, however, even second-class cars in which it is forbidden.

Nuremberg, where we have now been two days, is, as is well known, the most perfect example of middle-age architecture now left in the cities of Europe. A product of the rising power of the Bourgeoisie of the fourteenth and fifteenth centuries, it rose to eminence by the industry and commerce of its people, built its streets and walls, its churches and towers under their inspiration, and fortunately has continued to our day substantially what they made it, unharmed and unchanged by modern innovations and reconstruction. Its streets have the irregularity of a town built by its inhabitants as their convenience prompted, without official direction or restraint. Its houses have the individuality of their original owners. The fortunate irregularity of the surface, which rises in parts to precipitous hills and is everywhere broken by ups and downs, has given a charming variety to the streets and put the genius of architects to all sorts of shifts to accommodate the growing population, at a period when the prosperity of the city outstripped the compass of its walls, and as yet there was no safety outside of them. Every inch of room, therefore, has been economized. The Pegnitz, a narrow and shallow mountain stream, running through the heart of the city in two branches, and making an island in the middle,

ιs made numerous bridges necessary. The houses not only
owd its banks, but actually constitute them, while their
cond story overhangs the river, making it look more like
ι artificial canal than a living stream. The roofs—built at
e sharpest angles, abutting on the streets in pyramidal ga-
es, pierced with small windows, sometimes in tiers of five or
x stories, and all covered with red tiles, and rising to differ-
·t heights with varying surface—present against the horizon
e most irregular lines of jagged architecture. Looked
down upon, you see a city of tiles and sky-lights, rolling like a
sea in waves of earthenware, and from my window on the
Baierischer Hof on the Pegnitz, as I look up to the Church of
St. Lawrence, and see the roofs of successive streets climbing
the rising grounds, I see an Alpine region in crockery, with
all the competition of rival mountain-ranges, and the breaks of
the sky-line by aiguilles and gaps, and all the tumult and in-
terlacing lines that so beautifully torment the eye when "Alps
on Alps arise."

The characteristic features of Nuremberg are of course
the same as those of the commercial free cities of Belgium.
Indeed, there are many souvenirs of Amsterdam here.
The overhanging top of the gable, with its lifting-tackle; the
protruding oval window—here the central feature of every
important house — the elaborate finish of the upper story,
and the windows at the eaves, are all familiar in the Flemish
towns. The perpendicular finish in five or six stories of the
gable-front, with rectangular notches in each story, seem to
have been the favorite style of the rich burgesses ; and it is
still preserved. Many of the finest of their old mansions are
carefully maintained in all their old architectural lines. The
hotel in which I am writing must have been one of them.
Interiorly, its court, built in stone, wears the look of a castle.
Its inside architecture is costly in the extreme. A magnifi-

cent spiral staircase of stone, marked exteriorly in carved stone, with an ornamental line following the inner winding, is worthy of a princely castle, while the galleries opening in the court have open-worked parapets worthy of the exterior of a cathedral. The private mansion known as the *Pilatus* house is still more rich. Indeed, its vaulted court and the pillars and balconies about it make it one of the most impressive and beautiful examples of the wealth and splendor of the mansions of the merchants of the fifteenth century to be found in the world. One room, wainscoted in mahogany of the most beautiful cabinet-work, is left to show what the interior finish of this princely house was. The rest of the wainscoting, it is sad to say, was sold to an agent of the Emperor of Russia and transferred to one of his palaces.

The name of Nuremberg appears for the first time in a document of the reign of Henry III., in 1050. It was first colonized by Slavic emigrants, and was made a city of the Germanic Empire as early as 1112. An occasional residence of the Emperors, it soon outgrew its first walls, which extended only from the citadel to the right bank of the river. The present walls date with their towers, bastions, and large ditches, from 1427. The four great towers at the four chief gates, originally polygonal, were rounded a century later, 1552, it is claimed, by Albert Durer. At one period, it is asserted, the walls were strengthened by more than three hundred towers ; about a hundred, including every thing that can be possibly covered by that name, may be counted to-day. These walls are still nearly complete, and form for me the most interesting feature of the place. I have driven around them completely, with an ever-increasing wonder at the labor and cost expended upon them, and a deepening insight into the state of society that rendered them necessary. They make the city one great fortress. At one of the chief ·

gates, you drive in darkness, even at midday, through the casemate that protected this passage, and gather a formidable conception of the thickness and strength of the walls these wealthy burghers thought it worth while to throw around their hoards of money and luxury. The old citadel, often an imperial palace, and now restored after various baser uses to royal service, is magnificent in situation, commanding the country far and wide, and overlooking the city it did so much to protect. In its court-yard is a tree said to be eight hundred years old. Its chapels are in admirable preservation, and contain precious wood-carvings by Veit Stoss, while in its small collection of pictures are a few good specimens of the Flemish school. In the court is a well of eight feet diameter, cut to the depth of three hundred feet in the solid rock. Letting down a light to the surface, or throwing, by a small mirror, a reflection upon it, the water is made visible from above at this immense depth. A subterranean passage from near the bottom of the well connected the castle with the Hotel de Ville, a half-mile off, and furnished a possible means of throwing relief into the citadel in time of siege, or of escape from it. The presence of a beautiful grand piano, finished in maple, in the sitting-room of the King, furnished a proof (as he is here only ten days in the year) of his devotion to music, a passion which is not a little ridiculed in his youthful majesty, as if it absorbed time due to more serious matters. But considering that Ludwig II. is only twenty-one years of age, and not yet married, we may pardon him some reluctance to take the reins of State at this eventful period of his kingdom, when even the oldest monarch would have his hands full to defend it from Prussian avidity. These Bavarian kings have been in our century gentlemen of art, architecture and music. Munich testifies loudly to their taste, and we can only hope that in the absence of warlike propensities or talents, they may not love worse things than music and architecture. The young King is to marry the daughter of Prince Max of Bavaria in the autumn. Their portraits hang together in all the shop windows, both likely-looking.

Nuremberg was among the earliest of the German cities to adopt the principles of the Reformation, and it did it so thoroughly that small traces of Catholic influence have been found there for two centuries and more. The original hold of the old faith is, however, testified in the beautiful churches which still remain full of Catholic emblems and workmanship; but converted to Protestant use, if we ought not rather to say to Protestant neglect. As precious historical monuments they are greatly valued and carefully preserved, but as churches they can hardly be said to be in considerable use. It is indeed melancholy to look upon the glorious architecture of Saint Lawrence or St. Sebald—the two chief churches on opposite sides of the Pegnitz, giving their names to the two great divisions of the city—and to observe how feebly the Protestant life of Nuremberg animates their majestic frames. Once they throbbed with fullness of life. The old Catholic faith, which lifted their costly stones into order, decorated them with elaborate altars, and filled them with sculptures and pictures from the hands of native artists, who drew inspiration from their own religious convictions. Throngs of devout worshipers breathed their incense and bent at their altars. Protestantism came and drove priest and ritual from these gates, and doubtless at first expelled crucifix and altar, while it set up its own simple worship with an intense enjoyment of its bare but sincere doctrines and forms. At first probably there was little falling off in the congregations that gathered at these shrines. The Catholics becoming Protestants burned with zeal and faith, and laid the offering of new and fresh convictions upon the old hearths, where their ancient devoutness had smoked. Now, alas, another change has come over the people. Victorious, free from persecution, and able themselves to be persecutors, if they had the zeal to prompt that pernicious excess of feeling for their own convictions, Protestantism clothes itself in political and social, not in religious, forms, and wears the appearance of Christian apathy or indifference. I could not learn and I saw no evidence of the existence of any living spirit of faith and piety in the community, where the splendid churches invite worshipers, but are left almost wholly to women and children, or to very humble people. The intelligence, the wealth of this still flourishing and important city, if I am rightly informed by citizens of the place, is characteristically indifferent to Christian worship. It is conceded generally that positive faith in Christianity as a divine institution and a public religion is widely declining in Germany; and Nuremberg, prosperous, commercial and independent, is certainly a strong witness to the decay of Christian worship and the prevalence of naturalistic ideas of religion. A candid and sober citizen, himself apparently of that opinion, spoke of doubts as to the existence of a personal God, as very prevalent and on the steady increase. He thought a faith in immortality of some kind less shaken; but surely it can not long survive the doubts which beset the cardinal doctrine alike of natural and revealed religion—the being of a personal God. It is no wonder that in this state of things the old and magnificent churches of Nuremberg seem the empty husks of a faith that has withered and turned to dust. Protestantism rattles like a dry kernel in its shell within these vast walls.

There are still six thousand Catholics in a population of about seventy thousand, and they have yet in their hands one or more of the smaller and more ancient churches, especially Notre Dame (the Frauen Kirche) which has a lovely porch and some valuable carvings and pictures within. Saint Sebald is said to have been begun in the tenth century, and contains an iron font of great antiquity in which King Wenceslaus of Bohemia was christened in 1361. Some of its altars were adorned by Cranach, Adam Krafft, and Albert Durer. Its chief ornament, however, is the sepulchre of St. Sebaldus, the work of the great Nuremberg founder, Peter Vischer, on which he and his five sons were engaged for ten years—1508–1519. It rests on twelve snails, and around its sides, shaped like a temple of perhaps ten feet long by four broad, are arranged exquisite statues in bronze of the Twelve Apostles—all first-rate works of art. Above them, in very diminished size, are twelve figures of Christian fathers, while the infant Christ surmounts the whole, holding the world in his triumphant hand. The sarcophagus within is wrought with exquisite art, in what looks like silver discolored. On the high altar are three figures in wood, carved by the illustrious Veit Stoss. Adam Krafft has a stone, " Jesus on the Mount of Olives," on the outside of the church, which has lost much of its original power through the decay of time. A lamp still burning is supported by a fund left by the first Baron of Tucher in 1326, and the Protestants on taking possession of the church have respected the will and bequest of the founder, whose family had long continued benefactors of the church, which is full of their memorials. The bottle of oil from which the lamp is recruited stands near, and the boast is (believe it who can) that, in all these centuries of revolution and change, the light has never gone out! The organ, still in use and of a beautiful frame, was built in 1444.

The Church of St. Lawrence was built between 1278 and 1477, is 322 feet long and 104 broad, and presents Gothic architecture in all its stages, from the period of its greatest purity to the time of its greatest decline. The glass is specially fine in color, and belongs to the close of the fifteenth century; the general effect of the church is profoundly impressive, despite the partially dismantled condition in which it is—which is less than could be expected. Protestantism has restored many of the old Catholic symbols in these tolerant or lukewarm days, and the church, with its nine-tenth Catholic and one-tenth Protestant look, wears the appearance of being kept for exhibition and not for use. The special ornament of the church is the famous Tabernacle or Sacrament-house, the work of Adam Krafft. It rests upon three kneeling statues, one being Krafft himself and the other two his sons, who labored with him for six years at this work of love. It is divided into four members, and rises sixty-three feet in a pyramid of exquisitely carved openwork of stone, ending in a bishop's cross. The figures that support the chest, the columns and garlands of flowers, and all the details are so delicate, that it has been said of Adam Krafft, that he had the art of softening stone and then of impressing upon it any form his imagination called for.

Nuremberg possessed, at one time, a most extraordinary number of artistic geniuses. Albert Durer, architect, sculptor and painter, a man not unworthy by the variety of his gifts and the dignity of his character to be compared with Michael Angelo; Adam Krafft, a sculptor of great boldness and great patience, who wrought in a sad sincerity whatever he wrought at all; Vischer, the founder; Veit Stoss, the chiseler in wood, and Hirschvogel, the painter on glass, all names well known to-day, were, in the first third of the sixteenth century, lending their united powers to this favored city. The brothers Schonhofer, 1361, had left in "The Beautiful Fountain" a splendid incentive to the genius of their succes-

sors in iron-work.   It is with Durer only, however, that posterity keeps up a close and ever-increasing acquaintance.
A society exists in Nuremberg devoted to the memory of his
genius.   His house is in their charge.   His best portrait is
still in the hands of the family for whom it was painted, and
is a wonderfully living work, fresh as if painted yesterday.
He seems indeed always the most spiritual of all that wonderful Flemish school, who made thought and feeling take
the place of grace and loveliness, and gave to painting the
severity of the unfading character of sculpture.   If they had
worked in enamel, their colors could hardly have been more
permanent, their surface more transparent ; and they had very
generally the ideas and feelings worthy of the immortal touch
of their pencils.   I visited Albert Durer's grave with profound interest.   He lies in the midst of hundreds buried
like himself under the heaviest monoliths I remember ever
to have seen used as grave-stones—a simple, solid, immovable stone, with a plate of bronze let into the top, on which
his history is briefly engraved.   On three sides of the block,
the single words, Painter, Sculptor, Architect, are cut.

In the modern part of the cemetery, much like our own,
there is a house, pleasantly arranged amid flower-beds and
shrubs, to which all the dead are at once carried, after being
laid out, and there placed on beds, each with a bell-pull so
connected with the hand, that the least motion of the supposed corpse on reviving, must arouse the attendant and
bring instant attention.   All this humane precaution has
never yet been rewarded with a single call upon its watchful-
ness.   Once, however, in a case where the deceased had
died of dropsy, the subsidence of the water caused a fall of
the arm which rested on the stomach.   The bell rang, and
the attendant who had been watching for years for the sound,
when it came was so frightened that he ran from his post and

alarmed the neighbors, who, after some time, rallied and discovered the occasion of the alarm. This method of guarding against premature burial is quite common on the Continent. It seems, however, attended by too many inconveniences, and to have too little occasion in any real uncertainty in the evidences of actual death, to be worth adopting in America, where it may, in passing, be said, that burials are commonly much too early for decency, not to speak of more sacred reasons.

There are very valuable collections of middle-age antiquities in Nuremberg, especially one in an old cloister, under the control of a private association, which shows an admirable spirit and skill in getting together in classes whatever illustrates, in the most lively way, the fashions of the old time. The history of printing and engraving is excellently illustrated here. A truly antique collection of musical instruments occupies one room, where various of those monochord viols are seen, to which the monks droned their vespers. A curious instrument in which the bow was applied to wire pegs of different lengths—still not wholly out of tune—is to be seen here ; a parlor-organ, worked by hand-bellows, with a quart or two of wind at a blast, and a spinnet too complicated and funny to be described. After seeing the tournament in most elaborate plaster on the ceiling of the Hotel de Ville (in one of the upper galleries), it was gratifying to see the very armor and the very lances with which these jousts were made.

Here, and still more plainly at another dungeon of the city, we saw the very instruments of torture which are described in all histories of the Inquisition, but which most readers charitably ascribe to Protestant exaggeration or credulity. But here in actual wood and iron, and in all their horrible deformity were the rack, with its pulleys for stretching the joints asunder, and its rollers of knotted wood to bruise and

F

mash the body laid upon it. These hellish inventions of bigotry I will not farther describe, excepting one, found only
twenty years back in a vault which had been carefully stoned
up, and called "the young maiden." It is an image of wood,
shaped to the human body, which closed looks more like a
mummy-case erect than any thing else. Its front opens,
however, like folding-doors on hinges. These doors are
armed with sharp spikes of steel, of perhaps eight inches
long, two being in the head, and twenty others in other vital
parts of the body. The victim, bound, was forced into this
box, and the doors suddenly shut upon him and held by a
vice. Pierced by twenty mortal wounds he perished, and just
beneath the instrument of his execution opened a well into
which his mangled body dropped to make room for the next
victim. The place of this torture was many rods under
ground, where sound or light could not come, and it was really some relief to the terror of the recollection to reflect how
impossible such cruelties would be in civilized countries in
our own day. If we have lost somewhat of the old faith and
the genius that accompanied it, we have certainly gained virtues and charities it knew little of, and learned to hate customs and practices it found very tolerable. Would it not be
well to inquire, however, whether in the American treatment
of the insane, there is not still in many county hospitals, spite
of Miss Dix's life-long crusade against such barbarities, conduct as atrocious for our age as the tortures of the Inquisition were for the sixteenth century?

Nuremberg is on the Ludwig canal, connecting the waters
of the Rhine and the Danube. It has an important trade in
looking-glasses, iron and brass ware, manufactured leather,
gloves, papier-maché and toys, with America. It is a purely
trading community—with no nobles, and little political stir—
but independent in spirit and alive.

XIII.

MUNICH.

MUNICH, August 5, 1867.

THE modern air of Munich, by no means a new town, is very striking after the antiquated aspect of Nuremberg, which, old as it looks and is, possesses a thoroughly modern spirit. Munich, on the contrary, is largely Roman Catholic and unprogressive in political temper and policy. Here the old Church seems still alive, and its temples swarm with worshipers. In the Frauen Kirche (Notre Dame), an immense church of brick, ugly as possible without, but grand within from its height and lofty columns and rich decorations, I attended mass yesterday in the midst of a great congregation of devout worshipers. Peasants in picturesque costumes— the women with bonnets that defy description, some in velvet mitres, others in gold lace snoods, just covering the back hair, the men in jackets and waistcoats covered with silver buttons — formed an interesting portion of the assembly. But the congregation was wonderfully diversified, containing rich and poor, beggars and beaux, young children and extremely old men and women. The absence of any special fashion is a great relief in Continental gatherings. There is none of that monotonous adherence to a freakish pattern which gives us in America five hundred women at a party with their hair dressed all horribly alike, and their dresses cut by one pair of scissors after one tasteless model. The chief charm of the cathedral service was the music, from a full choir, accompanied by the organ and a complete orchestra. They sung the music of Pergolese and Palestrina, and never have I realized so perfectly what sacred music was and ever should be. No solos, no secular airs, no light and meretricious ornament, unspiritualized this music. It was strictly religious in origin, adaptation, style and execution—a fit concurrence and succession of tones to bear the prayers and aspirations of human souls up to their divine and all-harmonious source. The music of the modern Church is characteristically barbarous, and wholly unworthy its own genius and mission, or the civilization of which it forms a part. It is either a dull, monotonous and inartistic droning of hymns— not one in ten of which has any lyrical quality—by a feeble choir or an undrilled congregation ; or else an operatic performance, in which strains associated with the capers of the ballet and the gayeties of the theatre are wrenched from their proper service without being successfully accommodated to any other. I verily believe it would be better to do without any music than to continue these wretched performances, full of worldliness, and directly antipodal in their whole effect to the true ends of worship, and even the general aim of the pulpit. The better they are as mere vocal displays the worse they are as religious exercises. There is, however, no incompatibility between the most artistic music and the most sincere religious praise. But religious music must be written by religious men for religious purposes, and then rendered in a religious spirit. That this can be done is abundantly proved by the immense quantity of such music now in possession both of the Catholic and the English Churches. How people acquainted with Handel and Haydn, Purcell, Bach, Pleyel and Mozart, not to speak of names before mentioned, can continue contented with our modern patchwork called sacred music or psalm tunes, is marvelous. One of the greatest of modern mistakes is that of supposing that good words will consecrate bad and undevout music. Religious music is essentially independent of words, its proper language being tones. Its meaning lies in its expression, and its proper accompaniment is the prayerful or worshipful sentiment it awakens in the hearer's heart. The words are usually merely in the way, and except in the original service they may now and then have rendered of moving the composer's mind, are nearly useless. Above all, until we cease to marry together ideas (or words) and sounds not originally pledged and adapted to each other, we shall have that hodge-podge which now occupies and disgraces the place that really belongs to sacred music in Christian worship.

I heard a military mass in St. Michael's a·few hours later, which was truly solemn. It was very widely distinguished from a military mass I attended in the Church of the Hotel des Invalides in Paris, a few weeks ago. There an excellent brass band accompanied the altar service with operatic airs skillfully performed ; here a still better band performed truly religious music in a way to thrill and purify and soften the soul, and send it up in thanksgivings and yearnings toward its Maker.

The road-sides all the way from Nuremberg to Munich tell you that you are in the heart of the beer country of Germany. Here the hop fairly beats the vine. Instead of wine bottles, casks and mugs, glasses of beer meet the eye at every corner and at every railroad station. The abundance of this pale and pleasant drink, light and nutritious, called Bavarian beer, is something astonishing. Last evening, for instance, I think I must have met a thousand people in the English Garden (a mile out of Munich) at Gungl's open-air concert—men, women and children of the better class. I doubt if, with the exception of a few visitors like ourselves, there was a man,

woman or child that did not drink at least a pint, and most
of them from one to two quarts, of beer.   They sat, indeed,
perhaps three hours, listening to music and slowly drinking
glass after glass of their mild potation.   It costs $7\frac{1}{2}$ kreutzers
a mass (that is a quart mug), about 5 cents, and can not be
purchased at retail at less than 6 kreutzers per quart, the
whole profit of the retail sale being about one kreutzer per
glass and the saving made by the fact that the foam in each
quart mug lengthens out the measure of the barrel about a
sixth part.   About three quarts a day is the average drink
of a sober workman, and with this he requires only one solid
meal.   But twice as much, and even four or five times as
much as this is not uncommon, and many of the people are
kept heavy and poor by the abuse of this beverage.   The
general attachment to it is something half amusing, half saddening.   The Bavarians will stand any governmental abuse,
it is said, except a rise in the beer-tax.   That has really made
and often threatened a revolution.   It is said that the brewers
are putting less malt in their beer, and that the effect has been
to increase the use of *eau-de-vie.*   Drunkenness is almost unknown, but systematic hard-swilling is terribly common.
The effect of this beer is very obvious in the paunchy ponder-
osity of most of the older men, and it tells on their noses as
well as their stomachs, and does not improve the German
face, never very handsome.   There is, however, a delightful
cordiality and genialness in their manners, and a quiet enjoyment of leisure, chat and music which is very refreshing
to see.   Their politeness is almost ludicrous in its painstaking excess.   They bow and touch hats, and bow again and
uncover, and cover again and then bow once more, and uncover, finally, smiling most deferential and benigant smiles meanwhile, until you begin to suspect it is a joke.   But there is
nothing less jocose or more serious than German etiquette.

They can not put Martin Luther into their Walhalla without belittling the name with his title of Dr. Martin Luther! The definition of a hat in German must be not a thing to cover, but a thing wherewith to uncover, the head.

Munich is a beautiful city, and quite astonishing as the capital of so small a power; for in public buildings, and in galleries, libraries and theatres, it is second only to Paris. It is, like modern Paris, a city built essentially by one man, and built to be looked at. Bavaria has about 5,000,000 people. Munich has 160,000, of whom only 16,000 are Protestant. But the palaces here, especially of art, are worthy of London, and it will be a great while before London will equal Munich in statuary and pictures. How so small a kingdom has furnished the means of so lavish an outlay in the great structures devoted to art and literature, and in the magnificent collections of treasures they contain, is inexplicable. Bavaria has possessed, in the Wittelsbach house of sovereigns, a royal family equally distinguished for bigoted Roman Catholic and Austrian sympathies, with a high sense of their prerogative, and a heart devoted to the fine arts. Ludwig I., the grandfather of the present King, who abdicated in the revolution of 1848 in a combination of follies in which Lola Montez had a conspicuous part, is still alive, and still a devoted patron of literature, art and music. A poet himself, he is a true connoisseur in art, and in his reign laid the foundations of the architectural beauty and artistic wealth of Munich. He still owns in his private capacity the New Pinacothek. He has lately ordered from modern artists a hundred of the largest-sized historical pictures, for a building now erecting to receive them. His son, Maximilian, who died much regretted three years ago, followed up his father's plans, with even greater vigor. The street named for him is a wonderful monument of his energy,

boldness and success. Ludwig Street—his father's—ends in
a magnificent trio of temples designed to exhibit each a strict
example of the Doric, Ionic and Corinthian styles. The
triumphal arch surmounted by Schwanthaler's magnificent
bronze group—"Bavaria driving a chariot drawn by four
horses"—is one of the most gigantic and imposing pieces of
modern architecture. Indeed, wherever you turn in Munich
you come upon some reproduction or imitation of world-renowned buildings, or style of decoration peculiar to other
countries. As the Palace Museum contains admirable models in cork of all the great temples in Rome, Athens, Pæstum, ·
so the city itself is a museum of copies in full size of the most
celebrated buildings and styles. Of course the general effect
is much that of the mongrel collection of Greek, Roman,
Christian, Pagan, Oriental and Western models in the outer
court of the French "Exposition." Stumbling at one time
on a Greek temple, and next on an Egyptian idol, faced here
by a wall painted in Pompeiian fresco, and there opposite by
another in blank and modern mortar—you are as much puzzled to know where you are, as you would be to know your
friends at a masquerade. The absence of a numerous and
lively population, or of an active and earnest business, neu-
tralizes very much the general splendor of the public buildings. The immense post-office, war-office and palace, and
other public structures provoke a constant comparison with
the small amount and importance of the business they represent. Ruins have a significance and interest of their own,
but empty, deserted, or quarter-part occupied buildings, fresh,
splendid and costly, are merely melancholy impertinences and
monuments of wasted ambition. The same criticism is to be
made of the great statue of "Bavaria"—the Colossus of modern times. Fifty-six feet high, and placed on a pedestal of
fifty feet, this immense woman in bronze, from an admirable

site, two miles out of the city, overlooks the capital and the distant Bavarian mountains and no small part of the whole Bavarian kingdom. The artist, Schwanthaler, has managed the gigantic work with great skill, and Miller, the celebrated founder, has cast it with admirable success. It is indeed a beautiful as well as colossal work; but in its signification it fails to win the sympathy of the stranger, who asks, What is little Bavaria, that she should swell up to this monstrous self-assertion? France, or Russia, or America might take on such a symbolic self-representation without provoking the feeling of the ludicrous, but not Bavaria. The collection of busts in the open gallery, around the statue—which is finely conceived—is an interesting illustration of the history of Bavarian genius and patriotism, and of the Catholic taste of Maximilian, the late King. Statesmen, soldiers, artists, priests—all the really conspicuous and useful citizens of the country in its long career—are here represented in colossal busts, ranged in two rows, against the wall of the open gallery. They can not fail to enrich the common air of Bavaria, which blows freely upon this open court of genius and worth. I have not seen the Walhalla near Ratisbon; but there the late King has attempted on a still larger scale to show his appreciation of great men, by bringing into one temple the chief benefactors of Germany and mankind. It is impossible not to admire the large-mindedness of so liberal and cultivated a prince, even if we see something a little presumptuous and inappropriate in his endeavors. It is hard to find words to convey an idea of the wealth of the Munich Gallery devoted to the old masters, and known as the Old Pinacothek. Its affluence, its admirable management, its inexhaustible treasures, must be seen to be credited. If one could animate its figures, Munich would not want population. I have not yet seen the Dresden Gallery, and it is many years (nineteen)

since I saw the galleries at Florence and the Vatican ; but
certainly the Munich Gallery, however surpassed it may be
by these others, is for the time being of overwhelming interest
and satisfactoriness.   Unequaled in its collection of the
Flemish and old German schools, here are found superb
Rembrandts and elegant Vandykes, a whole room devoted
to some of Rubens's greatest pictures, the first satisfactory examples of Murillo, a few delightful Raphaels, and, above all,
some tender, holy examples of Perugino's exquisite purity and
devoutness.   There is enough in this gallery to account fully
for the presence of the thousand artists said now to be living
in Munich.   Munich is celebrated for its cheapness as a
residence ; but certainly its hotels do not favor its reputation.
They are excellent, but dear.

The collection of modern pictures in the New Pinacothek
is a very interesting and wonderful one, and places Germany
far before all modern countries in the courage and learning,
the inspiration and mechanical skill of its artists.   What
country can give us living or lately living names as historical
painters worthy to be set beside those of Overbeck, Corne-
lius Hess, Schraudolph, Schnorr, Kaulbach ?

I had long had the greatest admiration for the genius of
Kaulbach, as exhibited in his illustrations of German poetry,
mythology and history.   To the penetrative intelligence and
spirituality which marks German art, he seemed to add a grace
and elegance commonly wanting in it.   His great affluence
and facility have not made him careless, and every thing
from his pencil is delicate, refined and exquisite, without lacking dignity and force.   He seems to possess a most tender
appreciation of childhood and womanhood, and no modern
artist, to my eye, throws such grace and elegance about the
human figure.   It was like meeting an old friend to see the
great artist in his studio.   His manly form is robust and

erect, the bloom of health is in his cheek, gentleness and power in his eye, ease and grace in his manners, and all softened by seventy years of an existence which can have had few idle hours. He sat, as we entered, before his easel, at work upon the drawing of the loves of two characters, in one of the very old German minnesingers. The youth and sentiment of the picture suggested the power which genius possesses of carrying its own youth with it into extremest age; and Kaulbach is really as young as ever in feeling and in the nature and handling of his subjects. He showed us several of his more recent pictures, and especially one elegant portrait of a Copenhagen merchant, full of power and beauty. He talks with freedom and charming insight about America, which interested him, as it does most Germans, who seem the only people capable of looking at countries with reference to the ideas they stand for, and their relations to human progress. He bade us not to expect a period of art in America until we had got farther through with the great and heroic period which gives art its inspiration and its subjects. He thought the late American war would in some future time be a prolific source of artistic ideas and themes; but artistic eras come: they can not be made.

The library, the richest, after Paris, in the world, contains over eight hundred thousand volumes, in eighty-six rooms, and twenty-two thousand MSS. The books are admirably arranged in the alphabetical order of their author's names, each nation by itself. The American books are separated from the English, and fill a large-sized apartment. I could hardly have believed that we had written so many since that short time ago when it was asked, without malice, "Who reads an American book?" There are many very curious MSS. of critical and theological value, and some specimens of the earliest printing, which prove that we have made no progress in the art, except in rapidity and cheapness. We may well revive the old typography.

The famous Munich foundry of bronzes is intensely interesting in its methods, and specially gratifying to Americans, because its collection of models (full size) contains so large a proportion of American works. There is indeed nowhere such a collection (in plaster casts) of American sculpture as is to be seen in the museum of this foundry. It is a little mortifying that we have to send abroad to get this work done.

Schwanthaler's gallery is well worth visiting, if only out of gratitude to an artist and sculptor who has set up monuments of his genius and industry in every church and temple and public edifice in Bavaria and neighboring countries. His fertility is truly astounding, and his general excellency is marked. There is no striking originality about his works, but he is always graceful, careful, and equal to what he undertakes. His lions over the "Gate of Victory" at Munich are very fine, and all four markedly different, which is not to be said of those at Nelson's column in London.

One of the most popular collections in Munich is the portrait series of modern beauties, of which King Ludwig formed a special exhibition in one of the great halls of the "Neue Residenz." A thoroughly impartial tribute is here paid to beauty, which the King recognized in the peasant or the princess with equal readiness. I could not think that the result was very creditable to the loveliness of the sex in this quarter, for I think I could pledge myself to beat the whole collection in the gathering of the beauties seen in one morning's walk in any considerable American city. The Neue Residenz is a magnificent extravagance in its interior, and adds another to the thousand superfluous palaces which have been built out of the bones and cemented in the blood of overtaxed and half-consenting dupes to the pretensions of selfish, idle and corrupting courts. They have been the curse of Germany, and are not yet duly abated—but on the way to correction.

The famous Glyptothek, a collection of sculptures, contains one ancient statue, which may well have come from the fingers of Praxiteles or Phidias, called " The Barberini Faun." It is a sleeping satyr, in which perfect *abandon* and perfect grace are united. The marble is soft as flesh, and the sweetness of healthy sleep breathes from the warm limbs, as they droop with light but perfect slumber. The creature looks as if he might spring up and advance at any moment. There are many other greatly-praised statues or fragments in the collection, but this single statue to me was worth all the rest. The paintings on porcelain and on glass are a specialty in Munich. They are lovely and of great immediate charm— of lasting brilliancy, without lasting interest. It is impossible not to enjoy a few views of them, and a specimen or so may well enough be sent home by those who can afford it ; but they compare with the pictures they represent, as ivory miniatures do with their originals ; they substitute *finesse* for fineness, and finish for perfection. " A Columbus in Chains," by Wappers, was the best copy of what must be an admirable picture in the fine collection of the dealer, Mr. Wimmer, very much patronized by American travelers.

Of the many other things in the churches and palaces of Munich, time would fail me to speak. Iser still " rolls rapidly" through it, and has not very lately had its blue stream stained red. The young King leans to the side of Prussia, contrary to the tendencies of his house, and perhaps with more credit to his sagacity than his honor. Bavaria is, I trust, more alive than Munich would indicate. If not, its industry, its agricultural wealth and its long independence will not save it for another generation from absorption in the common German Empire. The young King marries in October the daughter of Duke Maximilian, one of his own subjects. One of his sisters was Queen of Naples ; another is Empress of Austria. There are too many soldiers riding about Munich for its own good. A cavalry band wakes me at 5 every morning, leading a regiment of horse to exercise. The music is pleasant, but it smacks of the ruin which befalls states always armed, and never able or ready to fight. The smaller states of Germany have long been in the condition of knights crushed under the weight of their own armor.

XIV.

SALZBURG.

Salzburg, Austria,
August 12, 1867.

FROM Munich to Salzburg, about one hundred and ten
miles, the railroad runs parallel with the Bavarian Alps,
and just far enough from them to command a series of enchanting views of their ragged tops and snowy shelves and
green flanks as they descend to the cultivated fields and great
lakes that lie at their base. When I visited Europe twenty
years ago, I received a very impressive charge from a man
of eminent taste and experience not to come back without
seeing Salzburg and the Tyrol. But it was not so easy
then to run over Europe as it is now. Railroads had not
then superseded post-roads, and I came back without having
obeyed orders. My friend, Dr. Bartol, celebrates this region
in his " Pictures of Europe," and on no part of his travels have
I heard his eloquent tongue more eloquent than on his visit
to Salzburg and the Königssee. Yet, after all this warning,
I was not prepared to find Salzburg what I am now disposed
to call it, the most beautiful spot in Europe—certainly the
most beautiful I have ever seen. I am looking, as I write,
on this loveliness. The Hotel de l'Europe, from which I
write — charming for situation and for architectural beauty,
is half a mile out of Salzburg proper, and brings the city
within the panorama it commands. The river Salza runs
through the lovely plain sprinkled with villages and beautiful
trees, often planted in colonnades of half a mile long, and

finally divides the city, which is crowded in between steep hills
crowned with old monasteries. A castle of five hundred
feet elevation, the old seat of the Prince Bishops, who ruled
over the body and soul of this neighborhood, overhangs the
little city with its proud towers, but is separated from it by
its immense height and inaccessibleness, as far as bishops in
the days of its foundation were raised above common Christian men. On the narrow plateau of the city proper ample
space is first secured for the cathedral and the churches of
St. Peter, with the monasteries and nunneries and spiritual
houses of all sorts now vacant or turned to civil uses, but
which were once crowded with an ecclesiastical population.
In the noble squares round which lie the palaces and libraries and hospitals of the old archbishops, are the costly fountains they built to adorn their successive reigns. Into what
little space their pride left was crowded the narrow streets
of the people's homes—which towered up into the air to find
the room denied them on the ground. The unevenness of
the surface, except for the few acres occupied by the churches
and palaces, and the precipitous character of the hills on
both sides of the defile, have given an unequaled picturesqueness to the appearance of the city, which is greatly aided by
the admirable Italian architecture of the town. The cathedral without and within is a most grand and solemn edifice,
and stands amid domes and towers that enhance its beauty
and dignity. Seen near or far, from within or without, the
city is a feast of beauty. There is nothing incongruous in it.
And yet it is the smallest part of what I see and call Salzburg.
If it were wholly blotted out of existence, this delicious landscape would remain essentially unimpaired. Far around the
open, smiling plain, with the river gleaming through the
beautiful trees that hang fondly over its meadows, stand as
sentinels the most sublimely fair peaks of granite, spotted

with snow, relieved by lower mountains clothed in darkest green to their very tops. If nature had cast each one of these mountains in a separate mould, with a direct eye to variety, contrast and picturesqueness, and then placed them where each would best support the general effect, they could not better meet the craving for artistic perfection. Here are gathered into one landscape all the beauties which, scattered widely, give distinction to the scenes in which they are separately found. The eye, satisfied with Untersberg, whose awful comb saws the sky with its marble teeth, falls on Hohenstaufen, rising in a regular cone, and is then relieved by Schmidteustein, whose rocks resemble the walls of a fortress.

But why dwell on particulars in a landscape so harmonious that it compels the eye to take in the whole effect at every glance? There is not an empty inch in the sky line, and not one repetition. The distances are graded so that every focus of the eye presents a new charm, and it is impossible to say whether the foreground, the middle distance or the far view is most delicious. The meadows just now are hazy with the midday heat, and the mountains seem to swim, like beautiful black monsters, in their radiant sea of emerald. This morning early, the mountains were mottled with black and white, and it seemed as if Beauty, Love and Terror were contending for their possession; last evening the sunset clothed them in roses and gold, and then the moonlight heaped more beautiful cloud mountains on their heads and flooded both ranges with its silver tide.

There is no crushing sublimity in the fair scene to make the heart ache with a majesty that never veils its terrors. Nobody of true sensibility can stay amid the high Alps for weeks at a time, or cares to look day after day upon Niagara or a storm at sea. But one could live here in Salzburg forever, and find it always beautiful and always sublime, and yet

never be dazed with the beauty or tired with the grandeur.
For it is the perfect balance of those two qualities, beauty
and sublimity, that characterizes this spot above all others.
The open, broad, smooth meadows breathe only peace and
cheerfulness.   Light in amplest abundance bathes the land-
cape.   Civilization, delicate culture, artificial gardens, fountains, shrubs, vases and statues keep all-comforting and pleasing images steadily in view.   But up there against the sky
stands that circle of marble walls broken into ruins, clo-
ven here almost to the meadow, and lancing up to the zenith
there in spikes of snowy marble, or in rifts of marble snow.
Winter bares his icy arm and reaches over into the valley to
pluck the summer rose ; while spring runs up the mountain-
side with emerald feet to meet brown autumn, holding court
midway.   The charming contrast is so vivid and yet so harmonious, that it satisfies without cloying, and compels attention without fatiguing the senses.   This is no unusual thing
in landscapes ; but it is commonly only landscapes that are
full without being striking, that soothe and permanently
charm.   This is the most striking of landscapes, and yet it
soothes and rests and satisfies and holds the heart.

How hard it is to tell what it is that so exhilarates in this peculiar scenery !   Sometimes it seems the majesty and beauty of
form, and sometimes the subtle charm of color.   The noonday is a great disenchanter.   Beautiful things, with their different charm in the morning and the evening light, are often
merely indifferent objects seen under the meridian sun.   We
had an experience of this at the Königssee.   The ride of eighteen miles from Salzburg was, I think, the most enchanting
drive I ever took—one ever-varying succession of pictures, as
individual each as geniuses among common men, of mountains
seen in mountain frames.   It was as if the mountains had
got up an exhibition, in which all agreed to show each other

off to the best effect, in a series of tableaux. A peak of pure cream marble would suddenly lift itself six thousand feet high into a notch formed by two green mountains, as perfect a picture as if ordered by Bryant from the studio of Gifford. Then again, a gulf of snow would open down between the two warm summits, as if Greenland had suddenly thrust·its bosom in between Teneriffe and Vesuvius. When we arrived at the Königssee about noonday, the vertical sun poured such a direct light into this rocky bowl, that its precipitous sides refused to cast one shadow of enchantment on the water. Under cover of a stout awning, and rowed by a company of peasants, of whom three were women, modest and pleasant-looking, though brown and brawny with work and exposure, we went down to the King's hunting-lodge, some three or four miles, and roused the echoes with pistol shots and songs as we glided over the purest water in the world. Really there seemed not more than half a dozen places in the whole shoreless lake where a landing-place could be made. The place strongly resembled the Yo Semite Valley in California, substituting only a floor of green grass for the green water. The mountain-sides were just as precipitous in both cases, and the dimensions and height about the same. On the way back, we stopped an hour at Berchtesgaden, to go into the salt mine.

The region about Salzburg is known as the Salz-kammer-gut, and is the source of large revenue to Austria, from the immense yield of salt. One-eighth of the national income comes from this source. The mine we descended was a succession of chambers three or four hundred feet square, and perhaps twenty or thirty deep, out of which the salt had been extracted by a curious process. The salt lies in strata, so mixed with clay and pebbles that it can not be hewed out in bulk. Fresh water is pumped into a chamber hollowed out by the pick and shovel, and the chamber is then sealed, until the water has become brine. This water is then decanted by pipes into receiving vats, where it is duly crystallized by evaporation. Large quantities of it are carried in pipes twenty, and in one case, sixty, miles across valleys and around mountains to reach some spot where fuel is cheap. The salt chambers, always enlarging as they yield their salt, are filled again and again with fresh water, which is converted into brine in periods varying from three weeks to a year, according to the percentage of salt in the walls, and this is repeated until they become so large that their unsupported vaults will not allow them to be made any larger without peril to the works. They lie one above another, or side by side, with only a few feet of thickness between, and occasionally a perilous caving in has destroyed life and property. We descended about half a mile, chiefly on foot, following our guide in solemn procession through long galleries, and sliding down steep balusters (without stairs) in a way that brought back the coasting down hill of boyhood very vividly, only our lanterns made poor moonlight, and the salt rather dirty snow. The air was cool and sweet, and tasted salt. We passed one of the briny seas in a boat. It had been illuminated for our benefit, and was as gloomy as Acheron-darkness made visible. We were disappointed in seeing no stalactites or sparkling crystals. A salt mine is not a whit more lively than a gold mine, and in fact there is a very general resemblance between them. The exit out of the mine is effected by striding a long wooden horse, on wheels, which, on a narrow tram-road, tears through the darkness at a fearful rate, and in a few minutes brings you out of the bowels of the mountain into very grateful day-light. The costumes worn on this occasion by the ladies and gentlemen are more convenient than elegant, and are slightly confusing to the general prejudice in favor of a difference in the apparel of the sexes. As a matter of taste, I decidedly prefer the usual distinction.

Emerging from the protecting darkness into the full light of a public road, we became somewhat painfully impressed with the absurdity of our habits, of which we had experienced the decided benefit in our subterranean life. The leathern aprons, worn in this case behind, made the sliding on the poles comparatively easy; and although I expected my leathern hand-shoe (as the Germans would say) to frizzle up with the heat of the friction, as I held vigorously on to the rope —having two very valuable packages pressing on my shoul·ders—yet I escaped with a whole skin. I can't say that the experimental trip would incline me to a repetition of the journey—various as the methods of progress were, and novel as the scene and agreeable the company—but it was worth doing once. The work goes on day and night. Laborers stand ten hours of this underground existence without injury to health. We saw this salt in transit at Ebensee and Gmunden. It is formed into loaves, very much the shape of a rimless hat, and weighing about twenty-five pounds each. A file of laborers, each with a wooden trough on his shoulders, fitted to hold three loaves, and with a linen bonnet on his head to protect his face from the salt, was carrying the salt from the covered flat-boats which fetch it from Ebensee to the railroad at Gmunden. Immense quantities were in daily transit over this road, which is one of the oldest in Europe.

Our next excursion from Salzburg was one of three days, to Ischl, the Traunsee, and Gmunden. The distance to Ischl is about thirty-five miles — a pretty hard day's drive over the mountains. Our party was of eight, in two carriages. A mile or two out of town, at the foot of a sharp ascent, we found an extra horse clapped on to our pair, and this was repeated as often as necessary on the journey. The constant use of the shoe and the brake enables them to dispense with any breeching to their harness, and is the greatest saving of horseflesh. The abandonment of the check-rein is another sensible improvement. The horses, without an ounce of superfluous flesh, carried us over the mountain-road in a stout carriage, with five persons and no small amount of luggage, very safely and without distress to themselves. The drive lay through the mountains, and ran round the lake-sides, and furnished a constant feast of varying surprises. Nothing could exceed the charm of the view, as we came suddenly upon St. Wolfgang, and pitched by a sharp descent into the village of St. Gilgon. After dinner, we lay stretched out upon the banks of this lovely lake, feeling that we could willingly pass a week doing nothing but watch its surface changing under the shadows of clouds and of its own mountains. The color and translucency of the waters, the combination of blackness and fertility in the mountain-sides, the picturesque shape of the hills, the gleaming of giant towers and steeples in the distant villages—all made this a delicious scene. Our afternoon drive lay directly round the western side of the lake, and scarcely left it until we got within five miles of Ischl. Here the mountains begin rapidly to close in, and finally, as you turn the shoulder of one of them, you find yourself in a stronghold of mountains, without a place in the horizon where the eye can escape. A closer prison of hills can not be conceived. It is very refreshing to those who covet a total change from the milder forms of nature, but not the kind of beauty that satisfies me. A single day of it was quite enough. Ischl is near enough to Vienna to furnish a summer retreat for the Emperor and many Austrian nobles. It is not, however, as much like a German Spa as I feared it would be. We found no crowd there, and no obtrusion of fashion and nonsense. The Traun river, a lovely mountain stream, which strings the Tyrolean lakes upon its thread, furnished our escape from Ischl.

Putting our luggage and our persons aboard a row-boat, manned with two oarsmen and a helmsman, we started down the rapid current of the Traun to float to Ebensee, a distance of ten or twelve miles. The river is broken by rapids every half mile, and is indeed a torrent in all its course ; but its navigation, after a short experience, was wholly free from alarm, and indeed became to the most timid of the party full of delicious excitement. We slid over waters generally not three feet deep, with varied-colored pebbles at the bottom shining clear in view, now in the sunshine, and now in the shade of mountain precipices, hurrying over boiling rapids and shooting round corners, which illustrated the skill of the boatmen and gave us all the exhilaration of a race-course. It was the most charming ten miles in all our journey. Reaching Ebensee, we found the pretty little English steamer that navigates the Traunsee waiting, and in one hour, passing through that famous water, were landed at the beautiful village of Gmunden. This lake has the charm of being locked up in rugged mountains at one end, and opening on to smiling and cultivated hills at the other. The bold Traunstein, 6000 feet high and naked from base to crown, is the rocky genius of the lake, and everywhere characterizes the landscape with his sublime and awful presence ; but a most verdant mountain stands just next to him, as green and richly clothed as he is white and bare, so that the general effect of the lake is beauty and not sublimity. A lovely esplanade runs for a halfmile along the shore in front of Gmunden, and furnishes a charming morning or evening walk. The romantic portion of the party went out on the lake for a moonlight row. I contented myself with a row before breakfast the next morning, and spent the forenoon upon a hill a half-mile back in the shadow of an old church and in full view of the whole length of the lake. Ten miles of hilly road brought us to the railroad at Vocklabruck, and two hours more by rail back to Salzburg, after a most thoroughly enjoyable trip, and with a feeling that, spite of all the beauty, nothing as beautiful as Salzburg itself had fallen under our eyes.

One more moonlight evening at Salzburg completed the gracious and ever-to-be-treasured impression of that peerless place. A few hours the next morning carried us by rail to Rosenheim, where we struck the beautiful Inn, and turning at right angles directed our journey toward Innsbrück. The day was intensely hot, and the European cars, though they exclude dust better, do not admit air as well as ours. We sweltered through the noontide hours, getting what refreshment we could from an occasional glimpse of some " frosty Caucasus " that did not much abate the " fire in his hand" of this present writer. But if ever lovely and glorious scenery could make one forget the fatigues of his journey, it would be in this noble valley, where open fields and snow-topped mountains, with flanks covered with fertile farms, diversify the course of the swift and snow-fed river. Every few miles a new valley opened far up on the right and left, tempting the traveler off his way. The features of the Inn valley up to Innsbrück are all large. Extensive districts of cultivated land cover the sides of the successive mountains. Large hamlets are gathered far up on the slopes, and little churches dot the stormiest and most inaccessible parts of the habitable region. Along the valley of the Inn, thickly peopled, innumerable spires repeat the claims of the Catholic faith. Nearly uniform in appearance, their slender towers support a sharp spire, usually painted green. Along the road shrines are sprinkled in excessive abundance, and every village has on the nearest shelf of rock a Calvary, with a shrine at each bend in the difficult path, completing the ten stations in Christ's passion. The notion of penance runs through the whole system. Instead of placing the churches with reference to the convenience of the worshipers, there are always many expressly made most inconvenient of access, that some merit may be acquired in getting up to them. The Tyroleans are the devoutest Catholics we have met. Their churches are full of worshipers, and the houses and barns and fields full of sacred images and pictures. They are a serious, self-respectful people, quite unlike the Bavarians, who are light-hearted and merry, or the Swiss, who are thought mercenary, and have been much demoralized by the constant visitations to which their beautiful country is subject. They keep up a faithful allegiance to Austria in this part of the Tyrol, and resist all temptations to desert her cause in the days of her darkness.

Innsbrück, the old capital of the seven circles, is a singular remnant of middle-age antiquity. Right at the German end of the easiest pass over the Alps (the Brenner), she has laid in the track of the armies that have surged against that rocky barrier for ages. Nothing but the importance of the position could account for the presence of so substantial a city at so high a point—nearly two thousand feet above the sea level—and in the immediate presence of such lofty mountains. Peaks of eight thousand feet high fling their shadows into her streets, and in the moonlight it is difficult to distinguish the angles of her roofs from the tops of the mountains as they mingle their outlines against the sky. Viewed from the bridge, which gave the city its name, there are few sights more striking than this substantial town, with its quaint gables and time-worn walls disputing possession of the ground with the river and the mountains, but holding it for centuries

G

in unchanged dignity and beauty. The stone arcades of its main street are most formidable-looking places. Its chief interest centres in the church built as the sepulchre of Maximilian I., Emperor of Germany. His tomb is one of the costliest in the world, and is unique. Twenty-four marble tablets contain the sculptured history of his life, worked in a miniature of perhaps a quarter-inch to the foot, but with a delicacy and truth that has never been surpassed. A group of colossal statues, of the chief ornaments of the Austrian house, surround the sepulchre. They are the finest bronzes I have ever seen, both in conception and execution, and make Innsbrück worth a visit for themselves alone.

XV.

THE TYROL AND THE ALPS.

Coire, Switzerland,
August 26, 1867.

WE left Innsbrück on the 17th of August for a drive of a week through the finest part of the Tyrol. Having joined a party of very old friends, whom it had been our good fortune to fall in with very unexpectedly, and whose company had half restored to us the feelings of home and parish life, we set out, eight in all, just two carriage loads, to try the charms of that most independent and delightful mode of travel, known so well to journeyers on the Continent under the name of *vetturino*. With a stout pair of horses, a good-tempered and "indifferently honest" driver, a roomy carriage, a mountain road, and an occasional extra horse or pair, according as the hill was longer or steeper, we made about forty miles a day for eight days, over roads uniformly excellent, through the fairest and grandest scenery in the world.

The valley of the Inn, celebrated for its wonderful beauty since interest in natural scenery took any place in literature (and it is wonderful how modern this taste is, and how difficult it is to find any thing answering to it in classical poetry —where the landscape is never painted), maintains the character it has fifty miles below Innsbrück, for fifty miles beyond it. It is a rushing, copious torrent, navigable only for rafts, turbid with the calcareous matter it washes down from the hundred mountains that feed it. Its beauty is sadly impaired by absence of all transparency ; but it is so full and free, and broken by such constant rapids, that it never ceases to be an interesting object even in the midst of the charming and magnificent hills and mountains that overhang it. The valley, up to the opening of the Finster-münz pass, is broad and noble.   Vast fields, smiling with grain and grass, checker its occasional meadows and more frequent mountain slopes ; but its chief feature is that it is broken at intervals of every few miles by immense lateral valleys, which open magnificent vistas back to snowy peaks, while they diversify the main valley with an endless variety of beautiful and often sublime prospects.   Here, in perfection, may be enjoyed that most exquisite thing, the natural hanging garden known as " the Alp," and giving its name to these ranges of mountains.   Three or four thousand feet above the valley of the Inn, and on the edge of a precipice or the slope of a rugged and barren mountain, appears a little island of exquisite greenness and fertility.   It looks in the distance almost as if you could cover it with your hand, and yet it is diversified with grain-fields and trees ; a few chalets and perhaps a little church gleam through their branches.   A dreamy, far-off, half-heavenly charm invests this inaccessible spot !   A thousand feet above it, another still more dimly made out inlays the mountain-side, and here on the opposite slope is another, and at one view a dozen similar ones adorn the scene.   They are the chaste jewels in which this stately mountain queen arrays herself ; and certainly for picturesqueness and suggestiveness to the imagination, nothing can exceed these Alpine *oases*, in the midst of their craggy and uplifted deserts of rock.   Nowhere are these mountain meadows to be seen in such perfection as in this valley of the Inn, if my memory of Switzerland serves me right.   Certainly since leaving the Inn I have seen none as beautiful.

Far higher up, where our path finally took us, we came across these spots of beauty, and found them of course far larger than they looked below and less interesting on a nearer view. As you climb higher and higher, green pastures without the cultivation that marks the islands of verdure that adorn the lower ranges, are always charming the eye, and especially when speckled with cattle, that look from even what appears a near view hardly larger than mice. The cattle in the Tyrol are all of one dun color, small and agile. They have the habits of goats, and hang upon the side of fearful precipices, seeking the tender, short grasses, with what seems the greatest risk. Early in the morning, you see hundreds of cows filing out of the narrow lanes of the dirty little stone towns upon the mountains, each tinkling its bell, and all taking the familiar path to the upper pastures. One shepherd goes before, and one behind, and if the flock is large several others are added. The well-trained dogs must not be forgotten. They seem animated with even a graver sense of responsibility than their masters. Following a flock of sheep or cattle through a road, you see them sweeping from one side to the other, with the regularity of a pendulum, so that every other moment they are barking at the heels of every possible laggard in the herd. Tending a flock of sheep in the mountains, the dog does ten times the work of the shepherd, who lies upon his side, with his peaked hat and red vest, his leather breeches and his staff, looking as if he were posing for his picture.

The patience of these herdsmen, passing oftentimes twelve hours of the successive days of many months in their absolute solitude and at their monotonous business, is something fearful to contemplate. I have often longed to penetrate the thoughts of these isolated shepherds, standing immovable and watching their charge. Their lives seem so vacant of

interest, that it is not strange that religious superstitions of
any kind find welcome in their hearts.   Nowhere have shrines
and crosses and pictures of saints seemed to play so important a part as among these Tyroleans.   The spirit of inquiry and intelligent doubt has not invaded their domain.
These valleys are bristling with church towers.   Every hill-
top has its chapel, every town on the road its shrine, and old
as their churches are, they are generally in good repair, and
new ones are still going up.   It is manifest that the priests
are honored and revered among them, and that their duties
are neither few nor small.   The merit of the images and pictures seen everywhere in this rude country is surprising.
The common road-side paintings, protected by a little stone
shelter, are far from despicable.   It is well known that the
Tyroleans have great skill in the use of tools, and especially
of the penknife.   They are poor and remote, and must needs
study economy and invention.   They make their own tools
and farm implements and wagons.   They are all rude and
shackly-looking things, but they answer the purpose.   They
bind their fences together with withes to save nails, and resort to every device to economize their humble resources.
As to industry, nothing can surpass the spur to labor their
mountain home and hard climate supply.   One-tenth of their
soil is all that is properly arable ; but it is said that they
have subdued a sixth part of it.   The pains and labor expended upon every inch of redeemable soil, show how precious land is in this overcrowded territory, where too many
mouths are seated at a most meagre table.   Distance, difficulty, toil present no sufficient obstacles to the cultivation of
the least acceptable and least productive parts of these
mountains.   Whereon any thing will grow by any amount of
pains and labor, there it is carried.   It is positively distress-
ing to look upon these bleak hill-sides, stony and precipitous,

but perhaps two or three miles square, and every rod of it terraced and every foot enriched with dressing carried on the backs or heads of women to gain a poor and uncertain harvest, and then to reflect upon the millions of level acres in the New World unpeopled and unclaimed, waiting to bestow abundance and emancipation upon these needy and over-worked mountaineers, would they emigrate. I could compare the hill-sides, in the regularity and closeness of the lines that mark their terraces, to nothing coarser than ribbed cloth, so close and fine is the labor expended upon them !

It is not to be wondered at that gravity describes such a people. I listened in vain for songs from the mountain-sides, and heard their *jodel* only on one or two chance occasions, and then in towns. They cultivate music in the towns, and several rustic bands of instrumental performers were roaming about playing very respectable music under the windows of travelers, and then sending in their chief, hat in hand, for a contribution. On several occasions, stopping at village inns for dinner, two or three musicians, unheralded, have come into the room and played and sung for a half-hour, and felt themselves abundantly rewarded by a couple of francs. Everywhere the memory of Andrew Hofer, the Tyrolean Tell, is held in reverence. In 1803 this noble peasant led the Tyrolese against the French invaders of their liberties, and succeeded for a time in exalting the feelings of his countrymen to a wonderful pitch of self-sacrifice and self-control. He had for a short time a kind of rustic court at Innsbrück, and governed his people with patriarchal simplicity, making their personal morals and domestic usages the subject of his official regulation. But his pure and fervid spirit was soon cut off by the invaders, and he perished by order of a court-martial, whose verdict, it is said, was inspired by Napoleon himself. His monument occupies a conspicuous place in the

Maximilian Church at Innsbrück. It is strange that the love of independence among this people should co-exist with a most lively devotion to the house of Austria. But Austria has made an exception to her usual spirit in dealing with the Tyrol. Her government has been mild and considerate among a people whom she knew would resent too much interference. But the spirit of liberty can effect little when unsupported by intelligence or when hampered by superstition. The Tyroleans are seemingly content with their lot, and their lot will continue to be a most narrow and unimproving one until a noble discontent with it is awakened by closer contact with the rest of the world. Their present adherence to their local costume is an indication of their isolation. Picturesque as these tribal badges are, their continuance is always the evidence of backward spirit, and their disappearance indicates the growth of intelligence and the progress of freedom. Happily they are rapidly losing their hold upon all peoples. The civilized people of all countries are beginning to dress much alike, and it is not the least of the evidences of that community of intelligence and feeling which is the hope of the world. Near Silz, where we stopped to dine, we met a wagon-load of Gipsies on their vagabond pilgrimage. A dozen children, their eyes as black as sloes, their hair curling and glossy, lay in all possible positions sprawling on the wagon-top, and as we passed held out their hands, from the oldest down to the baby, as if their first instinct was to beg. At Rouen and at Homburg I met other parties of these privileged vagrants— as handsome creatures as ever crossed my path, spite of tawdry jewels and dirt. They looked as if the three Kings from the East had started out of the canvas of an old master and commenced a modern progress. I have seen no genuine royalty in our day half as impressive as the mock majesty of these untameable savages, who, half-brothers as they seem to our Indian chiefs, are likely to outlive them.

We stopped at an old monastery near Silz, tempted by the size of the buildings, and especially by the external pretensions of the church, which we found quite as costly and elegant within as without. It was not without difficulty that we waked up a single representative of this nearly extinct community. Six monks are the sole survivors of a large brotherhood. The vast corridors, once so resounding, are now given up to cobwebs and silence. One of the monks, a most civil and obliging gentleman, showed us about the monastery, and led us to the grave of one of his late companions, which was still strewed with flowers. One of the company chancing to sneeze, he raised his cap reverently and pronounced a blessing, apparently as unconscious of the singularity of the act as if he had been returning a salute. It is plain that even in Austria the days of monasteries and nunneries are numbered. We passed our first night at Imst, in the midst of solemn mountain shadows, relieved later by brilliant moonlight. The quietness of the town as we drove in about sunset, was intensified by the tinkle of the bells from a herd of goats just returning with swollen udders from the mountain pastures, and finding their way each to its owner's door, where they bleated for admission. Beautiful creatures, in their speckled coats and mild eyes, they seem half human in their strange intimacy with the households where they are brought up, companions of the children and sharers of the domestic accommodation. The stabling of the cattle within the same stone walls with the family gives a peculiar odor to the whole in-door atmosphere of the Tyrol; and even in the inns it is impossible to escape the stable smell. It qualifies all the food, and abates sensibly the pleasure of being in the country.

Our second day's ride carried us, still keeping the banks of the Inn, up through the famous Finster-münz pass, a rival of the Via Mala, in solemn and awful severity. The magnificent road which conquers the natural inaccessibleness of this rocky gorge, through which the Inn forces its impetuous way, is a triumph of engineering audacity. For a mile or two of the road it is a ledge hewn out of the solid rock, and seems to hang between heaven and earth in a way to make the traveler upon it shudder to gaze up or down. The snow peaks look over into the chasm to see what has become of the river born in their glaciers. Shrunk to a milky line, it sends its faint murmurs, almost like expiring sighs, up to the traveler's ear, who, a thousand feet above, listens for the voice that has so lustily cheered him on his way for a hundred miles back. We passed the night at a little tavern beautifully poised upon the summit of the pass, from which a most commanding view of all its glories was to be had. The grandeur and beauty of the scene haunted me on my pillow, and when the late moon had won its way high enough to shine into the pass, I rose, about 2 A.M., to see the deeply-buried Inn reflect its rays, and to enjoy that magic which only moonlight throws about mountain scenery. The next day carried us, by a sudden bend, away from the valley of the Inn over into that in which the Adige takes its rise. We passed the fountain-head of its waters, and already felt ourselves down in Verona.

We had now crossed the Alps, and by merely following the stream could, in a few hours, have been on the shores of Como or in the streets of Milan. But our purpose was to cross the Stelvio—the highest carriage road over the Alps, and for all who have made it and the other passes, incomparably the most striking. So we turned off at Mals from the descending valley that leads to Botzen, and took the upward path that, by the way of Trafoi, carries the traveler over to Bormio. The road steadily ascends by the side of a stormy and turbid torrent from Prad to Trafoi—a corruption of Tres Fontes, a name derived from the bursting out of three fountains, side by side, in a ledge of rock a mile or two above the little filthy hamlet, in whose cleanly inn we passed the night. As I am striving to bring my muscular system into better habits, I make it a point to walk up all the mountain passes, and five miles walk up to Trafoi gave a very good relish to the mountain trout, for which the region is famous. I rose early enough to see the cows, the goats and the pigs start on their daily pilgrimage to the upper pastures—an event which, with their return at sunset, seems to constitute the only excitement of these lofty villages. Five hours of hard pulling at length brought us to the summit. But what scenes of wonder and beauty had we not passed through on the way? The Ortler Spitze, almost the equal of Mount Blanc in loftiness and awful majesty, was the intimate companion of our way. It seemed so near, at times, that we could fancy ourselves stepping across the abyss and standing on its very crown. The great glaciers of the Ortler hung right in our view, their viscous constitution perfectly evident, so that one half-waited for them to flow. The contiguity of such vast masses of snow and ice cooled the August midday. I chose to be alone in my walk up this fearfully grand way, and it is hard to say whether pain or pleasure prevailed in the emotions aroused by the awful beauty of the precipices and torrents, the oppressive bulk of the masses that surrounded me, the desert waste in which the imagination wandered and was lost, with all the dizzy sensations that come over sensitive brains, looking down bottomless abysses or up inaccessible precipices. The road is a miracle of daring and of success. It takes the bull by the horns, and instead of winding its way round distant sweeps, zigzags its path in the face of the precipice, climbing in one place a thousand feet in a compass of a quarter of a mile of square surface. The immense difficulties overcome in this passage give this road a superlative claim to admiration. It is a real work of art. One is amazed to hear that it cost only $1,500,000. It could not be built in America for $10,000,000. There are no open views on the Stelvio, or indeed on any of the mountain passes I have yet made. The mountains are too much in each other's way for that. The eye is shut in and has nothing to compare them with but themselves. The whole world becomes a mountain tract; there is nothing to see or to think of but mountains, and after a week or two in the upper Alps I can conceive of an almost entire forgetfulness of any existences except mountain peaks and snow summits. The height of these mountains is felt only by those who climb them, and my experience is to feel their height more in descending than in ascending them.

After descending quite as much as you can remember to have ascended, you find yourself, after a brief enjoyment of a level which you mistake for the bottom, beginning a new descent which seems quite equal to the one that you had accepted for the whole descent, and you are like enough to repeat this experience three or four times if you are actually going to the level of the country from which the mountains rise ; for great mountain ranges are not got up without enormous buttresses in the shape of side ranges, and after coming down the central pile, you have all the outlying terraces to descend before you reach the bottom of the bottom. The descent on the Italian side of the Stelvio is far less fine than the ascent on the Tyrol side, and it is a misfortune to any traveler who makes this pass to approach it from Italy. We were in company with friends who had tried it both ways, and their testimony was very strong in this direction. We came down to Bormio Baths and passed the fourth night of our journey at the excellent inn, so charmingly overlooking the valley of the Adda, at the new baths of this most ancient place, known to the Romans and much resorted to. Descending the valley the next morning, we found ourselves unmistakably in Italy. Not only had the language changed wholly, but the appearance of the people and the country. In place of the mountain ash which had accompanied us all the way from the German baths (and nowhere are these beautiful trees more perfect and abundant than on this line of journey), and the barberry bush, which to a Boston boy seems a sort of Yankee notion, we found the mulberry and the fig and the walnut. The country looked softer, and the people far more picturesque in costume and manners, and fairer in face and figure. The peasants at work along the road-sides rested in attitudes that an artist would have posed them in, and their rags were all arranged as if they were playing charades. It was a charming change, and struck every member of our party in one way. The road-side was less marked with shrines and the people seemed less superstitious.

From Bormio to Tirano our way followed the valley of the Adda, another of those mountain streams liable at any time to be converted into a furious torrent, sweeping bridges and houses and even towns before it. The wide and stony beds of these Alpine rivers show now, when shrunken by the heats of the whole summer, what they must be in copiousness and rush when the snows are first beginning to melt. They are always fearful objects in my eyes—images of unrestrainable passion and destructiveness. At a narrow defile in the gorge, about two miles above Tirano, a land-slide blocked up, in 1803, the course of the Adda, when the river rose and flooded the country for many miles back, and only after eleven days forced its passage through the obstruction, carrying away and destroying a large part of the town of Tirano. We passed on to Madonna, a village just at the opening of the Bernina pass, and quitting the valley of the Adda, which would have led us by night-fall to Colico, on Lake Como—re-served for a later visit—we made our way up the beautiful gorge that leads by the charming valley of Puschiavo over into the valley of the Inn at Samaden. Crossing within a mile of Madonna the Swiss frontier, we found a disagreeable evidence of the existence of cholera in Italy, in the estab-lishment of a smoke-house through which all travelers com-ing from the Italian side are obliged to pass, by way of dis-infecting themselves of any possible contagion. It was a short but very disgusting process, and as useless as disagree-able. There was no thoroughness about it ; our luggage was not smoked, and several of the party escaped by remonstrat-ing. One of the young ladies, not accustomed to chemicals, was so suffocated by the disengagement of chlorine gas that she implored with frantic earnestness to be released, and her cry, I think, emancipated us all a minute or two earlier than the regulations required us to stay. The *douane* just here appeared solicitous only on the subject of tobacco— which I find everywhere to be the first and commonly the last question at the frontiers. If you can answer promptly, No ! to the inquiry, "Any tobacco ?" there is little danger of any ransacking of baggage. A very generous method of dealing with travelers' luggage prevails at the European cus-tom - houses nowadays—a great improvement on twenty years ago.

We passed the fifth night of our drive at Le Prese, a little mountain watering-place on the shore of the fairy-like lake of Puschiavo, a most romantic spot. A party of Italian gentlemen amused us greatly by the complete abandonment of their usual quietness to the temptations of some gymnastic apparatus in the court-yard of the hotel. If they had been trained monkeys, they could hardly have shown more agility or made more fun. So much noise and such tricks upon each other, were accompanied with such admirable good temper, that I formed a very favorable opinion of the amiability of a people usually considered somewhat jealous of their dignity. The next morning, an ascent of five hours carried us to the summit of the Bernina pass, which after the Stelvio is rather tame, although it carries one up to the line of the snow, which could be gathered from the road-side in an occasional patch. The diligence runs daily at all seasons over this admirable carriage road. The descent on the northern side is far more interesting than the ascent on the south, on account of a series of magnificent glaciers, presenting the best possible views of themselves from the road. One of them, and a very glorious one, is easily approached and crossed without danger or special fatigue. A long descent brought us out near Samaden, by way of one of the chief tributaries, if not the very head of the Inn, a river we rejoined with gratitude and delight. At this point we gained the famous valley of the *Engadine*, or narrows of the Inn, which is divided into the lower and upper Engadine. We took the lower part, and passing the now frequented places of Pontresine and St. Moritz, we brought up for the night at Silva Plana—a pretty spot on a green lake just at the opening of the *Julier* pass. This, one of the inferior passes and over a secondary range, is nevertheless full of charm, especially on the first mile or two of the ascent from Silva Plana. It brought us up for the night, after a drive of only twenty-six miles, at Tiefenkasten, a romantic inn, at the spot where the road to Coire cuts the Albula river and pass at right angles.

Our inn seemed coiled up in the folds of the swift brook, that filled the house with its brawling and the eye with its foam. It was a watering-place indeed, and it needed pretty quiet nerves and a very weary frame to sleep in the midst of such a whirl of waters. The road to Coire, only eighteen miles distant, was over another pass of no mean height, and the descent into the valley of the Rhine was full of beauty and grandeur.

We had made five mountain passes in seven days, and become so accustomed to hills that we had almost forgotten what level ground was. The opening of the broad Rhine valley was a delightful surprise and refreshment. The mountains around Coire are half superbly rugged and severe, and half wondrously wooded and verdant, and the open plain gives the advantage, so much missed among the higher Alps, of a foreground and a contrast. Not willing to be so near the Via Mala without visiting it, we here turned off our direct route, which was toward Zurich, and drove eighteen miles south to Tusis, up the Rhine and at the very gates of the Via Mala. The scenery, going and returning, was such as to revive all the charm which hung around our recollections of the week spent on the Rhine two months ago. There seems hardly a mile of the course of that enchanted stream which is not worthy of special visit. Its waters refuse to run where beauty and grandeur cease, and hide themselves in morasses and sand when they can no longer reflect overhanging cliffs and vineyards. We stopped on the way at Reichenau, to see the house and the room in which Louis Philippe had passed a few months, disguised as a school-master, and where he was at the time of his father's execution and his mother's banishment from France. Two portraits, one as he was when he came to Reichenau, and one as King of France, sent by Louis Philippe himself, in grateful remembrance of the hospitality he received and the faithfulness with which his secret was kept, hang in this chamber and are full of significance. There is a charm in the melancholy of the young exile, disguised in his simple yet elegant bourgeois dress, which the Marshal's uniform and royal orders of the King in the days of his prosperity, with his full face and somewhat heavy good nature, do little to replace. Tusis, like Ragatz and Emps, is one of those little Romansch towns, whose names preserve the peculiar dialect once universally spoken in them. It is still spoken in some villages exclusively, but not in this, where a very corrupt German seems to prevail. It is for its size and promise one of the noisiest spots I ever sought to pass a quiet Sunday in. All Saturday and Sunday nights the jodel was shrieked in the streets, in every form of caricature and extravagance which the love of noise and mischief could inspire. There being eight in our party, we had a private religious service in our own parlor, and in the course of the day walked or drove into the Via Mala, not the fittest temple for thoughts of a God of love. Every body knows all about the Via Mala, which has been described a thousand times.

The Rhine here finds its way through an awful crack in the mountain some three miles long and a half-mile deep. The fissure is so narrow and the walls so steep, that it was for ages after the settlement of the country impossible to get through the gorge ; but Pocobelli, a bold engineer, blasted a road in the side of the precipice, now clinging to one face, and then passing by a bridge (there are three on the gorge) over to the other, until an excellent way for the high-road was achieved. The gloom of this place, even at high noon, is fearful. It is grand and awful to look up at the walls of stone that overhang the narrow way, and then five hundred feet below to see the Rhine shrunk to a brook of a yard's width, burrowing down for unknown depths to find the room

denied it on the surface. At times the river thus compressed rises within a few feet of the bridges, and it is hard to
conceive a scene of more terrible magnificence than this
gorge must then present. I walked up three miles and back
again through this horrid defile, with shuddering nerves.
About half-way through a green expansion occurs, where a
few houses and fruit-trees and a little breathing-room rest
the heart heavy with the desolation and the suggestions of
peril and imprisonment. There was, I confess, no view in
the Via Mala so agreeable to me as the view out of it ! The
green valley and the pleasant village of Tusis, seen from the
gorge, a half-mile before reaching the northern gate of the
defile, was like a glimpse of Heaven to a soul in Tartarus.
One can not wonder at the passion which humanity has
shown for harsh and cruel views of God's nature and character, when he considers the taste for horror which seems to
prevail still among travelers. If there is any place of special
gloom and awful desolation, where Nature has been most violent, abnormal and hideous in her workings—there the most
numerous feet are found, and there the greatest interest and
admiration centre ! Are the majority of people so dull in
sensibility, that nothing but pepper and mustard on their
food, rape and murder in their reading, and precipices and
abysses in scenery, can touch their appetite ? I may be very
weak in my tastes, but I confess I can stand only a very
moderate amount of awful and desolate scenery. A very
few hours amid horrors of snow and glaciers and perpendicular walls of rock above and below, satisfies my stomach for
the sublime. I find myself returning from such scenes, as I
came from the Via Mala, glad to have seen them, and very
glad not to be obliged to stay long with them. Returning to
Coire, we started for Ragatz, and at 2 P.M. found ourselves at
the ravine that leads to the famous baths of Pfaffers.

XVI.

SWITZERLAND.

August 23, 1867.

THE town of Ragatz has a beautiful situation on the Rhine, commanding a most striking view of the picturesque and architectural cliffs that stand still, inviting castles to come and perch upon their half-finished buttresses, and holding the ruins of such as long ago accepted the hint. It is chiefly visited, however, as the entrance of the remarkable chasm, bold and precipitous, which leads, by a ledge-sustained road, to the Baths of Pfaffers—a warm spring bursting at blood-heat out of the mountain-side in a cave of rocks, which grows more and more grand and curious as the traveler follows up the excellent path to the fountain-head. Visiting this place at noonday, we did not experience all the awe which it is fitted to inspire at a later hour, when the direct light is withdrawn; but even after the Via Mala and the Finster-munz, it is a defile of wonderful grandeur and beauty. The violent stream that disputes the roadway in this choked gorge, last year acquired a still more gloomy interest from becoming the grave of three English women who, by the fright of a horse in the carriage in which they were driving, were precipitated into the river, and all lost. There is still no sufficient protection to the road on the precipitous side, a strange omission now in Europe, where most frequented places are carefully fenced against slips and missteps. Schelling's tomb, with the expressive and beautiful monument erected by King Maximilian of Bavaria to the "First thinker of Germany," adorns the church-yard at Ragatz. However this confident title may be disputed, Schelling's bust indicates the presence of a masterly genius, and it is always most refreshing to see hereditary monarchs paying tributes to men who are kings in realms not reached by tax-gatherers or won by blood and ancestry. The railroad from Ragatz to Zurich is as lovely as cultivation, carried to lofty heights, bold palisades of rock and distant snow peaks, can make a road which is bathed for a portion of the way by the transparent waters of the charming lake of Wallenstadt. The easy motion of the rail and its swiftness were delightful after ten days of creeping in our voitures. Darkness, without a moon, came on an hour or two before we reached Zurich, but not before we were satiated with beauty.

ZURICH.

August 27.

The intense interest which the natural beauty and sublimity of Switzerland excites, deadens observations of her political and social life. She is buried in the shadow of her mountains, and so trampled over by tourists, and hid behind the crowd of summer visitors, that it is hard to find the Swiss people or to measure their present condition and prospects. Entering the country at Zurich, and having to submit to a couple of rainy days which made scenery-hunting useless, I have had time to look a little at the present life of this important town, which I am glad to say presents an appearance of enterprise and activity quite worthy of the nineteenth century. The old home and fighting-ground of Zwingle, the earliest and stoutest friend in Switzerland of the Reformation, it has retained its thoroughly Protestant character, and shows the fruits of this intelligence and freedom. The old church where Zwingle thundered, and out of which he drove the organ and all the symbols and insignia of Romanism, still keeps its solid base, and is largely attended as a Protestant church on every Sunday. There are five Protestant churches in this town of twenty-five thousand inhabitants, and only one Catholic church. The people are church-going, and not inclined to desert the severer dogmas of their fathers. The freer theology, which has so extensively illumined the Genevan end of the cantons, seems not to have touched this. Some of the professors in the university are suspected of liberal theological tendencies, but there is no church in town under the new-school theology.

Here I sought with lively interest the place, and stood in the pulpit where the mild and curious-minded Lavater preached for thirty years, devoting, I fear, his most lively hours to his physiognomical studies ; and then I went with pious care to visit his grave in St. Anne's church-yard, where a modest tablet records his birth in 1741 and his death in 1801. He was shot, it will be remembered, by a French soldier, at the door of his house—in wantonness—but, lingering in agony three months, refused to designate, although he knew, the man who murdered him, notwithstanding he had been giving him bread and wine just before the atrocious deed. Perhaps his physiognomy may have struck Lavater as one from the owner of which violence was to be expected, and in the essential coarseness of whose proclivities he founded a charitable excuse. He seems to have been thoroughly beloved as a man in Zurich. I could find no trace of Pestalozzi, although this was his birthplace. The Gessners are remembered — the naturalist and the poet—both natives here.

A museum of armor (admirable in its arrangement and quantity) contains the sword and helmet reported to have been worn by Zwingle in the battle of Kappel, where he lost his life, and had his body burned by the enemy. Whether Zwingle actually wore and contended with these carnal weapons is doubted, and many of his disciples are anxious to clear his reputation from the charge. I confess I should think only the better of him for knowing that he was willing to repel the enemies of his country with sword in hand, as he did the enemies of the truth with his sharp-edged tongue. There is a hole struck in the hemlet through which perhaps ·his mighty soul went up to the God of truth and of battles. Among the armor are two suits of sternest steel, designed for women and unmistakably accommodated to the female form. For what Joan of Arc these complete suits of mail were forged I could not discover, but they were curious evidences that women's rights were not without assertion in very backward times, and that some women are ready to accept the sternest duties of manhood with its larger privileges. Mr. Curtis, whose speech in the New York Convention on woman's right to the suffrage I have so much praised and blamed, ought to see these iron arguments for his cause here in Zurich.

Fuseli, who was born here but lived so long in England that one always thinks of him as a Londoner, and associates him with Northcote and Reynolds, has an ambitious picture of the famous Oath of Grutli hanging in the Rath-haus. It is theatrical and bad in action and tint, but has a redeeming quality in the expression of the face of the central figure. But it was neither the antiquities nor the art of Zurich that interested me most, but its present life. It is thrifty and prosperous, with something better than toy-carving or cheese-making or petty industries.

The silk factories here are large and active. The famous iron works of Eschel employ two thousand workmen, and turn out engines for steamboats and locomotives which suppľy Switzerland. These marine engines were carried in parts over the passes of the main Alps, and set up on the various lakes where they were needed, before rail communication had become so common and so thorough in this country. There is a magnificent Polytechnic School here—in a beautiful and stately edifice, three years in building, overlooking the town—which has fifty professors and over five hundred students. The highest branches are thoroughly taught here, and the professors are selected for merit, without regard to religious or political biases. There are many Catholic as well as Protestant professors. There is no chapel connected with the institute. The catalogue shows that the Swiss students are from twenty different Swiss cantons, (two hundred and forty-three in all), and the rest (three hundred and eight) from thirty-four different countries, including one from England, one from North America, and one from South America. This shows a world-embracing popularity, or else indicates some extraordinary circumstances of cheapness in the cost of education here in Zurich. I do not find in the list of professors any names of European note except Kebler's, who has written on Lake Village Remains. Herr C. Kappeler is President of the Faculty. One course of lectures attracted my special attention. It was entitled " The History of the English Novel," by Dr. Behn-Eschenberg. A beautiful collection of casts, carefully arranged, shows the attention given to æsthetic culture here. A university with fifty professors also exists at Zurich, but I had no time to visit it. A costly and elegant railroad depot of stone, now building, indicates the fine public spirit of this place. Elegant residences, chiefly on the hill-sides, attest the prosperity and refinement of the city. " Rude as a Zuricher," though a Swiss proverb, seems to have less foundation than most popular sayings.

I am sure it would have done my friend Mr. Jackson S. Schultz's heart good to have accompanied me on my visit to the new stone *abattoir*, which Zurich has built by the side of the swift river that carries off all its impurities. Large and lofty, with every possible accommodation of tackle for lifting carcasses, gutters for disposing of offal, special apartments for the slaughter of beeves and of calves, in another place of sheep, and in still another of swine—with polished stone floors, keeping no stain and most readily washed—with every arrangement for cooling the meat, and keeping it sweet while duly ripening for market—with beautiful stables near for stabling cattle fatted for the knife, and with butchers' offices in rows adjoining the butchery—the whole arrangement was such as to command my great admiration. It was too near the town (in fact in it), and the odor of the place was not inviting, but no butchery is fragrant ; if it can only be made wholesome it is all we can ask. A market-house, fully worthy of such an *abattoir* and of the city which possesses it, next engaged my attention. It was a model of fitness, cleanliness and attractiveness. Made of iron and marble, there was nothing about it to collect or retain dirt or odors. No community with such indications of civilization can be kept in the rear of the times. I regarded these tokens of enlightened self-interest with a feeling which wholly reconciled me to the curtain of mist that hid the snow-mountains, and limited the lake views which most persons visit Zurich to see. Zurich is not merely interesting to look *from*—it is interesting to look *at*.

LUCERNE.

August 30.

We came from Zurich to Lucerne by rail, through a smiling country that rested our mountain-tossed spirits and prepared them for a fresh enjoyment of the wild scenery that was before us, as we plunged again into the Alpine region. The lovely lake of Zug, with its inviting inns upon the very shores, tempted us to linger, but we resisted the spell and pressed on to the famous centre of so much romantic interest at Lucerne. Its old towers, all in a row, greeted us with their quaint square forms, capped with purely utilitarian sheds, as we stepped out of the depot and made our way on foot across the antique bridge, roofed with rafters, each one of which holds a triangular painting commemorating events in the lives of its two patron saints, St. Leger and St. Maurice. The architecture of all the houses, except the numerous hotels, is of the most ancient middle-age type, solid, with loop-holes for windows, and with jutting cornices separating the stories. That peculiar style of rafters, built in between with stone and mortar, and showing themselves externally in quaint patterns, is here seen in elaborate perfection. The modern buildings are all of the new Parisian style, and are clearly the growth of that pressing demand for accommodation produced by the annual influx of pleasure-travel, which within the last quarter of a century has converted Switzerland into one great and splendid caravansary.

The moment we struck Zurich we found ourselves in this mighty current of summer tourists, and saw at once how deluged with travelers the land was. Lucerne is even more marked with this tide than Zurich. Its quay, commanding one of the loveliest prospects in the world, is wholly occupied by elegant hotels, crowded with guests. Its waters swarm with graceful and swift steamers, hurrying to and fro from village to village and ferrying this restless crowd of scenery-hunters to the various points of interest along these enchanting shores. Row-boats, with gay awnings, keep up the appearance of an endless water-party. The shaded walk running along the quay is the scene of constant rencontres between acquaintances ignorant of each other's whereabouts, but seemingly not more surprised to meet here than though it were in the streets of London or Paris.   Indeed, from every diligence or voiture in Switzerland one catches a bow from some familiar face, and is hardly astonished if our own brother or next-door neighbor opens the carriage-door as he alights at a way-side inn.   What Paris is as a city, Switzerland is as a country, the spectacular centre of all pleasure-seekers.

It is difficult to conceive a position in which more of the elements of beauty and sublimity are mixed than that of Lucerne.   Backed by mild hills, green as lawns and cultivated as gardens, amid which lovely houses look out from trees that do not too much hide their inviting roofs—with a foreground of gentle slopes, which in successive points overlook each other, as they glide into the lake, and which are richly dotted with festive-looking cottages and some stately houses, —the middle distance is occupied by stern Pilatus on one side, and the cheerful, verdant Rigi on the other, which let the eye out over waters blue as heaven, into a sublime vista of rugged mountains reflected in every shape on their bosom, and fashioned round great bays that strike in four directions deep into the heart of the hills, while over all hang the distant snow peaks, the crowning charm of the grand and bewitching prospect.   Whether it is sweeter calmly and fixedly to watch this delicious scene from the shore, or taking the light steamers to change it, making the rounds of the lake and sounding its bays, and coming with every twist of the helm on some new combination of beauties—it is hard to say.   But every cloud in the sky and every change in the wind and every variation in the temperature alter the prospect ; for this sensitive beauty wraps herself one hour in misty drapery, and the next flings it suddenly off and discloses charms that were not missed till they appeared. We tried both ways, studying the scenery from the slopes just back of Lucerne, and the next day making the tour of the lake to Fluelen.

Here, of course, we visited Altorf and saw the native haunts of William Tell, and the famous spot where tradition declares he shot the apple from his son's head and then drove the remaining arrow through Gesler's tyrannical heart. A little chapel by the water's edge embalms Tell's memory, while Schiller's genius, who has done more than all others to brighten his fame, is celebrated by an inscription on a rock that stands isolated on the brink of the bay of Uri, eighteen feet high, and bears the name of Schiller's Monument. Men like Schiller are their own monuments ; but it is delightful to find all over that vast Central Europe where German is spoken, the pride and affection felt for his name manifested in bronze and marble statues and in inscriptions of praise. The bust in the Central Park at New York is only a becoming tribute from a city that is probably the third or fourth in the world in German population. But if German love and pride did not commemorate Schiller in New York, American gratitude and admiration would !

Saint Gothard Pass opens below Altorf, and the splendid preparations the mountains were clearly making for a sublimely beautiful road, made it very hard to turn back without following the invitation to enter their glorious gates. But back we turned and made our way to Weggis, anxiously watching the sky, which for four days had been sulky and weeping, to know whether it were prudent to make that now indispensable climb, the ascent of the Rigi. The clouds were still many and thick in some quarters, and especially heavy on the mountain itself, as we disembarked at Weggis about four in the afternoon, and, mounted on horses which, with the ad-

dition of friends picked up on the boat, counted up thirteen.
The wharf at Weggis looked as if a cavalry regiment were
drawn up to receive some military visitor, so closely stood
the horses side by side waiting for their riders.   So great a
trade is now driven in this ascent, that we found the boat
full of rival horse-furnishers soliciting our patronage.   The
legal tariff fixes the price at ten francs a horse, but competition has reduced it to seven, and even to five francs.   About
half the visitors ascend on foot ; a few are carried up in
chairs by two strong porters, usually relieved by a third man.
We found the ascent about five miles long (it is called nine),
and by no means as steep or uneven as any of the old horse-
paths up Mount Washington.   The road is in excellent order, and has nothing dangerous or trying to ordinary nerves
about it.   I rode up and down without one single misstep
on the part of my sure-footed beast.   The ascent took two
hours and twenty minutes, the descent one hour and three-
quarters.   There was no serious fatigue to the young ladies
whom I accompanied, who rode, or even to the young gentlemen who walked, both ways.   The views on ascending from
Weggis are a perpetual feast, as one after another the turns
in the path bring the climber into wider and loftier views of
the lake with its bold or verdant shores, or of the outer
ranges of mountains which come gradually more and more
into the prospect.   The lower flanks of the Rigi are beautifully green and productive, and all the autumn fruits were offered to us as we passed through them — peaches, pears,
plums, figs and grapes, the last two in high perfection.   A
little farther up a magnificent precipice, like the Palisades,
lies directly across the path, its beautiful blue rock tiled into
courses of diagonal masonry.   The boulders that have fallen
from it lie in grotesque shapes, tending always to the pyramidal form, along the path of the ascent, and the path winds

in and out among them in a delightful way, often producing a kind of cave effect. The stone is, curiously enough, the same old pudding-stone that prevails in such perfection in Roxbury, Mass.

The path surmounts this precipice by a lucky shelf, and after shouldering what from the bottom looks like the only mountain to be climbed, emerges upon the real Rigi, and by a somewhat more precipitous but still easy ascent passing the Kaltbad—a hotel inaccessible to any wheel vehicle, two-thirds the way up—where many people pass months and whole summers as the most attractive and wholesome spot they can find ; and the Rigistatter, within a half-mile of the summit—another comfortable hotel—attains the Kulm or crest of the Rigi. There a large hotel of most comfortable accommodations, and a pension about as large, stand ready to afford shelter and food to about three hundred persons at a time; and there we found ourselves on this somewhat un-certain night (when very prudent mountaineers predicted no prospect), in the midst of what seemed to us, for such a place, the astonishing company of from one hundred and fifty to two hundred persons, perhaps only about the average gathering every night during the season of four months. At about half the distance up we had come suddenly into a stratum of cloud quite dense and cold, which obscured perfectly every thing below and above, and shut us up in a world of mist, which, for aught we knew, reached to the zenith. But a half-mile of climbing carried us out of it quite as suddenly as we came into it, and in a moment more put it at our feet as completely as a lake lies at the feet of one walking on its bank. A half-mile farther up, this world of cloud, as it had seemed, was a little layer of cotton-wool floating in a clear heaven, and obscuring only that particular and exceptional portion of the landscape over which it hung. Above, a cloudless day reigned supreme, while another brilliant day was shining below it.

We arrived at the summit about 6½ P.M., in ample time to enjoy the sunset and to study the effects of the too-swiftly fading light. The sun descends so slowly upon mountain-tops that there are few of those lightings-up of the clouds and higher grounds which often in sunsets seen from plains or low places make the after-glory more brilliant and beautiful than the moment of the great luminary's disappearance. The sun sets on Rigi once and for all. His slant-beams, while he is above the horizon, gild the snow peaks with a peculiar splendor, and all the mountains round look as if gathered, with their crowns upon their heads, to pay homage to their returning lord! It is a beautiful and a solemn sight to behold! The moment he is gone the world is changed, and glooms gather quickly around all mountain faces. I confess I did not pay much attention to the landscape at our feet in the midst of these pinnacles of snow and rock. Seven great waves of rock, tossed into granite spray, with foaming caps of snow and ice, were before me; gulfs of yawning space separated these mountain waves. A Titanic storm stood petrified in the prospect. An ocean of molten rock, lashed to fury by volcanic blasts, caught in the acme of its rage, lay frozen in its wrath, rigid and changeless.

The prettiness of blue lakes and happy villages and fertile cultivation seemed impertinent, and I saw nothing of them until the next morning, and only then after having exhausted wonder and delight upon the upward vision. The horn (no dryad wound its horrid changes) waked us at 4¼ A.M., and with a hasty toilet, fifteen minutes found us in a company of one hundred and fifty expectants (evidently very few of them acquainted with either the time, place or manner of the sun's rising) watching the break of day and the appearance of

Apollo. Some looked with desperate obstinacy at the place where the sun went down, as if they expected him to return in the same spot. Others near me were disputing which was east and which west, and one gentleman frankly confessed that he had all his life been under the impression that when the east was on his right and the west on his left he was always facing south! Already a belt of delicate rose went the complete circuit of the horizon, the eastern half of it low down, the other half a little above the highest mountain-tops. As the sun suddenly shot his first rays from the upper limb, the range of the Jung-frau melted into a delicate yellow, and deepening in tone, soon glowed with golden hues. The lower ranges caught up the theme, and soon a chorus of praise, all in tones of light, resounded from the mountain-tops, inaudibly singing Milton's sublime hymn, " Hail, holy light! offspring of heaven, first-born of the eternal," etc., as the sun *swiftly* rose, for he comes rejoicing like a strong man to run a race. The forms of the outer mountains began to show themselves in shadow upon the slopes behind them ; the mist which lay stowed away in solid coils in the holds of the valleys began at once to stir and turn over, and slowly rifts opened in what seemed a firm and motionless lake of flaky snow, and showed the blue waters of Zug below. An hour after sunrise the mountains looked as if they had never known night—all brilliant and wide-awake, and more beautiful, if possible, than earlier. For, bating the force of contrast and the charm of the level rays, there is a superior glory in the ampleness of the light for an hour or two after sunrise, which makes it finer than sunrise itself. Nine-tenths of all the company on the Rigi evidently did not think so. They came up to see the sun set and rise, and ten minutes after he rose they all went in to breakfast, or to their toilets, as they would have gone away from a play when the curtain fell.

The sheep-like way in which the crowds of tourists follow their leaders through Switzerland, doing up the things to be done, admiring what is set down to be admired, and seldom asking themselves one serious question as to what impression is really made upon their own minds and senses, is something incredible till one has seen it, and half makes one doubt the possibility of freeing the masses of human beings from the moulds of a few shaping minds.

The descent from this point brought us rapidly into those charming half-height mountain views which, for all details, are so much lovelier and more enjoyable than the sweeps from the summits. The lake of Lucerne, just as blue as the sky, seemed the other half of an azure globe of crystal, which, with the concave above, had caught the mountains on the shore, and held them in the centre of this beauteous sphere of solid light. Nothing since the shores of the Mediterranean and a few miles of the coast at Beverly, Mass., ever seemed so lovely as the notches in the shore, green as emeralds, which, jutting and retreating, give, on the north of the little town of Weggis, a paradisaical aspect to a half-mile of the lake bank. We could hardly bear to descend from our coignes of vantage to the level of the world, which lay below us; but hunger gave swiftness to our horses, and, after all, emotions weary in proportion to their intensity, and I will not deny that, at 10 A.M., we drank our bitter beer at the foot of the Rigi with a capital relish, in spite of all the romance which had sweetened the five morning hours of that memorable day.

Sunday, Sept. 1.

This morning a dozen Unitarians, who happened to be spending Sunday in the same hotel, met privately at the usual hour of worship, 10½ A.M., and had a regular religious service. Unitarians have the great advantage of respecting all forms of Christian faith and worship, and of being able to join, without any offense to their consciences, or any surrender of their personal convictions, in all serious acts of praise and prayer, however erroneous may be the dogmatic form in which the worship is couched. The toleration and liberality of construction in which they are reared, makes them less anxious when abroad to enjoy their own special creed and worship than most Christians ; and it is, I believe, better, when people are traveling, to mingle with and participate in the Christian worship that prevails in the place, than to set up or seek out their own. For so only is true knowledge of others' religious opinions and customs to be obtained, and that breadth of view and charity of judgment encouraged, the want of which has created the persecution, bigotry and fanaticism of the Christian world. Still, it was very sweet, when it came in so unforced a way, to meet "according minds," and to worship God in a foreign land after the manner and spirit of our simple faith, with a knot of Unitarian Christians.

The English Church deserves praise, and it certainly thus pursues a very self-saving policy, for the efforts it makes to establish its missionary chapels in all parts of the world where its disciples are likely to spend any fragmentary portion of time, or to be found in any numbers. Nothing can give a better impression of the power of the English Establishment than the overflow of its energy and working strength. Not a town of any magnitude, not a watering-place of note is to be found on the Continent, in which an English Episcopal service is not heard on the Sunday mornings and evenings of the traveling months of the year. Doubtless the punctiliousness with which the English hunt up their own church, prayer-book in hand, does something to continue the narrowness and formality of their faith ; but on the whole, the effect is good. The English piety is formal, ritualistic, but it is robust and substantial. It does not diffuse itself like a universal spirit through life, but it keeps certain precious truths and principles under a very strong police, and makes them efficacious and fruitful. In the absence of better things, which can come only with great pains, the religion of England in its Establishment is to be vastly respected, and its spread over Englishmen encouraged. It is curious to notice how strictly *national* it is, and how little power it has to carry itself beyond the sway of the English flag. It is as insular as the politics of Great Britain.

Lucerne is as Catholic as Zurich is Protestant. I found the old cathedral here thronged with worshipers at seven in the morning of an ordinary week-day. There must have been at least thirty priests engaged in the service. The vitality of the church is indicated by a magnificent organ four years old, which equals in power and purity any I ever heard. It was built in Lucerne by Haas. It is played twice every day for one hour, and furnishes a favorite resort for travelers. I stumbled into the church first at the very hour the organ was being exhibited, and with no knowledge of its merits, and of course without any special expectations. But the hush of the little audience showed that something unusual was going on; and it required only a few minutes to bring me wholly under the spell of the most magical stops that I had ever listened to. The player, I found after a second hearing, was not a very great one, but the organ itself was wonderful, and he understood perfectly how to exhibit it, undertaking only what he could do with entire success. The power of the full organ was immense, and as sweet as it was powerful. I could compare it only to the effect of a great park of artillery heard at a distance sufficient to mellow the thunder. But the *vox humana* was the specialty of this organ, and certainly nothing more successful in the way of imitation was ever done. At first, after a bold introduction of the full organ, we heard a choir of children's voices, singing apparently in a neighboring cloister; then a chorus of men's voices took up the strain, and came nearer and nearer as if one and then another door between us and them had been opened. I could not persuade myself for a long time that a choir was not concealed in some adjoining apartment; but it was finally clear that no choir could keep such time and agree together in such expression. Nothing by tones more human or more angelic was ever permitted to visit my ears; at times the mighty instrument was subdued to the gentleness of an infant's breathing, and we all held our breath not to lose the least sigh of its decaying harmony. It seemed as if a choir of seraphs had strayed out of heaven and were overheard by chance as they flew by.

A few moments after we had a *storm*, which, however offensive, considered as an abuse of music, was a marvelous exhibition of the quality and power of the instrument, and of the practiced skill of the performer. The first sobs of the rising tempest, the distant thunder, the shrilling of the breeze, the sweep of the winds, the pattering of the rain, and all the voices of troubled nature were given with telling power. I of course was eager to know the master of this famous instrument. What was my surprise to see a grave old gentleman, in knee breeches and silk stockings, crooked and scholarly, come down from the organ loft, and answer—to my self-introduction—as the organist of the cathedral. He was modest and dignified, and might have been old Handel himself so far as fitness of looks was concerned. It was quite charming to talk with him in bad German about his instrument, and about sacred music generally. We promised

to come again in the evening, about twilight, to hear the
organ. A half-dozen tall tapers lighted the dim cathedral,
and a hundred persons sat for an hour in absolute stillness
while the old man played. It was very charming, but it was
the *second* time!

The lion, of Thorwaldsen's design, cut in the living rock of
the stony hill-side just out of Lucerne, continues, just what it
struck me as being twenty years ago, one of the most
thoroughly expressive and pertinent monuments in all Europe. It commemorates the fidelity of the Swiss guard, who
at the peril of their lives protected Louis and his family in the
storming of the Tuileries in 1792. " It represents a lion of
colossal size wounded to death, with a spear sticking in his
side, yet endeavoring in his last gasp to protect from injury a
shield, bearing the *fleur-de-lis* of the Bourbons, which he holds
in his paws. The figure, hewn from living stone, is twenty-
eight feet long and eighteen high." The human expression
of anguish and fidelity which the artist has thrown into the
lion's face, is something more suggestive of the common nature that binds the animal creation together than compara-
tive anatomy could ever tell. If men are sometimes beastly, beasts are sometimes more human than their masters.

XVII.

SWITZERLAND.

INTERLACHEN, September 3, 1867.

IT was hard to say farewell to such loveliness as passes under the name of Lucerne! The early morning light had converted her proud diadem of mountains into a rosy crown, as we turned for a last fond look on the fairest Queen of Lakes, to whom we vowed eternal loyalty. How blue those calm waters, how green those overlapping tongues of land, how grey those jagged precipices of rocks, how white those pinnacles of snow, how red those tiled roofs, how black those shore-shadows! Proud Pilatus, whose ruffled crest sternly bounds the Southern horizon ; mild, social Rigi, over whose crowded inn no cloud hangs at sunrise this morning, adieu !

Our road to Interlachen lay as far as Alpnach mostly on the lake shore, between which and the crowding flanks of Pilatus it had often hard work to find room. The abundance of stone and the cheapness of labor secure a quality of road in Europe never seen in America. Endless walls of rock, sheer as a plumb line, lift up the lake and mountain roads of Switzerland, and bring the traveler in his cushioned carriage face to face with the wildest scenes. What is to be reached elsewhere only by perilous and fatiguing exposure, is here attainable without labor or danger. The tenderest invalid may travel in the most picturesque parts of Switzerland, and find everywhere the most skillful and luxurious ar-

rangements to carry him to every point of interest without personal exertion.   Strong porters, with easy-chairs, make light
of carrying a hundred and fifty pounds of asthmatic or rheumatic or consumptive flesh over a mountain pass seven hundred
feet high.   With money in one's pocket (especially with French
Napoleons) one may go anywhere in Switzerland—man,
woman or child—in the arms of never-tiring guides.   All the
life of this people is passed in carrying burdens.   The little
children of four years old are seen with baskets, fitted to their
years and their backs, making their mountain climbs.   The
young women, buried beneath sixty and seventy weight of
grass—great walking hay-cocks—come down from the upper
pastures as briskly as though they carried nothing but their
light hearts.   All the wood burned in the frequent hotels up
near the snow lines, with all the food for horses and man,
goes up on the backs of men and women.   I found the
women carrying sixty pounds five miles up the Rigi.   The
guide said he often walked up and down three times a day.
Such training of muscles is wonderful.

One sees in these mountainous countries how literal is
the force of sayings, which have become purely metaphorical
in level and modern lands, such as, " The back is made for
the burden."   Every Swiss and Tyrolean back certainly is.
The wooden buckets in which these mountaineers carry their
milk and their water are very deep, and flat on the side that
comes to the back, oval rather than round.   The pails or
piggins with which they go to the fountain (they have no need
of wells, and their water is usually running) are without bails,
with a long handle on one side, the lengthening of one of
the staves.   They manage them very deftly.   The fountains
—every village has three or four—are the centres of meeting ; horses, dogs, goats, men, women, children, are always
coming to drink.   The family washing is usually done there.

Nobody drinks from a cup at the fountain, but applies the mouth to the water-pipe, without choking or getting drenched. The hot horses from the diligence, trained not to drink when warm, come and stand obediently to have water dashed in their nostrils without presuming to touch the trough with their panting mouths. By the way, the only horses with freshly polished hoofs I ever saw, were in the post at Sarnen this morning. They looked as if they might have left their shoes outside the door to be blacked, as the passengers had done. It is strange how little effect the immense incursion of foreigners has had upon Swiss architecture. It preserves, either from policy or from persistency of habit, its ancient forms. And although very heavy in timber, it is curiously like the Chinese pagoda style in general effect. The base is the narrowest part of the house, which spreads like an umbrella. It is no wonder that with the immense purchase which its broad eaves and the copings over the successive stories give the wind, the houses and barns should require to be ballasted with very heavy stones on the roof, to keep them from blowing away. They are usually without cellars, the basement answering that purpose. The windows are usually glazed with very small glass. Sometimes very pretty carving decorates the timbers and string-courses. The furnishing of even the best seems very meagre, and the ideas of domestic comfort exceedingly low and poor. The barns are very solid structures, and often better than the houses. The general idea given in all the smaller villages and on the mountain slopes is that only ceaseless and very laborious industry keeps soul and body together. Hemp and flax are grown in small parcels near every cottage, and the people are often seen, especially on the southern side of the mountains, tending cattle or goats, with the distaff in their hands. The beating of flax is another common occupation. They spin and weave their own linen. The women work as hard as the men ; and the old people (and many are very prematurely old) are often seen carrying crushing burdens. While the children are numerous and singularly pretty, spite of their tow-heads, exposure and hard work seem to coarsen the girls so rapidly that even their picturesque bodices and white, stiff, leg-of-mutton sleeves can't redeem them. The men are better looking than the women—which is true wherever women work as hard as men. The drivers of carriages, the guides and the men we fall in with, please us by their seeming integrity and unspoiled manners. Really few people could stand the corrupting influence of an annual invasion of pleasure-seekers, so well. The main roads are, at this season, thronged with carriages and foot travelers, so that at the little village of Lungern yesterday, where we stopped to dine at noon, there must have been, at a poor little inn, in a mean little town, twenty voitures, and at least fifty travelers waiting for dinner. A daily *table d'hôte* for a hundred guests waits to catch at the half-way place the appetite of the crowds swinging between Lucerne and Interlachen. At every inn there is a sale of Swiss wooden-ware. It is the chief mechanical industry of the country, and at the main points, dozens of shops are opened for its sale. Much of it is really artistic in style and execution. It is so common as to destroy its own charm. The difficulty of getting it home safely is another obstacle to its purchase, but spite of that and of the duties, few travelers, for the first time in the country, can resist the temptation to burden themselves with these carvings of wood.

A beautiful road has supplanted the bridle-path by which, nineteen years ago, I passed over the Brunig. A heavy shower covered the whole lower part of the lake of Brienz, as we looked down the valley of Meyringen and the course of the Aar as it shot into the lake. The celebrated water-falls of Meyringen were all in view at one moment. They hang this deep valley with milk-white garlands. Some of them plunge, in their united bounds, over a thousand feet. By 6 o'clock the clouds broke into beautiful silver-edged masses, letting the deep blue through in charming splendor and under the welcome of the clearing shower. We passed Brienz and the cataract of the Giessbach on the opposite shore, and by a rapid drive through wooded fields and under towering cliffs, but always *on*, or just over, the lake shore, we watched the approach to Interlachen, waiting impatiently to see the Jung-frau peering through the gorge that faces that unique spot. But crane our necks as we would, that cold-bosomed nymph reserved her charms. Either veiled in mist as we feared, or else changed in place (or was it only we whose memory had failed?), we got no glimpse of that fair damsel, until in the very town itself, she suddenly looked out, her white neck blushing with the sun's directed gaze, but her head lofty and glistening with a radiance of diamonds, and seemed to take at once complete possession of the place. The valley of the Lütschine, with the Schynige-platte on one side and the Morgen-berg on the other, forms the glorious frame through which the great picture of the Jung-frau is seen, and, green and snowless, they present the most vivid contrast with this solitary peak, which, isolated, or rather cut off by the narrowness of the view, is grandly distinct, and like a wondrous "pearl hung in an Ethiop's ear." The world has occupied the mouth of this valley (Lauterbrunnen) with the finest look-outs—in the shape of a row of elegant hotels—a dozen, probably, accommodating two thousand visitors at a time, the number of persons that daily come to pay homage to this prospect. Perhaps there is no parallel to this costly compliment. Niagara itself has not such a collection of prepara-

tions to meet the influx of daily visitors. A smooth meadow
lies between the range of the hotels and the mouth of the valley down which the Jung-frau looks. Back of the hotels rises
a sheer precipice, leaving only room for a Kursaal and public
grounds. Last night the young moon had little power, but
this immense precipice, as black as ink in its shadow, lay
against the starry sky in an outline as sharp as steel, and
while the head lay back on the shoulders to reach the place
where heaven began, I thought I had rarely seen so magnificent a contrast as this under-gloom and the glory above.
This morning the Jung-frau bade me "Guten-tag" as I rose
from bed with the sunrise, and in cloudless beauty, all day
long, she has been sending her ice-cold smiles down into the
hot valley to cool our thoughts if not our tongues. It is hot-
ter here this 3d Sept. than perhaps at any previous day of
the summer. Yesterday, Sept. 2, we climbed the Jung-frau-
blick, a little pyramidal hill, posted one side of the gorge in
front of the Jung-frau, as if nature, in love with her landscape,
had ended with making a gallery to see it from. The two
lakes, not visible from the plain below, came into the prospect here, and at the Thun end, some mountains so perfectly
regular in shape, that the Egyptian Pyramids can not surpass
them in artificial outline. Between the foot of our outlook
and the opening valley of Lauterbrunnen, stretched meadow
as level as that at the foot of Holyoke, and green as that is in
early June. The white roads glistened like chalk lines upon
a blackboard, as they wound round boundaries and through
scattered trees, and lost themselves behind the slopes that
overlap each other at the entrance of the gorge. No way
seemed open or possible for any carriage road, yet the great
road to Lauterbrunnen and to Grindelwald lies through it.
The Jung-frau revealed half her own height, and spread her
shoulders until she seemed to cover all the southern hori-

zon. The silver horn for the first time came into view. It was near sunset, and whatever views Mt. Blanc and Mt. Rosa may have in reserve for us, it is hard to believe that any snow peak can ever charm and awe us more than this did. Usually the grand views lack unity. They are picture galleries and not independent pictures. I remember nothing in all Switzerland which possesses the emphatic unity of the Jung-frau seen from twenty points at Interlachen.

We went at 9 P.M. into the Kursaal to hear a special concert from a choir of Tyrolean singers. They were peasants refined by traveling; three men and two women; all stout, mountain-grown persons, broad in the shoulders, erect and vigorous in the extreme. Their voices were truly national and characteristic, as if formed to drown cataracts, out-distance dividing valleys, and reach from lower to upper pastures. The women possessed a quantity and quality of voice such as I never heard proceed from female lungs before. With as much body as any masculine voices, they were clear as bells and capable of a shrillness that pierced your marrow. The contralto might have beat Alboni at her best in profundity. Their songs were all Tyrolean, and they gave us every variety of the jodel. It is hard to call that curious *falsetto* singing. It seems to be a kind of change from the throat notes to the head notes, with a deliberate disappointment of the full note, which is flatted a quarter instead of a half-tone. It seems to be an imitation of the way in which animal and other sounds are broken and modified by great heights. It was a wonder to see how little the natural quality of the voices of these singers was injured by this trick, which must be a terrible strain on the vocal chords. The *zither*, a sort of violin without a hollow body, was skillfully played by one of the company. It has great plaintive power but little body of sound. An instrument made of bits of resonant wood, with tones like the babbling of water over stones, was very pleasantly beaten with two little mallets in waltz time, and made a curious variety in the concert. The natural, unpretending, yet self-possessed manner and bearing of these singers was thoroughly prepossessing.

GIESSBACH.

September 5.

We spent the night at this celebrated spot, which draws daily two or three hundred visitors off their route to witness the illumination of the Falls. About ten miles from Interlachen and nearly opposite the town of Brienz on the lake of that name, a torrent precipitates itself, by a series of five leaps, into the lake, over a finely wooded but most abrupt mountain face of perhaps 1500 feet in height. The Fall is very pretty, seen from the lake, where, however, only a small portion of it is visible. About two hundred feet above the lake an unexpected plateau of charming shape opens, on which the steamboat company have erected a large hotel, inaccessible by any carriage road along the shore, but to which they furnish very pleasant conveyance in their steamer. Here, amid delightful prospects and well-arranged grounds, is a resort of unique description, so enchanting that it forces a continued stream of travel from its course, to make at least the pilgrimage of a night to this out-of-the-way spot. The Falls themselves, by day-light, are beautiful, but by no means more so than twenty others in Switzerland. They are neither more copious, bold, lofty, nor finely situated than several in the valley of Meyringen close by. A steep climb of half an hour carries the enterprising visitor to their top, giving him pleasant views of the lake below, and of each shoot, passing him directly behind the finest, which looks more like a violent snow-storm than any thing else, seen from its rear. The

tug up the hill, over roots and rocks, especially in the twilight, when we made it, hardly rewarded our painstaking,
except as a preparation for the succeeding illumination. At
about half-past eight of the moonless evening, when heavy
clouds added special darkness to the night, the three hundred visitors who had assembled at the proper point of view
—most conveniently furnished near the restaurant, twenty
rods below the hotel—began to see mysterious lights, moving briskly by zigzag routes up the face of the black precipice before them. The faintest ghost of the Fall could be
just made out in the gloom, by a broken line of less perfect
blackness on the face of the mountain. At least a half-hour
passed while we watched these human Will-o'-the-wisps that
were fitfully dancing in the forest and establishing by degrees a
line of lights from the bottom to the top of the Falls. Carefully shaded as the lanterns were until the proper moment,
enough of their beams escaped to mark out the course of the
Fall. A great hush of expectation came over the company.
Suddenly a signal rocket blazed out from the very top. A
minute later it was answered by another from the very bottom, and a half-minute later, by a simultaneous firing of Ben-
gola lights, there opened upon us a more surprising spectacle of fairy-like, if I must not say heavenly, beauty, than I
ever saw before. The five shoots, and indeed the whole
chasm for a thousand feet long and a hundred broad, were
in a blaze of light, exceeding the brightness of noonday,
while absolute darkness buried every thing else. The water
seemed visible in every drop—the whole series of falls in perfect view at once—and I can compare the magical effect only
to a staircase such as might open from the gate of heaven
itself, on whose successive flights choirs of angels—here in
garments of white, and there of blue, and then of rose and
green—were posted, to welcome the expected guests. Ja-

cob's ladder could not have been more lovely in his dream. In fact the ecstasy of this prospect was almost painful. I. found myself expecting that something in me would give way under a vision of such supernatural beauty, and was afraid, as men have been afraid when angelic messengers have appeared to them. I can not say that the many-colored lights added to the effect. The first minute, when only pure white. light illuminated the whole series of falls, was really far the most effective. Falls of red wine or green vitriol are not natural enough to please, and it is impossible not to be a little vexed with memories of stage-spectacle, when red and green lights intrude into scenes which Heaven itself has fashioned. But I will not complain of any part of a vision which gave me such exquisite pleasure while it lasted. It was long enough, although I believe the watch reported only three minutes' duration. The lights were skillfully made to die out of the successive shoots rapidly, but in succession, beginning with the lowest. One by one, those heavenly gates closed! The highest, which was red as blood, closed last, and with a longer interval, and we were shut out and left in the darkness! I would not for the world have had the spectacle repeated. It would have become theatrical the next time, and I dare say hateful after a few repetitions; but it has left an image on my senses and my imagination so vivid and so enchanting that if I should live a thousand years I could never forget it. I expect to have it return in dreams, and should not wonder if in the shadows of expiring nature it presented itself as a foreshowing of the glory that is to be revealed.

Yesterday at dinner, at Interlachen, who should most unexpectedly greet me as I rose from table but my old teacher and friend, Rev. Dr. Palfrey of Boston, and with him a knot of Unitarian friends. The Doctor was just flitting through Switzerland by a swift detour on his way to England, where.

I surmise he has a few weeks of work before him examining historical documents. Meanwhile he represents the country at the Anti-Slavery Congress held in a few weeks at Paris. It was delightful to see this accomplished scholar and faithful historian getting a little relaxation. New England owes him some leisure in his declining years. America owes him lasting honor for his illustrious fidelity to anti-slavery principles in days when it cost reputation, place, and almost a livelihood, to be an avowed Abolitionist, especially if the avowal was not itself made a trade of. Dr. Palfrey was never a fanatic nor a revolutionist; but his labors in Congress and out, and especially with his pen, in behalf of national purification from slavery, entitle him to the abiding gratitude of the American people. His pupils in theology do not forget their personal obligations to his learning and his conscientious criticism.

September 6.

The Hotel Belvedere, where we are staying, has the reputation of being the scene of Longfellow's Hyperion. I expected to find it lying about in the inn, but have not laid eyes on a copy. But books have a poor chance in the midst of such scenery, and, above all, of such troops of friends as one meets in this rendezvous. Bostonians and New Yorkers, and almost all of them Unitarian friends, make more than half the guests at this hotel. Twenty-five I counted in the *salon* at one time. Not that this is an American haunt especially. I see from my window a gentleman and lady breakfasting out-of-doors, in the public drive-way, directly in front of the hotel, and I know they must be French. That other man, smoking his pipe before breakfast, must be German. There, by his peculiar robes, is, I judge, a Russian priest; and near by, an English High Church minister, who enters his name in the book, Rev. J. H. Davidson, *Priest*, England.

It is no wonder that one sees at Interlachen, on two doors, side by side, entering the same building, the notice, on one, " English Church," and on the other, " Catholic Chapel." It would be very easy to knock away the partition if these sentimental Ritualists had their way.

We have the refreshing company to-day of Mr. Wood of Rev. Mr. Hale's church, and Mr. Kennaird of Dr. Hedge's, and Mr. Moses Kimball of Dr. Lathrop's, and Mr. Bouve of Dr. Putnam's, not to mention a half-dozen ladies. I saw yesterday *eight* of my own parishioners. I can not feel very far away from home. But I sat down to say something about our flight over the Wengern Alp yesterday, but I see that I can not get it into this mail.

XVIII.

THUN, September 9, 1867.

JUST opposite the line of brilliant hotels at Interlachen opens the famous valley of Lauterbrunnen ("nothing but springs"), through whose magnificent gorge bursts out the violent torrent of the Lütschine, whose deposits, it is supposed, · have built the isthmus of two miles level land that so charmingly separates the two lakes of Brienz and Thun, which, by the way, are at different levels, Thun being twenty-five feet lower. Through this gorge bursts, also, the glorious beauty of the Jung-frau, in a prospect of unrivaled grandeur and sublime unity. Following up this valley four or five miles, you come to the end of the lateral valley of Grindelwald, through which the black Lütschine pours its gloomy waters. Following the other branch of the torrent, the white Lütschine, you are led to the village of Lauterbrunnen, which, amid the greenest and most cultivated slopes, is overhung with precipices which delay the sunrise and anticipate the sunset by a couple of hours. That part of the valley, in the midst of which the " Staub-bach " hangs its scarf of mist, reminds me strongly of the Yosemite valley in its general features, though wanting in equal beauty. The famous " Bridal veil " of the Yosemite is a finer fall than the " Staub-bach," although it has not had Byron for its poet nor Longfellow for its historic romancer. It is best seen from a half-mile distant, and is poorest when viewed directly in front.

I

At Lauterbrunnen, after having with partial success dodged all the benevolent old and young women, who wanted us to buy sour plums and juiceless pears to an extent that would. have given the dreaded cholera to a regiment, or else to lay in wooden-ware enough to stock a toy-shop at Christmas, we mounted our horses—in a party of nine—to cross the Little Sheideck, and from the Wengern Alp to face directly the snows and precipices of the Jung-frau, perchance to hear the roar and see the fall of its famous ˙avalanches. Some wag has called the Wengern Alp the "Boulevard of Switzerland." Certainly over its steep and narrow bridle-path file daily more visitors than over any other foot-pass, unless we call the "Rigi" by that name. I met an acquaintance made in California, on the passage over, who knew me after three years' separation, in the disguise of my grey whiskers and unclerical wardrobe, and saluted me, as if it were the most natural thing in the world for men living on opposite sides of the globe to meet four thousand feet above the ocean in a mule-track of Switzerland. The ascent for the first two miles is steep and uncomfortable, but from the top of the first ridge to the summit the path is neither precipitous nor rugged, nor is there any thing that need discourage persons of ordinary strength from riding up or down. The general views are superb.

The Wengern Alp seems a mere gallery for seeing at close hand the sublime precipices, the noble glaciers and the towering peaks of the Jung-frau. The last two miles before reaching the summit are the great lookout, from which the sight of falling avalanches and huge snow-fields and immense perpendicular walls of rock is commanded. It looks as if you could toss a stone across this valley, which must be a mile wide. It is really only just far enough to allow the best possible view of the Jung-frau, which, in all its savage majesty and frozen wrath, stretches up and down the valley as if its roots spread from horizon to horizon, while its snowy top seems to support the sky. It was wholly bare of vegetation—all rock, ice and snow—while the Wengern is green and covered to its top with pastures, full of cattle, filling the air with the music of their tinkling bells. A half-dozen refreshment saloons, with two excellent hotels, measure off the way, so that civilization, comfort and verdure are here brought *vis-a-vis* with desolation, sterility and Arctic savageness. Every half-mile that gigantic bassoon, the Alpine horn, a rude wooden instrument, called for a tribute of pennies to its success in waking up the echoes of the mountains, and now and then Tyrolean melodies were choraled at the door of chalets by women, who dropped their lace bobbins to take the small price they asked for stopping their noise. We began to fear, as we approached nearest to the shelves from which the avalanches usually drop, that the season was too late for this coveted spectacle. But a heavy rain of the night before had loosened the snow, and a hot sun was untying its last bonds, and just as our despair began to culminate, down came a torrent of snow and ice, which for a few seconds eclipsed the Staub-bach in copiousness, and when it reached the ground, shook the valley with thunders and a tremor that was palpable, while a smoke went up from the gulf equal to the torrent that forever boils in the basin of Niagara.

The sight was vastly more impressive than we had anticipated ; and, indeed, the avalanche was an exceptional one in its magnitude. Seven of unusual size had followed each other in as many minutes, at an earlier hour in the morning. A second of large proportions fell when we were on the summit, and many smaller ones beguiled our way up. We felt amply rewarded for our pains. An hour's rest, with some bread and cheese, a mountain custard and a bottle of Swiss wine, prepared us to descend on foot to the glacier of Grindelwald. We were two hours and a half riding up, and less than two hours coming down to the glacier—a fact well enough to mention, as the innkeepers, horse-furnishers and guides call it an eight or nine hours' journey over, and charge in proportion. To get from Interlachen by carriage out to Lauterbrunnen, then sending the carriage round to meet us at Grindelwald, to cross on horseback with a guide, visit the glacier and get back to Interlachen, cost three of us eighty-five francs and just twelve hours' work—a great deal more than in fairness it should have cost. We had in our patriotic tenderness selected from among the guides a fair-faced boy of sixteen, who speaking good English had excited our curiosity, and who turned out to be a lad from Indiana, who had got across the water, he did not seem inclined to tell us why or how, and was now studying French and German practically to qualify himself for success as a guide to travelers. He had, evidently by his lingual accomplishments, especially by talking English, aroused the universal jealousy of the native guides—speaking only a patois of German and a little bad French. But it was clear enough that it was not in language alone that he was their superior. In intelligence, cunning, self-control and the arts of getting along he was worth a dozen of them, and moved like a superior being among them. I am very much afraid his superiority was not a moral inspiration. We found him as grasping and artful as he was clever, and did not care much to present him as an American product. But it was instructive to notice how much finer textured and more subtle and active the brain of this Yankee boy was than the brains of the grown men about him.

We find the Swiss, like other mountaineers, narrowed in

intellect as much as they are expanded in the love of freedom. They have all a little of the Savoyard softness and
sentimentality. It is in their eyes and voices. Very little
self-assertion or enterprise attaches to their personality.
Good-natured, unambitious, poor, and contented to be poor,
they are living on the crumbs of rich men's tables—in short,
supported by the pleasure travel of the world, and I see few
evidences that their country is any the better for the use it
is put to ; but of that more after a little more experience.
Of course, hot as we were, we went into the glacier, where I
suspect a great many people get their death o' cold. The
gallery *in*—which is twenty feet above the foot—penetrates,
by a tunnel of perhaps ten feet square, some two hundred
feet or more into the heart of the glacier. It has three or
four angles in its passage, and ends in a chamber of twenty
feet square. The ice, of a bluish tint, is wonderfully clear,
and lighted, even poorly, gave very brilliant crystalline reflections. The temperature, after our hot walk, was painfully
and perilously cold, and allowed a much shorter visit than
we all coveted. Before we had advanced half-way, sounds
of distant music, as if from spirits imprisoned in the glacier,
aroused a painfully interesting attention. I was meditating
on the possibility of sounds reaching us from the surface,
when the increasing loudness culminated in bringing me face
to face with two shrouded and doubtless shivering women,
who were playing the zither, and singing in the heart of this
glacier. It was a most disagreeable entertainment in all its
suggestions and all its concomitants. The poverty which
could drive women to this perilous exposure, the unsuitable-
ness of the thing—as if glaciers were like other ices, to be
served up to the sound of an orchestra—and the unexpected-
ness of having your pocket picked by an appeal to your pity
in the heart of a glacier—all combined to fill me with disgust,

as, shuddering with cold, I retreated out of this crystal cavern, to find sunshine and freedom in the open air.

Grindelwald itself is fully entitled to its reputation as one of the grandest and most beautiful valleys in Switzerland. People make a great mistake in hurrying through it as we did. It is a place in which all possible mountain effects may be studied at leisure. The faces of the precipices are so bold, the horns of so many towering peaks glisten through its gorges, its slopes are so fertile, its chalets so sprinkled about, that I know no spot more attractive when the charm of its two glaciers is added. Finer glaciers are easily found, but none so accessible. The drive to Interlachen was all down hill, and accomplished in two hours. We could not believe that we had left so many hundred feet to be descended, as we pitched from Grindelwald down the steep road into its dark valley. The mist was just rising from the Lütschine, as the snow-cooled stream came into warmer air. As we descended, the sunset turned the tops of the mountains into precipices of ruby, while a few clouds outblushed their florid faces. We drove furiously down the declivities, saved from peril by a very ugly guardian angel in the shape of a stunted boy-man, whose missing height had gone into his thickness, but who kept up with us for at least four miles, applying the chain and shoe to our wheels and loosening it at proper moments—a sort of benevolent hobgoblin, whom a half-franc converted into a smile such as brought out the human heart from within his rough hide.

It is impossible to get out of Interlachen in the direction of Thun, without passing through Unterseen, and it would take all the waters in both lakes to wash out the fœtid odors that stifle those who ride through its streets. Pig-sties, barnyards, sewers, butcheries, tanneries, combine to pollute the air, and the children who grow up in its disgusting atmosphere show the poison they breathe in their stunted stature, and deformed and idiotic appearance. It will be idle to charge the Cretinism of Switzerland to its waters, so long as the filthiness of its lower population remains such an active source of domestic malaria. It is strange that the pure air of its mountains should not create a distaste for a foul, reeking air in its dwellings, or that the charming purity of its lakes and rivers should not provoke a spirit of cleanliness and a love for bathing and washing. But the very reverse is true. They wash their flannels, it is said, only yearly, and change their linen quarterly! Their basements are always damp, dirty and disgusting, and you can only reach the dining-room in many of their houses by passing by the stable and the piggery. . Doubtless there is something radically wrong in the architecture of the country. In all the towns it is enormously heavy—commonly built in stone arcades, very low in the arches, excluding light and air, and of course both. gloomy and ill-ventilated. The houses would all stand a siege, and look more like fortresses than habitations.

The lake of Thun, beautiful as it is at its western end, with the glorious peaks that rise over its smiling slopes, is not equal to Lucerne. The town, built on the Aar, which divides and leaves part of Thun on an island, has hidden itself from the lake view, as if only cold winds and bleak prospects came from its lovely waters. It is a picturesque old place to look upon from any neighboring height, with its raised sidewalks and its lofty four-towered castle, and the broad meadows, flat as a sheet of paper, that offer themselves in such beautiful contrast with the conical mountains around. There are charming houses, or rather castles, on the banks of the lake, one belonging to Count Portalis, former lord of Neufchatel, and another still more elegant, the property of a French gentleman. The view of the lake from the summer-house on the height behind the beautiful grounds of the Hotel de Bellevue is magnificent, and richly repays the sharp climb that leads to it. The enterprising proprietor of this extensive establishment, which embraces four houses in a large garden or park, has found it for his interest to erect a chapel for the service of the Church of England in his own grounds. The zeal of the " Establishment" keeps it open for four months, and the guests of the hotel and town supply its choir and fill its pews. The Continental hotels are all placarded with notices of these English Church services, by ministers duly licensed by the Bishop of London, and doubtless many poor clergymen get their summer run only on the terms of supplying some such Continental chapel for a few weeks. Such poor stipend as they receive, you are carefully notified, proceeds only from the contributions of the worshipers. The service is long, repetitious and formal. The Lord's Prayer is repeated three times in the morning, as if it were a cabalistic charm, and there is an air of superstitious observance in the whole service which is offensive to an enlightened spirit. I heard lately of a blasphemous bet made by the ship's doctor on one of the transatlantic steamers, to whom, as the "aftest man" aboard for that duty, had been committed the task of reading the service. He bet that he would publicly read the service in thirty minutes, and did it in twenty-nine.

Thun contains a very costly barrack for soldiers, just built, not without great opposition on account of its cost. The Swiss Diet in purchasing the postal service from the cantons, who formerly derived considerable income from it, agreed to pay back a certain proportion of the net profits of this lucrative business to the cantons annually. But the Diet is always in want of money, and the cantons are in debt, and fear every federal expenditure may diminish their prospects of receiving their dues from the Diet. The railroads are some of them productive, and others not. They can divide only six per cent., and Zurich is now building a most costly depot, with a surplus which really, in the spirit of the act of incorporation, belongs to the government. Skipping Berne, where we passed three days, and to which I must devote my next letter, I pass on to Freybourg, known to travelers for its famous suspension bridges and its grand organ. The organ, although well played by Mr. Voigt, who has been organist for over thirty years, is not as pleasant an instrument to hear as the organ at Lucerne. There is a peculiar harp-like twang in the quality of its tone, which is like a nasal tone in the human voice. Its "vox humana" is far inferior to the stop in the Lucerne organ. Had it not a start of a quarter of a century in reputation of many other fine organs in Europe, it would hardly hold its renown. None of the great organs abroad I have yet heard are superior to the Boston organ ; but they have the immense advantage of being in buildings precisely adapted both in size and shape to their full expression, which the Boston Music Hall is not.

The two suspension bridges in Freybourg are really wonders of courage and skill. They accomplish their difficult object of bridging gulfs which for ages had subjected the inhabitants to daily and most serious inconvenience with the smallest expenditure of means. Usually suspension bridges are imperiled by the very weight which is adopted to make them secure. Their own gravitation exceeds any pressure which is put upon them. Here the engineer has had the faith and boldness to avoid every pound of iron not indispensable to the practical strength of his bridge ; and with probably less than a tenth of the avoirdupois in the great suspension bridges over the Menai Straits and Niagara River, he has built a bridge of a single arch, the longest in the world and the highest, which has stood forty years. There is a very perceptible, and I must confess to me a very disagreeable oscillation in these bridges when a single heavy wagon is crossing them ; but they have borne a train of wagons reaching from one end to the other, and are safe beyond any question. Freybourg, like Berne, and I may add Lausanne, is one of the most difficult cities to get about in in the world. All these cities, originally jammed into chasms not unlike that at Niagara below the Falls, have run up the precipitous banks, and created stories above stories, connected with stone stairs and almost inaccessible steeps, which render locomotion about them almost as difficult as in mountain passes. They are, however, wonderfully picturesque. The view from the terrace of the Hotel Zahringer at Freybourg is extraordinary and fascinating.

Five Franciscan monks were our fellow-travelers in the cars from Freybourg to Vevay. I could not help envying them their compact costume, so admirably adapted to traveling in Europe, where luggage is such a nuisance. Most travelers are sacrificed to their clothes. But these ascetic saints, with their single cloth garment, which seemed to answer all the purposes of a complete suit, besides being furnished with a cowl which covered their shaven crowns when they condescended to such a weakness as a head-piece, were equipped for a journey of a month when they added a wallet of a few ounces to their wardrobe. Their gowns were sewed up in front from the waist down. Their sleeves they used as pockets, tucking their handkerchiefs up them, and any thing else they wished to dispose of. They snuffed and chewed tobacco, but in other respects looked like self-denying men, not without intellectual expression.

Freybourg was the seat of Father Girard's admirable educational influence, which was felt all over Switzerland, and to no small extent in Europe. His benevolent face is perpetuated in a bronze statue in one of the principal squares. He was a monk and an earnest Catholic, but none the less a profound and practical philanthropist and friend of science and popular education. His memory is venerated and blessed in all this region. Switzerland, through his influence in large part, possesses a school system which educates her own children and attracts thousands from every part of Europe. Zurich, Lausanne, Vevay, Geneva, are full of schools, patronized by English, French, Russians and Germans. Great numbers come to them from all countries to be perfected in the French language. It is unhappily true that the better sort of Swiss youth are compelled to leave their own land for a livelihood. Paris is full of Swiss clerks, and they are scattered all over the cities of Europe. Their excellent education stands them in good stead in these positions. Several Swiss parents have told me that their own country furnished no career for their sons. The new railroads are improving business to some extent, and their hotels, with their enormous summer business, have actually re-created some towns. Ouchy, the port of Lausanne, has grown into a thriving place from nothing since the beautiful and popular Hotel of Beau-rivage was opened there. One man, by omnibus and livery business, from a poor voiturier has become in a few years the capitalist of the place, and lately gave 160,000 francs for a piece of property which he will doubtless turn into a " pension " — the destination of all large houses on the Lake of Geneva. There is a truly American air in the bustle of travel about Lake Leman, and with so many American faces about, it is hard to feel very far from home. But this beautiful and classic region must not be disposed of in the concluding paragraph of a letter, so I will adjourn the Lake of Geneva to a later communication.

XIX.

BERNE.

SWITZERLAND, September 10, 1867.

BERNE, the political capital of the Federal Union of Switzerland, occupies a noble bluff, round which the Aar sweeps, holding the city almost encircled by its beautiful arms. The blue river, deep in its bed, meets the eye of the stranger from a dozen terraces that overhang its waters, as unexpectedly he comes upon the narrow boundaries of this natural fortress. And yet, high as Berne is, it is overlooked in every direction, excepting toward the Oberland (where the prospect is so important), by commanding hills, beautifully wooded, and at convenient points laid out in drives and gardens, from which Berne, with its grand old minster, and its rich roofs bristling with picturesque chimneys and gables, presents a most inviting prospect. The old city stands there as if made to be looked at.. It appears almost like a toy city, built to amuse a prince, so gem-like and artistic is its form and place. I wished to take it up as I looked down on it from the Enghe, and carry it off to America, to give the good untraveled people at home (if there are any left) an idea of what a place a thousand years old comes to be under favorable circumstances. That grand cathedral tower, unfinished as it is, need not hide its head in the presence of the grandest chain of mountains in Europe—the Bernese Alps—so visible from its turrets. The snow peaks, that rest on the granite summits yonder, seem to own that venerable tower as a part of nature, so long have they been exchanging looks with each other, and so solidly and sincerely did art and piety work when they heaved up that enduring pile. These arcades of stone, strong as casemates, on which whole streets of houses, four, five, perhaps seven hundred years old, are resting, and may continue to rest as many hundred years more, how they bring back the days when a man's house was his castle, and when domestic architecture was upon the military model. Italy has evidently set the copy which Berne, Innsbrück, Basle and other Alpine cities have followed in their street architecture. Berne has broken up its old walls, but pieces of them, and old towers and gates, are still wrought into its present charming surroundings.

The chief ornament of Berne, however, is the unrivaled prospect it commands of the Bernese Alps. They seem almost to belong to the city and the city to them. Thirty miles off, at least, they are only just distant enough to be seen to full advantage, as a part of the grand landscape in which they are set—a mighty necklace worn on the bosom of Central Europe. Amid the Alps, the Alps are a world in themselves, and can not be seen in their relations. They tyrannize over the imagination and crush the senses. They are not things over which man feels his rightful superiority. He walks in their dark gulfs a prisoner; he trembles on the verge of their precipices; he drags his weary limbs up their endless ascents, and feels how weak and miserable a creature he is before their crushing glaciers and overwhelming avalanches and inaccessible heights. But a remove of fifty miles reduces this exclusive and imperious tract of mountain territory—which bars out all the world and makes itself an unrelated district—to its real proportions—a furrow on the face of mother earth, a wrinkle on her brow, so venerable yet so fair. What was painfully sublime, seen in its isolation, is only grandly beautiful seen in its relations. The Alps are only beautiful, nay, are only really seen, when seen in whole chains and from a sufficient distance to give them their full place and no more, in a landscape embracing the plain from which they rise. Even the White Hills (let us never more call them mountains, but retain the dignity which first named them so proudly and modestly hills) are not really seen from any. point nearer than Littleton or Lancaster. And the Alps, of which the Oberland is the real jewel, are not seen to perfection from any point nearer than Berne. Here in fair weather—which I am afraid is a rarity—they hang with the clouds, their natural playfellows, in the eastern horizon, things of beauty. The doubting eye, unused to such heights, refuses to acknowledge them as solid and mundane substances, as they now melt into heaven and now freeze to the ground. Mocking the clouds or mimicked by them, the clouds seem mountains, the mountains clouds. The granite precipices look like snow, the snowy peaks like granite. Blushing in the sunset, they become like the walls of jasper and amethyst in the heavenly Jerusalem. Phantoms of glorious loveliness, they sink with the sun and rise with him ; the ghostly presences of the day, haunting the horizon, but coy and uncertain, never to be counted on at any given day or hour, yet sure to return, and always the same enchanting objects. If any body wants to enjoy the Bernese Alps, let him come and get a room, facing the view, in this admirable " Bernerhof," the pleasantest inn we have yet occupied, and stay here till a thoroughly fine day, and then he will never forget the mountains of the Oberland, or doubt where to place them among the other ranges of the Alps.

This is, of course, the place, here in the capital of Switzerland, to make some brief study of Swiss politics, and under the guidance of our intelligent and obliging Minister, Mr. Harrington, and of his enlightened friend, Mr. Ninet, I have done my best to understand the working of the Swiss Republic. Of the history of old Switzerland, older than Christianity and coeval with classic times, this is no place to speak. It is sufficient to remember that the Rheti from Italy and the Helvetii from Gaul are commemorated by all Roman historians, and that Cæsar gives no small part of his commentaries to his record of terrible struggles with these, the fiercest soldiers he ever encountered. Switzerland has been the mountain wall against which the surges of two vast forces have for nearly two thousand years been beating; Roman conquest and ambition, making the madness of one tide, and Gothic and Vandal barbarism the fierceness of the other, until the rival ambitions of the Church and the State, and of Northern and Southern empires, took up the old strife of Roman eagles and Gothic spears. Every torrent in the Alps has run blood; every mountain pass been the tomb of hosts of armed men. Switzerland, never homogeneous in its population, has belonged in parts to so many countries—has been conquered and abandoned, sold and partitioned, freed and bound so often—that it is wonderful it possesses any unity now, or that, under all circumstances, it has preserved so much liberty.

The Swiss, under that name, do not appear until A.D. 1114. Arnold of Brescia, an Italian monk, living at Zurich, a disciple of the free-thinking Abelard, was among the first to stimulate the spirit of independence in the Swiss against the domination of the Church, which by its monasteries was always oppressing the mountaineers of the Alps. Henry V. and Conrad, emperors, (1144) supported the pretensions of the Abbeys, which were ever striving to abridge or deny the right of the people to sell in the markets of Lucerne and Zurich, where the Abbeys wished a monopoly. Arnold of Brescia denied celibacy, and maintained that the clergy ought not to possess either property or temporal power. St. Bernard denounced him as one who " in a vase of honey distilled the poison of heresy." Arnold, six years after, passed the Alps, followed by 2000 men, and by their aid stripped the Pope of his temporal power and founded on the borders of the Tiber a republic which was very short-lived. He was delivered up by the Emperor Frederick I. and burned by the Prefect of Rome as a heresiarch, in 1155. The mountaineers who had accompanied him may have all perished, but the reformed faith he had sowed in Zurich could not die.

The foundation of the Swiss confederacy dates from 1291, when the three cantons, Uri, Schwytz and Zurich, entered into a perpetual compact—" All for each, each for all " being their blazon. They did not propose treasonably to throw off their due allegiance to any rightful rulers, but simply to protect their just rights. Lucerne came into this league in 1315. Later, and after defections and wars, eight cantons formed a perpetual alliance, which lasted from 1353 to 1415. The Grisons became allies of the Swiss in 1400. The Council of Constance—1415, 1418—was followed by terrible civil wars at Zurich, and by little foreign wars for a whole century. Zwingle, the natural successor of Arnold of Brescia, took up the work of Reformation at Zurich in 1518. In spite of the efforts of the Catholic cantons, the Reformation was established in Berne, St. Gall, Appenzell, Schaffhausen and Basle. Then followed the separate leagues between the Catholic and the Protestant cantons, with the wars growing out of them. The Anabaptist persecution and other troubles succeeded, until, under the religious and political dictation of Calvin, Geneva became, in 1536, 1564, the Protestant Rome. The Catholic reaction in Europe and in Switzerland then followed. Austrian, Spanish and French occupation of Switzerland darkened the sixteenth and seventeenth centuries, and especially desolated the Grisons, who only recovered their independence in 1640. The independence of the Swiss was guaranteed in the treaty of Westphalia, 1648. Then came the peasant war, and the revolutions at Basle and Geneva. The struggle to drive the Jesuits from their stronghold at Freybourg and from the other cantons, was raging from 1712 to 1774.

The French Revolution had its strong echoes in Switzerland, and the invasion of the French under Generals Menard and Brune lasted from 1790 to 1798, when it may be said that old Switzerland ended and new Switzerland began. It is not strange that a country with so large a French element should have sympathized with the ideal democracy of Robespierre and the French Directory, or that one with so large a German element should have contained a strong opposition to purely French principles and inspirations. Many of the larger cantons welcomed with enthusiasm the " Republique Lemannique," of which Laharpe had sent them the plan from Paris, and, putting on the green cockade, constituted themselves a representative assembly, and called Stanislaus Poniatowsky (Secretary of the last King of Poland) to preside over them, under the name of Citizen Glayre (24th June, 1798). On the other hand, the noble Charles Louis d'Erlach, a true and magnanimous Swiss, of a family long distinguished for patriotism, led the opposition which, with patriotic rage, had sprung up in the smaller cantons. Under him occurred some of the most heroic and bloody battles ever fought, battles in which women and children participated, and in large numbers were slain, when Gen. Schauenbourg was sent to put down all resistance to the wishes of the French Directory, who had resolved that Switzerland should be a copy of Republican France. The glories of their ancestors at Morgarten, Laupen and Morat were renewed under D'Erlach and Alois Reding.   But resistance was in vain to so over-whelming a power as France, forcing, in the name of Liber-ty, a constitution on Switzerland which she might have glad-ly accepted under other circumstances, not compromising her independence.   Berne was surrounded, and the French took armed possession of it March 5, 1798.   The new constitu-tion—in which the cantons were essentially reduced to coun-ties of a common State, and the *old thirteen* (like the Ameri-can) were, by additions, annexations and partitions, divided into twenty-one—went into operation.   Few or none of the historic associations of the Swiss were respected in the new government, yet it achieved immediately many very benefi-cent reforms.   The abolition of torture, and of the tax im-posed on Jews ; the conversion of the post service from a can-tonal to a federal one ; the purchase of many exclusive priv-ileges of feudal origin from the proprietors, were among the chief benefits.   Dr. Albert Rengger and Albert Stapfer, men of high views and great gifts, showed excellent administrative skill in their respective departments, one as Minister of the Interior, the other as Minister of Arts and Sciences.   Many distinguished men adorned this period.   Charles Louis Hal-ler, the historian Fuseli, Zschokke, Pestalozzi, Girard, were encouraged by Stapfer and employed in the public service in literary ways.   But it was in vain.   A pure democracy was not yet possible.   Many of the cantons revolted, and finally Napoleon intervened in 1803.   A new constitution cre-ated under his inspiration caused insurrections in and about Zurich, and the incorporation of Valais with France.   The allies came to Switzerland.   The power of the Patrician party was confirmed, and what is known as the federal pact was formed in 1815.   Under this the Jesuits were established at Freybourg, and new struggles of the liberal party became in-evitable.   A democratic revolution occurred in 1830.   Political and religious revolution followed in many cantons. The convents in Aargan were suppressed in 1834, 1843. Civil war raged at Lucerne, and in the Valais. The Pope finally abandoned the seven cantons. The Swiss Diet voted the expulsion of the Jesuits in 1847. The existing federal constitution was adopted in 1848. Those interested in filling up the great gaps in this running history will do well to consult Mr. Alexander Daguet's "Historie de la Confederation Suisse," from the most ancient times to 1864, a learned and eloquent work, which has passed to its sixth edition. It is published at Lausanne, and is a recognized authority, being, I believe, adopted in the Swiss colleges.

This hasty sketch will give some imperfect idea of the antecedents from which the present condition of Switzerland has sprung. She is a democratic republic, having a patrician element in her population of great exclusiveness and much social dignity, and holding a large share of the landed property, but without a particle of political influence, and standing aloof from all that is characteristic of the new regime. She is also a confederation of cantons, with the State-right principle, rooted by a thousand years of independence in the separate cantons, slowly surrendering to the advantages of a more perfect union and homogeneous nationality. There is nothing in the United States, speaking one language and all of comparatively modern origin, to compare with the divisions and local peculiarities and antagonisms which tend to maintain State-right jealousies in the Swiss cantons. Of three main origins, German, French and Italian, and still speaking these three tongues in their legislative halls at Berne, with interpreters sitting by to explain their meaning to each other ; with some cantons wholly Protestant, like Zurich and Berne and Geneva, and others wholly Catholic, like Lucerne, Freybourg, and Uri ; with traditions reaching back a thousand years, and old families and old monuments that have become a part of the very life of special neighborhoods—Switzerland finds difficulty in accomplishing an effective unity between her states, which few nations could have to contend with, and which have been so far overcome as to surprise us at the result.

Switzerland is a thorough democracy. Her executive power resides in a Council of seven ministers who elect one of their own number President for two years. He takes the portfolio of foreign affairs, but in other respects, except in receiving the representatives of other powers, is on a par with the other ministers. His salary is only 10,000 francs, theirs 8000. There are two Houses corresponding to our House of Representatives and Senate. The cantons send a Representative for each 2000 of their population, and two Senators each. The houses meet twice a year, for very short sessions, one for a few days, the other session for perhaps three weeks. The debates are purely business-like, and relate to local details. There is no chance for eloquent discussion, and the speeches are not reported. The people retain the right of assembling in mass and revising any act of their Legislature. When 50,000 signatures are obtained, a general meeting in each canton may be called, and a popular vote taken from a high stand in the open field, " yes " or " no," for any proposed change in the laws or policy of the government. And this right is actually exercised from time to time. The people here thus keep the " veto," we have found so troublesome in the hands of our President, in their own hands. Lately, in Uri, a citizen was publicly whipped for having written and published an article against the Catholic faith. The event created an immense excitement and discussion in the Protestant cantons, and meetings were held to protest against this outrage on religious liberty ; but the right of the canton of

Uri to whip its own citizens for opinion's sake is not yet restrained by any federal law! Efforts have been made to abate the odious tax upon the Jews, which exists in several cantons. French and Belgian Jews in Switzerland are protected by treaty, but Swiss Jews are not their equal in their own country, and it properly excites great indignation.

The population of Switzerland is about 2,800,000. It is divided into peasants, artisans, bourgeois (including shopkeepers, merchants, bankers) and patricians. The last class has no political recognition and is tranquil, but lives on its recollections, its pride, its titles of courtesy, and above all, its money. Switzerland is poor. In a few cantons, Zurich, St. Gall, Appenzell, Basle, Geneva, it has some enterprise and industry. The rest are purely agricultural. Its resources are the manufacture of silks (especially ribbons), embroideries, muslins and cottons, chiefly for the Oriental market; its timber, its cattle, and its cheese and its wooden ware. It has, of course, no port, and conducts its foreign trade chiefly through Havre. It sends commercial agents to North and South America, to India, China and Japan—and instead of forcing its own patterns upon foreign markets, like England, it studies the taste and copies the fancies of all the nations it trades with, and makes its goods to please them. But for its immense water-power, it could not compete in its isolated position with the industry of England and Belgium, or France and Germany. It is striving to be allowed by the other powers to purchase a port outside its own territory—but America, mindful of the use to which neutral ports, especially of feeble powers, are put in time of war, objects very properly, and Switzerland can not afford to incur the displeasure of America—from whose citizens, first in trade and then in pleasure travel, she draws so large an annual income. Basle and Geneva are the moneyed centres of Switzerland; Zurich

and St. Gall its industrial centres ; Geneva and Zurich its
intellectual centres ; Freybourg the centre of its Catholicism.
There is very little wealth in the country, and no superfluous
capital. Berne is a slow city, with a sluggish population, and
a reputation for much addictedness to carnal sins—its common people drinking themselves stupid on *schnapps* and
smoking themselves copper-colored with tobacco as coarse as
cabbage leaves. Still the Bernese have shown themselves
patriotic and brave, and when aroused, very capable and determined. There are very fine buildings now going up under
the inspiration of companies, who borrow capital and build
on speculation. It is painful to hear the low accounts given
of the public morality. Purity and fidelity to marriage vows
are considered exceptional in Berne. The peasants and artisans are very careless of chastity, and illegitimate offspring
are frightfully common. Some old customs connected with
the intercourse of affianced parties are too shameful to be
any thing more than thus hinted at. I always distrust
sweeping charges of dishonesty, unchastity or falsehood,
against any class or community, but the testimony of people here on the spot touching the moral life of the Bernese
peasantry is very discouraging. Wages are better than I
feared, from 30 to 50 cents per day, and in skilled labor, 75
cents. The prisoners in all the cantons do a large part of
all the public work. They are farmed out in gangs to private persons, under a guard, and are preferred to ordinary
labor because better controlled. " They don't listen so much
to the birds," said my informant. I saw both women and
men returning at sunset, from their daily tasks as hired laborers, to the prison at Berne. The band of women was
under an unarmed woman-superintendent, and what kept
them from running away, I could not see.

Switzerland has 200,000 men capable of bearing arms,

who, without much expense to the cantons or the federal government, are kept for six weeks every year under drill in encampments or at barracks, and made well acquainted with the life and duty of soldiers. Besides a uniform and their living, they receive about three cents a day in wages. The young men make a frolic of it, so far as is compatible with the severity of the drill. A staff of about 150 officers are in constant service and under government pay. They are the teachers and organizers of the rank and file. The Swiss, mercenary as they have so often been, are good soldiers and take naturally to arms. The federal government has an income of about twelve million francs. Berne offered the central government a palace, or National Congress Hall, if the Legislature would make her chief city the federal capital. She has accordingly erected a handsome and suitable edifice, containing an upper and a lower chamber—the meeting-place of the popular House and of the Senate, or Council of State. It is a costly and creditable building. A picture here of William Tell pushing off in his boat after having killed Gessler, led me to inquire of a competent authority how well-attested that world-renowned story was, and I regret to say that the antiquarians of Switzerland are much inclined to give the story a mythic origin and interpretation. The tale will, however, survive all historical scepticism, having been accepted as true to humanity, if not to fact. In short, it ought to be true, if it is not.

The pecuniary importance to Switzerland of the annual influx of pleasure-seekers, is confessed to be immense. Independent of purchases, the mere money expended at hotels is estimated at not less than $3,000,000. The trade in carved woods last year was nearly three millions of francs. When it is considered that probably not less than 300,000 visitors go through Switzerland every favorable year, the importance of this tide of strangers, with loose purse-strings, becomes very obvious. Last year the German war and the financial distress in England kept both Continental and English travelers very generally out of Switzerland, while the cessation of our war encouraged so many Americans to visit Europe, that it is confessed that they alone saved the larger hotels from ruin last season. Ordinarily about as many English as Americans annually visit Switzerland. Last year and this, it is said that the proportion is as three to one in favor of America. Americans are known at once at the hotels by their freer expenditures, their pronunciation, and their paler visages. The Britishers call them " faded Englishmen," they think themselves cuter and sharper, and only less fat and bloated than their British ancestors. " I am *taller* than your Majesty," said one of Napoleon's marshals, as he handed him a book from a shelf which the Little Corporal was straining to reach. "*Longer*," replied the Emperor. There are two ways of looking at most things. I confess I see very little of the disagreeable qualities of John Bull as a traveler. His growl, his reticence, his exactingness, I have not yet encountered. His pronunciation of his and our language I think better than our own, *i. e.*, in the traveling class. The influence of all this travel on the character and fortunes of the Swiss can not be good. For four months Switzerland stops her national life to wait on the traveling world. To make the greatest harvest out of this pleasure-seeking throng is her sole occupation on the ever-expanding lines of travel through her territory. Her hotel-keepers seem to be among her most important citizens. Intellectual-looking young men are waiters in her inns. The only good-looking women in Switzerland, so far as I have seen, are those connected in some way with the wants of strangers. An immense system of beggary is carried on by children. The Cretins and Goitres trade in their afflictions. The eight months when the country is empty of visitors must leave a very large set of idlers and persons demoralized and broken up in business. Then the great hotels are closed, or do no supporting business. The spirit of the country must become mercenary and petty, or tend to become so, under these circumstances. Greece had "the fatal gift of beauty," and perished of her own loveliness. Switzerland is in danger of losing her freedom and her national life, in waiting on the world round her mountains and valleys. It becomes her to look to the effect of all this seductive publicity of life.

The peasants in Switzerland live poorly and work hard. They are up and out at their labors in the summer-time at 2 o'clock, A.M. (in winter at 4 A.M.), and, with an hour's intermission, keep at it till 6 P.M. The cheese business, very modern in its origin (not more than forty years old), but now immense, deprives the peasants of the milk of their cows and goats, which has disastrously ceased to be the national food. They have substituted coffee and schnapps, and poison themselves and their children by their use. Their cretinism is the result of their terrible intermarriages in their small valleys, their insufficient food, their schnapps, and their abominable pipes, to which add their filth, and their cold, stone basements, with the malarious air of their unsunned valleys? Goitre, hard and soft, comes from the same general causes, and the lime in the water acting on feeble and overworked constitutions.

There is an unspeakable poverty in Switzerland. From ten to twenty per cent. of the population are paupers, living on their respective cantons! And, alas! this is so common that it hardly seems any disgrace. The almshouse appears to be the expected retreat of the old age of many thousands. There is even an almshouse for the bourgeois in Berne, in

K

which it is said that some decayed patricians find a home.
By paying about a thousand dollars, a Bernese citizen may
purchase the right of being comfortably provided for at this
place in his old age, while he has a certain immediate right
to an annual amount of fuel and a small percentage of income (in all say $50 worth) per year.   There are abundant
evidences in Berne that the old mischief of substituting public care for private industry and thrift, has found too much
favor.   How to live with least work and least self-providence
is a fatal question.   Domestic life is at a low level in the
artisan and peasant class, and, I suspect, not high in the
bourgeois.   Men of families spend all their leisure at the
wine-shop and the club-house.   The women are left to themselves, and they take their revenges.   On the whole, Berne
does not present a very encouraging show for the moral and
social future of Switzerland.   One of the testimonies to the
degradation of labor is seen in the present general use of
the tread-mill as the approved method of raising stone in
house building.   In a hollow wheel of twenty feet diameter,
tread, like a squirrel in a rotary cage, these poor human beings—all day long throwing their avoirdupois into the scale,
as their sole function.   Such brainless, handless business for
grown men, struck me with disgust and horror.   Six of these
wheels, some of them forty feet in the air, were going all day
at the corner of the street, where a public saloon was in
process of building.   I have not seen in all Europe a worse
indication of the backwardness of public opinion ; and this
in democratic Switzerland !   The fact is, with a thoroughly
free constitution, there is an immense practical restriction
on liberty in Switzerland.   The cantons do not permit each
other's citizens to move freely from canton to canton.   They
must first give elaborate evidence of their self-supporting
power before they can come in.   They can not marry with-

out a great many expensive formalities. There are hundreds of local restrictions upon industry. There is no career open to enterprising young men. Honest failure in business is permanent ruin. To be in debt is to be without character or hope. Jealousy and solicitude about being saddled with more paupers increases cantonal narrowness and magnifies State-right feeling. It is the bane of Switzerland. Doubtless it decreases slowly, but it is still in full force. Religious freedom practically is very weak. The Catholic cantons allow very little expression to Protestant opinion, and the Protestants are intolerant of Catholic feeling, and both oppress the Jewish citizen. If there were more fervor and earnestness of faith, this would be more excusable, but there is little evidence of a deep religiousness in either Catholics or Protestants. The women keep up their pious usages— but the men are negligent of public worship. The Prussian compulsory school system prevails, and education of the best kind is cheap and accessible. But education without equal political rights and an open and inspiring life, with opportunity to rise and acquire personal and family independence, has never yet done much to stimulate and develop general intelligence—and it does not do it in Switzerland.

The bear, the symbol of this capital and canton, is a sluggish animal. On the gates and upon the public monuments he presents himself with his small head and bulky body, his short legs and good-natured, easy air, a somewhat faithful representation of the people who are so proud of his name and figure. In the famous bear-pit at one end of the city, a crowd of idlers may usually be seen looking at him as he lazily lolls about his small estate. Berne would do better to imitate some more active animal. The chamois or the deer would set a happier example.

The United States are fortunate in having so intelligent

and active a Minister as Mr. Harrington, at Berne. His kind attentions to American visitors entitle him to the gratitude of his countrymen, and his watchful care of our public interests is no doubt well understood at Washington.

XX.

SAVOY AND GENEVA.

September 15, 1867.

IT is Sunday, and I have just returned from the morning worship in the English chapel, where the very long service was excellently read by an English clergyman, who, by the red-scarf at his back, must have been a University man. The church was full of English people—and very devout and well-instructed in the service they were. There was none of the wandering attention, none of the silence or muttering in the responses, observed so often in American Episcopal services. They seem, too, to have agreed in the English Church upon a few hymns, set to well-chosen tunes, which whole congregations can join in. The chants are simple and appropriate. I must say that the English Church service, as I hear it on the Continent, formal, long, repetitious as it is, has a body and substance to it which, after the thinness of other Protestant services, at home and abroad, is refreshing. It has good sound English muscle in it, and if it is a form, it is made of English broadcloth and not of paper-muslin or shoddy. The power and influence of the English Establishment is felt at the remotest extremities of the nation, in all its colonies, and wherever Englishmen journey. There are 150,000 English citizens who live, for cheapness, on the Continent, and probably as many more who are always pleasure-traveling there. It is a matter of first-rate political and religious importance to bring these people under the influence of the national religion, and great pains are taken to do this. It is plain, however, that the English Church is largely a political institution. It is used to maintain the English ideas of monarchy and of nobility, and the prayers and litany keep up offensively in God's house the distinctions, social and political, which it is so desirable to forget there. On the other hand, from an English point of view, nothing can be conceived better adapted to the support of the national predilections or principles than their Establishment. And, considering the essential unspirituality of the race, perhaps the liturgy proposes a set of grooves for religious thought and feeling, which, if not thus economized and directed, would mainly evaporate or dry up. Any one who watches the girls and boys, the young women and young men, saying the creed of the English liturgy, with an implicit reverence, into which thought and choice evidently enter very little, sees plainly that the theory is not to encourage any thought or choice about it, but to take the best means for stamping a faith, which has been thought out and agreed upon by competent persons, upon those who are probably to have no faith, or only a very foolish and ineffectual one, if they are not thus furnished. There is an immense deal to be said in favor of this side of the question. It is the Roman Catholic notion of the rightful authority and solemn duty of the Church to provide the people with a sound creed. The English Establishment adopts it just as far as the Protestant atmosphere in which it breathes will allow, and with excellent effect, so far as a faith out of which intellectual life and personal spiritual struggle for a satisfactory theory and experience of religion are systematically struck, can produce satisfactory results. The English people are really reverential—decidedly under the influence of belief. They believe in the being and providence of God ; in the reality of Christ's mission and the efficacy of his death; in the immortality of the soul, and in a judgment to come. The average mind, the middle station of the English, appears to be in a state of Christian belief which one looks for in vain in the same class on the Continent. And it is doubtless very much due to the influence of an Established Church.

Every Unitarian Protestant knows what is to be said on the other side, and how immensely important to the emancipatiǫh of the intellect and to the freedom of the conscience an entire absence of any Establishment and of any creed or liturgy whatsoever is thought to be. But those who carry out their confidence in the entire competency of each and every human soul to discover and adopt a faith for itself, and who assert and feel that no faith which has not been thus personally thought out and adopted is of any worth, must be prepared to see Christianity set aside as essentially and historically a superstition and an offense, by men who are honest and influential; and not only Christianity, but religion of any sort or kind.

The Peace Congress at Geneva, which rose on Thursday last, was composed of one of the most earnest bodies of men ever assembled, and of men of obviously excellent and humane dispositions—men who had, many of them, made life-long sacrifices to their love of freedom and to their sense of the wrongs of the oppressed masses. The speeches were eloquent and earnest, almost without exception. I have carefully read the report of all that was said and done, and have been very much impressed with the sincerity, courage and ability of many, not to say most of the speakers. But it is perfectly plain that the vast majority of that Congress regarded the Christian religion, and all religion, as one of the main obstacles to human equality and the progress of society. The Church, and the priests, and all its ministers were ac-

complices with the privileged class who had fastened arbitrary governments upon the nations.   They had come together in the name of Peace, universal peace, and to put an
end to wars; but it was maintained by one of the speakers
that Christ—whom the world has called the Prince of Peace
—was on the contrary an avowed advocate of war, and had
declared that he came to bring not peace but a sword—and
that his words had been fulfilled by the wars which religion
had never ceased to inspire from the time of Constantine to
the late war about the holy places.   Not only was the Papacy
attacked as the chief buttress of political absolutism, but it
was declared over and over again, with applause, that the
world owed nothing to religion good or needful, and had out-
lived it, as in every way a puerility and a bugbear.   Garibaldi himself, pure and worthy man that he is, and seemingly beyond the reach even of the corrupting flattery of which
he is the subject, pronounced religion to be identical with
science, and Newton and Galileo and Arago its only true
priests ; and one of the speakers declared that Garibaldi was
the modern Jesus Christ, who had come to do away with religion and substitute social justice and political equality for
it.   There was enough caution and common sense left in the
Congress to prevent these private expressions from being
made a part of the action of the whole body, but no policy
could hide the sympathy felt for them by the majority, or
prevent the impression they will make upon the world.
Here, in the only free State on the Continent, the philanthropic enthusiasts of all countries have met in the interests
of universal humanity, to deprecate wars and fightings among
men, to inaugurate the reign of political economy, free trade,
arbitration of all differences, and lasting peace among men.
They have found the source of wars to be the existence of
hereditary families and prescriptive rights, the existence of

personal rulers, instead of laws administered by democracies ; and they have found what men call religion, in all its forms, to be a distraction, a substitute for justice, an ally of tyrants, a buttress of inequalities. Since the times of Robespierre, and the union of Red Republicanism and Atheism, under the French Directory, nothing has appeared so much like it as the debates of this Peace Congress. It was, in short, the old political and social idealism of that day dressed in modern costume, and Quakerized by the pacific object of the gathering.

I believe that great good will come out of this event. The tendencies of a rising school of naturalists and humanitarians will be exhibited on a high platform, and by men having a right to speak for their fellows. These tendencies are to a purely scientific and logical ordering of society. The instincts and passions are left out of the account. Nothing that is not demonstrable by science is to be credited, nothing that is not level with human reason is to be tolerated. There is nothing sacred in any of the traditions of the race, nothing providential in the method of its unfolding. The place which reverence and faith have held in the heart and life of the world are to be henceforth filled with the latest maxims of political economy. An enlightened self-interest is to occupy the vacant throne of the universe, and for prayers men are to learn the multiplication table. This, I believe, is what Secularism, Positivism, Naturalism, all point at, and, left to themselves, would finally come to. They are striving to root out all the historical and providential faith in the world, to plant their patent philanthropy in its place. So far as they succeed they will bring evils they little dream of in place of those they are aiming to expel. This wretched, priest-ridden, superstition-darkened world, out of which, according to Mr. Edgar Quinet—one of the most

K 2

distinguished members of the Convention — all conscience
has died, is, in my poor judgment, a paradise compared with
what a world would be under the Providence of the Peace
Congress.   Welcome war, Cæsarism, social inequalities, Roman Catholic superstitions, welcome all existing evils, with
some faith in one overruling Providence, a living God and
Father of men, a guiding spirit which has never left the
world without some witness of itself—a Church which has
foundations in a living corner-stone—rather than everlasting
peace, universal democracy, perfect free trade and general
equality, in a Godless, Christless, faithless, self-worshiping
world, such as political economists and Peace Congresses are
striving to prepare for us.   Were there no immortal and unseen interests involved, the mere decay of imagination and
passion out of this utilitarian world would make it hateful
to dwell in.   Religion, if it were the superstition these theo-
rists make it, would be a blessing, compared with the light
which is to banish it from the world—a light that would
blind with its fierceness.

War is an immense evil ; but there are far greater evils,
among which is a stupid, money-worshiping, calculating, materialistic peace.   Society, without great passions, great powers of self-sacrifice, great hopes and great experiences, would
be like the ocean without winds or storms—a sink of corruption, a vast puddle.   In proportion as the world grows
richer, safer, more populous and more industrial, religion
must become a more vital and ethereal power, must do not
only its own ancient work, but also the work of Poetry and
Romance—or the world will become a mere workshop and
restaurant.   As to extinguishing wars by Debating Societies
or Peace Congresses, we may hope as soon to establish Com-
munism and Fourierism by Lyceum lectures.   It is not war,
but the inevitable conflict of human interests, prejudices,

passions and convictions that is to be abated, and a society for abolishing war is a society for bringing in human perfection at once. But for past wars society would still be in barbarism. The very freedom to debate the question of universal peace has been won by war. Slavery has just been extinguished by war in the United States. The independence of the United States of America, the model of all future States, was established by war. War is not an essential evil, like falsehood, selfishness, vice and crime. It is to be classed with storms and elemental strifes, the only method known by which, under certain circumstances, the balance of forces is restored. It is good or bad, right or wrong, according as it is waged, and the motives impelling to it. There must need be offenses, but woe to him by whom the offense cometh. Let us ply all the means of education, of political emancipation, of moral and religious inspiration we possess, and wars will take care of themselves. We shall always have them when political and social knots can not be untied and yet must somehow be loosened. War is the knife that cuts these knots. If we would avoid wars, we must see that these knots are not tied.

It is important not to allow the excesses of Rationalism to drive us into reactionary measures. I do not wonder that the present tendencies of scientific thought and philosophical speculation have provoked a Ritualistic zeal and a Roman Catholic fever in England. The more I see of religion abroad, the better satisfied I am that American Unitarians, of the historical and positive school, possess a type of Christianity precisely adapted to the present wants of society, and unspeakably precious to the cause of Christ and the Church. If Christianity, as we know it and maintain it, were known in Europe, it would reconcile some of the most perilous antagonisms now existing, and enable men to distinguish between

faith and superstition, and the Church and priestcraft. The
prevailing impression that life here and life hereafter have
no common term and can not be resolved in one equation, is
one which American Unitarians have done more, practically,
to correct than any other branch of the Church.   Our precious faith has weathered successfully the storm of the nineteenth century—not by going into harbor and suffering the
dry-rot while waiting for tranquil weather, but by throwing
overboard or cutting away what could not bear the winds or
float on the waves sent by an all-wise Providence, keeping
only what was precious in the cargo and indispensable in the
vessel.   Accordingly, with sound and tried timbers, we are
ready to face the hard weather of the times ; and I believe
millions would take passage with us, who now suppose the
voyage of faith an impossible venture, if we only had our
principles duly advertised.   Unitarians who know themselves
to be Christians in belief, and love and prize that name
above all others, are called to a new zeal and courage.
They are not a hundredth part as confident and self-assert-
ing as they should be.   The world is waiting for their guidance.   They are capable of making a new reformation,
would they only accept their mission.   With a rational and
historical faith that is evangelical in its origin and spirit,
they have broken away from the dogmas which are now sinking those who continue to cling to them.   As our own
church re-opens to-day, Sept. 15th, after the summer vacation,
I have spent much of this Sunday, here in the shadow of
Mont Blanc, reflecting upon its interests and those of the denomination with which it is so closely associated.   Clouds
and darkness, wind and rain, obscure the sky and envelop
the summits around this narrow valley, but I hear the sound
of the Arve rushing under my window to the Rhone and to
the sea.   It speaks of a way out of the darkness and storm,

the way of faith. I take the lesson of this voice. Fed from eternal snows and nursed at the bosom of the glacier, cradled in this rocky valley and passing its stormy youth amid dashing precipices and falling avalanches, the wild, cold torrent is pointed for the sea, and will find itself at last in the warm and tropic-shored Mediterranean. Our faith has had its cold and stormy time, its day of small things and of public indifference or opposition. *If we will,* that day is over. May God dispose the heart of the church and congregation over which he has set me as minister for so many happy years to do its part toward upholding and illustrating the power of pure Unitarian Christianity! And may this new ecclesiastical year, opening under the benignant influence of Brother Collyer's prayers and preaching, be richer than any past year in works of mercy, in acts of faith, and in the demonstration of the spirit of holiness and love!

XXI.

CHAMOUNI.

September 17, 1867.

THE road from Geneva to Chamouni lies through the valley of the Arve, which is broad and not specially picturesque. It is infested with beggars, who, after a generation of experience, have learned all the arts of moving compassion or profiting by the impatience of their victims. They know just how to approach the old and the young, the sensitive and the frigid, the wary and the careless. No airs of indifference or pretended ignorance of their presence disconcert or discourage their purpose. They reckon very little on sympathy or pity. They know that the traveler has seen hundreds of just such beggars as themselves within a few hours, and has exhausted his sensibility. They know that they are regarded as engaged in a sort of business, and are of the nature of petty highwaymen. And they pursue their calling on business principles. A shelf on the road, where after a severe ascent the horses must breathe, is a very favorite position for infirm beggars. They have you shut up to their importunity long enough to make pretty sure of your resistance giving out. A long hill, where younger beggars can keep up with the carriage for half a mile, is another choice position. Armed with a few faded flowers or a half-dozen unripe plums, the sturdy beggar is more than a match for most temperaments. If you don't surrender the first quarter of a mile, you will have to pay double for it in the course of the second quarter. Running beside the carriage for a whole mile, without asking for any thing, is a method adopted by girls of ten and twelve, who expect such silent and breathless devotion sooner or later to be handsomely and piteously rewarded. Mothers with a babe in arms, followed by a troop of children; old men, looking hungry and childless; cretins, goitres, the lame and deformed, all train in this company. And yet I feel bound to say that this class does not seem so large as it did twenty years ago. Since Savoy became a part of France it may have fallen under its influence, which steadily opposes mendicity, and very successfully suppresses it in Paris and throughout its home provinces.

Beyond Bonneville the valley becomes narrower and the mountains steeper. The geological formation of the cliffs, the circular bend of the strata, as if giants had been playing with dividers upon the flat walls, and the architectural effects of the broken summits, make the road interesting to St. Martin or Sallenches, where Mont Blanc comes into view. To those who have enjoyed the magnificent views of the mountains from Lake Leman, between Morges and Geneva, this nearer prospect will not be very impressive, as indeed none of the near views of Mont Blanc are. In short, so large an object requires a very large space for its exhibition and a very considerable distance to take it in. Near it you see it in parts, and are almost in the condition of a fly walking on a statue, who, if he thought at all, might mistake a finger or a toe for the whole figure. The parts hide the whole. There are great charms in the valley of Chamouni; and the vicinity of Mont Blanc, independent of any good view of him, is exciting. You see the route by which, with such peril and fatality, the summit has been sought. The magnificent Aiguilles, that fence in the southern side, are in full view, and play an enchanting part when bathed in moonlight or bidding adieu to the sun, or floating like islets in the clouds. The smooth, cultivated valley, fifteen miles long and three-quarters of a mile broad, is always offering its green and checkered surface as a place of repose for the eye weary with up-looking and with wild sublimity. The village which has grown up here, with its half-dozen grand hotels in the midst of humble chalets, is a wonderful testimony to the love of nature and the passion for its wildest and most inaccessible scenes which distinguishes our modern civilization. It is an equal evidence of the superfluous wealth which enriches society in these days of steam and machine labor. Indeed, the amount of money everywhere expended on pleasure travel is one of the extraordinary indications of the times. In place of hunting and fishing, horse-racing and the ring, the lovers of athletic sports and adventure have taken to climbing snow peaks and "taking down" the pride of challenging aiguilles ; while the tour of Europe and a summer in Switzerland has become almost the necessary finish of a young lady's education. To meet these tastes, a prodigious investment in vehicles, steamers, ho- tels, horses and mules, guides, etc., in the most out-of-the-way places, exhibits itself all over Europe, and specially in Switzerland, where every fine valley has its costly hotel, every commanding point of view its place of shelter and refreshment. In Chamouni, high and cold, the valley seems to hold an uncommonly handsome and interesting native population. Roman Catholic, and secluded for eight months in the year, there is no business going on but the care of the herds and the service of the guests who annually inundate the valley.

Every grown man under fifty that one meets here is a guide. A tall, broad-shouldered, mild, courteous, interesting class of people they seem to be, and their wives and children are attractive, and have taken on some polish from their intercourse with the world. So important to the population is this business of guiding strangers, that it is reduced to very rigid law. There is a Bureau, under a chief, which furnishes guides, where they are registered and numbered, and take service in turn without any liberty of choice on their own part or on that of their employers. There is a strict tariff of prices, moderate enough, which protects strangers from imposition. But simple and saving of trouble as the arrangement is, it of course takes away from that life of all occupations, free competition, and robs the guides of the stimulus to distinguish themselves by intelligence, enterprise or special caution. As a consequence, there is no preparation on their part to answer any questions which inquisitive travelers desire so much to put, excepting always the most simple ones. There is not one out of twenty who knows what an English mile is, or can give you any idea of distance except in hours. No man is competent by their rules to become a guide until he is twenty-three years old. He may be a porteur at an earlier period. The difficulties of ascending Mont Blanc, though mainly those of endurance or fatigue, are not, I judge, exaggerated. Although done every year now by many travelers, it is not a feat which loses dignity or importance by repetition. The names of all those who accomplished the ascent before 1854 are prominently enrolled and paraded in the public hotels of Chamouni. The statues of Balmat, the guide who made the first ascension, in August, 1786, and of Dr. Saussure, the savant, who went up with him the following year, very fitly decorate the entrance hall of our Hotel d'Angleterre. Balmat lost his life by falling from a precipice forty years afterward. One might almost think such a death and such a grave the most becoming a man whose whole life had been passed among the Alpine heights, chasing the chamois, or leaping the crevasses of the glaciers to make a path for

others.   The guides themselves seem to respect, even
more than novices, the dangers of the higher ascents.
Tempting as money is (it costs about five hundred francs
to each person ascending Mont Blanc, of which the
largest part goes to the guides), I have not found any
eagerness on their part to repeat the enterprise.   They go,
of course, as a sailor goes to the top-mast in a hurricane ;
but I doubt whether Jack enjoys it, and I believe the guides
are honest enough to confess they do not like the summit of
Mont Blanc.   The shoes, stockings, two watches, fifty-nine
pieces of money, belonging to three guides lost in a crevasse
forty years before, were found with their remains, a foot here,
and a hand there, mangled and sundered into innumerable
pieces, in the year 1863, eight thousand feet below the place
where they were lost, brought down by the glacier in its down-
like flow—noiseless, invisible, but irresistible and constant.
Such objects do not increase the appetite for the more difficult ascensions.   " The mountains don't interest me any
longer," said a pretty young woman who waited upon us at
the Schanzli, the most commanding prospect of the Bernese
Alps, as she witnessed our enthusiasm when the setting sun
had set the whole chain into a flame of gorgeous beauty.
She had seen too much of them.   " All the world comes here
to see this great mountain," said to us another peasant girl—
returning from the fair at St. Gervais to her chalet near Les
Ouches at the opening of this valley—" and I wish they
would carry Mont Blanc away with them—a great snow-
bank, spoiling our harvests in autumn, and carrying away our
bridges in spring, and killing our husbands and brothers who
have to climb it for you strangers, so curious about such a
common thing.   Every body wants to come here, and I only
want to get away.   I am saving all the money I can get to
go to Geneva, and perhaps to Paris."   The woman was the

village tailoress, and more than usually intelligent ; but she only better expressed what is, I suspect, a general feeling in the valley.

Saturday night, the moon rose over the Aiguilles de Charmoz and Lechaud at about 9 o'clock. From the porch of the Catholic church, just above the Hotel Imperial, we watched its slow coming for an hour before it appeared above the battlements of that beauteous ridge of mountain rocks. The sky was full of clouds, tumbling and foaming as they broke upon these barriers. They caught the upshoot of the rising moon and reflected it in magical ways, now down into the valley, now up to the Breven, and then far away down upon the mists that were slowly steaming up from the Arve, ten miles westward. The pinnacles of the Aiguilles were often perfectly separated from their bases by a sea of clouds, which, floating at a level, gave them the appearance of a castellated city in the sky, the tower in ruins, but lighted from behind with a glorious brightness which was full of enchantment. The moon threatened for a whole hour to break through now one and then another of the deep depressions in this lofty ridge. She cheated our expectations and baffled our longings, as if we had been lovers and she at her old tricks of coy evasion. But while our expectation grew to almost painful impatience, what magical transformations were going on in the sky, shifting its forms and colors from one spell to another until the heaven seemed to have won us away from the earth and to have become our real residence ! At last, struggling like any common climber over a picketed wall, one limb of the moon caught our side of the ledge, and soon her whole fair figure stood on the mountain gap, looking down at us as if she had been at willful play and was now enjoying her long sport with our desiring eyes.

Yesterday, Monday, we visited the Fall " Du Dard," near

the Glacier du Bossons, and then by a climb of an hour reached the vast moraine of that vast and beautiful glacier, at about a mile above its foot in the valley of Chamouni, where we crossed it by an hour's hard work, and, coming down the opposite side, walked home—an excursion of three and a half hours. The rain of the previous night had washed this always specially pure and transparent glacier until it shone with an extraordinary splendor, and glistened with a polish altogether more beautiful than safe and convenient. Indeed, with only a small boy for a guide (a very imprudent provision for inexperienced travelers on the ice, like ourselves), my son and I found ourselves very much embarrassed either to proceed or return at several points in our transit. Comparatively even as the surface is, looked at from the shore, we found it heaved into furrows and broken with deep crevasses, and running with small streams, slippery to a perilous degree, and with so few stones upon its surface that no good hold for the feet was to be had. Then there was no path whatever indicated, and a very uncomfortable sense of possible obstacles between us and the opposite shore kept our spirits at a level decidedly below the jubilant. By scrambling on all fours, or sitting down in the water at glacier temperature and so sliding down some declivities, or by cutting steps with the points of our batons, we succeeded in picking our way, without breakage of limb, to the other side, having had quite enough of glaciers — unattended by guides and hatchet-bearers — to satisfy our present ambition. The day was an exceptional one, and the state of the glacier peculiar — perhaps the place where we crossed unusual. With properly armed boots (with iron clogs) or with stout woolen socks, and a proper guide, there need be no serious difficulty in crossing the Bossons, which is one of the most familiar of all the glaciers, and probably to experts hardly presents difficulties enough to be interesting.

The four glaciers of Taconey, Des Bossons, Du Bois (foot of the Mer de Glace) and of D'Argentiere give their most distinguishing feature to this valley. The village of Chamouni is situated between the glaciers " Des Bossons " and " Du Bois "—which put a great silver fringe upon its prospect, up and down. Mighty ruffs of ice, they glisten like diamonds in the sun, and in the gloom they seem to emit a light of their own, which is in its effect like the glow of phosphorescent water. As you approach them, they lie in their steeply-inclined valleys great compact masses of ice, stones and earth, made up into a consistency of frozen mortar, which, under great pressure, would flow and take on somewhat regular lines of direction. The weight behind pressing hardest, deepest down, cracks the surface of the glacier at certain places into splinters which are finger-shaped and thickly crowded. White beneath, they are smouched atop, and not beautiful on a near view. But a few feet beneath the surface, and especially in the Bossons, the ice is of a crystal clearness, and as solid as though it had never moved and never intended to. The smaller crevasses, ten or fifteen feet long and as many deep, and a foot or two wide, are usually nearly full of water, and while very dangerous to careless walkers, are very beautiful to look upon. I have not yet seen any of those vast fissures of which I have often read, which reach down to the bottom of the glacier and yawn ten or fifteen feet in width, and which have become the tombs of so many unfortunate explorers. The force of these mighty ice rivers, which ebb and flow, shrink and expand, is such as to grind the surface they cover, to tear the banks that hold them, and to pile up as they melt on the surface, and fling out their mighty arms slowly like a swimmer, a great moraine at their sides, which rises a hundred feet above their bed, for a half-mile above their foot, and covers with a great delta of stones and earth their mouth. The ice at the foot of the Bossons seems about a hundred feet thick. A strong river flows from the foot, which never wholly ceases. The water comes from the surface of the glacier, trickling through the crevasses and uniting at the foot to form a torrent, which is seldom clear, though in many of the rills which are found on the surface, and in the crevasses, the water is exquisitely pure.

Tuesday, September 16.

It rained all night and is raining still. A deep and obstinate mist envelopes all the near and all the distant mountains. For the time, Chamouni is a plain. It is the only chance the natives have for knowing how it must seem to live away from the mountains. A hundred guides are chaffing each other in the little square before the Imperial Hotel, giving guesses to anxious travelers about the prospect of fair weather, and regretting their own lost day, which doubtless the mules alone, of all creatures except the waiters, are really enjoying. The bustle of caravans packing off for the Montanvert, the Flegere and for Martigny ; of voitures gay with newly-arriving travelers, or departing visitors, each with precious alpenstock in hand, duly labeled with the names of ascended passes or places of interest visited ; the packing of mules with shawls and overcoats, all this which yesterday made Chamouni so gay, is now suspended. A few guides are flinging through the air heavy wooden balls at nine-pins, in an alley without floor, and at double the usual distance. I am sorry to see them exchange their hard-earned francs, as they win or lose on their throw. The village is still as a New England Sabbath. One man seizes his staff and is off to the source of the Arveron, four or five miles, saying encouragingly as he leaves, " If you stop for rain this month in Switzerland, you might as well ' put up ' for the season, and done with it." It is a dripping, melancholy day. The cows and the goats hung their tails very despondingly as they filed along the narrow streets last evening and this morning. Every thing hangs down—mist, rain, the faces of the landlords, guests, guides—every thing but the mules' ears, which I doubt not would be found in a very cheerful perpendicular ! We had such good weather in the Tyrol, at Lucerne, Interlachen, Berne, on Lake Leman, that it would be ungrateful to complain of a couple of days' rain now ; but rain at Chamouni is very unpopular, and, not to speak improperly, inconvenient—and really, it may be bad for the crops and quite unChristian—but we do all very anxiously wish it would clear up. Just after breakfast, Mont Blanc put his nose out very plainly, and took a look at the weather, and then went to bed again, drawing the curtains with fearful closeness, as if he foresaw at last twenty-four hours more of freedom from all interruptions of his peace from visitors and gazers. My solace in such weather is letter-writing. Reading will not dispel the melancholy of such disappointing weather. It is not absorbing enough ; but with a fair sheet of paper and a pen and ink, I can always defy blue-devils, without shying the inkstand at Satan, after Luther's example. Bad spirits are very much in fear of ink — especially printing-ink. I find even the poor fluid furnished us in hotels, under the name of " Tintre " or " Encre," quite efficacious enough to banish all the imps that haunt me.

Wednesday.

The bad weather has its compensations. I could not have believed that mist could be so beautiful and make such a variety of landscapes, if I had not watched its pranks

yesterday in this valley, flying from side to side, rolling
itself now in winrows and sleeping on the ledges, and then
heaping itself in hay-cocks and spotting the hill-sides ; now
mounting like smoke, until the woods seemed all afire, and
then scudding in level flows like rivers of wool. The whole
Breven would be bare one moment, and almost before the
head was turned, lost again in impenetrable vapor. The sun,
which never appeared, was yet near enough to give the thin
mist on the mountains the appearance of chased silver, while
the bare places stood out like relief in the same metal;
Every now and then a mountain peak, absolutely free from
clouds, stood out for a few hundred feet, resting on the mist,
and looking, we observed, much higher in that condition,
than when " fit body " was joined to " fit head." Mont
Blanc woke up and turned over, and went to bed again a
half-dozen times in the course of the day. Meanwhile it
kept up at intervals a solid pour. In the afternoon, we
footed it in the rain three miles down to the foot of the
Glacier de Tour. The air was chilling, the ground muddy,
and the pastures soaked, but in every field, where as many
as two cows were feeding, stood one old woman, sometimes
with but usually without an umbrella, " minding " the cattle.
One philosophic old soul, covered with a stout straw hat, two
feet over, sat in the middle of the field, with a goat-skin
on her lap, calmly knitting, with her eyes on the cows—the
rain pouring and the cold chilling our flesh—but with as much
serenity and as little seeming consciousness of any hardship
in the position as if she had been on a satin *fauteuil* in a parlor spread with Turkey carpets. One young woman, in a
coat of furred goat-skins, looking like an Esquimau, gave us
a sample of the winter-costume of this region. These watch-
ers of the cows appear to serve the humble purpose of fences.
The most economical form of fence discovered in Switzerland,

appears to be a watchful old woman past other work. I could not help thinking that our New England grandmothers, in their warm corners, had a somewhat more enviable lot. We passed through two poor villages. The women were busy watching the precious heaps of manure, seeing that the rain did not run away with its juices—packing its sides, and working it as only the Swiss know how. Children and some men were collecting carefully the droppings in the road. They manage to get four small crops of grass in these cold valleys, by careful culture. The moment one crop is sheared —for it is treated more like wool than grass—the field is immediately sprinkled with liquid manure. This is repeated after every cutting, except the last, which is followed by a thorough dressing.

The foot of the Glacier de Tour is approached through a ghastly moraine, in which some tremendous blocks of stone exhibit the carrying powers of the ice, the melancholy hills of ground stone which, from the sides of this frightful river, lift themselves one or two hundred feet, spreading like the sides of an open fan, and leaving a broad channel for the Arveron which flows from the glacier's foot. The ice is blue, but dirty; in thickness at the foot, perhaps a hundred feet; but not as handsome as the foot either of the Bossons or the Grindelwald. The ice grotto is not half the size, and has little of the purity of the grotto at Grindelwald. The wonderful rush of the river from the jaws of this glacier is very impressive. It seems to spring to full life in a second, and have all the energy and rage of a torrent at its birth—like Richard III., "born with teeth." The fact is, like a good many other seething things, the river has run several miles under the ice before it appears. Things never *begin* strongly.

The weather still continuing misty or rainy, we ascended the Montanvert, with a party of at least twenty, who like our-

L

selves had been waiting for a more favorable sky, but had despaired of fine weather. The sturdy mules, without a single stumble, carried us up the muddy steep in a couple of hours. Some fine views of the valley and its half-dozen hamlets opened through the clouds, which for the most part floored the valley with a soft fleecy carpet, but now and then suddenly opened. The Aiguille de Dru, as we approached the small inn at the summit, welcomed us with its military salute, presenting its pike with erectest precision, and then the sublime semi-circle of Aiguilles about the Mer de Glace stood in soldierly silence and order, raising their mighty bayonets around the awful field of ice. The majesty of the prospect can not be exaggerated. No familiarity with it can take off the edge of its sublimity. If Mont Blanc, invisible, but present in its tremendous glacier, had been the Northern Pole, and we, voyagers with Parry, or Kane, or Dr. Hayes, tumbling about amid the floes of polar ice, to find a nearer approach to the axis of the world, we could hardly have felt more the strangeness and awfulness, the desolation and grandeur of the scene. The temptation to go up to the " Jardin," or over the " Col du Geant," was immense ; but overborne by the consciousness of inadequate vigor for the exposure and fatigue at this uncertain season, we clambered down the vast moraine, whose deceptive height aids in correcting, as one passes down its long side, the imperfect testimony of the senses to the unaccustomed magnitudes of this colossal region. The blue crevasses opened their treacherous eyes and smiled an icy welcome, as we stepped on to the Mer de Glace. The rain had washed the surface and made it too slippery for comfort, and we were too much occupied in keeping the perpendicular and watching for the safety of the ladies, to enjoy any thing except the mere excitement of the adventure. The last third of the way was more or less difficult, the ill-marked path leading round many a deep crevasse, into which stones weighing a ton or more had fallen and hung twenty feet below, between the sides of the icy vise. A misstep would, in many places, prove fatal. It is surprising, considering what multitudes cross at this place every summer-day, that some serious accidents have not occurred. It is not until a mile down the opposite side that the glacier is seen to best advantage. Here the vast frozen Niagara is visible at the sharpest part of its curve, where the current is most broken and splintered. At first it hangs over in great waves, mightier than any in a stormy sea, and then it cracks into vast pinnacles, and stands bristling like the back of some mythic boar, leagues long, whom Titans had hunted into rage. The glacier appears swollen and greatly rounded at the middle. It is as crimpled and curled as a ruff in Queen Elizabeth's time. Now and then the snap of some new crevasse might be heard, and once a heavy block fell from the crest of one of the waves and gave us a lively sense of the actual life of this icy opossum. On the ice the feeling of a possible movement adds to the terror of those who possess tyrannical imaginations. We hardly regretted that the clouds, by excluding distant views, shut us up so wholly to the presence and influence of the glacier. Certainly few objects in Nature are so beautiful and terrible at once. Frozen storms, suspended avalanches, arrested cataracts, glittering and jeweled, yet sullen and implacable—fixed, yet in ceaseless motion—imperishable, but in everlasting decay—sleeping, but grinding their teeth in silent rage and foaming at the mouth —these enormous creatures, infinite elemental forces half-organized and subdued, fill the soul with a fascinating terror. The "*Mauvais Pas,*" a path cut in the face of the precipice, was, in spite of its rocky steps and its iron balustrade (on the *wrong* side of the traveler), altogether too long for the com-

fort of persons troubled with sensitive nerves. It is fully entitled to its ominous name. We passed some beautiful cataracts on the road down, one of them, which flows in a full
stream over the back of a rounded precipice, of a peculiar
beauty. Some welcome refreshment at " The Chapeau,"
which might as appropriately be styled the boot, or any other
article of human attire, prepared us for the sharp descent to
the source of the Arveron.

XXII.

VALLEY OF THE RHONE.

Switzerland, September 19, 1867.

DESPAIRING of any view from the Flegere, we left Chamouni, with a rising barometer and some promise of better weather, at noon, Sept. 18, for the Col de Balme, taking a carriage as far as Angentiere, and there mounting mules for the ascent. The fine glacier of Angentiere hangs over the village in a very threatening aspect, and looks as if it might at any time advance and sweep it away. The church here has been twice destroyed by the violence of the Arve. The valley narrows and grows bleak and desolate from this point, and the wretched hamlet of La Tour, the highest village in Savoy, looks hardly habitable. It has a lofty glacier for its cold neighbor, and all the diligence of its small population barely suffices to raise a few starved crops of grain which the people were busy harvesting as we passed by. A dark, crumbling cliff of shale furnishes a fine *debris* with which the peasants sprinkle the soil in the spring, thus absorbing the rays of the sun and melting off a few weeks sooner the snow. Last winter 15 feet of snow fell in this place, and for seven or eight months out of the twelve the ground is covered with it. The mule-track here ascends rapidly, and soon carried us into the clouds, where a smart rain made every wrap we could muster necessary to save us from being drenched to the skin.

Misery loves company, and we soon met a caravan of eight

mules carrying a very disgusted party down from the summit we were seeking. They had seen nothing, and took some excusable comfort in thinking that we should not be more fortunate than themselves, a fate to which we were already resigned. The rain made the path both muddy and slippery, and every now and then the mules gave us a fearful lesson how far they could flounder without coming down. We reached the "Hotel Suisse," a decent cabin at the crown of the Col, by 4½ P.M., in the midst of a mist that made a twilight of that early hour. Three young Englishmen, foot-sore from their first adventure in mountain-climbing, were the sole guests at the summit, and were deploring their inevitable loss of all that had brought them so high. But almost in a moment, at 5 P.M., the mist broke away and dispersed, revealing the valley of the Rhone on one side and of Chamouni on the other, in nearly perfect clearness. Then opened for a half-hour the whole sublime view of Mont Blanc, with the Aiguilles about the Mer de Glace, and on the other side of the valley the solid and regular peaks of the Aiguilles Rouges, with countless other mountains, all circling round the deep valley of the Arve, which seemed scooped out to the very centre of the earth, while the snow peaks gained immensely in apparent elevation by the height from which we surveyed them—6000 feet above the sea-level. It was the first prospect from a great height which has not seemed to me to lose in general obscurity of all details what it gained in sweep and relation of parts. If I should say that it was the most striking view I have ever yet seen, I should imperfectly convey my sense of its wonderful beauty and power. It has been celebrated for at least thirty years, but has not yet had its due merit assigned it, at least in my guide-books. The mist closed in a half-hour later as suddenly as it had scattered, but such good fortune made us bold, and we climbed the summit north of the Çol—a rise of 300 feet perhaps—to take our chance of another clearing at sunset. After waiting in the thickest mist for a half-hour, the clouds again opened, and gave us a still finer view of the prospect in both directions. But the exhibition lasted scarce a quarter of an hour, although the regathering of the clouds was as interesting as their temporary lift had been. A great bank of mist came swelling up the hill like an incoming tide. The clouds advanced like a park of flying artillery lost in its own smoke, but intent on taking a hill which lay in its track. Swift and irresistible, the smoke of its invisible cannons swept up the slope, and it seemed as if every moment horses and men would appear through the gloom. After this play at storming practice, we had another game from the clouds. One valley, full to overflowing of mist, emptied itself over the Col de Balme, just below us, into the valley of the Trient, with just as much precision as ever a pail of water was poured into a tub. The current never broke until the reservoir was exhausted and the mist sunk into the receiving valley on the other side. The tinkling of the bells from a herd of over two hundred cows, a mile below us, made a regular tattoo, as the whirr of the commingling sounds reached our ears. It was a wholly new effect, and very charming. The sun set to the sound of this music, and we came down to our inn and our supper, thoroughly in love with the Col de Balme and impatient for the dawn of to-morrow morning, when we have the best hopes of a clear sky.

September 20, 6 A.M.

The sky is clear overhead. The rising sun, invisible to us, gilds the clouds on the mountains. Mont Blanc is "nowhere." The "Aiguilles ranges" are like ocean rocks beaten by a tremendous surge. "Le Dru" and the "Buet" are visible from time to time. Occasional glimpses of the valley of

Chamouni are presented as the clouds open below. The Rhone valley is buried in fog. We shall wait an hour or two to give the prospect a fair chance to redeem its reputation, and then descend. We have been made as comfortable in this little inn as good and well-cooked food and clean beds could make us, when offset by an odious smell of the mule-stable in the cellar. The bread, butter, eggs and tea have been excellent. The family interest us by their intelligence and kindness. A child of two and a half years old toddles round among the rocks and irregularities of the summit, with the self-possession of a woman. Her cheeks are bursting with health, and she is almost as broad as long. Her chief amusement appears to be soaking her shoes in the various " cow-stockings" (alias puddles), although the thermometer is at fifty degrees. She came up to my daughter, who was looking through an opera-glass, and said, " *Je voudrais voir Mont Blanc.*" Permitted to look through the glass, she pretended to see the mountain, which was invisible, and putting out her hand for a penny, went away rich and happy.

MARTIGNY, 8 P.M.

Some charming views came out after breakfast this morning, but Mont Blanc witheld his summit, although the Dome de Goute was bare. " High on a throne of royal state he sat" — and Satan himself could not have been more malicious in deceiving the expectations of his victims, than this monarch of mountains was in hiding his face from his friends. The winds seemed to drive every thing before them except his veil. That was closer than a nun's —and would not lift a corner. So, after giving his Majesty two hours to repent of his obstinacy, we left him to his moody fit, and descended to the valley of the Trient, by two hours of hard work for knees not accustomed to such long stairs. The views from the cliffs that surround this deep valley are on all sides very grand—whether from the "Forclaz" on the opposite side, which we reached later in the day, or from the side of the Col de Balme. An impressive sight of the Glacier of the Trient is got here. It is said to be next in magnitude to the Mer de Glace. Here Geneva gets its supply of ice—by a road from the glacier to Martigny, whose excellence we experienced on our way down. There is really no reason why wagons should not run from Martigny to the inn at the Tete Noir, saving full half the arduous mule-ride between Chamouni and Martigny, which ladies find so fatiguing. Few country roads in New England are as good, and a farmer's one-horse wagon would run over the whole distance in two hours. . But it seems the policy of this region to maintain these mule-rides as a source of profit to the people of the country ; and so ladies and invalids will, I suppose, for some years yet be compelled to cross this most interesting piece of country wholly on jolting beasts, out of whom neither whip nor spur can get more than two and a half miles an hour. We made a detour of an hour, from the little village of Trient to the inn on the Tete Noir, and explored the road for a half-mile each side of the Turmel, to recall the recollection of the dizzy precipices which twenty years ago had curdled our younger blood. They are very striking still, but after the Via Mala and the Finstermünz, hardly worth going much out of the way to see. Precipices are as plenty as water-falls in Switzerland, and there is not a pass through the Alps that does not present both in perfection. One cataract was advertised at Argentiere thus : "La cascade de—*Folly* facile promenade." But I had seen it so often in all countries—and it had always appeared a promenade more facile than I approved, and so I did not visit this particular Fall of Folly. We found the descent from the

Forclaz to Martigny, down a hill six miles long, full of interest from the continual views presented of the valley of the
Rhone.   Broad, and level as a floor, with the bright Rhone
meandering through it, and villages and roads conspicuously
marked upon its surface, it was in such vivid contrast with
all the broken and precipitous country immediately about us,
as to derive a great charm from the comparison.   The slow
descent, at every turn in the circuitous road brought us into
closer views of the plain ; but it seemed almost farther and
farther off as we approached it, and were in some degree
able to realize our height above it.   Long after Martigny
seemed within stone's throw, it took us an hour to reach it.
Our two days' ride appeared a week as we looked back to
Chamouni, which was indefinitely removed, although it was
less than forty-eight hours since we had left it.   The bless-
ings of civilization appeared in the cleanly, sweet-smelling
inn we reached here at 6½ this evening, and we improved
them with sharp appetite.

The next morning we took the cars for Sion, about an
hour's ride up the valley—a picturesque town, with two castellated pinnacles on either side of it.   It was market-day,
and the streets of this little depot of the trade of the miserable Valais were crowded with a wretched-looking population
overwhelmed with poverty and disease.   Almost every third
person was afflicted with goitre or cretinism.   We entered
the church and found as many as ten ecclesiastics sitting in
the choir droning out a liturgical service, to which there was
not a single listener except ourselves.   They were duly
dressed in surplice, and looked fat and sleepy.   They had
the service by heart, and used no books as they rapidly recited the prescribed prayers.   The empty church echoed loudly their buzzing voices, as they flung from side to side their
task-work of evening prayer.   At the end they filed out, from

the eldest to the youngest, making very formal courtesies at two altars, and retreated into a neighboring monastery. The town is full of the remains of former ecclesiastical importance. The Rhone valley must, two centuries ago, have had a better climate and a more fertile soil than now. At present, it is the opprobrium of Switzerland, barren, bleak, devastated by the Rhone, full of miasmatic disease, and crowded with a hopeless and helpless population. The landscape is itself leprous—a spotted, livid and repulsive scene—with here and there a fertile interval or mountain slope, to make only more melancholy the general view. It is fit only to be looked down upon from a great height, and then it is very grand. The valley is fenced in between mountain ranges of moderate height, too straight in their trend to be interesting, and too equal in height to allow of intermediate views. The whole road from Martigny to Visp is monotonous. We drove up from Sion to Visp in six hours. Visp, another wretched Valais town, with some relics of ancient importance, in the shape of large houses, formerly occupied by the old Swiss nobles, but now abandoned to the poor, was, about twelve years ago, the centre of an earthquake, which lasted at intervals for a year, and shook the country for thirty miles about. Every stone house in the city and neighborhood bore evident marks of its destructive work. Great cracks in the walls of the churches and habitations and barns, filled with fresh mortar sometimes, indicated the universality of the misfortune. That the church, overhanging the Visp, escaped as it did, shows how much firmer the structures of three and four centuries ago were than our modern edifices. It is however, now tottering with the actual wear and tear of its exposed position, and looks eaten with storms of wind and sleet. We slept at the comfortable inn at Visp, and next morning started on mules for St. Niklaus, about fifteen miles up the Visper-thal.

As we rode through the stony, narrow streets, out of the town, we were struck, as always in Switzerland, with the pretty *faces* of the children and their poor *shapes*, and with the decrepit and ungainly looks of the adults. A few luxuriant fields, with lovely chestnuts rich with fruit, varied the general sterility. The Visp, with its sandy bed, broad and bare, filled up almost the whole bottom of the narrow and gloomy valley. The well-made mule-path, spite of stones, and ups and downs, and spite of the ill-sunned vineyards, opened upon striking prospects. The Breit-horn, a noble snow summit, bounded one end of the valley, and another snowy peak seemed to close up the view behind us, as we entered this dreary but fascinating pass. We felt every step as if we were stealing into the fastnesses of the Alps, and leaving civilization and almost humanity behind us. Yet wretched black hamlets, hung like bees on a high branch, with a white church acting as queen bee, clustered on the almost inaccessible cliffs above our heads.

A church festival had assembled the people at two or three villages in the valley, and showed us how populous those silent and deserted-looking slopes really were. The hats of the women, which a stiff wide ribbon in a few loose plaits converts into a sort of many-colored crown, gave a kind of picturesqueness to their otherwise dull and heavy faces, and thick, short-waisted forms. The children kissed their itching palms to us as we passed, and then looked down for their expected penny! One little rogue clung to our char above St. Niklaus for a mile or two, silent, but with asking eyes, until we purchased relief for our overburdened horse by tossing a penny over his head, which he dropped instantly to find, and stood looking at us gloatingly until we were out of sight. The road after awhile mounts the edge of a precipice and runs fearfully on its verge for several

miles, giving those dizzy views of a gulf a thousand feet below, which so many enviable people enjoy the imagination
of falling into, but which afford me nothing but pain and a
sickly terror. My mule, much of the disposition I so much
envy, appeared to enjoy the prospect highly. He insisted
upon keeping as near the edge as possible, and now hung
his nose and now a hind leg over the abyss. If I could have
pushed him in without going too, I fear I should have sent
him, in my chagrin, to that "*horse* heaven" (in New England
I learned in childhood to name all steep ravines lying below
traveled roads by that irreverent title) which would not have
rejected even mules. For those who enjoy Tete Noire and
Via Mala roads, I know nothing finer than this precipitous
mule-path. The approach to the point where the Saas valley joins the Visper-thal, is peculiarly grand, and makes one
hesitate which of the two forks he would choose to pursue.
We had, however, made our selection, and kept on through
the poverty-stricken hamlet clinging like a fungus to the
rocky hill of Stalden, where it shall not be forgotten that a
boy, unsmitten with mercenary passions, flung us of free will
a bunch of grapes—and so on to St. Niklaus. Let me not
pass the poorest habitation, where the patron saint of my
adopted city is baptismally honored, without respect! It is
doubtless in this cool and quiet place, where wood is cheap,
and carving common, that Santa Klaus comes in the summer
months to superintend the fabrication of the toys he scatters
so freely at Christmas! Doubtless here he refreshes his
mind, after contemplating our highly artificial comfort and
enervating luxury, with the strictly natural inconveniences
and tonic severity of a life as nearly savage as is consistent
with any thing not absolutely troglodytic. St. Niklaus is
conveniently situated under a precipitous cliff of a thousand
feet high, just at the angle and in precisely the spot where

the snowy avalanches of the winter are accustomed to descend. Its church has twice been thus destroyed. It is now and then shaken by añ earthquake, to vary the monotony of avalanches. To its disjointed, crowded and ugly heap of houses, it adds any amount of dung-heaps and pig-sties, and is a model of filth and disorder. There is no road for any sort of wheel-vehicle out of the valley. The church and the inn are the only places where decency appears. Here Santa Klaus, tired of the exquisite order and cleanliness of New York, can fly to enjoy the blessing of an absolute contrast. Might it not be well to send our city government, exhausted with their self-denying labors, their fastidious purity and their exacting standards of public convenience, to St. Niklaus on an annual excursion—not to exceed twelve months—to unbend their minds and loosen their grasp, so fatiguing to them and to us, upon the public interests, and allow them to enjoy the proud comparison between St. Nicholas at home and St. Niklaus abroad?

Beyond St. Niklaus, a very good though narrow road, wide enough for a New England wagon, runs up to Zennatt. Of course all the vehicles used upon it have to be built on the spot, as there is no access for carriages at either end of the valley. But a good wagon-builder is a great desideratum here. The axle-trees of the existing vehicles are built of wood. The seats are hung upon leathern straps, and the springs are supplied by the natural elasticity of the human body, when not too old and lean. Some hard mules had prepared us to think almost any thing short of riding a rail tolerable ; but the St. Niklaus *char* convinced us of the haste of our illogical anticipations. A jolt which lasts a dozen miles is with difficulty rendered pleasant by any amount of natural elasticity. Our bounding spirits had not cushioned us in the right place. We were jarred from sole to crown. I felt as if a grater had mistaken my head for a nutmeg. The road was one pretty steady pull up the valley, and it took us nearly four hours to make the twelve miles. The dull speed saved our lives, which must else have been shaken out of us. Nothing but a special providence saved them again when we had to return, and found—not to our surprise—the road running all the other way! How we survived the thumping of that char, when it made five miles an hour on the return, even the English physician who accompanied us was puzzled, notwithstanding his full knowledge of the exquisite stuffing Nature has applied to the more exposed bones and joints, fully to explain.

XXIII.

September 19, 1867.

ZERMATT, which we reached by 3 P.M., is a poor hamlet at the foot of the great Gorner glacier, and the head of the Visp valley. *Matt* means meadow, and if Zer is any corruption of sour, the place is well named. Such starved fields I never saw except in some parts of Cape Cod. And yet, all the artifices and labors and prudencies of the most encouraging soil were evidently brought to bear on this ungrateful tract of land. It was hedged and bounded and drained and planted precisely as if it had been a meadow in Devon, England, or in Chester county, Pennsylvania. But such poor, discouraged crops I have rarely been called to sympathize with. And no wonder! Here, in the very presence of tremendous glaciers—with snow mountains all around the horizon, at a height of nearly 5000 feet above the sea-level, dwells a set of peasants, with their cows and their goats, trying to make believe they are in a habitable region. What they did before the scenery-hunting Englishmen found them and chose their village as a sort of jumping-off place from all civilization, a farewell to fatiguing comfort and facility of motion—what they then did for the means of living, it is hard to conceive. At present they rear their poor little crops and tend their cattle (how they got so fat and big is a mystery), and wait on the visitors from all countries who have come to think Zermatt "the thing" to do after Chamouni, so long the *ultima Thule*

of tourists. And Zermatt merits its honors! For over it
hangs the Matter-horn, the famous Mont Cervin—the most
emphatic mountain in the world.

It answers best to the ideal mountain which children, unlimited in their fancies, always have in mind and imagination
when they dream of mountains—something steep and peaked
running up into the clouds and perhaps grazing the moon.
I never saw any mountain except the Matter-horn that looked high enough to satisfy me! Higher mountains there are,
Mont Blanc and Monte Rosa, not to speak of Chimborazo
and Mount Hood and Himalayas. But what is the use of
being high and looking short? I have been half-way up the
Sierra Nevadas, without once suspecting I was on a mountain-side, and Mont Blanc and Monte Rosa, too, lose much
of their height by the gradualness of their rise and the company of their lofty neighbors. But the Matter-horn suffers
no rival to approach it! For miles on either side of it the
mountain chain falls away to a low level, leaving the Matter-horn, rising like an iron wedge, 4000 feet above the
line of its chain ; and this 4000 feet is on the shoulders of
10,000, which form its noble base. Only this beautiful
wedge is seen from Zermatt, the base being all hid ; but it
hangs in the air as if unsupported, an elegant, regular obe-
lisk, rising over the whole landscape in unapproachable beauty and grandeur. It was utterly obscured when we reached
Zermatt and started on mules to climb the Riffel, 2000 feet
above the village. We dared not in the late season lose our
chance of the sunset and sunrise of a single day, and so,
tired as we were, we left Zermatt a half-hour after arriving,
for the hotel on the Riffel. In the grand old woods, with
their gnarled roots and rugged Norway pines, with the glaciers peering at us, like the frozen serpent of the North
seeking its evening prey, and with cataracts dashing the air

into strange sounds, we chanced to look up, and through the
leaves of the trees and through the rising mists a vast ghost
of a pyramid stood between us and the upper sky! The
form was definite yet visionary—the substance chased silver
with spots less bright upon its surface, the size enormous, and
the height incredible. It vanished almost as suddenly as it
came ; but if we had never seen it again, we should have
felt that we had seen the most wondrous mountain on the
globe. We gained the large and comfortable hotel on the
Riffel by a steep and needlessly rough mule-path of 2000
feet ascent by two hours' incessant climbing.

There we found a nearly deserted hotel, with ninety beds
— until the middle of September usually crowded every
night—but now having only a dozen guests, including our own
party of three. The weather was cold and rough, but the
promise of the sunset kept us all out-of-doors. Every moment some one of the half-circle of mountains to be seen
from the Riffel cleared its head from the clouds. The
Rhymfisch-horn, the Allalein-horn, the Roth-horn, the Weiss-
horn — most elegant of peaks — the two Gabel-horns, the
Dent Blanche—all came one after another to bid the sun
good-night, with faces smiling and with beaming eyes. But
the Matter-horn behaved like a prima donna spoiled with
admiration and playing sick to test her power with a doting
public. For two days our fellow-guests had been waiting to
see Mont Cervin, and in vain, except at 5½ in the morning,
when for two days at that precise hour he had come like a spirit at cock-crow, and departed, " no sooner seen than gone."
But he had clearly been waiting for visitors from America
—Englishmen were too common and came from too short
a distance to interest him! Accordingly, just at sunset, he
came out from a rift in a bank of clouds that for miles long
were passing slowly before him, in a most tedious procession.

Nothing ever annoyed me more in the shape of a procession, except St. Patrick's procession, which for several years has broken up all possible connection between Union Square and Wall Street for all the business hours of the day. But this cloudy procession had a gap big enough to let the Matterhorn through, and before it closed we had enjoyed one short, clear vision of that majestic, exceptional, nay, unique summit, which eclipsed beyond comparison all single mountain views ever under our eyes. It was unusual and almost unwelcome to have the horn of Mont Cervin so completely covered with snow. Usually it is quite bare, with spots of snow upon it. But the weather had created a peculiar sleet which sheathed the upright blade of the Matter-horn with silver. The contrast with its base and neighbors, which it commonly presents in its rugged black pinnacle, was lost. How much was gained in harmony, I can not say until I have seen the other effect. There is such a splendor in the other snow Aiguilles of this extraordinary view, that it is difficult to say how much the prospect owes to the Matter-horn alone. But doubtless the view is distracting, and lacks the unity of a true picture.

This became still more obvious the next morning, when, with a sunrise of cloudless beauty, we climbed by an easy though long ascent the Gorner Grat, 1700 feet above the Riffel, and 10,000 feet above the sea-level. Here broke upon us the three great masses of Monte Rosa, Lyskamm and the Breithorn, which, in their lumpish vastness and absence of features, present a great contrast with the pinnacles of the other half of the panorama. The great waste of unbroken snow and ice which this chain exhibits is sublime, especially when the eye gains, by attention to details, some conception of its vastness. The tendency to the dome rather than the peak in its forms is a little oppressive after the lightness of the exquisite Aiguilles opposite, but each side lends the other

interest, and doubtless enriches the panoramic effect. Monte
Rosa, I must confess, as a mountain by itself and separated
from its chain, greatly disappointed me, as seen from this
side. It has no obvious elevation above its neighbors, and
is even exceeded in effect by Lyskamm and Breithorn. Its
summit is a rather mean little horn, with nothing to distinguish it from a neighboring knob, and in every way inferior to
twenty peaks in full view. The great Gorner glacier, which
lies in majestic length and breadth below the Gorner Grat,
stretching its glistening bulk up near the very summit of
Monte Rosa, and then winding in vast curves its way down
to the Zermatt valley, is a most impressive spectacle.
Breithorn is a far grander and more individual mountain, in
my eyes, than Rosa. His sides are spotted with rocks which
give him a brindled appearance that is pleasing. Castor and
Pollux, two lower summits, just vary the Monte Rosa chain,
by interposing a gentler feature in their harmonious duality.
If panoramas are ever satisfactory, the Gorner Grat may
claim to present a perfect specimen. I confess that my æsthetic instincts are always wounded by pictures that have not
a beginning, a middle and an end, or in which beginning and
end take each other's places. But, putting pictures aside,
the sublime effect of being encircled by a horizon of snow
mountains which is so high as to make a world of its own,
can not be overstated. There was an exhilaration in the
position of transcendent charm.

The Riffelberg, a sort of natural castle, black and forbidding, we had passed on the way up. Although the special
ascent is not five hundred feet, it cost a clergyman, a year or
two ago, his life—slipping from its craggy sides, which he
had mounted safely in the morning, on a second trip in the
afternoon. It was deemed inaccessible until Mr. Wilson
climbed it. The Matter-horn showed us plainly the track,

on the edge or angle of its two hither sides, up which the
party, headed by an English clergyman, went when year before last they scaled the peak, and four men lost their lives in
descending. They were bound together by a rope, and when
the weight of the four men strained it, held in the hands of
the remaining three, it broke and they fell three or four thousand feet down the most precipitous side of the peak. Since
then, and in spite of this warning, repeated though infrequent
ascents of the Matter-horn have been made. It is clearly a
matter of mere endurance and carefulness to ascend any of
these mountains. Mont Blanc is now considered the easiest
of the half-dozen most difficult. A gentleman of our party,
who ascended twelve years ago, said that it was disappoint-
ingly easy in every respect except mere plodding fatigue in
winding about crevasses or walking miles and miles in the
snow. There were no terrific scrambles, or dizzy scaling of
precipices, or, in short, any thing to prevent a woman or a
child whose muscles could hold out from making the ascent.
The Alpine climbers on the Riffel with us were making difficult snow passes every week. Two a week they considered
about a dose. Their faces were moderately skinned, their
lips cracked, and their general appearance not enviable.
And yet they were "in condition," and could make their
twenty miles' tramp over glaciers and *cols* eleven and twelve
thousand feet high, without serious fatigue, and with great
enjoyment. According to their representation danger upon
the ice is always the result of foolish neglect of well-known
precautions. The open crevasses are not dangerous to people of any steadiness of footing and a proper preparation of
the shoes with hob-nails. It is the snow-bridges across the
hidden crevasses that constitute the only serious peril. A
crust capable of bearing a man is often thus formed over a
crevasse ; but it may look firm and be weak, or it may not

differ in appearance from the ordinary surface, and yet give way and let the traveler down fifty or a hundred feet. A perfect security is obtained by using "the rope." A party of three or five—the more the better—thus bound together by the waist, with an interval of ten feet between each two, may cross any glacier with impunity. If one slumps in, he is caught by his companions and immediately lifted from his fall, which can not go far with a *taut* rope. The gentlemen on the Riffel had crossed the previous day a glacier-pass, thus roped together, and had in turn fallen into crevasses as many as a dozen times in their passage over, without any penalty except a momentary fright, which after a little experience passed away. In short they quite laughed at the popular ideas of the difficulties of the high Alps. The Theodule pass, for instance, which lay in full view to the left of Mont Cervin, although a lofty pass, over many miles of snow and ice, has been crossed by ladies in a *chaise-a-porteur*. Cows are occasionally driven across it into Italy, and it was long a favorite pass for persons running the customs, and smuggling silks and laces and tobacco over the frontier.

We returned to Visp without any fresh experiences on the road. The sheep and goats are commonly marked like the mountains, white as snow and black as rocks in spots. The goats, in their white trousers and black jackets, looked almost like school-boys in procession as they filed into town at sundown. The lambs were comical enough in their marking, muzzle, tip of tail, feet, black as ink, and all the rest white as chalk. I am greatly in love with the Swiss goats, they are so tame and yet so agile and graceful, so useful, and so ornamental.

We made an effort to cross the Gemmi, and drove ten miles up the marvelous and beautiful road that runs up from Leuk to the Baths of Loeche. Nothing in the way of road-making, nothing in the way of valley-views, nothing in the way of precipices, can be finer. The situation of Loeche les Bains, under the most architectural cliffs I ever saw, is superb. But, alas! a fearful storm of wind and snow baffled our farther progress at this point. The people at the hotel declared the mule-path over the mountain dangerous, and as we had almost had our heads blown off in getting thus far, we concluded not to risk them any farther. We accordingly drove back to Leuk next morning, and so on to Sion, and there took the rail for Lausanne and Geneva, where we had resolved to lay by for a week and "repair damages"—a phrase which to foreign tourists means renovation of the wardrobe, which is sadly tried by much travel.

Gen. Meigs, U. S. A., our energetic and patriotic Quartermaster-General through the war, is now recruiting his shattered health in Europe. He recommended the guides at Chamouni (who lie by nearly idle for eight months in the year) to employ their leisure in making a railroad between Chamouni and Geneva, for the transportation of the glacial ice of Bossons and Du Bois to Paris. Certainly if we had such reservoirs of beautiful ice, we should economize them in some such way, especially if labor was as cheap with us as in Europe. But there is little invention or enterprise here. They go on working by hard hand labor, when a little pains would do it all away. There is great need of some new stimulus to mechanical improvements. They want a hundred thousand Yankees in every European country to supply men with "notions."

GENEVA, September 28.

We chanced to return to Geneva on a day of peculiar interest for its religious history, the day when the "Salle de la Reformation," just finished, was dedicated, in the morning by special religious services, in the evening by a historical address from the venerable Merle d'Aubigné, "The Arrival of Calvin at Geneva." The morning service we know of only by report; the evening address we had the pleasure of hearing. "The Hall of the Reformation" is a plain building without external shapeliness or show, but capable of holding two thousand persons in its chief audience-chamber, and having numerous rooms and offices suited to committees and other small gatherings. It seems that the project was conceived in the Conferences of the Evangelical Alliance held at Geneva in 1861, and received its final shape at the commemoration of the third centenary of Calvin's death, 27th May, 1864. The erection of the building has been effected by contributions from the United States, Scotland and England, principally from England. Little or nothing has been contributed in Geneva. Several thousand francs are still due upon it, and efforts are soon to be made to raise that sum here. The editor of the *Semaine Religeuse* (No. 38, Sept. 21, 1867), the only Protestant organ in Geneva, and apparently in the interest of the Orthodox party in the National Church, regrets, in giving notice of the consecration of this hall, that in rendering homage to Calvin (for one of its names is Calvinium, or house of Calvin) a larger spirit and one more in accordance with public sentiment had not been observed. He regrets that the building should have been founded on the ground of a special confession of faith—the Confession of the "Evangelical Alliance"—instead of being based upon that larger platform on which the National Church of Geneva is built, viz., "The divine authority of the Holy Scriptures." He acknowledges that the project was started by the Evangelical Alliance, but thinks that it will lose some of the ends aimed at by having excluded many of the living forces of Protantism at Geneva, by its too narrow platform. This is a very remarkable concession from an understood organ of the self-styled Evangelical party in the National Church. Before going farther, it will be well to give such information as we have been able to gather from competent sources at Geneva, touching the present condition of Protestantism here.

The Cantonial, or State Church, is Protestant. It has about fifty ministers, of which half are in Geneva and half in the country. Geneva constitutes a single parish, divided into sub-parishes, and served by a Collegiate Pastorate, who preach in turn in the various churches, of which there are six or seven. The old cathedral, St. Gervais, the Madeleine, are among the principal churches. The Genevan Church is modeled evidently upon the French Protestant Church, and experiences many of the social difficulties and reflects all the theological phases of that Church. It possesses a Liturgy whose creed is very broad, and which it is perfectly possible for Unitarian and Trinitarian interpreters of the Scriptures to use in good faith. This Liturgy is publicly used without variation, and has long been used by pastors of both schools of theology. Since 1822, a very strong Liberalism, precisely equivalent to the Unitarianism of Channing and Ware, has prevailed in the Genevan Church. Every body knows the active part which the now venerable professor and pastor, Dr. Cheneviere, took in the discussion which terminated in a large accession of the people to *Unitarian* opinions — actually such, though not called by that name. For awhile it seemed as if Calvinism were actually dead in the place of its birth, and those who had killed it too fondly believed it would never rise again. But the fall of Calvinism at Geneva was not a mere local disaster in the estimation of its friends in all other parts of the world.

The tendency to Unitarianism, or the actual liberality of the pastors and people in the seat of Calvin's ancient autoc-

M

racy, were blows of fatal significance to the system everywhere. Accordingly, outside influence has been at work for thirty years and more to stay the liberal current, and to restore if possible the prestige of Calvin in his old home. Dr. Merle d'Aubigné, still living at the age of 75 years—professor and pastor here, has been perhaps the chief champion of the reaction. Gaussen, with whose popular little work on the verbal inspiration of the Scriptures most students in theology are familiar (and a work of unusual audacity and ignoring of all inconvenient learning it is), has been another strong fighter for the reaction ; but is now dead. Malan is the third name specially entitled to mention, but he is lately dead also. Vinet, who lived and labored in Lausanne and had much influence in France in his day, but is now dead, does not seem to rank with these in importance, if measured by the respect of their opponents. He is said to have become liberal in his last days, and it is even asserted that his latest writings were suppressed by his family. Dr. Merle (they seldom use the family name in referring to him here) has abandoned new theological studies and given himself up to ecclesiastical history. He is not a thinker, but a dramatic describer of situations. His theological opinions have apparently undergone no growth or development for thirty-six years. He has a fixed and never-questioned creed, which he has apparently not thought about since he first adopted it, and he holds it precisely as if it had never been doubted or denied. Meanwhile he has written, as every body knows, the history of the Reformation in a highly interesting and dramatic way. Chalmers gave it its first renown by announcing its author as the greatest living historian ! Few who know his own imaginative character will think him a very competent authority. The feeling among scholars and thinkers in Germany seems to be that Professor Merle has written very interesting sketches under the name of the History of the Reformation, but hardly permanent and wholly reliable history. Every body gives this gentleman credit for integrity and Christian purity of life and character ; few judges seem to think him entitled to the reputation he enjoys in Scotland, England and America. It is evidently in part factitious, and due to his theological opinions ; it is still more due to the incompetency of those who feel most the charm of his dramatic style to estimate its historical accuracy. Dr. Merle was not thought very sound on the question of our late war. Of the thirty pastors connected with the Protestant Church in Geneva, it is said that twelve or thirteen are liberal, that is to say, essentially Unitarian in their theology ; and as a proof that the people are in sympathy with them rather than with the Orthodox party, every new election to a vacancy, it is affirmed by my informers, is in their favor. On the other hand the native aristocracy, the wealthy and conservative element in Geneva, supports the Orthodox side. There is (to explain this) a special relation between the religion and the political tendencies in Geneva—an embarrassing connection. Democracy has always struggled here with the old aristocracy, and there is a sort of Red Republican party in Switzerland which keeps the sober intelligence of the country in a perpetual alarm, and impels many with moderate views to lean rather to the aristocratic than the popular side. The Calvinists in theology use the political fears of the Moderate party to enlist them on the Conservative side in theology, and it is not safe to infer any real sympathy with the theological opinions of the Orthodox, from the support they thus receive on political grounds. It must not be forgotten, either, that Calvin has a national prestige, aside from his theology, in Geneva, to whose moral reputation and political liberties he rendered such substantial services. His immense personal weight of character and vigor of mind make him still the central figure in Genevan history, and his bust stands with those of Fabbri in his bishop's mitre, De Candolle, J. J. Rousseau (a curious collocation), upon the cornice of the new Athenæum in the city; yet, after all, from the best information I could get, Calvinism as a theology is a shadow and not a substance in Geneva. It is sustained on grounds of policy by an influential class, not intelligently embraced by the people as a free choice of their hearts and minds. It is upheld by foreign influence; by money from abroad; by a policy which is animated by English, Scotch and American sects in sympathy with it, and not by the affections or convictions of the native population. Its throne, like many a political fabric leaning on foreign bayonets, is of course unreal and uncertain. Geneva is not a Calvinistic city in any proper sense. Liberal religious thought steadily advances among the people, and there is no prospect of any reaction of a genuine kind in favor of the Institutes of John Calvin. Such at least is the testimony of the intelligent and candid men whom I have consulted on the ground. Let me now return to the meeting in the Calvinium and to M. Merle's address.

At seven o'clock, we found ourselves in a great crowd of Genevese, entering the new " Salle de la Reformation." The people were of all classes of society, but composed largely of plain, roughly-dressed but respectable persons of both sexes, including a percentage of youth. It was more like the audience of a country lyceum in a large manufacturing town in New England than any collection of people I have seen in Europe. The hall, exceedingly plain, but lofty and not without a certain harmony of color and form, was furnished with unpainted and cushionless seats—benches with backs. It had two galleries running down both sides, like our Boston

Music Hall. The rostrum was occupied by forty men of a ministerial appearance. From 1500 to 2000 persons were assembled—a very orderly, intelligent and attentive audience. M. Merle d'Aubigné came in quietly and took his place in the pulpit, and after a short prayer gave out a familiar hymn, which was heartily sung by the congregation. He then begun his address, which he read like a practiced orator. Our view was a distant one. Bald, with heavy eyebrows, an erect and commanding form, a thin French face, a clear, strong and audible voice, it was difficult to believe that a man of 75 years was addressing and making himself generally heard in this vast audience. With great vivacity, highly dramatic action and unflagging vigor, he spoke an hour and a half upon his theme—the arrival of Calvin at Geneva. He sketched the history of the man and the time ; the condition of things political and religious in Geneva at Calvin's coming ; his struggle with the Savoy princes ; his preaching, and the renovation of the public morals. He passed with a light and judicious hand over Calvin's theology, presenting what he called his principles only in a very general way, and painting them in their aspects toward political liberty and freedom from the Catholic yoke. But his real subject was an attack, well deserved, upon the irreligious implications of the late Peace Convention, and an assertion of the absolute importance of a positive faith in Christianity to the moral, social and economic prosperity of Geneva and the world. His address was highly dramatic, interesting and judicious, but indicated no freshness, originality or peculiar force of thought. It had no critical merit, and no illumination in it for persons in the least acquainted with the subject. It was easy to see what the magic of his personal influence was over his pupils, and over hearers who demand only to be pleased. I was fully repaid for the two hours I gave to the *seance.* It was difficult to reconcile the presence of this great audience with the alleged unpopularity of M. Merle's theological opinions among the people of Geneva.   But the newness of the hall and its free seats had moved the curiosity of hundreds to go, and M. Merle, apart from his opinions, is a speaker whom those who least agree with him must often desire to hear.

I hope to attend upon another meeting in the Hall of the Reformation to-morrow evening, Sunday, when various ministers, native and foreign, are expected to speak.

This hall is not a church.   It is designed to promote the interests of Orthodox Calvinism, by various religious, educational, philanthropic and literary appliances ; by evening schools of a secular character, and by a lively interest in the wants of the common people.   It will be supported by foreign funds, and is a skillful and politic arrangement for carrying forward indirectly what could not be as well advanced by more direct methods.   Orthodoxy in England, America and Scotland is thoroughly alarmed at the free religious tendencies of literature, politics and philosophy.   It sees that the old theology of the Reformation is against the grain of the nineteenth century. ` It hopes by a vigorous and careful policy to arrest the current of popular thinking.   It does not recognize any thing providential, necessary and irresistible in the tendencies which have cast Orthodoxy, as a snake casts his old skin.   The more effort it makes in the direction of this new movement at Geneva, the better.   If it really seeks to educate, interest, or even amuse the people, it will only unwittingly confirm their incapacity for being Calvinists.   It can only make them such by adapting Calvin himself to the times.   If he is to continue Captain of Genevan thought and Genevan theology, he must himself be made a nineteenth century theologian !   Whatever may be the motives or exnectations of the supporters of this scheme, its results, I have no manner of doubt, will be such as American Liberal Christians could desire and well approve.

I called, with a letter from Dr. Palfrey, upon the venerable Cheneviere, the champion of religious liberty and an un-Calvinistic faith in Geneva forty years ago, and who has never ceased to contend with it in a Christian spirit and with unfaltering courage and faith. He is now eighty years old, and in delicate health, but alive in spirit, affection and intellectual convictions. He maintains a perfect confidence in the essential progress of religious liberty and Liberal Christianity in Geneva ; said that Calvinism was continually falling, and could never rise again in any substantial reality. It was charming to see this finished French gentleman, with his graceful manners and *esprit*, sitting in his library, still at work on theological questions, and adding to the ease of the man of the world the gentleness and dignity of the Christian minister. He had known Tuckerman and Ware, Palfrey and the younger Channing, and spoke of all of them with affectionate respect. He has a son, he told me, settled as a teacher of a young ladies' school in Brooklyn, N. Y., a man of character and talents, and a successful extempore lecturer, whom, for the sake of his venerable father, I desire to introduce to our Unitarian ministers in Brooklyn, and to our Liberal friends there, begging their attention to his school and himself—a stranger in a strange land. I called, also, on Rev. Pastor Viollier, of the National Church, whom I found to be a thorough Unitarian, and a man of marked intelligence, candor and worth. He half promised to write me an article for the *Christian Examiner*, on the present attitude of Liberal Protestantism in Switzerland. It would be, I doubt not, a valuable contribution, and correct any errors into which I may have run in this somewhat hasty sketch, which, however,

I have done my best to make exact. M. Chéneviere named the Rev. Messrs. Cougnard, Guillermet, Oltramare and Viollier as among the most able Liberal ministers in the National Church of Geneva.

XXIV.

GENEVA.

SWITZERLAND, September 29, 1867.

GENEVA is the most cosmopolitan of all cities of its size. It seems to be a sort of European centre of exiles for political, religious and socialistic opinions. Jews and Christians, Catholics and Protestants, Infidels and Believers, Orthodox and Heterodox, Greek and Roman churchmen, Rationalists and Supernaturalists, Progressives and Reactionaries, Anti-Government men and Imperialists, Red Republicans and Conservatives, all are in activity here. The proper character of the city and people is swamped in its foreign population. It is a sort of fulcrum on which all modern powers of thought and aspiration are resting their levers. Perhaps it has less original mental activity than it once had, and has fewer distinguished exiles ; but it is the refuge and halting-place of thousands of restless and self-banished persons who find in its political freedom, its central situation, its attractive scenery and unrivaled facilities for living pleasantly and moderately, a reason for choosing it as a temporary home. Here travelers in Switzerland are apt to terminate, by a stay of a few days or weeks, their laborious pleasures among the mountains. Here, too, the more enterprising portion of traveling-parties leave the less active members of their company to rest. Parents establish their children at its schools, and many Americans, Russians, English, live here the year round. The new part of the city is truly

Parisian and cosmopolitan in its aspect. What can be finer than the street about the foot of the lake, and on either side the broad yet arrowy Rhone, that shoots fiercely blue and swift out of Leman, with all the force and beauty of the Niagara river, broken with slight falls, but exquisitely pure and grandly copious? The Pont du Mont Blanc, a new bridge, wide and long, is surely one of the noblest bridges in the world. Low in its piers, it is so solid, wide and commanding in its position, that nothing on the Seine or the Thames strikes me as so attractive. This part of the city is composed almost wholly of magnificent hotels—the Beau Rivage; the "de la Paix," with its Pension; the Hotel des Bergues, on one side; the Metropole, the l'Ecu; the Couronne, the Hotel de la Porte, and others, on the opposite side. What can be finer, architecturally, or give a stronger notion of the immense hospitality of Geneva to strangers? The upper town — quite separated by its steep and narrow approaches from the lower town—with streets and lanes and flights of stairs, and irregular places, that could only have originated within straitened walls two or more centuries ago, is the ossified heart of Geneva, which once beat with earnest life and motion. It is still occupied by the relics of the old noblesse and the would-be aristocracy of the city—the Genevan St. Germain—and still keeps up a little of its arrogant contempt for the lower, newer, and living city. The new town returns its disdain, and on occasions when this antagonism has taken on an active character, has brought the upper town to terms by cutting off its water, which is supplied by works from below.

J. J. Rousseau's island is between the two main bridges, and, while it commemorates his name, affords a point of view for the lake and the range of Mont Blanc. That wonderful pile of mountains is seen in fine weather, from the Quai du

Mont Blanc, to great advantage; indeed, far better, to my view, than at any nearer point—as its relative magnitude may here be duly estimated.

September 30.

A showy and picturesque Jewish synagogue in the lower town, I visited yesterday; a Greek Church on the hill, of a rich Saracenic style, where a Russian priest says mass on every Sunday morning: This morning at 9 A.M. we attended divine service at the Oratoire—one of the dissenting chapels—attracted by the announcement that Rev. William Monod, of Paris (in attendance upon the *séances* of the " Salle de la Reformation "), would preach. His elder brothers, Adolph and Frederic, are both dead. The church, hidden in a narrow lane of the upper town, is mean though venerable in its exterior ; plain and dark in its interior, lighted from above and at the end, much like our old church in Chambers Street, of which both in size and shape it reminded me affectingly. M. Monod was in the pulpit, and had already begun the services when we entered. The congregation—about six hundred—filled the chapel, and was composed four-fifths of women and children. A few substantial men, of evident position, sat on the pulpit platform. The minister was in a reading-desk, in front of the pulpit. The chorister stood near him and conducted the effective congregational singing. The liturgical service was thin and meagre, without responses or vocal participation, except in the singing. Indeed, the whole service was too much like our own, or any other congregational form, to satisfy my wishes or expectations. The prayers were extempore ; one of them, addressed directly to Jesus, was highly dramatic, and, despite its fervor, offensive to my feelings. So bald a piece of anthropological worship I do not remember to have heard from any other thoughtful and accomplished divine.

Certainly, neither the Episcopal nor the Catholic Church would venture on any such protracted and exclusive prayer to Jesus, to the absolute forgetfulness of the Infinite Spirit. The other prayer was addressed to God, the Father, and I was able to join in it with sympathy and satisfaction. The sermon (the whole service was of course in French) was from the words "*Heureux les debonnaires pour les inherirent la terre.*" I had quite forgotten that the French had no better word for the meek than "*les debonnaires,*" and it hardly surprised me that M. Monod should find it so hard work to explain how the "debonnaire" were to inherit the earth. This celebrated preacher has a charming and saintly countenance, sharpened by labors and self-denials. He is apparently about sixty-five years old, with a benevolent, drooping nose, a bright yet tender eye, a little bald but with abundant hair, grey and soft, an expressive mouth, a voice sweet and plaintive, which he swings through all the minor keys, an earnest, half-dramatic manner, wide and graceful gestures, and a presence altogether lovely and revereable. He preached extempore, though not without careful preparation, and, I think, from skeleton notes. His enunciation was so slow and clear that I was able to follow him perfectly, and really lost nothing of his meaning, and hardly any thing of his beauty and eloquence.

The sermon was a model of Scriptural preaching, so far as that consists in adherence to the words of the Bible, and an argument compacted from assuming an absolute identity in the authority and an unbroken unity in the argument of the Old and New Testaments—the greatest power and the greatest vice of Orthodox hermeneutics. He began with criticising the disposition which some ingenious but dangerous innovators had shown to explain away the apparent contradiction of the text, by showing that a yielding temper and a policy of concession was actually more favorable to worldly success than a violent, grasping or energetic will. He maintained, on the contrary, that "the earth" to which the Evangelist referred was not this world, but that "promised land" in the skies, of which the promised land sought by Abraham was only a type. He adduced at much length Abraham's history, and specially his amicable division of the land with Lot—to avoid scandal and unkindness, not from softness or policy—as a type of the kind of meekness which would really inherit the earth. It was the surrender of earthly advantages and policies, for God's sake, in the spirit of faith, and in the confidence of better things reserved for love and obedience — which alone deserved the name of Christian meekness — the meekness that should inherit the earth. Moses, Christ, Paul were meek, but they could threaten and judge and use the severest condemnations. There was nothing soft, pusillanimous, compromising in their spirits, traits which so often appeared in the meekness of the self-seeking. Christians must not expect worldly success, nor an easy life, nor an avoidance of strife and oppositions, persecutions and death ; they must not hope for peace and prosperity ; they must live in the spirit of the apostles and martyrs, if they hoped to inherit that earth which was alone in Jesus's thoughts in his glorious beatitude. After illustrating this idea very fully, the preacher referred, in closing, to the attacks on the unworldly spirit and character of Christianity lately made in the name of human progress and a tenderer humanity, a false liberty and a base secularism. He rejoiced in the triumphs of political freedom, of industrial improvements, of pacific policies ; but any dependence on these for Christian perfection, individual or social, was delusive. These were, indeed, lesser fruits of divine grace, charity and faith—but not their chief harvest, which lay in the future rewards awaiting the just. He gave a blow, not less felt for being left-handed and indirect, at the late Peace Congress, for its attacks on Christianity, and considered the *séances* of the Salle de la Reformation, in which his audience and himself had assisted, as providential in their character and their date, following so soon upon the infidel explosions of the philanthropists who had ignored the Prince of Peace. He apostrophized Geneva, by its ancient morals, its honor of Calvin, and its place in the Reformation, to be faithful to the great doctrines and principles of an Evangelical faith; and then he apostrophized France, by its Huguenot blood, and its great and sacred martyrs for purity of doctrine and holiness, not to allow worldliness, materialism and secular ambition to drown its spirituality and faith in Him who would give only to the truly meek in spirit and in faith the heritage of this world purified from sin, and a better world in the skies.

There was great warmth and eloquence, simplicity and truth, in this discourse. It was not pointed or brought home to the conscience or the affections as it might have been; but the personality of the preacher was so charming and saintly that it took the place of appeal, almost as much as example takes away the need of precept. It must be confessed, however, that the doctrine was not as high-toned as it should have been. M. Monod seemed to forget that Jesus ignored time and space in his teachings, placed the kingdom of God *within*, and made the real inheritance the actual possession of a Christ-like, or rather God-like, temper and spirit. The meek, in inheriting a true notion of life and in adopting it, win at one stroke time and eternity, this world and all worlds, for they win God and dwell in him, and own all he owns. The hymns were poor, in a sort of Methodistic sensualism of sentiment, which is unworthy a cultivated and spiritual taste.

After this service we went to the Greek church, a beautiful edifice of white stone, nearly square, with a square clere-story and crowned with fine pear-shaped and gilded domes, each surmounted with the cross springing from a crescent. From the arms of each cross extend gilded chains, which are attached to its dome. The Oriental origin and character of the church, which might easily be mistaken for a Turkish mosque, or a Persian kiosk, is very apparent. The interior is even more Eastern, being a square, richly carpeted, and without seats, except against the walls. It is frescoed in the richest blues, greens and gold, in arabesque patterns, and adorned with a picture of Christ on the ceiling and on the wall, and others of apostles and saints, especially one of Saint Alexander, a Russian prince, canonized for having built the first bridge across the Neva. The altar is separated from the auditorium by a wall pierced with five arches in white marble, through which open three doors. Behind the double open-worked central door hang thick curtains, which are drawn before it is opened. The service began when not a dozen persons were in the gem-like place, with a muttering as of prayers, by a voice concealed behind "the veil of the temple." We understood from a Russian lady, neighbor to us, that these were special prayers for the sick or separated, and not a part of the public service. At eleven o'clock a deacon in plain clothes took his place before the door of the altar, with his back to the audience, and commenced reading out of a liturgy, in a guttural, yet not unmelodious tone, with a curious prolongation of the final syllables, like, yet differ-ent from, the Roman Catholic intoning. After awhile the reading was taken up by the invisible priest on the inside, and then commenced a responsive service between him and the deacon, who seemed to act as the clerk in the English service, except that he had a great deal of going in and out to do, lighting candles and carrying them about, and changing their positions.   Presently, with a congregation which was gathering and slowly increasing, came in four men from out-doors, who took their places one side on a little raised and enclosed platform outside the altar, and began to sing the responses to the priest in a choral harmony which was exquisite in its chords and in the voices of the singers, but became finally fearfully monotonous from a continual repetition of the same phrases.   The "God be merciful to us sinners," or "Lord help us to keep this law," could not be more tedious in the repetitious portion of the English service.   Presently, the curtain was drawn and the doors opened, and a young man, in carefully-dressed hair and beard, of a pleasant and devout face, presented himself in gorgeous apparel—the priest whose voice, deep and gentle, we had been so long hearing.   He had on a rich white under-tunic, girded with a sash which reached to his feet, and over this a magnificent blue silk robe, covered with golden crosses, with a hem of gold lace, and a cape or cope of stiff, plain cloth of gold.   About his neck hung a heavy gold cross.   This gorgeous and elegant figure, who looked like a monarch prepared for his coronation, had a laborious work to perform. The service consisted in a long order of prayers, whose virtue depended apparently on the position in which they were said, so that the priest was walking about a great deal, now in at one door and out of another, now visible and now invisible, sometimes with the main door closed, and sometimes open.   He swung the censer from time to time at the altar, the pictures and the people.   He bowed to the very ground, and, if I mistake not, kissed it.   He brought out a Greek missal with great ceremony, into the cover of which five miniature pictures were set, and laid it on the altar.   He exhibited the vessels of communion, covered with gold lace, several times in the service, and apparently took the com-

munion himself at a certain solemn point, when the Greek
portion of the congregation were bending on their knees,
their faces near the ground. The amount of crossing done
by the priest and the people was something incredible, until
seen. Really, the arms of a jumping-jack could hardly be
kept in more active motion by a boy, on first possession of
his toy, than were the arms of the devouter portion of the
worshipers here. Had it not been sacred in their eyes, it
would have been ludicrous in mine.

Near the close of the service, a child of perhaps nine
months was brought forward in the arms of a pretty young
woman, dressed in the most elaborate way—in a sort of
glorification of the peasant dress of Russia—all white and
blue, with a gold embroidered blue satin cap, who almost
eclipsed the priest. After the young woman had been consecrated by some ritual process, the elements of the communion were administered with a spoon to the babe! The
mother, who was present, did not approach the altar. After
this short but very peculiar service, the nurse and child retired. Before the service was fairly through, the audience
relaxed the strict decorum which they had hitherto preserved.
The priest, having himself kissed the cross (of course the
crucifix is not used), extended it to the people, who quite
generally kissed it, and while this was going on, the choir
meanwhile singing, the people exchanged salutations and
chatted, as if the " opus operatum " was now fully perfected.
The congregation, including curious strangers, could not
have been over one hundred, of which perhaps half were
Russians. The two types of national face, Scandinavian
and Tartar — one fair-haired and well-featured, the other
dark-complexioned, with crispish hair and high cheek-bones
—were apparent in the congregation. A dozen Russian
children, in blue blouses and loose trousers tucked into

their boots, or with velvet tunics and white sleeves, gave a charm to the scene. On the whole, after having been now three times to the Greek Church, once in Paris, once in Munich and once in Geneva, I am impressed with its decided inferiority in æsthetic and ritual effect to the Catholic Church. Notwithstanding its married clergy and its opposition to images, its spirit and aspect are more obsolete than Romanism, and it seems to have less place in the world and less power to accommodate itself to circumstances. The coquetry which the English Church, aided by the American Episcopal Church, is practicing with the Greek Church, is an absurd attempt to reconcile things that have no real sympathy. It would be easier to effect a union with the scholars of the Roman Catholic Church than with the traditionists and formalists of the Greek Church, who seem to have nothing modern in spirit or manners. Every national worship is interesting and instructive, and particularly the worship of so vast and rising a people as the Russians. But I never have shared the artificial passion for an alliance between Russia and America, and her religion is an indication of the utter backwardness of the nation, and of the dead weight they furnish to the true progress of civilization and popular enlightenment. There is much to fear for all Europe from their overwhelming numbers and ambition.

Sunday evening we attended the first popular meeting for the promotion of personal religion, held in the " Salle de la Reformation." The hall was full. M. Barde presided and opened the meeting with a prayer of an impassioned and dramatic character, accompanied with violent gesticulations—as if not only the kingdom of heaven but the divine love and compassion were to be taken by storm. I can not get used to the Continental fury in extempore prayer. It seems incredible that persons realizing the divine presence should not be more awed and subdued by it. None of these saintly men would venture upon a tithe of the familiarity and the *abandon* they show to the Supreme Being, in approaching a little German duke or petty sovereign. After some good congregational singing, Rev. Pasteur Monod was introduced and made a touching and attractive application of the " Come unto me all ye who labor and are heavy-laden, and I will give rest unto your souls." " Come unto Jesus" was the key-note of the occasion, followed up by all the speakers. M. Monod touched the Calvinistic theory very clearly but lightly. He was followed by a pastor from Berne who told simple stories, such as we should address to Sunday-school audiences, but with the implication of the whole Calvinistic theory. The rough work of this international " Orthodox " meeting (for France, England and several of the Swiss cantons were represented specially) was given to a Mr. Baxter, an English layman, a man of sixty-five, with a large and fine head, confident carriage, great boldness and naturalness, without sentimentality or cant, of correct utterance, but with a terrible, good-natured, John Bullish narrowness of opinion and dogmatic certainty and definiteness, embracing the whole Calvinistic scheme in its original horrors, unshaded, unmodified, unsoftened, and without any suspicion apparently of any thing not wholly lovely and genial in its features. He poured this dogmatic hot lead, drop by drop, into the ears of the audience, for he had to be translated, sentence by sentence, by an admirable interpreter who did his best to soften the dose, although his faithfulness did not allow any omission of its essential vitriolic ingredients. It was wholly doctrinal, and chiefly an adroit piecing together of texts from all parts of the New Testament showing the utter ruin and condemnation of every human soul, the purchase of their forgiveness by Christ's blood, and their free offer of restoration to God's fa-

vor and eternal life by the acceptance of Christ as their
Saviour.   The horrid literality and hardness of the statement
could not be overstated.   The self-righteousness of the speaker appeared in every look and word, despite his doctrine.
He seemed to say, "Look at me, happy Christian that I am, an
Englishman, an educated and well-born gentleman, traveling
for pleasure, clothed in these nankeen trowsers, this white vest,
this handsome coat—with a capital dinner inside and a half-
bottle of wine to moisten it—look at me, blessed with all this,
and yet sure of eternal blessedness and everlasting life, and
all because I have accepted God's offer in his Son, have got
his bond for it here in my well-thumbed Testament, and am
going to hold him to his word."   "I am a stranger to you,"
he said, "but there are only two characters in this assembly
—saints and sinners—souls bound to Jesus and to heaven,
souls bound to sin and going to hell."   There was no excitement, no glow in the address.   It was cold-blooded, sincere, yet wholly self-mistaken and deceptive.   Had this Baxter had any of the temper of the "Saint's Rest" about him,
he could no more have looked and talked as he did than the
true mother could have seen her child cut in two and not
cried out at Solomon's judgment.   Instead of a comfortable
dinner on Sunday at his hotel, this gentleman would—had his
heart realized what his head was affirming, have been pulling
every door-bell in Geneva, and with tears and entreaties have
begged each and every soul to flee from the impending
wrath.   There was a manifest uneasiness on the platform as
this gentleman rubbed in his cruel lotion.   The blisters started, but they were not those of wholesome irritation.   All judicious friends even of Calvinism must have felt the impolicy
of such literal and offensive plainness.   The audience seemed wearied and worried, but although he looked at his watch
three or four times, it was only to protract the anguish of his

hearers. He had this prepared dose to administer, and he gave it to the last scruple, and sat down with the most cheerful aspect of having performed a most agreeable duty in a most acceptable manner.

A young man from canton Vaud followed him with a tender speech, proving how the same doctrine might be taught with far greater effect, because with genuine sympathy. I confess that it seemed to me as if I had receded into the sixteenth century. I think a few more *séances*, with Mr. Baxter present, would arouse a reaction against Calvinism which would undo ten times over all that the "Salle de la Reformation" has been able to accomplish in the way of honor to Calvin's memory and principles. Why can not Christians, who hope to make the Gospel acceptable to the race in the nineteenth century, see that they must show it to be more credible, rational, humane, just, free from caprice and worthy of infinite love, than any human system of faith and ethics? Surely it is so, or honest and brave men, unselfish and devoted to their great brotherhood, would disown it as a superstition, an antiquated prejudice and an undivine pretension. Thank God, Jesus Christ is not of the mind, never was of the mind of these perverters of his simplicity! Thank God, the real Gospel is broad, free, generous, patient and humane! It is eternal, because it has no corrupting principle of narrowness, nothing capricious, arbitrary, or dependent on mere critical and scholastic science in its composition. Bless God, Calvinism will never succeed in substituting its cast-iron image for the living shape of Jesus of Nazareth, the friend of sinners and the universal bishop of souls!

There are two theological schools in Geneva. The principal one, under the control of what is called "The Faculty of National Theology," has five Professors, all originally pastors of the National Church. Their names are as follows:

Munier, Professor of Hebrew ; Chastel, Professor of Ecclesiastical History (the author of various excellent and celebrated works) ; Oltramare, Professor of Exegesis ; Bouvier,
of Dogmatics ; Cougnard, of Homiletics. Of these, four are
emphatically liberal, that is to say, in sympathy with Unitarian views. Bouvier is Orthodox-liberal, and occupies essentially the position of Pressensé. The students (the term is
four years) are divided into two classes of persons ; first, candidates for the pulpits of the Genevan National Church, of
whom there are only six or seven ; and secondly, students
from France, candidates for the pulpit of the French National Protestant Church, of whom they are usually fifty or sixty.
It will be remembered that the French Protestant Church
has two theological schools at home, one in Strasburg, the
other in Montauban ; but Geneva educates the largest number of her ministers. The cost of a theological education in
Geneva is about 1200 francs ($250 gold) per year. There
is a charity fund, created two centuries ago, which affords
about 600 francs a year to each student needing it. The
professors receive only 1800 francs a year ! Their support
and that of the pastors of the Genevan Church is principally
derived from another fund, which was contributed by French
Protestants soon after Calvin's time. The pastors have a
meagre salary of 3700 francs, less than $800. They can not
live upon it, and are obliged to resort to other means of support. There is a fund for the relief of retired pastors. The
other theological school is of comparatively recent date, and
was mainly inspired by Merle d'Aubigné. There is what is
called a Societé Evangelique in Geneva, which is thirty-
six years old. It is made up mainly of Dissidents from the
National Church, who desire a Calvinistic creed in its original strictness and narrowness. It has a theological school,
of which Messrs. La Harpe, Binder, C. Pronier and Tissot

are professors, and Merle d'Aubigné is president. It has a department of foreign missions ; a department of Biblical work and colportage ; of home missions, with foreign correspondents in Scotland, England, America, Germany, France and Belgium. The Rev. Messrs. I. Proudfit, Dr. Cox, Dr. Sprague, Alex. Proudfit, are among its American correspondents. Its annual expenses are about 150,000 francs ; of this amount Geneva supplied, the last year, over 41,000 francs, Scotland 22,000, England 16,000, America 15,000, Holland 13,000, Ireland about 8000, France 5000, and the residue came from legacies and the Swiss cantons. The number of students was forty-nine, of whom twenty-three were French, thirteen Swiss, and the rest from various countries — one from Italy, one from Spain, one from Russia, two from Ireland ; nineteen, however, are in the preparatory school. There is no open strife between the Dissidents and the National Church, nor between the Liberal and Orthodox party in the National Church. The moral division and open antagonism which exist in the French Protestant Church has not yet occurred in Geneva—but of course this has been mainly due to the vent provided in the existence of a dissenting organization, which has as many churches as the National Church. The most popular preachers in the National Church are Orthodox, Messrs. Coulin and Tourmay. Brett, Oltramare, Richard, Guillermet, Viollier, are reckoned Liberal, and are popular preachers, also. It is evident that Protestantism has hard work to maintain its positive character, and to make itself effective anywhere out of Geneva and Paris. There is much excuse for the alarm which its friends feel, and for their endeavors to harden its shell by reviving the old dogma. But the success is small. On the other hand, Liberal Christianity does not visibly flourish any better ; the tendency is to no Christianity. And this makes even the Liberals cautious and self-distrustful. The ignorance touching our American Unitarianism seems dense ; and it is very important that a positive sympathy should be created by a better mutual acquaintance. The Theological School in Geneva ought to be furnished freely, and at the expense of the American Unitarian Association, with all our theological literature, and with our reviews and newspapers. Rev. Pastor Viollier, No. 3 Rue Tabazan, Geneva, would gladly receive them and see them properly commended to the attention of the professors, pastors and students in theology. I commend the suggestion with the utmost earnestness to the attention of the Board of the American Unitarian Association, and especially to my friend Rev. Charles Lowe, its ever enterprising, judicious Secretary.

The most interesting place in Geneva is the public Library, founded by Calvin, and containing precious mementoes of the Reformers—beautiful MSS. of the tenth century downward ; copies of St. Augustine's sermons, made in the sixth and seventh centuries, on papyrus, in uncial letters ; Greek Liturgies in rolls ; letters of Luther, Calvin, Knox, Melanchthon, Beza, Henry the Fourth's original order for the execution of the Edict of Nantes ; a kind of Encyclopædia of Brunetto, the friend and master of Dante ; and many autographic remains of J. J. Rousseau, with a table once in his use. One very suggestive antiquity was a map of the world, made before the discovery of America — in 1476 — where the great space now occupied by the Western Hemisphere presents not so much a void as an absolute nothingness, as if such a thing as another half of the world were not even missed, or suspected of existence. The library possesses a great number of original and authentic portraits of the Reformers, and the princes who befriended them. Among these Zwingle, with his protruding under-lip ; Melanchthon, looking so much like dear Henry Ware ; Huss, with his nose and forehead straight as a line ; Wickliffe, looking like a Jewish Rabbi. Beza, most modern of all in style of face, specially interested me. All the portraits of Luther are coarse and unsatisfactory, not to say self-disproved. But the immediate jewel of the collection is an authentic portrait of Calvin, which looks as Calvin ought to have looked, and which you feel to be the man himself. It is of a man of fifty, with a round cap (not a skull-cap), but a cap with a flat round top above the band which goes round the head, and with side lappets covering the ears, not untypical of one who listened to few outside voices and had his ears on the inside. His face is refined, but hard as steel ; his sharp nose, in line with long, retreating forehead, looks like a weapon ; his lips are thin and his mouth compressed. He has one hand on the Bible and the other raised, with a finger laying down the law and pointing to its source above at the same time. There is nothing warm in the portrait except the fur that borders the cape and collar of his robe. It is the figure of a scholar, gentleman and leader, polished, elegant, uncompromising, narrow, stern, cold, but with a will which no passion could render more vehement and firm.

There were portraits of Turrettin, Claude the antagonist of Bossuet ; and it is pleasant to see the names of the old pastors who succeeded Calvin's time re-appearing in their children's children, still in the ministry. There is a Turrettin of the present day among the ministers of Geneva, I think. I must not forget an original letter of Sir Isaac Newton's, dated Oct. 22, 1722 (addressed to Prof. Arland, at Geneva, Professor of Mathematics and Painting), a photographic copy of which has just been sent to London, on account of its bearing on the controversy which has lately arisen touching Pascal's alleged claims to the chief honors Newton has so long worn. The canopy under which Calvin and Knox preached so often, is still hanging over the pulpit of St. Peter's, and a chair in which Calvin sat as Professor of Theology is to be seen there. I sat in it, with strange feelings of reverence for the man and aversion for his opinions. But surely he was a great and ever-memorable personality.

The most honored living citizen of Switzerland is doubtless General Dufour. For thirty-two years he labored and brought to perfection, not many years ago, the survey on which he has made the exquisitely beautiful map of Switzerland, doubtless the most perfect natural map in the world. It is a perfect work of art, as well as a great victory of science. The surveys, from the nature of the country, involved enormous difficulties and exposures. One of his assistants was killed by lightning, another fell from a precipice. This map should be in all colleges. It is in twenty-five leaves, and costs about ten dollars here. A similar work would cost twice as much in America. But this is only one of General Dufour's titles to respect. He has been the most honored soldier of his day in the country, and the head of the army; the head also of every benevolent and generous enterprise. He was the shaper, it is said, of the present French Emperor, his tutor and governor. I found him a venerable man of over seventy—genial, highly informed, most kind in his judgments, and tender even of those who had wronged him. He thought great things were to come out of the American war, and congratulated the country on its charity to the soldiers, its firmness in trial and its moderation in victory. Switzerland is poor, and pays her benefactors illy, so far as money goes; but in every chalet and inn, if you see any picture, not religious, it is the picture of General Dufour.

XXV.

GENEVA AND STRASBURG.

SWITZERLAND, October 3, 1867.

GENEVA is a most difficult city of its size to find one's way about in. It is built on so many different levels, and these are approached by so many flights of steps, now covered and now open, going down from out-of-the-way corners, and coming out at the most unexpected places. Many of its streets are as crooked as snakes, and not much wider than anacondas. The new part of the town, however, is on a fine, open scale, and there is abundant room for a great spread. A wide common on the south (a military parade, I suppose) reminds one of Salem Common, and one of the suburbs on the Chambery road gives pleasant souvenirs of Roxbury. Under the high terrace, on which stand the " Maisons de Salon "—the term my coachman used in designating an elevated range of aristocratic-looking houses—is the spot (between the Theatre and the " Musée Roth ") where executions are conducted, and where, within four years, the *guillotine* has been used. Two men, one in 1862, one in 1863, were executed by this process for murder ; another was shot in the Park adjoining, for stealing *watches*—a very mortal offense in Geneva. The wonderful resemblance in customs of Geneva to Paris is carried out by the existence of an island in the Rhone, like the island in the Seine, on which a part of the city is built. The Rhone, more blue and swifter every time one looks at it, supplies water of the purest kind for the city. A hundred women are every day seen there washing the clothes of the people, and such a wash-tub was never yet seen !

It seems impossible to communicate impurity to its swift water. One might as well hope to corrupt Niagara by sponging coats in it. Such views of Mont Blanc as open from the doors of the Hotels de la Paix, Des Bergues and Beau Rivage, are marvelous ! Seen, too, through the opening between the little and big Saleve, the prospect is charming. The environs are superb—sprinkled with country houses and gardens. Coppet and Ferneay are still visited, although the public are not admitted to see Madame de Stael's tomb. The house is occupied by a Baron de Stael and by the Duc de Broglie. At Ferneay may be seen traces of Voltaire, and none less agreeable than the church with its impudent inscription—"*Deo erexit Voltaire.*" The Jura range with its level outline, and the Saleve, in the soft blue of the distance, are ravishing features of the town scenery. The " Athenée " has a few good pictures, and specially one group of statuary (below life-size) in which a Sybil with a Dantesque face is replying to a fair young girl who bends to seek guidance from her experience. The answer written in her face is also inscribed upon a tablet, "*Qui scit comburere aqua et lavare igne, facit de terra cœlum.*" A very heathenish answer to give a young heart aspiring to happiness. It is thus giving up humanity and its terrestrial home which has excused half the sloth and lowness of aim among men, both in religion and philosophy. But Gughemy of Rome, the sculptor (always with a reserve as to the pettiness of the size he has chosen for his work), has done capitally in this design. Diday, the teacher of Calame, is still living and painting. Calame, a great loss, died four years ago. The trees in Geneva all recall his pencil, especially those heavy Norway pines in the Botanic garden. He painted gloomy, rugged nature with absolute exactness. Loppé has two fine pictures, in which the exquisite blue of the glaciers is thoroughly caught in tone. Adolphe Potter (it is pleasant to find that name re-appearing in art) has two rich, original landscapes of bold and masterly coloring, small but of great contents, A. Veil-lon has one landscape. There are a few generous patrons of art in Geneva, but on the whole it is a workshop of ideas and watches, not an atelier of fine arts. The confluence of the Arve and Rhone is a striking scene, taken in connection with the view of Geneva and the Saleve. The Rhone shoul-ders its dark and vulgar neighbor aside with all the pride of the " sang azur." Its blue veins shudder at the contact with the coarse, cloudy blood of the Arve. Yet both rivers flow by different valleys from one range of pure mountain-tops. It was suggestive to see a *black* swan in the Rhone, divided from the white and brown swans by a fence of wire, and pecking at her aristocratic sisters through the web ! Only, with her coral beak and ebony coat, she looked much the more princely.

Being delayed in Geneva a day longer than I intended by the illness of an American gentleman, whose family interested me greatly, I had one more opportunity of seeking out the Liberal ministers of the city, and was so happy as to secure the company of three of them at dinner on the last day of my stay—Messrs. Cougnard, Oltramare and Viollier. We were together from 5 P.M. till 8½, and hours never sped more swift-ly. We had to carry on our conversation wholly in French, but I found out how much the desire to communicate with friends unlocks the lips, even in a foreign tongue. After an hour we all really forgot that we were not talking English, and I had no serious difficulty in saying all I desired, or in understanding every thing they said to me. Prof. Cougnard is a man of the loveliest and most engaging countenance and character.   He reminded me of Ephraim Peabody. Prof. Oltramare is a great favorite with the Genevan public. He is very liberal, but not as radical as Cougnard.   Viollier is a Broad Churchman, who believes that liberty and order in religion may be united, and that the æsthetic need not be sacrificed to the theological element in public worship.   I have rarely enjoyed any interview with kindred spirits more profoundly and gratefully than this.   I confess my excitement was too great to be often risked.• It was so thoroughly delightful to find, in a place wholly strange and under such different circumstances, ministers perfectly congenial and in absolute religious sympathy with our own dear brotherhood. I felt as if I had to pour into their hearts, in one great flood, all the hoarded love and confidence our whole denomination must feel for such noble and liberal souls, and to receive back a tide of sympathy which belonged to my brethren, but which I had to hold all alone within the flood-gates of my heart.   It was a memorable season ! We parted as dear friends, and with mutual vows of fidelity and co-operation.   I trust that none of our ministers will visit Geneva without an effort to see our clerical brethren.   It will be a lasting shame if we do not keep up the communication, which may be considered as now re-opened after being closed for many years. Thirty years ago there was much talk of our Liberal brethren at Geneva.   There is much more reason to rejoice in their prospects now, and to cultivate their acquaintance.

The Religious Tract Society of London has published a very charming little volume—" Footsteps of the Reformers in Foreign Lands "—which contains a passage on the 110-116 pages, which we feel misrepresents (under the influence of religious prejudice) the history of opinion in Geneva. After stating the general truth that Geneva was the Thermopylæ of the Reformation, it says : " Before the end of the eighteenth century her pastors and professors had nearly abandoned the doctrines of the Godhead and atonement of our Lord Jesus Christ, and were Arians and Socinians. Her Sabbaths were profaned and trampled under foot. On God's holy day the theatres were opened." "The names of Voltaire and Rousseau were held in higher honor than those of Farel and Calvin." This terrible state of things was interrupted in 1817 by the interposition of a Scottish layman, Mr. Robert Haldane, whose heart was greatly stirred by the defalcation from faith and the immorality he saw about him. He sought out some of the students of the Theological Seminary, and in spite of the frowns and threats of the Professors, soon engaged nearly all of them as docile hearers of a course of conversational prelections on the Epistle to the Romans, which ended in the conversion of not a few of them to Christ. Of these Rieu, Pyt, Gouthier and Adolph Monod—all departed—were notable instances, and Merle d'Aubigné, Galland, Guers, James and others still remain to testify to the thoroughness of Mr. Haldane's evangelical influence. Cæsar Malan and Gaussen were even then pastors, and had not strayed from Orthodoxy, but were greatly quickened by Haldane. Merle d'Aubigné has stated somewhere (according to this book) that when in the Seminary he presided at a meeting of the theological students of Geneva, assembled in the " Grand Hall " to consider and condemn a pamphlet which vindicated the doctrine of the Divinity of Jesus Christ. But afterward meeting Mr. Haldane at a private house, he heard for the first time, in his comments on a chapter of the Romans, of the natural corruption of man, which he took to heart and which became the means of his conversion to Calvinistic Christianity.

The mixing up in this account of the laxities in morals and faith which followed the French Revolution with the Ari-

an or Socinian theology, is one of those blundering assumptions which bigotry and uncharitableness are so often guilty
of. Is it Socinianism or Arianism which keeps the theatre
open in Geneva on the Sundays of this very year, 1867?
And why did not the doctrines of Calvin and Farel—never
preached with more faithfulness than in Geneva—so recommend themselves to that people, once so wholly under their
power, as to make it impossible for infidelity and immorality
to take possession of the chosen seat of the evangelical theology? If the question of social order, good morals and
public propriety is to be discussed as affected by Orthodoxy
and Unitarianism, we humbly desire to be fully heard before
sentence is given. It is our deep conviction that, whatever
may be the influence of our Unitarian faith on the future
fate of men—concerning which we have no misgivings—its
favorableness to veracity, justice, benevolence, freedom, de·
corum, is too generally recognized, even by its enemies, to
make it becoming or safe to associate with Unitarian theology either laxity of personal morals or carelessness of public
purity and order. Any defalcation which Geneva at any
period of her history may have made from her ancient asceticism of manners, must be ascribed to the fanaticism of her
Calvinistic teachers, bringing on the reaction by which alone
a humane and a wise moderation in manners is restored to
a long-repressed and perverted humanity. A much more
specific reply might be made to the weak accusations of this
injurious comment on Liberal Christianity in Geneva—but it
should come from Geneva itself.

●

BASLE.

October 4.

Basle is one of the most active cities in Switzerland, and
has a large amount of banking capital. Its chief manufact-

ures are ribbons. Looking across from the " Trois Rois,"
which fronts directly on the Rhine, we can see not only the
steam of these factories, but the bright dyes of its vats, which
color the threads it weaves into such silken rainbows, stain-
ing with their purples and yellow the blue river which receives their waste. The streets are narrow and winding,
and present a great appearance of antiquity. The old Catholic churches, excepting the cathedral, have fallen into secular uses and decay. The impressive and very ancient cathedral is in excellent repair externally, and preserves the old
cloisters in a state of remarkable beauty and interest. It
has within a very few years received internally a costly renovation, which gives it the appearance of an almost perfect
newness in painful contrast with its venerable exterior. It has,
however, been more successfully converted to Protestant use
than any cathedral I have yet seen on the Continent. It is
honorable to the Protestants of Basle that they make such zeal-
ous efforts to maintain the religion they received from their
fathers. It is not in vain that Erasmus's ashes rest in this
church. They still send their fragrance through the old city
he adopted as his home. A very costly Protestant church—
stone inside and out—with a parsonage and a parish school-
house, built by one man—a deceased citizen of Basle—at a
cost of a million dollars, is an indication of the zeal which
animates the leading citizens of this place. Doubtless it would
be a better augury if the church had been built by a congregation uniting the voluntary subscriptions of many self-sacri-
ficing hearts. Basle is evangelical in its Protestantism. It
inherits a certain narrowness from the early guides of the Reformed faith, who took under severe surveillance the domestic manners, the dress and the diet of the people. Something of the same jealousy of personal liberty prevails here
still. The Museum is the custodian of many excellent works

of Hans Holbein—the younger and more celebrated of the two—the father and son. His genius was remarkable, even at fourteen, and is testified to by two pictures, of bold and original drawing and coloring, still to be seen here. In his admirable drawings and paintings a genius of the most marked individuality is discovered, the most definite conceptions worked out with masterly precision and in a spirit full of intelligence, feeling and power. His reverence for truth was greater than his idealism, and he had no phantoms of beauty and delight in his brain. A grim humor and a cruel faithfulness are seen in his works. His Madonna at Dresden is the only evidence that beauty had ever impressed him. His figure of the dead Christ, laid out like a corpse straightened for burial, is one of the most terribly real of all pictures of death I have ever seen ; but while it avoids the sentimentality that weakens almost all other pictures of Christ, dead or alive, it leaves out the sacred beauty without which a dead Christ is only a well-painted corpse.

There is here a beautiful modern picture of Diday, the master of Calame—a view of Lake Brienz—which justifies his high reputation. He still lives to lament his more distinguished pupil, Calame, who died four years ago. One of his best pictures, " The Wetter-horn," hangs in the same gallery at Basle.

I went out to see the government " Fish-hatching " institution, about five miles out of Basle, on the route to Paris and on French territory. Here for ten years or more the French government have maintained a very careful, scientific and well-administered establishment, at a cost of $10,000 a year, for the artificial propagation of the more valuable kinds of fresh-water fish. Their object is to create a large amount of fish eggs, of trout, salmon, perch, etc., and to distribute them gratuitously to those who will engage to plant them in streams, lakes, ponds, not only in France but in her colonies, in order that the product of fish may be greatly increased. The arrangements for the artificial propagation of these eggs is a very delicate and skillful operation. It consists in procuring the spawn of the fish, and passing it down in running streams over pans which are floored with small glass tubes, each about the size of a knitting-needle. The spawn, in passing, catches where it will upon these glass tubes, and fastening there, is ripened into well-developed eggs, in about two months, in streams of water at a moderate temperature. This is all under cover. Although the end of the establishment is not to *raise* fish, but only eggs, yet a certain amount of fish is raised, probably for the sake of their spawn. We were shown trout at all stages of growth, from a few months to five years old. The several classes were separated by wire sieves from each other. The least neglect as to the purity of the water or its active motion was always fatal to many of the fish. The trout we saw were admirably grown. They are said to be as well-flavored as those which grow naturally, but are not so hardy. It is very important that all the art of Pisciculture should be understood in America. A son of the geologist Buckland has written a little book on the subject, which persons interested in restoring the fish to the New England rivers should procure.

STRASBURG.

October 6.

Strasburg, a German-French town, was, from the days of the Reformation, a wholly Protestant city, until Louis XIV. forced a Catholic population upon it, which has increased in our days, under imperial influences, until probably nearly two-thirds of the people are Catholic. Only one Catholic family remained here after the Reformation. Now the richest and poorest part of the population are Roman Catholic. The bourgeois, containing the best intelligence and worth of the public, is actively Protestant, and maintains its religious life with such zeal as an Establishment permits. The Protestant Church in Switzerland and in France, as in many other parts of Europe, is cursed with State support and State regulation. If every vestige of this fatal protection and guidance were swept away, and all the existing Churches were to perish, Protestantism would revive in Europe with something of the earnestness it now possesses in America. The national support is only a clog and a chill on Protestantism. The people, released from their obligations to maintain religion of their own free wills, and at their own cost, are without proper emulation or spirit. They compose their differences of opinion under false and mischievous truces and compromises, or are like people of wholly dissimilar tastes united by forced marriages, who keep up before company an appearance of union, and are secretly the scourges of each other's peace.

One of the two theological schools of the French Protestant Church is established here, on an old foundation. It is a part of the old " Academie de Strasburg," and is styled " Faculté de Theologie de la Confession d'Augsburg." Its present Professors are MM. Jean Frederic Bruch, Dean of the Faculty; Edouard Reuss, Professor of Old Testament Literature and Criticism; Charles Schmidt, Professor of Ecclesiastical History; Tomothee Colani, Professor of Practical Theology and the Art of Preaching; Frederic Lichtenberger, Professor of Biblical Ethics. Of these, Bruch, Reuss and Colani are thoroughly liberal men in their theology, and in full sympathy with the liberal professors at Geneva. The others are perhaps mildly " Orthodox." Colani, of whom American Liberal Christian scholars have heard most, is probably the most radical in his opinions. He is a man of extraordinary spirituality, of most various and versatile attainments, and capable of giving lectures—as he does—both in philosophy and theology. He is also an excellent mathematician. About forty-five years of age, he was for many years most attractive as a preacher, and, in spite of his advanced opinions, attracted even "Orthodox" hearers by the charm and spirituality of his preaching. It is to be extremely regretted that when appointed Professor, about three years ago, he gave up preaching, and has since devoted himself exclusively to his lectures to the students. He is a sufferer from some constitutional lameness, and is now, vastly to my regret, at Ragatz, Switzerland, passing his vacation, so that I shall fail to see him, having come to Strasburg mainly for that purpose. Prof. Reuss is most highly respected for his learning and liberality, and is the warm personal friend of M. Cougnard of Geneva; but he too is absent. The Dean of the Faculty, Prof. Bruch, I have had the pleasure of two long interviews with, and he has entered with lively sympathy into the desire I felt to establish cordial and intelligent relations between our American Liberal theologians and our Continental congeners. He is now an oldish man—reminding me not a little of Dr. Lamson at sixty—a truly accomplished, enlightened and comprehensive mind, in perfect sympathy with the best school of American Unitarianism. He said great pains were taken abroad to represent our Unitarianism in the United States as not only having seen its best days, but as fast dying out. I told him it was a device of the enemy, and that really we were never so strong or so truly national in our prospects as just now, at which he expressed unbounded satisfaction. There are about forty-five theological students here, and about thirty in the preparatory school, seventy-five in all. The buildings in which the students live are excellent, and the lecture-rooms attractive. It is regretted, however, that the small support given to the ministers repels young men of good birth and breeding from the profession ; that the unsettled state of theological opinion in the world alienates still more, and that the strifes in the National Protestant Church keep away another portion. Notwithstanding, therefore, that theological students are exempt from military conscription, and that a considerable fund exists for their support, the numbers who come are far below the wants of the Church. The preliminary examinations are severe, and would exclude nine-tenths of all our candidates.

It may be interesting to name the chief seats of theological learning in Europe at this time, with the more distinguished professors who attract students to them, for the benefit of young men coming abroad or clergymen traveling in Europe and desiring to make the acquaintance of theologians. Of course my list will be imperfect, but correct as far as it goes, and may convey some useful information at home.

1. Berlin, where Hengstenberg, an unqualifiedly Orthodox, and Dorner, a broad and generous theologian of the same type, are the great ornaments and attractions.

2. Erlangen in Bavaria is now, after Berlin, perhaps the most frequented of theological schools. It is intensely " Orthodox," and Prof. Hoffman is its leading spirit.

3. Halle, where Tholuck and Julius Müller—mild and enlightened men of a Broad Church spirit—are the world-known Professors.

4. Göttingen, with Ewald and Ehrenfrickter.

5. Heidelberg, with Schenkel and Hitzig. Rothe died two months ago, a great loss.

6. Jena, with Hase, Grimm and Schwartz.

7. Tübingen, where Baur, at sixty-eight years of age, died two years ago, leaving no successor. His learning is con-.

ceded to have been immense, and his candor and sincerity
equal to his attainments. Out of his study he had the simplicity of a child. His influence was vast, and continues, although nobody has arisen to take his place, and a very Orthodox professor now rules at Tübingen.

8. Leyden, where Scaolten has a great and deserved reputation as a Liberal theologian.

9. Copenhagen. Profs. Sharling and Claussen are leaders in Liberal theological studies.

10. In Holland, there are numerous and ever-increasing
friends of the Liberal theology. Reville, at Rotterdam, as a
preacher and writer carries a great weight. He belongs to
the French Protestant Church in its Liberal wing, theologic-
ally. The Memnonites are said to be in sympathy with Unitarian opinions.

It is very evident that the present direction of serious
theological studies abroad is thoroughly Liberal, and favorable to that theology which is dear to us. English influence,
so far as it goes, is adverse, except in the half-heretical and
wholly noble defection of scholarly English thinkers and di-
vines whom Maurice, Stanley, Jowett, Williams lead forward.
I am much impressed with the narrowness of all English
churchmen I meet on the Continent. Their seemingly willful
blindness to modern illumination in theology, is dreadful.
One does not wonder to see Archdeacon Denison, as reported in the London *Times* of September (and he does not
lack a most sprightly wit), maintaining that the positive dem-
onstrations of science must yield to the assertions of the inspired writers; as though, if the Bible should say the earth
was flat, good Christians would not believe it to be round !
What greater folly of statement could be indulged in, or what
sort of credulity could be more fatal to any final faith in the
sacred writings ? Let me mention here the names of the two

French theological reviews most likely to interest our ministers who are properly curious about the opinions and doings of their Continental brethren. *Le Disciple de Jesus Christ*, a Liberal Christian Review, published under the editoral care of J. Martin Paschoud, who is assisted by all the writers to whom the recently remarkable progress of Liberal Christianity is due in France—such as Michel Nicholas, Albert Reville, Ernest Fontanes, Felix Pecaut, Charles Verhuel, Jules Steeg, Leblois, Goy, Theophile Bost, E. Paris, Colani, Coquerel fils, Grotz, Albarie, Veges, Gaufrès, Dide, Cruvellié, Pelissier, Fermaud, and others. It is published the 1st and 15th of each month, in numbers of three or four octavo sheets, and forms annually two thick volumes of 600 pages. Price of subscription twelve francs a year. Paris : Germer Bailliere. New York : Bailliere Brothers, 410 Broadway. The other is the *Revue de Theologie*, a quarterly, published at Strasburg under the editorship of Colani, which appears to be supported mainly by the same writers, but contains somewhat more elaborate articles. It costs eight francs, and may be had of Cherbuliez, 33 Rue de Seine, Paris, or Williams & Norgate, Henrietta Street, Covent Garden, London.

Strasburg is a walled and fortified town, full of soldiers at all times, and specially so now when the neighborhood of the Prussian frontier and the present stir in German politics make French vigilance and preparation for defense or offense peculiarly active. We rode through an immense stronghold of fortifications within fortifications, with the modern theory of the superiority of earth-works over stone walls in evident application. Thousands of men are employed in giving impregnability to this important post, within a mile of the Rhine, from which would probably be launched the bolt of war, should Napoleon ever think to realize the French hankering to regain their Rhenish provinces. Vast quantities of munitions of war are heaped up in the yards of the huge arsenals just out of Strasburg. The soldiers evidently think that their hour is approaching. Strasburg is too commercial not to dread a struggle, which, turn as it would, could not fail to damage all her existing interests.

The cathedral, so famous in all the earth, is the great architectural feature of Strasburg. Its spire is the highest in the world—four hundred and sixty-eight feet! I remember very well clambering up into the lantern twenty years ago ; and yet, when a kindly cicerone asked me yesterday if I would not ascend, I indignantly asked him if he took me for a fool. I was trying (I found on reflection) to cover up under the name of wisdom the decay of my enterprise and the weakening of my tendons! The façade is a curious basket of stone, through whose lattice-work the grim under-walls appear. Of the two towers, only one is finished. It is impossible to realize either the size or height of this building from any point nearer than a mile off. From the farthest fortress wall we got our first true idea of the relative vastness of this enormous mass, by seeing how all the largest buildings in the city and almost the town itself were dwarfed in its shadow. The proportions are said not to be very good. The interior is superb in its majestic pillars, lofty nave, vast space and exquisite windows. Nowhere have we seen more beautiful glass, and it occupies every window of the church. Just as we entered, a choir of nuns' voices burst out in a hymn of praise and made the vast aisles echo with harmony. This cathedral was once in Protestant hands, and it was respected and even renovated by its somewhat unnatural heirs.

But one can hardly regret that it has reverted to its original owners. Protestants have no use for cathedrals. They are not fit to preach in—and they require a spectacular worship such as we can not use. I must confess, however, that

I heard the end of a very bold and earnest sermon from a Catholic priest in this very cathedral, and was glad to see a thousand people listening to it. It was a melancholy change, the afternoon of the same Sunday, to attend Protestant worship in St. Thomas's Church (a fine old place, better known · for Marshal Saxe's monument than for any thing else), and to hear a sermon in German from Professor Baum, on the old Union of Protestants, their unhappy divisions, the appearance and prospects of a better understanding among them, the uprise of Protestantism in Italy, where Sunday-schools have already gathered in six thousand children, and the encouragements to work with fresh zeal and courage. The sorrow was to hear this excellent sermon delivered in this great church to a hundred hearers, of whom nine-tenths were women! The prospects of Protestantism will not be very brilliant while such indifference exists among its own children. There is evidently a lively competition between Romanism and Protestantism here and everywhere else in France. But it is carried on very differently by the two parties to it. The Protestants use the press, fill the air with *brochures*, and array science, philosophy and criticism against the old enemy. The Catholics fill their churches, meet the religious wants of the common people, ply more actively all their safe methods, point to the lukewarmness and external impiety of the Protestants, and hold by these means the bulk of the common people with them. It was not surprising to me to see a pamphlet in a Catholic book-store to-day—" Protestantism—Is it a Religion?" Certainly it must learn some new ways before it will become the religion of the people of France, Italy, or even Germany.

I passed my last evening in Strasburg at Prof. Bruch's hospitable fireside, and in the midst of a charming family circle. The unusual coldness of the weather makes fires already necessary. Snow covered considerable portions of the Jura a week ago, and between Salzburg and Munich snow lay quite deep on the railroad track the 1st of October, a very unusual promptness in the advance of winter. There are very poor preparations against cold in the hotels. Stoves (usually of porcelain) abound, but one misses the open fire and a chance to toast the feet. The German feather-bed cover begins to vindicate its value in our eyes, as we enter the stone-floored and often immense rooms of the Continent. I slept last night in a room thirty feet square, larger than a good drawing-room. It makes one shiver to enter such apartments after a day's journey in cars that are never heated.

XXVI.

HEIDELBERG.

DUCHY OF BADEN, October 9, 1867.

EVERY body goes to Heidelberg! Its famous castle is perhaps the most picturesque ruin in the world. Just high enough to command the landscape, and just low enough to form a part of it ; enough in ruins to gratify the passion for age and decay, and enough preserved to leave the full impression of its ancient magnificence—itself a lovely mass of reddish sandstone, framed in the greenest and most luxuriant foliage—there is nothing wanting to give dignity and charm to this best known of all ruins. There is an extraordinary massiveness and an extraordinary delicacy in the architecture of the castle, and enough remains to exhibit both nearly in perfection. Food for a whole summer's dreaming is stored away in its winding walks or its subterranean passages. Its various terraces are places where one might linger away a hundred twilights without monotony. The vast champaign of the Rhine, level as a prairie, stretches away twenty miles in every direction, so that the opposite hills are rarely seen in clear outline ; the Neckar, just unsheathed from its lovely scabbard of vine-embossed hills, strikes its glittering blade out into the plain ; Mannheim, Spires, and other numerous towns stud the wide field with their towers ; trains of cars mark their swift ways with smoke that curls and melts like a frosty breath. The dull old town, crowded in between the river and the mountains, contracts its streets and pares away its sidewalks and stretches out its length to meet its narrow circumstances. Its grim old church, with its nave divided by a stone wall, shelters on the choir end the Catholics, on the opposite end the Protestants. Like other cities in these little German States, whose people have changed their religion as their rulers have chanced to be Catholic or Protestant, Heidelberg has had three or four revolutions in its ecclesiastical history, to say nothing of the sieges, bombardments, conflagrations and political upsets it has suffered. That wretched Louis XIV. has made all this part of the country hate his memory. His generals were monsters of cruelty, and made nothing of ordering all the inhabitants out of a city at twenty-four hours' notice, and then burning the whole town to the ground.

Heidelberg has about eighteen thousand inhabitants, of whom two-thirds are Protestant. The Protestants form one parish, with three churches and five ministers. Their religious affairs are directed by a committee of citizens, about seventy in number, who are the ultimate appeal of a smaller committee of about twenty, who have immediate charge of the interests of religious education and religious worship. They nominate pastors to any vacancy. The ministers are said to be all liberal in their theology—as the people are. By liberal we must not understand Unitarian, for they do not own and hardly know the name in Germany. But they have essentially the *thing*. The Lutheran Church in Germany is orthodox, as a rule, in the American sense of that word. The Reformed, as they call themselves, are not orthodox. But they do not make a dogmatic confession. They are not Trinitarians any more than we are, but they do not call themselves Unitarians, and they try to propitiate the intolerance of the Lutherans by devoting themselves to practical preaching and dogmatic silence. Some of the liberal teachers avoid a schism or scandal by mysticism and obscurantism. Those teachers of theology who are not connected with pastoral charges and are not members of consistories are of course more free in their utterances and of course correspondingly clear in their thoughts—for what one must not say one tries not to think.

Heidelberg may now be said to be the head-quarters of the Liberal Christian theology in Germany. Not only are her pastors liberal men, and her population, too, but her University is thoroughly liberal. Her theological faculty, in its *ordinary* (that is, full and permanent professorships) consists, or did consist until a few weeks ago, of Rothe, Hitzig, Schenkel and Holtzman, of whom Holtzman alone was "Orthodox," and he has just left and gone to Bonn. One of the professors told me that with him departed from Heidelberg the last of the Orthodox school! I inquired if there were left no Orthodox laymen among the professors. He knew of not one.

Richard Rothe, born in Posen, Jan. 28th, 1799, was educated partly at Breslau, then from 1817–19 was at Heidelberg, and finally concluded his University studies at Berlin. He made the acquaintance of Bunsen when at Rome, and formed a warm friendship with him. For a short time he was Professor in the Theological Seminary at Wittenberg. Afterward he was at Bonn, and finally at Heidelberg, where he finished his laborious and honored life, August 19, 1867, only two months ago. His works are too numerous to mention here, and are well known to theological scholars in most countries, especially his great work on Christian Ethics. I was greatly grieved to find Rothe dead, for I had counted specially on making his personal acquaintance, having become greatly interested in the man and his thoughts, chiefly through the interpretation of my friend and colleague, Dr.

Osgood, for many years a student and lover of Rothe. All I could do was to collect such an idea of the man—his mental, moral and spiritual quality—as conversation with his old colleagues and friends could yield.

It was plain enough that Rothe was no ordinary man from the profound sorrow his death had left in Heidelberg, where personalities are not too much recognized in the supreme interest accorded to ideas and facts. But from all quarters Rothe's loss was met with grief and profound recognition. He was by universal concession a man of immense learning, research and diligence—greatly distinguished for the spirituality of his temper, his moral purity and the heavenly gentleness of his disposition. He not only had no enemy, but he had not even an opponent. Broad and liberal in his spirit, he was yet constitutionally disqualified from being a leader in theological reform by his anxious desire to promote harmony and maintain peace. His colleagues, who knew the absolute freedom of his own mind and his genuine sympathy with their more aggressive Liberalism, say that his gentleness and his spirituality exhaled in a kind of mystic vapor which took the edge off his thoughts, and perhaps hid their form even from himself. His somewhat vague and mystic theology was favored by the practical seclusion of his own private life. His wife for many years was reduced to childishness by an illness which ended only with her life twenty years later. During this long period Rothe devoted all his leisure to watching over his sick wife, whom he soothed with little stories, as he would have amused an infant. He wholly gave up general society, and this increased somewhat a certain eccentricity of mind, although it developed a most lovely disinterestedness. Rothe, by his character and general talents, commanded universal love and reverence. His ethical work, the chief labor of his life, will hold a permanent place in

Christian philosophy, and his death leaves a void in the theological faculty it will be difficult to fill.

Hitzig is the Hebrew Professor, a profoundly learned and most liberal-minded theologian, whose influence may be compared here to that of our own Dr. Noyes at Cambridge.

Dr. Schenkel, left by Rothe's death essentially the head of the theological faculty at Heidelberg, is a man of about fifty. His hair is still unturned. In appearance he is not unlike Dr. Chapin (though not so stout in figure), and has a good deal of his fervor of speech, and much of his pulpit reputation. But he is above all a scholar, and has written twenty volumes, of which, after his "Character of Jesus," the most important is a work on Christian dogmatics. Dr. Schenkel is of Swiss origin (from Schaffhausen), but a thorough German in blood and nature. He is recognized as a man of much sharper intellect and much clearer expression than Rothe, and of a totally different sense of duty in regard to the advancement of theology. He is out and out a Reformer, and inherits the temper and courage of the early German and Swiss breed, who were never disposed to conceal their teeth behind too close or too soft lips. Schenkel knows, by his profound and universal learning and by his quick sympathy with the nineteenth century, just to what form Christian faith has come ; he knows that it will not do to leave the people to their natural tendencies—which are either to fling Christianity aside, as an outworn garment, or to buckle the rags of the old theology with a stouter strap round their chilled limbs and declare it a sufficient cloak. He knows that the cry which Hengstenberg (whom he respects as a brave and straightforward man) and his school are maintaining, that Christianity is to be weighed in different scales from all other kinds of truth, is a cry which in the end buries beyond memory the very Gospel it temporarily hides from rude investigation. He knows, too, that the rationalism of Baur and the destructive school of mere critics in Germany does no justice to the testimony, which the unwritten tradition of the living Church hands down, of a solemn verity in the Gospel, and he is working to reform without destroying or disturbing the continuity of the Christian consciousness in the Church.

We are sometimes wont to deplore—in our efforts at a sublime candor—the definite and somewhat antagonistic outline which our American Christian Liberalism took on when it assumed the shape and name of Unitarianism. But nobody who observes in Germany how those who left Orthodoxy were, for the want of any existing theology organized into a definite Church like our own, obliged to step off into vacancy or to float like feathers blown by a high breeze off a bird's back down the wind, can doubt the good providence which gave us a positive even if it were a circumscribed position—a fortress if not a country. A few of the nobler minds in Germany are doing just now what we did half a century ago. They see and feel that the prosperity of theological reform can not be separated from a Church life—that Christianity is an act as well as a thought, a life as well as a theory, a Church as well as a creed, and that the cultus and the dogma must be kept together. Schenkel is, I suspect, the leader in this movement. I could not quite find out how far he was the prime mover of the union recently formed in Germany of pastors and theologians, which extends now to several thousand members, whose professed object is to encourage Christian worship and increase the co-operation of the laity with the pastors; to build up churches upon a practical Christian foundation, leaving each and every member to an absolute dogmatic freedom. It is chiefly Reformed pastors (not Lutheran) who are in this union; but there

O

are Orthodox members.   Mainly, however, it is composed of Liberals who know and own their sympathies, and Liberals who, not knowing their own tendencies, suppose themselves to be " Orthodox."

Schenkel has not escaped persecution in Germany from Lutheran ecclesiastical bodies.   Only three years ago, after the appearance of his " Character of Jesus," a protest, signed by several thousand Lutheran ministers, called for his removal from his position in the Heidelberg Faculty of Theology. The Grand Duke of Baden, who seems a liberal and sensible man, replied that scientific theology had its rights ; that scholars studied theology to advance the science, and if they published books which were not sound, objectors had it for their duty to answer their arguments, not to silence their writers.   Schenkel answered this persecution by an able volume.   He is of a calm, strong spirit, brave and self-sustained. He understands himself and his duty.   In wide correspondence with the advanced minds in Europe, he is a kind of centre of our Liberal Christian movement on the Continent. He knew Channing's and Parker's writings well, and theirs only.   Parker he had personally seen.   He had never heard of James Martineau, although he knew of the English " Essays and Reviews."   On the whole, English theology had not interested him.   It was a derivation from the German, not an original shoot.   He looked with much livelier sympathy upon the American Liberal Church.   It was so practical and so loving.   There is no manner of justice done to our American thinking or scholarship among savans in Europe.   I have seen no men abroad whose total manhood made me feel the inferiority of our first-class Americans.   What we lack in scholarship, we make up in a wide scope of actual life.   Our men are really more cosmopolitan in mind than any I have met, and with all Schenkel's charm, his learning

and his eloquence, his purity and nobleness, I did not feel
that he was greater than several of our own ministers. At
my first interview we talked two hours on the prospects of
Liberal Christianity in Germany. Our talk was in French,
and hampered by imperfect facility of speech on both sides.
We had an hour or two of conversation on the evening of
the next day, at the house of a mutual friend, Professor
Winslow, an American, to whose courtesy I was greatly in-
debted for the opportunity of seeing just those Professors
whose reputation attracted my curiosity and admiration.
Schenkel gave me a half-dozen letters to theological friends in
Europe, and we parted cordial friends, equally solicitous to
keep up future correspondence and to aid in bringing Liberal
Christians on both sides the ocean into practical communion.
Schenkel is now engaged on a Bible Dictionary, as editor,
with a large force of helpers. It will be a very important
work for our cause. He had never seen Dr. Furness's trans-
lation of his work, which has been translated into several
languages. He received from the A. U. A. our monthly
journal. It is delightful to come unexpectedly upon traces
of Lowe's missionary zeal in distant parts of Europe! I
hope my colleague, Mr. Allen, will see to it that the *Christian
Examiner* reaches some of these men, whose acquaintance
with our work is so important to the general cause.

I called upon Professor Bunsen, the Professor of Practical
Chemistry here, and found in his plain and noble face and
simple manners the model of a genuine, modest, yet assured
man of science. He has usually about seventy pupils at his
lectures, and thirty in his laboratory, and his work is laborious. He had recovered from a somewhat alarming illness
by spending his vacation at Ragatz, Switzerland. Professor
Kirchhoff, Professor of Physics, and his companion in the
famous researches into the constitution of the sun, is a deli-

cate-looking scholar, who parts his hair in the middle. His acumen is at least equal to Bunsen's. He is now lame and a sufferer from overwork. I find that the old tradition about German scholars setting at naught the laws of health with impunity is a fable. They are not a bit more enduring than we are, and perhaps work no harder. Professor Helmholtz, of the Medical Faculty, impressed me as a man combining in an extraordinary way physical and metaphysical insight and knowledge. We talked of the tendencies of modern thought and modern science. He exhibited a seriousness and dignity as well as comprehensiveness in his views, too seldom observed among physicists. His person was unusually grand and commanding, not from size, but carriage and expression. Professor Zeller, of the Philosophical Faculty, is the son-in-law of Baur, of Tübingen, and a disciple of his great relative. He was educated to theology, but driven out partly by persecution and partly by philosophical preferences. He has a most ethereal delicacy of face, a keen, sharp outline in all his phrases, and a purity and dignity which none dispute. He is the author of a standard work on Greek philosophy. I found him much interested in the account of Liberal Christianity in America. Professor Otto, of the Modern Language department (his German grammar is the best), a most clever and enlightened man, and a warm and truly Liberal Christian, tells me that out of the hundreds of students here, there are not five a year disposed to study French or English. These languages are taught in the public schools, and are considered unworthy to employ the time and energies of adults. Want of acquaintance with English is, in my judgment, one of the radical defects in the training of German savans. They don't know enough of the language to derive the correction from its literature which the more practical understanding of the English would afford their too speculative intellect.

The University in Heidelberg, founded in 1316, and one of the oldest in Europe, has about a hundred Professors, ordinary and extraordinary, and about eight hundred students. Its Professors are divided into the four great Faculties of Theology, Law, Medicine and Philosophy. Each of the great universities has its special eminence, and law is the specialty of Heidelberg. Mittelmeyer, who died a few months ago at eighty years of age, had been for many years the great ornament and attraction of the Law Faculty. He was very great in criminal law. But Vangerow, the greatest Pandectist in Europe, remains, and of late years has had a larger class of students at his lectures than any other Professor in any branch. Three hundred out of the eight hundred students are followers of his courses. Hausser, a most distinguished History Professor, and one of the greatest ornaments of Heidelberg, has lately died, and also a young Professor Weber, of the Medical Faculty, so that the university has suffered the bereavement of four of its chief pillars within a year. It is not the practice of German students, except the poorer class who are on charity foundations, to remain at one university through the whole period of their studies. They usually divide the time among two or three—going to each university for what it is thought to have best; to one for law, another philosophy, another theology, and so on. The regular ordinary Professors are supported by the government, and have salaries of from 2000 guldens to 3500 (a gulden is worth forty cents), according to their distinction. There is a rivalry in the universities to procure the more famous men, and they buy them by outbidding each other. They receive besides oftentimes their rent and such fees as students may pay them, perhaps twelve guldens for each half-year from each student who follows them. In case of a popular subject and a popular lecturer these fees become very considerable. The students are under very little discipline. There is a University Court which tries them for offenses against order, and imprisons them for days or weeks, according to their offense. They leave the college prison to attend lectures, but at other times are confined to it until their sentence is out. As to their studies, they are under no compulsion, except the necessity of submitting to a severe examination before they can receive their degree, or obtain employment in their profession. These examinations are not conducted by their teachers, but by government commissions, and are genuine tests of scholarship. With this admirable check, the freedom allowed the students is not dangerous. With the exception of a class of rich young men from noble families, the students are faithful to their opportunities. The dissipation, duelling and beer drinking, excessive and disgusting, are confined to about one hundred and fifty out of the eight hundred, young men of fortune who have too much money and too little concern about their future. They form themselves into clubs, distinguished by badges and caps, and cultivate duelling and beer drinking in a beastly way. It is no extravagance to say that a dozen duels a week occur in termtime. They are not mortal combats, for the vital parts of the body are protected. They fight with blunt swords, sharpened at the edges, and fitted to scar but not to stab. Their aim is to mark and slash the cheek, and many of them wear about as ornaments these disfiguring cuts. The clubs have also stringent drinking rules. The lowest qualification for entrance is ability to drink thirteen glasses of beer at a sitting. One of the more aristocratic exacts thirty-four glasses; a feat which is not to be performed without artificial emptying of the stomach in the course of the session. These vulgar details are necessary to stamp the proper character upon these semi-barbarous excesses. There is a slow tendency to decline in these time-honored follies. The knowledge of them ought not to deter young men of sober purposes from seeking Heidelberg, where excellent companionship and serious aims prevail among the vast majority of the students. Living is cheap here. One American gentleman, who has his family with him here, told me that it hardly cost him more to live, rent and clothes included, than his grocers' bills had been in Boston. Still, apart from the university life, there is little or nothing besides, and families not intent on education find it dull—as all foreign life is, compared with our own.

We made an excursion to Spires, for the sake of the memory of its ancient Diet, which stopped private wars in Germany and advanced civilization so much, and because of the glorious *Protest* here made by the princes and doctors in 1529 against the Imperial ordinance forbidding the rights of conscience to the early Reformers, from which Protestantism derives its baptismal and honored name. The old cathedral here, restored with pious care and Catholic zeal, is perhaps the noblest specimen in Europe of the Romanesque style. Its domes and towers are glorious to behold, and its nave and choir have an unequaled majesty. I doubted if the costly modern fresco painting of the ceiling and walls added to the effect, and this doubt was strengthened when I saw the next day the sister church in the same style at Worms. Its bare stone gave a finer impression. Outside and inside, the grand old minster harmonized. Oh, how solemn and splendid the associations clustering round that grim cathedral! The old Diet-house, where Luther argued his cause, lost before it was heard, and gained when it was lost, is gone, all but its foundations. " Here I take my stand; I can not do otherwise ; God help me." But the minster, in whose shadow it stood, remains essentially as Luther saw it. The narrow streets about it, now so empty and still, became again for me peopled with knights and princes and their armed followers ! The Catholic bishops and their gaudy trains were jostled by the glittering soldiers who came to lend steel arguments to their master's reformed opinions; and amid all the splendid retinue of proud ecclesiastics and electors, I felt Luther's great shade passing by, in plain gown and cap, but with a more than imperial majesty in his prophetic mien. Two miles out of town we rode, to stand in the shadow of the great tree, known as Luther's tree, a linden of eight feet in diameter, planted to commemorate the very spot where Luther's friends, directly in sight of Worms, dissuaded him most earnestly from keeping his purpose of answering the summons of the Diet; and there it was he uttered the ever-memorable words, " If there were as many devils in Worms as there are tiles on the roofs I would face my accusers there." And when they told him if he advanced he would be burned to ashes like John Huss, he replied, " Though they should kindle a fire whose flames should reach from Worms to Wittenberg, and rise up into the vault of heaven, I would go there in the name of the Lord and stand before them." Near the Diet-house the foundations of an immense monument to Luther's memory—surrounded by the chief Reformers—are already laid. All Protestant Germany has contributed to the fund of this costly memorial, which promises to be worthy of its subject. The statues will be speedily erected, being nearly ready.

At Spires I stumbled into a Jewish synagogue, with its front in an alley, as if still hiding away from persecution. Two hundred Hebrews were celebrating some high festival, perhaps the Feast of Penitence. A few of them were clad in sackcloth. The priest wore a turban, and they looked more like Arab sheiks than modern citizens.

The late harvest is coming in, and the fields are thick with laborers. Immense quantities of beets, turnips and potatoes are being gathered. Such heaps of potatoes I never saw before, and they appeared excellent in quality. They must furnish a large portion of this people's food. The frost must have seriously injured the grapes. Wine has gone up in price. The grapes are often sold standing at so much per pound. Oftener the wine is sold merely as grape-juice, at so much the ohm, which is eighty mass, or about a barrel English measure. It varies from thirty to fifty thalers, the ordinary kinds. Choice vineyards are sold at fancy prices. Travelers pay very much higher prices than the natives for the same articles. Ignorance is very expensive.

The cathedral in Frankfort, burned on August 15th, since we were here, we found not so seriously injured as reported. It is already covered with stagings, and will soon be fully repaired. Its tower is majestic, and it overshadows prodigious memories. The loss of such a storied monster as this would be a calamity for the world. Fortunately it is hard to destroy the noblest structures.

XXVII.

HAMBURG.

October 15, 1867.

THE carriage-and-four of the Prince of Wales stood in the Porte-cochere of the Hotel de Russie at Frankfort as we came down stairs to our own voiture. The Duke and Duchess of Nassau and the Crown Prince of Denmark were in the house, whither they had all come from Wiesbaden, and there had been all the morning a considerable embargo of the grand staircase by solemn footmen. The Princess of Wales, who is said to have profited in her lameness by the waters of Wiesbaden, was brought down stairs in a chair and placed in the carriage, before the horses were put to ; she is a pretty, amiable-looking woman, bright and cheerful, and was dressed in a plain traveling-suit. She looked pale but not ill, and was natural and simple in her manners, and as the carriage stood in the court-yard fifteen minutes after she got in (the outer doors being closed), there was a very good opportunity to see the royal party. Coming down stairs, I overtook a stoutish young man, with full face and light whiskers, in a white overcoat and low-crowned black hat, totally wanting in any air of nobility. He appeared to be waiting for something, and addressed somebody in German. Great was my surprise ten minutes afterward, to see this gentleman mount the carriage and take his place beside the Princess, the very apparent heir of the English throne ! There was very little needless display in the equipage. The royal pair rode

alone, and were followed by another carriage with their attendants. The Crown Prince of Denmark was our fellow-
passenger in the train for Hamburg. We had many opportunities in the waiting-saloons on the way of seeing him.
His dress was thoroughly undistinguished from that of any
well-dressed young man of twenty-four. He does not look
like a forcible or earnest person, or one with more than average abilities, but has a truly amiable, pure and prepossessing face. He traveled with two footmen in attendance, and
two friends in the same rail-carriage. I saw him in the early
morning munching a dry roll which he had bought at the
counter, and he did it with an honest appetite that spoke well
for his simple tastes.

We passed the night—our first—in the cars, leaving Frankfort at 5½ P.M. and reaching Hamburg at 10½ next morning.
We changed our train five times. Germany is a perfect net-
work of railroads, and it requires peculiar skill and special
accuracy in the time-tables, to secure the proper connections
in long stretches. We lost at least an hour and a half waiting for trains, and as the weather was cold and damp we were
not wholly comfortable when we arrived. Yet the cars of
the first class—which in long night-journeys are best—are
not bad sleeping-rooms if you are not called too often to
change them in the small hours of the morning.

Hamburg is an amphibious city, half in and half out of the
water. The broad Elbe, full of islands, opens into the city
on one side by numerous canals, cutting it up much like Amsterdam, although not in concentric half-circles. These canals, very ugly and dirty at low water, are flooded by the tide
every six hours. The wholesale stores all have their backs
upon them. This frees the city from burden-wagons and
trucks, and adds very much to its quiet and comfort. On
the opposite side of the city comes in the Alster, a small river,

which, by judicious dams, has been converted into a beautiful lake, around whose shores lie the finest houses of the city,
and which, extending a couple of miles back, is now drawing
the new and elegant part of Hamburg out of town, the city
ending in a beautiful suburban region fast filling up with elegant houses on charming grounds.   Hamburg is a low, flat
city in the midst of a level plain.   The blue hills of Hasburg
may be seen in a clear day—but clear days are very scarce
here, although it is very ungrateful in us, who have had four
superb days here, to say so.   The only settled weather to be
depended on is said to be from the middle of August to the
1st of October.   Usually up' here in 52 north latitude—10
degrees north of New York—the weather is damp and chilly,
when not wet and cold.   But it is said not to be unwholesome.   The regular Hamburger is a sort of petrel, who enjoys storm and wet.   His natural breath is fog, and he com-
plains of a weight in his head if the sun shines too clearly.
The people look vigorous, with good red and white complex-
ions, and when I am shivering, I see women with bare arms
and without bonnets going about their duties without the
least sign of discomfort.

Hamburg, for centuries a free city—and one of three survivors of that old Hanseatic League, which once assembled
at Lubeck, the representatives of ninety cities, and made independent treaties with great powers — is at this time the
most important commercial town in Germany.   It has nearly two hundred thousand inhabitants, possesses great wealth
and prosperity, and wears more the aspect of New York with
its forest of masts, its immense stores, crowded streets and
bustling ways, than any city we have seen since Paris.   There
is here nothing of the languor and shrunken look which so
many other Continental cities wear.   Frankfort is dead and
dull in aspect, compared with Hamburg.   The Exchange is

fuller and more charged with commercial life than any one
I ever attended. Three or four thousand merchants assemble at 1½ o'clock P.M., the hour of high 'change, in the grand
and convenient Bourse, and their voices, heard in the gallery
above, are like the roar of a cataract. Every commercial
house in Hamburg has its representative on the floor of that
Exchange at that hour. The floor is marked off in marble
squares, and the pillars or arches around it are all numbered.
Every merchant or broker has his fixed place, and by naming
the two numbers in the line of which he stands, he indicates
his position. The largest part of the business is done by
brokers, who are here strictly intermediates, and not, as with
us, persons doing business on their own account. An agree-
ment informally made between parties at their places of business is formally completed on 'Change by the broker, and is
thus legalized. Goods sold one morning are delivered with
the bill in the afternoon, and if not paid for the next day,
the purchaser's credit is lost, as much as if he had failed to
meet his note at the bank.

A great and even cruel strictness rules here in respect of
business credit. It is next to impossible for a merchant to
recover from even an innocent failure. Money is the god
of Hamburg, and no disrespect must even accidentally be
shown this divinity. If the citizens are themselves to be
credited, money measures sense, virtue, birth, every thing
here. Men bow at the angles due to a million, a half-million, a hundred thousand marks, with mathematical precision,
and seem to possess an instinctive adjustment in their spinal
cord to the demands of the occasion. In the absence of a
political or social aristocracy, it is not strange that money
should assume so much importance. But this is perhaps no
truer here than at home in certain cities, and of course it is
not true anywhere without great exceptions. For Hamburg,

though an intensely commercial city, is also a city full of public spirit and charities. It possesses admirable water-works, excellent hospitals, large churches, and shows a vast public ambition. Since the fire in 1842, which burned over the finest part of the town, destroying sixty-one streets and seventeen hundred and forty-nine houses, Hamburg has rebuilt the city on a truly splendid scale. Geneva itself hardly presents a finer view at the beautiful foot of its lake than Hamburg, when, in the evening, brilliant gas-lamps illuminate the fine blocks around the Binnen Alster basin, and the water, lit up by a full moon, shows off the architecture around them in a sort of magical beauty. The Alster is full of pleasure-boats, and what is more important, of little steamers, clean and snug, hardly bigger than gondolas, and covered in with glass, which perform omnibus duty and make, every ten minutes, the tour of the Alster (about three miles), calling at the several stations and connecting up town and down town in a most agreeable manner. The great commercial advantage of Hamburg, not to speak of its fine harbor (it is eighty miles from the ocean and can not be reached in winter by even the great steamers which stop at Cuxhaven, just at the mouth), is the fact that cargoes entering here pay only a duty of a quarter per cent. on the valuation, and that the merchants' written oath is taken without examination for this valuation. This advantage may now be lost. Hamburg is evidently preparing to be swallowed by Prussia. On Wednesday last her own troops were disbanded, and on Thursday two battalions of Prussians marched quietly in to take their places. Prussia has asked her to furnish 2000 troops toward the North German Confederate army. She is trying to get off with 1000. But shrewd people here foresee that in less than five years the strict independence of Hamburg will have departed. She was never in a condition to defend it. It has been guaranteed by the jealousies and interests of the great powers hitherto. But Prussia needs Hamburg, and she is strong enough to defy objections to so natural a demand, as that a city which she would be called on to defend should acknowledge allegiance and fall into the Soll-Verein, a customs-union, and in short into the German nationality, now so rapidly forming. Hanover has gained nothing by her squirms but a heavier hand, and Hamburg will probably yield with grace in due time. Doubtless the consolidation of Hamburg with Prussia and her union with the Soll-Verein would raise local prices ; but her wiser citizens seem to see more advantages in the union than disadvantage ; and Hamburg, with some wry faces among the middle classes, will follow Frankfort soon.

Hamburg possesses several fine commodious churches, including her suburbs. She has seven Lutheran parishes and as many churches, each with several ministers. The same division of sentiment found in all other German cities, between the "Orthodox" and the Liberal party, exists here. The Orthodox include usually the rich and conservative classes, and have perhaps the most ecclesiastical zeal. The Liberals include the active merchants and the thinking class, perhaps also the more careless spirits. Both classes possess even too great a freedom from Sabbatarian bigotry and asceticism. The substantial and discreet people, Orthodox and Liberal, make no scruple of attending the theatre or the opera Sunday evenings. There is, however, a growing feeling in favor of a stricter observance of the Sunday, which it is hoped will increase. Much account is made of confirmation in the Lutheran Church. At sixteen or seventeen the young people pass through a special religious course to prepare them for their first communion. There is no doubt a good deal of merely technical interest connected with this event, and it is too much after the pattern of a Catholic superstition to render it as useful as it might be made. Religious lessons are given with a good deal of punctiliousness in the schools, either by a pastor or a candidate in theology. Nobody is allowed to keep a school for more than twelve children without a special license. Most of the schools are private. There is one public school of much importance where an academical or commercial training may be had. Hamburg abounds in hospitals and infirmaries ; one for aged persons of respectable antecedents. An orphan asylum containing 500 foundlings or orphans enjoys a very generous support. On the first Thursday of every July a special festival is held in Hamburg, for the aid of this asylum. The children, at 6 A.M., boys and girls, form in procession and march through the streets, soliciting contributions from the inhabitants. They are led by older boys who are crowned with wreaths and who collect the general contribution. The " best boy " is " king," and comes in for a large special contribution. All of them walk cap in hand, and receive each what any citizen may be inclined to give. All they receive is taken charge of by their governors, when, at about 6 P.M., they return home and make over their gains. These are put to the individual accounts of the children, and returned to them when they leave the asylum. The rich merchants have an honorable fashion of endorsing public charities. One rich Jew has founded a hospital called after his deceased wife, which is open to Jews and Christians alike. There is a diminishing prejudice against the Jews, who are numerous and among the richest and best citizens, but it still continues in some force. They are not admitted into some of the schools or into most of the hospitals and asylums.

The wealthier citizens have founded a beautiful zoological garden, with most tasteful grounds, where the noblest and rarest animals are to be seen in great perfection. The ant-bear, a very rare animal, is one of the creatures here of which they are most proud. They have the finest aquaria I have ever seen, arranged with the highest scientific skill, and where the habits of fish and the growth of sea-plants may be studied with great facility.

The bank of the Elbe is adorned as far as Blankenese, nine miles out of town, with the beautiful and costly country houses of the wealthier citizens of Hamburg and Altona. No finer houses or more exquisite grounds are to be seen in the suburbs of any city I have visited. The Elbe, full of ships and steamers, affords a most lively prospect from these charming villas. The capitalists see from their own doors their richly-freighted vessels going out and returning to port, while the coast of Hanover and the pretty hills of Hasburg bound their prospect. The fishermen along this shore are celebrated for their neat housekeeping, and many citizens resort in the hot weather to their roofs for a change of air. Every thing along the Elbe indicates wealth, prosperity, activity and power. The harbor is a forest of masts. The streets running to the Elbe are crowded with business, and bear no mean resemblance to the vast commercial parts of London or New York.

The inhabitants of certain villages—the Fierlanden—belonging to Hamburg, have a prescriptive right to sell fruits, vegetables and fish in the city. They wear a very picturesque costume ; each village of four has a different one, which is hundreds of years old, and wholly unchanged. It is rich in color and embroidery on Sundays and festivals. In one of the Fierlanden villages the pastor has the custody of three crowns, which are worn by brides, who pay one, two or three *thalers*, as they can afford, for the use of these crowns on their wedding-day. They are of three degrees of richness.

The fee is a perquisite of the pastor's wife. The child's nurses of Hamburg are gay in ribbons and colored dresses and white caps. The maid-servants carry their market-baskets under a showy shawl worn very gracefully over one arm, beneath which they conceal their burden.

We visited the Rauhe-haus—the celebrated school established by Dr. Wichern at Horn, three miles out of Hamburg, on a small farm—the object of which is the reform of vicious boys and girls by a special treatment, in which kindness and skillful adaptation of occupation and wholesome inducements to order and virtue, take the place of punishments. The institution is a collection of separate houses, all either small or of only moderate size, scattered over the farm, the object being to separate and not congregate the children. There are here seventy boys and forty girls of the rougher class, and also twenty-five boys from good families, but of unruly tempers, whom their parents have found unmanageable. These last are separated from the rest, except in certain general chapel exercises. They live in a nice boarding-house, and receive a methodical instruction in the usual branches of high-school education. The rest are associated in squads of about twelve in family houses, where they eat and sleep and pass their leisure hours, under the special care of a brother of the "Inner Mission." These brothers are an association of young men, originally formed by Dr. Wichern, who devote their lives to the care of poor and exposed children in all parts of the world. They get their preparation in the Rauhe-haus at Horn, where the chief labor is thrown upon them. There are, it is said, some three hundred of them, and their influence wherever they are scattered must be excellent. There are perhaps a dozen of them at Horn always under Dr. Wichern's eye and care. A few sisters, also, of a similar devotedness, are in charge of the girls.

There is a Superintendent, or Vicar, who takes more immediate charge of the school, as Dr. Wichern has other duties
which carry him half the year to Berlin. The boys are instructed in the elementary branches for three or four hours
a day. They have each a little plot of ground to cultivate.
All of them learn some trade under a competent master on
the ground; printing, tailoring, shoe-making, smithery, car-
pentry, I observed going on in separate apartments. The
houses where the boys live were plain and neat. Every thing
on the grounds, indeed, had a commendable simplicity.
There was no superfluity and no over-refinement. In one
of the houses, laid out on a table, were the simple gifts which
his companions had bestowed on one of the boys whose
birthday fell on the day of our visit. A few coarse but instructive wood engravings, a rude toy or two, one handsome
marble (an *alley* we used to call it), a pair of wooden slippers, made up the assortment. In the chapel every morning,
the names of all the boys who have ever been in the school,
whose birthday the current day chronicles, are called out; a
short history of their career since leaving the Rauhe-haus is
recited, and any thing that can properly and honestly be said
of those still present, is also given. Thus a very wholesome
interest in each other and a very commendable ambition as to
their future career is excited. The young man who showed
us round the school was a candidate in theology educated at
Halle, and a favorite of Tholuck, I judged, as he had traveled with him in Switzerland. And no wonder; for his face
was as full of purity and benevolence as it could hold, and
his intelligence and civility were both instructive and charming. He was himself a perfect recommendation of the work
he was serving. Dr. Wichern, whom we saw for a few moments only, is a man of large mould, with strong blue eyes,
abundant hair perfectly white, and a face of great resolution

and perfect kindness.   He is a man of no sentimentality, but great practical sense.   This work is likely to remain. Eight hundred children have been under his care.   The school is not gratuitous.   All who can are properly required to pay for their privileges.   The work of the boys is also made profitable.   The institution receives many benefactions from an appreciative public.   On the whole, there was less to object to in its management than in any institution for similar objects I have ever visited.   The children (especially the boys) looked contented and under cheerful and inspiring influences. The girls pleased me less.   But bad girls are a worse class than bad boys, they fall from so much higher an estate.

We stayed in Hamburg one day longer than we intended, to hear Joseph Joachim, the most distinguished of living violinists, in a charity concert.   Joachim lives in Hanover, where the blind king, who has just lost his throne, has cherished him among other great artists, with peculiar fondness. But he has not been spoiled.   He has the rare character of being as distinguished for his personal worth and general culture as for his skill on the violin.   He is a savan, it is said, who still attends lectures at Gottingen, and is the peer and companion of learned and accomplished men.   He is about thirty-four years of age, stout and heavy of mould as to his features, of a decidedly lymphatic aspect, without token of skill, either in the grace or agility of his bearing.   Over a pale and flabby countenance a high forehead rises, crowned with abundant and flowing hair.   His square and heavy jaw promises little.   But when he takes the violin and puts it to his shoulder, and bends down his somewhat dreamy face to the instrument, a new life takes possession of him.   His serious, unsmiling face becomes lustrous with a spiritual beauty.   His eyes, which he half shuts when he plays, as if he would be all ear himself, add to the lost aspect he wears.

He seems to forget his audience and himself, and to be wholly absorbed in his business. His facility is perfect; he wholly removes the impression of effort or difficulty, and allows the hearer to be rapt in the music. Wholly without clap-trap, vanity or self-display, he plays only the best music in the most faithful and exquisite manner. In his most rapid passages no note is slurred; his transitions were exquisite, and his tone perfect. He played nothing for the sake of the difficulties to be mastered. On the whole, no artist since Jenny Lind has made upon me the impression of a stronger and nobler character. Joachim looks like a plain clerical Professor. He wears glasses, dresses very simply, and is altogether a very rare and delightful artist and man.

I must not forget to mention the Church of St. Nicholas now building in Hamburg. It is the largest and most imposing of modern churches, so far as my observation has extended. Of English Gothic, of a pure style, it is finished within with perfect elegance, and, for a Protestant and Lutheran church, overcomes the difficulties which an edifice without altar or cathedral-stalls has to contend with, most bravely. The usual emptiness and bareness of even the English cathedrals is overcome by the beauty of a marble screen and the sumptuous splendor of a white marble pulpit, which in exquisiteness of workmanship and richness of design is nowhere exceeded. The spire, which will be nearly as lofty as that at Strasburg, is going up slowly, by the aid of weekly contributions from Hamburg Protestants. It has been twenty years and more in progress, and will be finished in four years. The church will seat two thousand people, but I hear that except on festival days it rarely has more than five hundred at the chief service. It is built on the site of a former church burned in the great fire. It is still remembered that the chime of bells in the great tower began to ring of their own accord when the church and spire were wrapped in flames, and in the height of the vast conflagration which was devouring the city. The effect, it is said, was terrific. This church owes its re-edification, like many other churches on the Continent, more to the pressure of historical associations and local pride than to any present want of so vast a building. From the point of practical religion, I can not but look upon the size of the churches on the Continent as a great detriment to the interests of public worship. They are usually cold, thinly attended, and very difficult to be heard in, adapted to a spectacular worship or an altar service, and not to preaching. The multiplication of small churches is the most urgent interest of Protestantism, if we except the increase of Christian faith and zeal.

Hamburg is very sure, under the vast impulse which the union of Northern Germany must give to commerce and trade, to grow with surpassing speed into the first rank of commercial cities. It would not surprise me to see it doubled in ten years. Prussia is now the third among the nations in its commercial marine. Its ports are rapidly growing. Hamburg has an immense trade with North and South America, with England, and with the Mediterranean. She is destined to become, even more than she already is, the first port on the European Continent.

Bremen, near by, I did not visit. It is the seat of the Theological School of the German Methodists, who have a growing influence on the Continent. The old Hernhutters or Moravians have their theological centre at Niskau, which I fear I shall not have time to see.

Let me mention one book which seems to be attracting special attention among Ethnologists abroad, as an original work carrying Mommsen's method of dealing with Roman history a little farther still, and into a more difficult field.

While Mommsen seeks to draw out the true state of Roman life from an examination of the laws of the Romans, subjected to an exhaustive analysis, Adolphe Pictel seeks to infer the life of the Indo-Europeans from a study of the Aryan words. His work is brimful of suggestion, and carries even the most cultivated student into " fresh fields and pastures new." It occupies an untrodden field. " Les Origines Indo-Europeennes, ou les Aryas primitifs. Essai de Paleontologie Linguistique, par Adolphe Pictel." Paris : Joel Cherbuliez. 2 vols. Somebody will thank me for this title.

XXVIII.

BERLIN.

October 24, 1867.

BERLIN—the capital of Prussia and the centre of German power, material, intellectual and political—is situated on a small, stagnant stream, called the Spree, in the midst of a vast, sandy plain, which, on the north, stretches up to the Baltic, and is swept by winds that envelop it for a large part of the year in clouds and fogs. It is in north latitude 51°, and has a cold, damp climate, which, with its uninteresting situation, makes its growth almost a miracle. Yet in one hundred and fifty years it has become a city of 600,000 from perhaps not more than 50,000 at that date, and chiefly through the vigorous policy of Frederick the Great, in making it the centre of military and intellectual life. Trade and commerce have obeyed the attraction of these higher powers, and Berlin is now a vast capital, second only to Paris in importance and in magnificence upon the European Continent. Its streets are wide and well built. The French style of large buildings, with separate floors for private families, prevails. "Unter den Linden," its famous promenade, answers, though poorly, to the Champs Élysées of Paris. A wide and shaded walk for pedestrians, with a side-road for horsemen, runs through the middle of the street, which is lined on both sides with the principal hotels, cafés and shops. This street, which is about a mile long, is occupied at the southern end for a quarter of a mile by the Palaces of the King and the Crown Prince, the old Schloss built by Frederick the Great, the Arsenal, the Dom, or principal church, and other public buildings. In the middle of it stands the magnificent equestrian statue of Frederick the Great, around the pedestal of which are placed in life-size, and in strict historical portraits, the statues of his chief generals, and of the statesmen and philosophers that adorned his reign. Along the sides of the street are fine statues in marble or bronze of the military heroes and statesmen of Prussia. A bridge which crosses the Spree, near the Palace, is decorated with eight groups of fine statuary indicating the career of the Prussian soldier. Minerva inducts him in early youth into the profession of arms by holding up to him a shield on which is inscribed simply the names of those great warriors, Alexander, Cæsar, Frederick; in the next group she is teaching him to throw the spear; in the third, she gives him a sword; in the fourth, she crowns his first success in arms, and so to the last, when, holding him, done to death in battles, in her arms, she points him to the opening heaven for his final guerdon. Berlin is full of street statuary, and especially of military monuments. Above any place I have seen, it abounds in statues of horses, now with and now without riders. The Emperor Nicholas gave two beautiful statues of horses, which came in the days of the revolution of 1848, and are now set up before the old Palace. The cornices and tops of the public buildings are crowned with figures of horses. The Brandenburg gate—built 1789— at the opposite end of Unter den Linden, is surmounted with a chariot and four horses, which are of special interest from having been carried off by Napoleon to Paris, kept for eight years, and restored to Berlin in 1814, only after long and mortifying negotiations. The absence of any good building-stone in the neighborhood has made Berlin a city of brick, covered almost in all cases with ornamented and painted

P

stucco. This gives a faded and unsubstantial character to the architecture generally. The dampness of the climate, with the dust, rusts the exterior of the buildings, and there is nothing bright and fresh, as in Paris, about even the newest part of Berlin. The Thier-garden (garden of animals), just outside the Brandenburg gate, is the " Bois de Boulogne " of Berlin. It is very extensive and covered with fine trees, through which rustic roads and paths are cut, and among which a few fine statues are sprinkled. On one side of this the favorite residences of the richer class are found, and new and showy streets run from it, full of large and costly private houses. The United States Minister occupies one of them, in Regenten Strasse, where he exercises an elegant hospitality to his countrymen and to the savans of Berlin, among whom he finds himself so much at home. The country is fortunate in being represented at Berlin at this critical and pregnant moment by a man known so well beforehand to the literati and statesmen of Prussia. Mr. Bancroft has received a most distinguished welcome at the Court and among the savans. Bismarck, it is said, has shown him very unusual respect, and the King, receiving him at his own table, has expressed his satisfaction at being able, for the first time, to talk with an American Minister in his own German tongue.

The flatness of Berlin is so perfect that I have hunted in vain for any natural elevation in or around it from which the city could be looked down upon. The evenness is very unfavorable to any street effects, and indeed to any easy acquaintance with the topography. Excepting the main avenue, there is hardly a commanding street in Berlin. Wilhelm, Leipziger and other streets, very long and very monotonous, run at rectangles, and an occasional open square, always adorned with statuary, diversifies the vast extent of buildings. But the main effect is lack of expression and want of variety.

Not that there is any absence of stir and bustle. The streets are full of droskies and private carriages, many of them elegant, and all roomy and comfortable. Well-dressed people throng the narrow sidewalks. Deep gutters, down which a fall would be almost as dangerous as a slip into an Alpine crevasse, line many of these *trottoirs*. At other places the sidewalks are level with the carriage-way. Crossing the streets is perilous, and the sidewalks are insecure, at least in the feeling of a stranger. The hack-hire is very cheap, and the *pourboire*, or drink-money, is not rigorously exacted as in Paris.

The hotels are rapidly improving, and nothing could be more comfortable than the Hotel de Rome, where we have been for ten days past. The old Palace, the beautiful domed tower of which, though planned by Old Fritz, was not finished until the present reign, is a sort of imitation of the Louvre—a vast range of courts within courts, and halls on halls —many of them finished in the most costly and elaborate style. The marble columns, the beautiful inlaid floors, the tapestried walls, the collection of royal gifts from Russian, English and other sovereigns, the abundant ornamentation in silver and in gold—all make these show-rooms very superb. The most noticeable part of the palace is the chapel, finished within late years, in the richest marbles and adorned with frescoes from the most skillful modern artists. Round in form and immensely lofty in its dome, from which it is lighted, it is a most gorgeous place of worship, and compares not unfavorably, in brilliancy and splendor, with the most decorated Roman Catholic shrines. Protestantism seems here to have labored to see how near it could come in costliness and show to the standard of the old hierarchical display. An altar, surmounted with a crucifix of fabulous cost, occupies one arc of the circular room. The place is used only on occasions of festival and state worship. Passing through one of the halls, we were struck with what appeared to be a mantle-piece of solid silver. We were told that it was only a copy in plated metal of an original one which was actually of solid silver, but was melted into money by Frederick the Great at the close of his wars, wherewith to build the Palace at Potsdam, which he undertook, in part at least, to show Europe that his exchequer was not ruined by his last campaign. In the "White Hall," fitted up in gorgeous splendor and decorated with statues of the twelve Brandenburg electors, and eight allegorical figures representing the Prussian Provinces (the new ones are not yet added !), the first meeting of the Prussian Parliament was held in 1847.

To-day, the Prussian Parliament — which with so little criticism has sustained the late vigorous and confessedly unlawful measure of the government — was dissolved by the King in person. About 2½ o'clock the main body of the hall began to fill with the nobles, generals, state functionaries and deputies of the kingdom. Sitting among a favored few in the tribune, or gallery, to which tickets from our Minister had admitted us, we looked down upon the gathering of this gorgeous assembly. Entering informally as they arrived, one or two at a time, we had an opportunity to watch somewhat deliberately their individual appearance. Half, at least, were either soldiers or in military uniforms, of all kinds and degrees of splendor—red, white, green—but always profusely covered with gold lace, and commonly hung about with orders and stars, sashes and ribbons. Another portion were in the usual court-dress, which is a kind of Quaker coat that has broken out into colors and gold lace. A few ecclesiastics or professors, in solemn gown and cape, with an order or two on their breasts shining all the more brilliantly from its black background, moved in the motley throng.

Perhaps fifty gentlemen in plain clothes were mixed in the

assembly. There were no seats for this company, notwithstanding the venerable and infirm appearance of a large number of them. Indeed, the advanced age of most officials and
notabilities in Prussia is one of the characteristic features of
a civilization where routine and slowness of advancement
are painfully in the way of merit and vigor. A few chairs
on one side of the simple throne (a classic chair upon a
slightly raised platform) were reserved for the privy council
and ministers of state, and in these, at 3 o'clock, twenty dig-
nitaries took their places, with Bismarck at the left nearest
the throne. Suddenly a herald announced the King in a
loud voice, and William I. came unattended, and cap in hand,
and at once ascended the platform. He was in full uniform
of a dark green, and in boots and spurs, and after bowing to
· the assembly, put on his cavalry cap with its fountain plume.
One short, simultaneous and percussive "Owa" welcomed
him. Bismarck advanced, and, with a very low salute, put
the open portfolio containing the Royal speech into the
King's hands. He read it in a simple and rather awkward
manner, without pretension and without effect. One suppressed murmur of applause greeted the close of a paragraph
referring to the harmony of the session. At the close (the
reading could not have taken three minutes) Bismarck took
the address from the King's hands, and turning toward the
assembly, pronounced the Parliament, in the name of the
King, dissolved. The King bowed and immediately descended from the throne (he had not once sat down), and left
the hall amid a few hearty huzzas. Bismarck was dressed
in the same white uniform I had seen him in at the Emperor's ball at Paris. He wore jack-boots and spurs. His
fine, great head upon his tall, full figure, gave him a marked
superiority over the whole assembly. Power, prudence, self-
possession, capacity, success, are stamped upon his features

and bearing. If he is worn with care, he does not show it ; perhaps he carries it in those great sacks that hang under his eyes ! He seems about fifty-four, and thoroughly well-preserved. His habits are careful. He rides on horseback, and bathes in summer in the open river, a few miles from the town. He seems to possess much of the attainments of John Quincy Adams, with a tact ʻin statesmanship which never marked that powerful politician. If he had fallen from the skies he could not have come more opportunely, or with qualifications more out of the usual line of German states-manship. Knowing all that German statesmen ever know, he has a thoroughly un-German dash and practical quality in ʻhim which marks him out from his predecessors, and leaves him wholly alone in his kind. With unsurpassed courage and competency, he possesses distinguished prudence and self-control. He does not undertake the impossible, nor in-vent a policy. He merely shapes and articulates a public sentiment which for a hundred years has waited for its crys-tallizing moment. He is not a moral genius, nor are disin-terestedness and pure philanthrophy his inspirers. But he is a patriot, and sees Prussia's opportunity to lead Germany to her destiny, and probably no man could possess qualities or antecedents better fitted to the work. An aristocrat, he puts himself at the head of the party of movement, and ad-vocates all possible reforms in the interests of a larger liberty and a freer life. He swallows and digests his antecedents, and evidently despises all criticism which merely convicts him of disagreement with himself—where the disagreement is necessary and born of new circumstances and new opportuni-ties. He is clearly a whole head and shoulders above not only his contemporaries in Prussia, but European statesmen in general ; and the more I see of the slack, tape-tied, broken-spirited character of German politicians — dreamy, mechanical, wordy, theoretical and inefficient — the more I admire the prompt, incisive, practical and bold qualities of this redeemer of Germany. But I am getting on too fast. After the King left, Bismarck passed into the assembly and greeted personally a large number of the members.

General Moltke, who planned the late triumphant campaign with such prophetic wisdom, and executed it so precisely, was very conspicuous, and the centre of very special attention. Not unlike General Dix in appearance, although much older, and quite infirm, Moltke, dressed in a white uniform and covered with orders, had a most modest and quiet carriage, and looked very little like a hero covered with fresh laurels. I looked in vain for Prince Carl, the cavalry leader of the war, nephew of the King and a great favorite of the people. The Prince of Prussia, with his English whiskers and great mustache, was very distinguishable. He occupies a separate palace next the King's, and seems a fair enough heir to the throne. His wife (Victoria, eldest daughter of the English Queen) is a woman of special culture and of a practical turn of mind, though capable of literary conversation and possessing marked skill with the pencil. She has six children already. The King is seventy years old—a plain, robust, soldierly man, with a great native passion for military matters—of unquestioned personal courage, and of a fair average understanding. He has a bluff face, and seems to love a simple life. He is an honest man, but without any special qualifications for the exigencies of governing. His brother, the late king, whose decline was accompanied with so many painful and humiliating circumstances, was of a different order. Full of knowledge, taste, and power of thinking, if he had not been a king he would have been a savan, and possibly a distinguished one. Their father, Frederick William Third, who reigned through the wars with Napoleon, was a man of a mild but firm and excellent character, a warm and efficient Protestant, who left a very decided stamp upon the minds and the policy of his children and of the country. He was blest with a wife who had a character even finer and nobler than his own. A Princess of the Mecklenberg-Strelitz house, she had a lofty soul shrined in a most lovely and noble person, and her spirit, roused to an exalted patriotism by the humiliation which Napoleon was putting upon the nation, kindled her husband's feeble temper and the faint heart of all Prussia to the resistance which saved the honor and the future of the country. She died at thirty-five, wept and revered by the whole people. Her statue, carved by Rauch, whose genius she had discovered and whose career she fashioned, lies in fadeless beauty and grace in the temple erected at Charlottenberg to secure it. The statue of her husband is placed by her side. Rauch is said to have spent fifteen years in bringing this work of love to its final perfection, and it is a master-piece of elegance and fitness. The King is doubtless led by Bismarck, who has the tact and judgment to treat the monarch with profound deference, while the King has the sense to appreciate his Minister's superior knowledge and address, and to follow his counsels.

I attended two sessions of the Parliament which had just risen, in the temporary chamber where it sits. The room was too small for the company, and not worthy the work done in it. The Parliament is composed, like our own Congress, of two Chambers. The House of Deputies is composed of Representatives, one for each one hundred thousand of the people. To favor the smaller provinces another representative is allowed them where the fraction passes fifty thousand ; an advantage which Prussia, strong in her majority, can readily afford. The Deputies quite fairly represent all classes ; there are nobles, commoners and mechanics in the House.

Perfect freedom of debate is allowed. The Senators, or members of the Upper Chamber, and the Ministers, have the privilege of seats and of speaking in the House of Representatives, which they often avail themselves of. The Upper House has duties different in many respects from our Senate. It is a sort of Standing Committee, digesting and arranging public business in the interval of Parliament. Speakers usually, though not necessarily, mount the tribune, as in France, when they address the House. The speeches I heard were all short and pithy, commonly written and read. The vote was often taken, always by show of hands. A great deal of business (it was the closing week of the session) was accomplished quite quietly. The Chamber had little of the disorder of our House ; members listened, kept their seats, and attended strictly to business. There was a comparatively small attendance of spectators and a small accommodation in the galleries ; and it is at least doubtful whether our American free invitation to the public to attend the meetings of the Senate and House does not seriously affect their character as deliberative bodies, and disturb the sobriety of their judgment and the simplicity of their discussions, besides making a great obstruction to the business by inviting talk and encouraging popular displays. Something, on the other hand, is to be said in favor of the presence of the people, as encouraging their representatives to advance and maintain their sentiments, when in danger of being repressed by bureaucratic or mere Congressional feeling ; and then openness and publicity are always favorable to liberty.

There is enough to keep one busy for a long time among the sights of Berlin, and we have passed rapidly through them. The Royal Library, one of the four largest in the world, is beautifully arranged; and contains many most valuable and interesting MSS. and a rich assortment of illuminated missals. It is particularly rich in every thing appertaining to the History of the Reformation, and is redolent with the memories of the Reformers themselves—copious specimens of whose letters and MSS. are found here. Even more living are the traces of the philosophers and savans who illustrated the time of Frederick the Great, and the later poets and thinkers, Goethe, Schiller, Herder, Lessing, Uhland, Fichte, Hegel, Schelling. Nothing was more startling than to come upon the identical hemisphere of metal (about eighteen inches in diameter) with which Otto Guericke made the experiments which led him to the discovery of the air-pump. Here are the ropes and tackle to which he attached his thirty horses when he proved that their power was not adequate to separate these metal hemispheres, when the air between them was exhausted. The Museum is rich in a vast variety of gems and coins ; of mediæval antiquities ; of sculptures and vases (1600); of bronzes and terra-cottas. The collection of Egyptian antiquities, occupying five chambers, is probably the best in Europe ; since Lepsius added the immense acquisitions his vast learning and acuteness enabled him to make in Egypt in 1845. Rev. Dr. Thompson, of New York, has the credit here of having been a very faithful and successful student of Egyptology when in Berlin last year, and adding his recent to his old acquirements, he must be in condition to give the curious in such matters in America some fresh light. The collection of pictures here, while it is hardly marked by one first-rate picture of any great master, has a vast and admirably-arranged series of good pictures from all the schools, and affords an unequaled opportunity for pursuing the study of art history.

The royal stables are interesting. They contain at least a hundred horses, mostly black (black and white being the colors of Prussia), and carriages enough to open a livery stable. Some of these, handed down from the earliest date of the monarchy, are rudely magnificent, and illustrate in their proximity to recent coaches the immense progress which has attended the art of the wheelwright within a hundred years. Nothing pleased me so much in the whole stable as the application in many of the royal carriages of tires of gutta-percha to the wheels. About an inch in thickness, these tires are found, on smoothly-paved roads, more lasting than iron. They save all jar, and furnish a most luxurious relief to passengers of delicate and overstrained nerves. The rich people in Berlin have very commonly adopted this improvement, and I wish our streets of New York were smooth enough to make the trial of it there possible. Certainly oh earthen roads, pleasure-carriages might adopt it to the great comfort of invalids. I see no reason why ambulances and hospital carriages should not be fitted with these beautiful cushions for the wheels.

Rauch, who died a few years ago, was to Berlin and Prussia what Schwanthaler was to Munich and Bavaria. His genius and skill as a sculptor have laid his country under great obligations. The Rauch Museum contains models or copies in plaster of all his works, and presents an astonishing evidence of the fertility, industry and success of his genius. His favorite theme seems to have been " Victory," of which at least eight different statues came from his hand. It is very interesting to study in this collection the gradual perfecting of his plan for his chief work, the splendid monument to Frederick the Great. It grew in his mind very slowly, and attained its consummate finish only after eleven years of study. It is now called the finest statuesque monument in Europe. Rauch's history, character, genius and works are all profoundly interesting; he has stamped himself indelibly upon the face of his country and the hearts of his countrymen.

The churches in Berlin are not worthy of its general architecture. The Dom is large, and an important feature in the street view, but is a homely pile, both outside and in. We attended service there on Sunday morning—sitting opposite (in the diplomatic pew) to the royal pew, where one person was sitting. None of the diplomatic corps were at church. The church was fairly filled, as it usually is, but chiefly, it is said, by the attraction of its famous choir of men and boys, who give church music in unequaled beauty and power. They sing chiefly without organ accompaniment, and only the finest and most appropriate music. There seemed a hundred voices in the choir. A screen separated them from all view of the congregation. The officiating minister, in gown and bands, came in and knelt on an altar, on which was a crucifix and lighted candles, and with his back to the congregation. He then turned, and read the prayers and passages from the Scripture, from a book, in a simple way. As I had to preach myself at 11½ in the American chapel, I could not stay for the sermon.

One religious service we attended, on the last day of the ten penitential days with which the Jewish year begins, in the magnificent synagogue lately finished in Berlin. It is in Oriental style, holds four thousand people, and cost a million of dollars. The interior is gorgeous and dazzling, with lighted domes of glass, ornamental pillars and cornices and arches of fantastic complication. It was nearly full of worshipers. At least a dozen officiating priests assisted in the service. The chief function was performed by one man, dressed in a black robe and with a cap on his head, who, with his face toward the ark containing the sacred books, sung in a magnificent voice the prayers, and was echoed by a charming choir of boys and joined very often by the whole congregation. At a certain point in the service the sacred

books, in their rich caskets of silver and surmounted with
bells, were carried in procession up and down the aisles, in
the arms of men accoutred in white shawls, and of course
wearing, as every body did, the hat. There was nothing very
impressive in the aspect of these worshipers. The music
was fine, and the attendance remarkable ; but, with a few
exceptions, there was neither in the air of the priests nor of
the people any rapt attention or devout expression. The
whole thing seemed a pretty, heartless ceremonial ; the atmosphere was not worshipful. There are twenty thousand
Jews in Berlin, and they are far the richest portion of the
community. They own the lots " Unter den Linden " and
about the Thier-Garten. They are the millionaires, capitalists, bankers and great merchants of the city. They are divided into two schools, those who are avowedly reformed
Jews and confess themselves no longer bound by the Tal-
mud, and no longer expectants of a Messiah in the flesh ;
and the old-fashioned Jews, who are supposed to have no
very different opinion, but who still hold on to the old style
of profession. The synagogues they build are no special
evidences of their zeal or faith, as they are built by joint-
stock companies, who manage to make them pay an annual
income by letting the seats at high rates. They are still
held together by more or less of political or social persecution. But marriages between Jews and Christians are becoming common. Jewish women, it is said, like Christian
husbands, and Christian husbands like Jewish dowries and
Jewish beauty and brightness. There is evidently the same
change and disintegration going on in Jewish opinions and
usages, commonly deemed so stable and permanent, as in
Christian theology, and the rapid success of the Jews in
wealth and in moneyed and social influence is pretty certain
to be the ruin of their ecclesiastical life. They are really

melting into modern civilization, which they greatly modify by their æsthetic tastes, and their acute minds and fervid tempers. Disraeli is himself a sample of what all Jewry is becoming, and there was never less reason to forebode any growth of real Judaism than now, when its external signs are so abundant. It is only in Russia and Poland that the old Judaism of the middle ages survives.

I saw an old man in military uniform in the streets of Berlin, moving about like a sort of grandfather of the people. He looked faded and not quite clear in intellect, but seemed full of benevolence and geniality. He spoke to all the children, and I saw one waiter rush out of a coffee-house and shake his hand. This was the famous Field-Marshal Wrangel, so well-known in Prussian history. He is still the titular head of the Prussian army, but without any actual command. It was affecting to see the old man's place in the affections of the people, and the enjoyment he found in mingling with all classes of society. So great a departure from the usual strictness of German etiquette could only be accounted for by the approach of second childhood. The respect for titles in Germany is very much founded on their real value. If a man has a title, there is some actual office and privilege to which it corresponds. Titles are by no means matters of course. They imply labor and desert ; and it is only very slowly that they are acquired. But they entitle their bearer to rights and to a precedence which are very real. Moreover, there is a slow but sure advancement in the military and civil service which makes government employment very much desired, low and inadequate as its pecuniary rewards are. I paid a visit of respect to Professor Neumann, the author of a careful history of the United States, in three volumes. He was an old man, who had suffered lately a slight shock of paralysis, but who retained full possession of his mental faculties, and a most enthusiastic admiration for the principles and institutions of the American Republic. He is the author of a history of British India. A German Republican of the purest water, he has written the history of the United States from the most radical stand-point, with the profoundest sense of the evil which slavery did the country, and the intensest sympathy with the moral and political efforts by which it was destroyed. He proposes to publish a cheap edition of his work, which it would be a great stroke of political wisdom to disseminate among the Germans of America. The existing edition would cost $10 in America. He proposes, if he can find encouragement from America, to publish an edition at a cost of about $3. · I wish some German book-seller in America could see it to be for his interest to order five hundred copies as an experiment on the taste of the American Germans. I should be very glad to act as intermediary, and to procure and furnish any more specific information, should any book-seller, German or American, think it worth while to look farther into this interesting and important matter. Professor Neumann could not speak without visible emotion and even tears of the present trying aspect of American politics. He said his studies had made the success of American institutions a matter of deep personal solicitude, and that every blow given to his confidence in the American people was like a family affliction. His tenderness on this subject was most touching, and filled me with love and reverence. I have not read his history, but from what I learn of it from competent judges I anticipate great profit and instruction from a future examination of it.

We made a visit to Potsdam, which is eighteen miles from Berlin and corresponds to it, as Versailles does to Paris, only it far exceeds it in interest. The modern palaces are very charming, specially the summer palace of the King, and his favorite resort when he desires retirement. No palace could possess a more home-like and attractive character. Not too large nor too much overlaid with splendor for comfort, it is full of elegance and refinement, a sort of glorification of a Hudson River residence of a New York merchant of affluence and taste. The walls were covered with small pictures by the best modern artists. I hoped every moment to come upon an American picture, but did not. The palace looked in all parts made for use, and to be really in use. No part of it was so modest and homely as the King's own bedroom, quite high up in the palace and commanding a lovely view of the river and the well-planted grounds sloping toward it. The King's bed was single, without posts, and made, like the other furniture, of a native wood. No well-to-do farmer could sleep on a plainer couch. Over the foot-board, in the little recess where it stood, was a small crucifix, and over the head-board a water-color drawing styled "The Genius of Thought," a gift from the Queen, on occasion of their silver wedding. A copy of the head of Rauch's statue of Queen Louisa, his mother, was upon one table, and a bust of the Queen upon another. On his writing-table, which seemed in constant use, was a small picture of Old Fritz, and all the implements upon it were military in their style, and cast from bullets or balls that had come from victorious battle-fields, and in the shape of cannon or stacked arms. The old palace, built by Frederick the Great, is an immense pile, with an interior in very poor taste and having a tawdry and faded appearance. It is kept very much as he left it. You are told that the arrangement of the pictures (some lying against the sides of the rooms without frames) continues as his own hand had placed them. His library, small and very French, is as he left it. The historical chairs, whose satin covers his favorite dogs had clawed to tatters, are to be seen.

The graves of his canine favorites and of his war-horse are marked with marble slabs on one side of the little palace of San Souci. Voltaire's ugly visage grins through the glass of one of the book-cases. Frederick's portraits at various ages are found here, always carrying the same expression of the philosopher in uniform, the soldier-savan. His spirit haunts this place, and it is a mighty ghost! Carlyle has not exaggerated its features. Posterity will not improbably decide, when this great soldier and king has exhausted his influence upon the world, that Napoleon yields to Frederick in real greatness. The ashes of this wonderful man lie under the pulpit of the Garrison Church, in a plain vault and in a still plainer metallic coffin. Here every Sunday two thousand Prussian soldiers are reminded of the real founder of their national greatness, and drink in as a part of their religion enthusiasm for his genius and aspirations. The flags taken from France and Austria hang over his tomb and embellish the walls of the church, adding to the influence that is perpetually diffused from this spot, to keep Prussia a military and an aspiring country. I might spend a whole letter upon Potsdam alone, which is full of curious and interesting things, and of lovely rides and walks. But I will only mention one other object of special interest, and that is a collection of exquisite copies of all Raphael's works, made by order of King William III., and affording the best opportunity of seeing all together and comparing with each other the works of this miraculous genius. It was difficult to tear away from the enchantment of this spot. The copies were as good as the originals for all but the nicest discrimination, and here I saw for the first time, in color, works the originals of which are in Spain, Russia, Portugal, but whose fame is in all the world. It was a delicious treat.

XXIX.

LIFE IN PRUSSIA.

BERLIN, October 28, 1867.

PRUSSIA is a military country in even a more marked sense than France. It owes its existence, its growth, its safety, its self-respect to arms. Its people are educated by the musket; they are all under military drill. The uniform is almost the national costume. Berlin is a city of barracks and arsenals and guard-houses, and soldiers are the characteristic feature of its street population. A clean, fresh, straight, comely-looking set of fellows they are, with self-respect and order in every button and every line of their features and forms. The education to cleanliness, decent manners, good carriage and respectful behavior which this great camp, called Prussia, secures, is something most instructive to see. The soldiers do not look brutal, coarse, or sensual. There is some secret about their training which neither the French nor the English have caught. It must be a good deal in the German blood—which is not hot, but as if made of beer, not beef—a little cool and sluggish. The German military spirit is informed and corrected by the universal education of the people. German soldiers and sailors are different from American or English or French. They are neither drunkards, nor quarrelsome, nor reckless. The union of a careful elementary education with a universal participation in the soldier's calling, takes away the exceptional character and licensed rudeness which belong to soldiers when they are only a special class of the population. But, doubtless, this soldier-life, so favorable to order and decorum, and even so chastening to youthful passions, has another and a most painful side to it. It drills the Prussian youth to mechanical habits, represses personal enterprise, delays the self-relying qualities in their character, habituates them to being taken care of, encourages them to lives of busy idleness, and sacrifices each to all, the people to the country. Accordingly, there is a general spirit of listlessness, occupation with immediate pleasures, or magnifying of eating and drinking as very serious occupations, a contentment with humble means, a patient waiting for slow advancement, which it is discouraging to see in so well-educated, so respectable and so orderly a people. Quick as Prussia is in arms—because her military life is all reduced to machinery, and the machinery is in the finest order and can be set in motion in an hour— there is no other quickness about her. She is a slow country. Every practical interest lags. Her workmen are slow, and do not effect in a day three-fourths of the work of an English or American workman. It drives one nearly crazy to see how many arms there are on the levers by which the smallest object is reached. In the restaurants one man receives the order, another carries it, a third transfers it, a fourth executes it, a fifth receives the thing executed, and a sixth makes it over to the original orderer. It takes twenty minutes to get a chop which would be before you in five minutes in an American eating-house. There is a system of military subordination running through the whole social and economical life, and this narrows and limits every body's sphere, and contracts and paralyzes energy and hope.

The people are driven to pleasures and trifles, as a substitute for engaging occupations. They pass an immense amount of their time in beer-shops and gardens, listening to dance-music. They are not rude and drunken—far from it—but they are unaccustomed to the concerns and unfamiliar with the earnest purposes that characterize our life. And with all the freedom of which they boast, they are practically drilled out of the best part of freedom by a parental government that takes care of them like so many ungrown boys and girls. The very students in the University are numbered like state's prisoners, and carry round a card in their pockets which they must show on demand. The police, or some government functionary, are forever meddling with the freedom of the people, who are so used to being watched and ordered and instructed that they do not even know that they are imprisoned in government rules and bureaucratic regulations. If you would go to the opera, you must make a written application for a ticket the day before, and you will receive (or perhaps not) a written notice whether you may be permitted to purchase a place! A servant girl can not leave her place without notifying the police, nor go to one without her paper of confirmation and two or three other certificates. Every Prussian must carry a passport in moving from town to town, which any sentinel may challenge him to produce. The fact is, the people are tied with a very short string to every finger and toe, and can not move out of their places, and the misfortune is that they do not seem to know it. They talk very loudly and proudly of English and American license and disorder, and civic immoralities and drunkenness and crime, and admire very much their freedom from these misfortunes; but they forget that alongside these tares the strongest wheat is growing, and that their political soil is much like their sandy territory, unfavorable to any large growths of either weeds or wheat.

In regard to the political situation in Prussia, it may be said that the only two parties are those of Bismarck, aiming at the unity of all Germany mainly by military force, and the party which wishes to bring about the same result by voluntary concession on the part of the outlying southern states. There is no doubt that the *force* party is carrying the day. Already force has brought three-quarters of all Germany into union, and the other quarter is very sure to fall in. There is no outlet for the superfluous products of Southern Germany except through Northern German ports. The Danube brings them into conflict with markets already preoccupied. They must, therefore, join the Zoll-verein. But North Germany (that is, Prussia) will not allow them this privilege (which they would at once seize upon) unless they pay for it with confessing allegiance. This they will for a short time struggle against, but they must finally submit. What sacrifices of personal liberty this compulsory union may occasion, it is alarming to contemplate. A certain portion only of the Prussian Parliament, not sixty perhaps in all, see clearly the danger, but they are helpless to ward it off. The union of Southern Germany with Northern has two sides to it. It will add an immense Roman Catholic population to a now Protestant country, and complicate internal politics with new ecclesiastical questions ; but, on the other hand, the smaller states of Germany wrung from their princes, so far back as 1816, constitutions which they compelled them to respect, and they have enjoyed a far greater degree of liberty under them than Prussians now possess who only since 1848 have had a constitution, and who have always had a powerful government to prevent its too favorable reading. This freedom in the south is a great offset to the Roman Catholicism there, and will help to reconcile the liberal and Protestant party in Germany to the fusion. When Germany is a unit, there will no doubt be a glorious necessity for separating Church and State, as the only means of solving the Catholic and Protestant question. The overwhelming predominancy of Prussia will be abated by the union, and thus the general liberties of the German race greatly advanced. Many conservatives perceive this side of the consolidation, and are opposed to it as involving a peril for Prussian influence. "Union first and liberty afterward" has been here, as with us, the cry of patriots. But many who might like the union, do not like the liberty, and they prefer to keep things as they now are, with Prussian influence in Germany at the very highest point. But this can not be done. Bismarck has the good sense to see that Prussia must finally yield to German nationality. He is, therefore, in opposition to his old conservative associates, accepting the destiny of Prussia, and aiding it in a certain way to sacrifice itself to a larger interest. This is noble.

Bismarck has for his invaluable assistants in shaping Prussia and Germany General Moltke, the first soldier in Europe, and General Wrode, an admirable tactician and organizer. Having himself been embassador at every important court in Europe—Paris, London, St. Petersburg, Vienna—he thoroughly knows diplomatic characters and political tendencies, and can make his combinations with unfailing skill. He was a student of Louis Napoleon until he excelled his master in astuteness, courage and success. He is a sort of combination of Mr. Seward and General Grant ; with the dialectic and diplomatic acuteness and use of skillful means and patient methods, without much care for what people say, which has distinguished. the Secretary of State, and with the energy and pertinacity of character, the prudence and directness which have illustrated the career of the Lieutenant-General. Bismarck was once a Prussian captain, but does not claim a soldier's reputation. The King had made him a general, partly because he likes to see his Minister in military uniform and partly as a compliment. It is said that Bismarck finds his uniform a convenient excuse for wearing arms, which, since the attack on his life, became prudent. There is no habit in Germany of civilians going armed ; not one revolver is carried here for a hundred in America. Duelling, however, is still common.

One of the most striking illustrations of the repressive tendencies of Prussian policy is seen in the forbiddance to retail newspapers or pamphlets and books in the streets of Berlin. To have a newspaper, you must subscribe for it for the year. As a consequence, the newspapers are neither numerous, enterprising, nor universally read. There seems a want of acquaintance with current events — a difficulty about obtaining local information, which is unfavorable to liberty and practical intelligence.

There is a certain awkwardness in small affairs, a want of tact, or of a sense of fitness—of practical ingenuity and address here in Northern Germany which is unaccountable. The public buildings here, at the centre of physical science, are wastefully and stupidly arranged as to entrance and exit, and terribly unventilated. All windows and doors are awkwardly handled. There is no grace and facility in mechanical matters.

In respect of the custom of living in stories, or apartments —some poor people in the cellar, a *graf* on the first floor, a *hochrath* on the second, a shop-keeper on the third, and a shoe-maker on the fourth—there is much to be said on both sides. It abolishes special districts, in which rich or poor live. It brings the two ends of society together ; it makes the children of the various orders and classes acquainted with each other, and secures a certain democratic sympathy. It is favorable to external morality and order. On the other hand, it destroys the privacy and free development of class-life, which we see in England and America. It makes *home* a less sacred word, and depresses those marked qualities which grow up in a less watched and more castellated domesticity.

In regard to the general morals of Berlin (a representative city), it is unquestionably a place of extraordinary order and decency—a place where tradesmen and mechanics keep their word, where crime is unfrequent, and where drunkenness or furious orgies such as we have in England and America are rare. At one season of the year they go into the country and drink buck-beer for a few days (a very potent liquor), and indulge in a kind of saturnalia. There is an immense festivity always going on in beer-gardens—where the people flock, especially on Sundays and festivals. Wine and beer and schnapps have an immense consumption, but either because the temperament of the people is more lymphatic, or because they have learned by experience to regulate their appetites, or because there is more domestic companionship in their pleasures, there does not seem to be the same tendency to perilous excess. From a careful inquiry at the Municipal Bureau of Statistics, and from the National Bureau (over which the celebrated Dr. Engel presides), I have obtained the data for some interesting comparisons touching the use of alcoholic stimulants, and of wine and beer. By the concession of all, intemperance has abated in Germany. Five-and-twenty years ago, gin-palaces and brandy-saloons were as prominent and active in Berlin as in London or New York. They have been supplanted by beer-shops, which have steadily increased in number and in respectability, while brandy-saloons have been driven out of sight, into cellars or back streets. It is not considered decent to visit places where *only* brandy or strong drinks are sold. They may be had in the beer-gardens, but they are not much used there. There is, however, still an immense amount of potato and corn whisky made in Germany and consumed at home. One of the tables reports the average consumption at twelve quarts per head. But it seems to be used by the poorer classes as an article of alimentation, taken with their food, and not, as with us, a mere indulgence at irregular hours and in repeated doses. Some people try to show that the use of beer has greatly diminished the use of whisky in Germany. I find both whisky and beer, by the tables, steadily increasing in consumption ; but they are neither of them used commonly for purposes of intoxication, although beer certainly is used to a stupefying degree. On the whole, it does not seem safe to argue from Germany to America in regard to the use of stimulants. The temperament and customs and circumstances of the people are so different as to make any comparison fallacious. But I wish we could manage to fight intemperance in America with some other weapons than direct prohibition. It is not the radical cure, and will necessarily have dangerous reactions.

The ordinary beer in use here has two per cent. of alcohol in it. Lager beer has three per cent. ; light wine, seven ; port, eleven ; and brandy, perhaps twenty-five. Enough beer is intoxicating, and often the only difference is slow or quick intoxication, as one drinks alcohol in the shape of beer in small but very numerous doses. This view might simplify some discussions if fully developed.

The University in Berlin was founded in 1809, and has grown to be the largest and most important in Europe. It has countless Professors, and it is said had, at the two semesters or terms of last year, three thousand five hundred students. The distinguished men in the theological faculty, which comes first—I mean the men known in America and Europe — are Twesten, Hengstenberg, Nitzsch and Dorner. Twesten and Nitzsch are very old men. Twesten's first volume is still a classical authority in Biblical criticism. His second, published twenty years afterward, is inferior, it is said, in freedom and courage. The reaction since 1848 has influenced German theology exceedingly. Hengstenberg is one of the old Lutherans, and is the head and front of the State Church. He is a severe polemic, a reactionaire, and a stiff formalist in dogmas and cultus. He heads a movement not unlike Dr. Pusey's, and is trying to bring back a semi-Catholic influence. In the appointment to Church places he has great influence; but his views and spirit do not make much headway in Berlin, although they are more followed in the strictly Lutheran provinces of the kingdom. I heard him lecture. He is a round, good-looking man, with less scholastic air than most Professors in Germany. He speaks with emphasis and warm personal interest, rising often half-way in his chair and sometimes leaning over on one side as if he would get nearer his pupils. His tone is a little querulous and dictatory. I was glad to see he did not despise illustrations drawn from general literature. He put Strauss, Renan and Schenkel in one damnatory sentence. His whole influence is backward. But he seems an honest and good man, and an able one. His learning none dispute, and his personal character is high.

Dorner is just now the chief ornament of the theological faculty, and the best representative of the modern Orthodoxy of Germany. Those who are competent to judge say that he is a man of very comprehensive intellect, with a natural aptitude for philosophy, and especially for the history of opinions; acute in his discriminations, and with admirable power of statement; rising easily from particulars to generals; possessing a moral genius and a constitutional devoutness. I passed an hour with him in very frank conversation, and was highly pleased with his general views and his enlarged sympathies. He is greatly interested in American developments, and has a high opinion of Professor H. B. Smith and of Professor Shedd. Of course he is thoroughly Orthodox, but I should judge more of Smith's type than Shedd's. I heard him lecture on the relations of the historical and the universal elements in Christianity. He is about sixty-five, well-preserved, of a very well-shaped head and serious, thoughtful face, rather small in stature, but in full vigor. He speaks slowly and with beautiful distinctness, in spite of rather poor teeth—a very common defect in Germany, where American dentists are trying to introduce a reform. Dorner came in after his class had assembled, sat down and commenced reading his lecture, read three-quarters of an hour, and got up and went out before the class left their seats. The lack of any personal relation between the professors and the students is very marked here, and in all the foreign universities I have visited. Mr. Bancroft has a very high opinion of Dorner's mind and learning. He is a very admirable embodiment of the moderate views which are now popular in Germany, where sharp dogmatic statements are dangerous and offensive, and where theologians are trying to fasten attention upon the practical side of Christianity and upon the devout life, to relieve the strain of merely intellectual criticism. The age of sharp and positive or merely scientific theology has departed for the present. Indeed, every thing in Germany is now done to postpone a struggle which far-seeing men perceive must come finally, and which must be fatal to so-called Orthodox theology. *Après nous le deluge!* Since 1848 theology has dropped behind the sciences, and the practical experience of political and social freedom. There is an obvious and undisputed rupture between the intellectual and the ecclesiastical life of Germany, not to add of Europe. Science and philosophy go their own way, believing in truth and expecting its ever fresh developments, and saying as little as possible about religion. Theology takes its separate path, accepts the merciful silence of science and philosophy, claims that religion has a separate basis, and has no reason for expecting the support or accordance of physical or scientific facts, and imagines that it is thus honoring the Gospel and saving the faith of three hundred years ago. Meanwhile, the churches are few and empty, or attended mainly by women and the unthinking classes. All this would be impossible were the Church in Germany or France separated from the State. But a clergy supported by State endowments, after being selected by State authority, neither represents public opinion nor meets public wants. It is moored by the interest of its priesthood to a confession or creed which is interwoven with political considerations and a policy of dynasties. Berlin, for instance, has six hundred thousand inhabitants, of whom at least five hundred and fifty thousand are nominal Protestants. It does not number over fifty places of Protestant worship, including every chapel in a hospital or barracks. The average Sunday attendance on Protestant worship is estimated at less than twenty thousand, of whom two-thirds would doubtless prove to be women and children.

· But Berlin is a moral, intelligent and orderly community, of conservative tastes and habits. Its people are not irreverent in tone and speech, among the better classes, and, so far as I can see, are not unbelievers in the essential truths of Christianity. There was a time when the philosophy of Hegel and Schelling led many savans to Pantheism, and the science of Vogt and Virchou encouraged many others to adopt atheistic opinions. But the decline of metaphysical speculations and transcendental mysticism, under the brilliant meridian of physical science, has favored a return from Pantheistic wanderings, while the more advanced Scientists seem to be growing so far religious, as the result of their own studies into matter, as to have discovered that God is not to be ciphered or crucibled out of the Universe. Science here seems to be more theistic than it is in England, and the German mind, which is essentially religious, seems in a fair way, the moment Church and State are separated, to rally round the science of the true savans, and purify superstition by seeing and acknowledging that there is really nothing inconsistent between what true science teaches and what the Gospel of Christ teaches. I think that science has even got far enough here to see that man's creation is a miracle, and life itself an interposition of the divine will and power, and that there is nothing impossible in the New Testament miracles. But all this preparation produces as yet little or no effect upon the church life or religious institutions of the people— nor will it be free to effect any change for the better while Church and State are bound together. This union prevents any true choice of their own ministers by the people, while it hinders any development of religious methods adapted to present circumstances. Nothing of the interest, the free support, the private responsibility which individual laymen feel in America for religious institutions, exists here. The Church is a part of the State, and has all the faults which belong to the State and all the dislike which often follows the State.

The Prussian United Church, as it is called, is a composite of Lutherans and Reformed, or of the two schools of the Reformation—Luther's on the one hand, and Calvin's and Zwingle's on the other. It has adopted the views of the latter on the question of the real presence in the bread and wine, which it denies, and the views of the Lutheran branch on the subject of a more external ritual service, the allowance of pictures, the crucifix, and candles, which are usually seen burning in its churches. It preserves in its confessions essentially the theology of three hundred years ago, and it never wants conservative leaders, like Hengstenberg, who favor the most hard and literal construction of these articles. The Reformed Churches, left to themselves, would doubtless advance in the right direction, and soon occupy the position of at least our Orthodox Congregational liberals. But the patronage of the government favors so completely the old Lutheran party that "the Reformed" are obliged to practice great circumspection to keep the places they have. There are seven or eight liberal ministers in Berlin, who would be Unitarian ministers if they lived in the United States. But they would disown the name, and profess themselves more or less afraid of the thing in their present position, so unpopular with the government, and the Church council which directs all, are their tendencies. I have seen and talked with several of them, and found myself in full and hearty sympathy with them. They are popular, too, with the people, and their churches are as well attended as any. Two of them, I know, confirm as many as or more than any Orthodox preachers. They say they have the youth of Berlin much under their influence and in their train. But it is plain, and they confess, that the whole life of the National Church, of which they are parts, is sickly and discouraging, and that all earnest men are looking for some great change—some radical revolution in the whole ecclesiastical life of Germany. Dorner is trying hard to make the best of existing circumstances, and to hold the people to a moderate Orthodoxy. He favors the continued union of the two parts of the National Church, the Lutheran and Reformed. Hengstenberg would like to crowd the Reformed out of the National Church, and to restore a more thorough Lutheranism, with some modification of Luther's great doctrine of justification by faith, which he weakens with limitations and additions.

But, notwithstanding, I can not but feel that the great common life of the German people and the Prussian people runs in neither of these channels, and has left the Church high and dry. The people have unhappily become accustomed to living without religious observances and without church-going. They have discovered, too, that morality may exist and does exist independently of churches and Sunday instructions. They have invented a kind of piety of their own, and are not without many religious beliefs, hopes and fears. But there is, in spite of all, that decline in earnestness, purity, the sense of responsibility and the service of humanity, which must follow the absence of public worship and religious co-operation. I feel among the people here, with all their geniality and kindness of manners and decorum, a sad want of the moral enthusiasm, aspiration and tenderness which accompany the religious life of the same classes at home. And I believe that a much braver, stronger and more earnest grasping with theological objections, and a much more radical change in the Christian confession of the Germans is absolutely necessary to bring out and reconstitute in Church communions the great masses of the people. This change will come, and the political movements in Germany will hasten it. It can not come too soon.

Talking with one of the best and purest and most distinguished men of science in Berlin to-day about church-going, he reminded me that they had one excellent substitute for it —and that was the habit of attending funerals, where a religious address was always given. He said he got about a dozen sermons a year in this way, and that, given under affecting circumstances, they had more influence than sermons in church, and were better in character. He complained that the preaching at church was usually cold and formal, and that the churches were bad places either to get fixed sit-

tings in or to hear in. I found he wanted preaching addressed to the heart only, and that he was content to hear very
little of it, such as it was. Another member of the Upper
House of Parliament, after a conversation in which his own
liberal views were very apparent, told me that he ordered the
religious teacher of his children to teach them only the old
Lutheran catechism, for he had noticed that women especially went to the bad if they became free-thinkers. He added, men must! Now, what is to be inferred from conversa-
tions like these, with strong, right-minded men, who, unsus-
picious of the effect of what they are confessing, acknowledge
the utter want of seriousness in their own dealings with religion? But I must tear away before half completing what I
should like to say on this absorbing theme.

In the law faculty of the University, the chief names among
the Professors are Berner, Michelet (one of the few remaining disciples of Hegel), Bruns, and Holzendorff. Reichert
is very distinguished in Anatomy; Bois-Reymond, in Physi-
ology; Virchou, in Pathology and Anatomy; Professor Jung-
ken, in Surgery; Dr. Rose, as a demonstrator. Dr. Gräfe
is the great authority on the eye, and has troops of patients
consulting him. At the head of the Metaphysical Department stands Trendelenburg, who lectures on the History of
Philosophy and on Psychology. He is a man of profound
learning and great personal energy—with the head of a philosopher and the face of a saint. He reminded me of our la-
mented Dr. Nichols, who would have been a philosopher if
he had not been a preacher. Professor Dove is a great light
here. His work on " Storms and Winds " has been translated
into French and English. He acknowledged the great importance of our American Redfield's writings, and deemed
his discoveries strictly independent of his own, and entitled
to the name of original investigations. He said Professor

Henry had preceded him a little in some important electrical discoveries. He was a thoroughly genial man and a delightful dinner-companion, as he had been much in England and talked English very well. But time would fail me to speak of Hofmann the chemist, who is the peer and is here thought the superior of Liebig (who is at Munich); of Ranke, the historian, the chief light in his department; of Lepsius, the Egyptologist; of Mommsen, the Roman Archæologist, and of twenty others of only less distinction.

Berlin is the most attractive place of study I have visited. Here one feels the depths of his own ignorance, and sees the means of filling up the vacuum—but, alas! life is too short!

Of the attractions of a lighter sort, much might be said. The best opera I ever heard was at the Royal Opera House, where "William Tell" was put upon the stage more effectively, and sung better and with a nobler impression than I had supposed possible. Wachtel is far the best tenor it was ever my good fortune to hear. Lucca is a great favorite here, but I have heard much more electric and sympathetic voices. The acting at the theatres is said to be very clever, without strain or self-consciousness. There is almost every thing in Berlin, except scenery and sunshine and popular liberty.

I find here an old friend, Hon. Theodore S. Fay, so long and honorably connected with our diplomatic service here, and for a term our Minister to Switzerland. His ardent patriotism through the war will be fresh in all memories. He has just finished an atlas and geography which has been the labor of nearly twenty years, and which is both beautiful and admirable. It ought to have the attention of all teachers. Mr. Putnam is the American publisher, and I hope no want of appreciation on the part of the public will prevent its immediate introduction into all private schools. It makes geography almost a new science. Dr. Abbott, Mr. Fay's son-in-law, is not only the most distinguished dentist in Berlin, but universally known for his patriotism, intelligence and worth.

I have experienced great aid in various statistical inquiries in Berlin from Dr. Engel, Dr. Schwarb, and specially from Mr. J. J. Stutz, who is crammed with knowledge on the subject of emigration, who has been both in North and South America, and has the most enthusiastic interest in our country. As a German he has been indefatigable in the dissemination of the truth in relation to American affairs, and his authority is generally acknowledged for exactness and thorough competency to form an enlightened opinion. He ought to have some position connected with the emigration of Germans to America. Let the proper authorities look to it that so worthy a man is in his right place.

The American chapel is just ready for consecration. I preached last Sunday week in the little hall, where worship is temporarily conducted, to a hundred Americans, and last Sunday heard there the Rev. Mr. Briggs, an Orthodox minister, with much satisfaction. It is under Methodist control, but is liberally conducted. The new chapel is very pretty and convenient, and will be a great comfort to Americans resident here, and to young American students specially. May every blessing rest on this enterprise! The English Congregational Bible Society has an admirable representative here in Dr. Simon, who is quietly doing a great work.

XXX.

WITTENBERG AND HALLE.

October 29, 1867.

WITTENBERG, " the Protestant Mecca," is about fifty miles south of Berlin, on the Elbe, in the midst of a flat country, and, although a walled town containing eleven thousand people, is so quiet and with so few suburbs that you must pass its gates and get fairly into it before you can be convinced that any city is there. Even then its demure and sleepy air gives no sign of the stirring life that emanated from it and once beat with fiery vigor within it. If this is the cradle of Protestantism, and was rocked by Luther's sturdy foot, it has certainly no present marks of the agitation which that noisy child made in his infancy, or of the amount of business he gave his devoted nurse.

But how that a town containing even the ashes of Luther can look and be so dull and mouldy, I can not see. Two chimney-sweeps, snaking along in their skin-close black leather suits, were the only brisk things I saw in town. And yet what a place of mementoes and memories it is ! Here, in this homely church, a part of the Elector's old palace, beneath this pavement on which I tread, sleeps the dust of Martin Luther ; here, a few paces on the other side of the aisle, lie the ashes of Melanchthon ; united in their lives and not divided in their death. What an aroma fills this place ! There, just over his grave, against the church wall, hangs the portrait of this glorious hero, painted by his friend, Lucas

Cranach, a native of this city, and looking every inch a king.
That broad, burly man, with a great sensuous nature and
frame, purged and refined by intellectual and spiritual life,
was made to reform the Church and to overturn the Papal
power—the mightiest foe human courage ever yet single-
handed was called to assail and defy. How homely, nay
ugly, that bull-throated, jumbled-up, low-crowned, square-
shaped visage is ! Yet, what genial sweetness, what moral
dignity, what largeness, what confidence, what humor and aspiration are commingled and embodied there ! That small,
inexpressive nose is the only unaccountable feature. The
eye, the mouth, the double chin, the great throat, the full
blood, the ample paunch and chest, all are as we would have
them. But, faithful Cranach, did Luther have that insignificant nose? Well, Socrates had a small nose, and Luther must
have carried his courage and firmness in some other member.

Melanchthon looks in his portrait, which hangs opposite,
just as Luther does not—the very complement of his great
friend and companion. His high and overhanging brow
speaks of the scholar ; his sharp, delicate features of the more
shrinking temperament he had ; his whole aspect, so saintly
and gentle, of the man of thought and affection, in contrast
with the man of passion and will. There, in what used to be
the old choir of the church, are the effigies, in iron castings,
from Vischer's skillful hands, of Luther's great friends, the
two Electors, Frederick the Wise, and John the Steadfast ;
and outside, upon the church door, where bronze gates now
occupy the place of the original doors, is a copy of the nine-
ty-five theses which Luther fixed in this spot, when he first
challenged the Pope to the combat which has already lasted
three and a half centuries. It seems as if the news from
Rome to-day must flatter Luther's ashes here in Wittenberg,
or even brighten the letters on these bronze gates. Garibal-

di, a victor at her doors, and with Luther's cry in his mouth, seems almost the fulfillment of the motto which stands round the mask taken from Luther's face after death—"Living, I was the Pope's pest ; dying, I shall be his death !" Such•faith is its own fulfillment !

From the graves of Luther and Melanchthon we went to their statues, noble figures raised on beautiful pedestals of polished red granite, and set up within a few years, one by a society devoted to Luther's memory, the other by the King of Prussia, in the market-place and in front of the venerable town-hall, on whose harmonious front Luther and Melanchthon must so often have looked. In this town-hall are various interesting memorials of Luther, especially the top of his beer-mug, and, what was more curiously suggestive, the very rosary which he used as a Catholic priest. I handled the beads, expecting to feel the marks of Luther's fingers on them, for such Paternosters and Ave Marias as he must have told off on this string could not fail to have imparted virtue, even to dull beads. Here is preserved the hand of a woman, cut off after her execution, which took place in front of the town-hall, who murdered the four children of the first wife of her husband, from a retrospective jealousy. Cranach's house is within view of Luther and Melanchthon's statues, if their spirits ever use these brazen eye-balls to look up the haunts of their life-time. The guide pointed us to Hamlet's house as we passed a venerable wine-shop ! Because Shakespeare sent his brain-child to college at Wittenberg, they have actually hunted up the lodgings of that fancy. So solid and actual are the men whom Shakespeare created, that they count in the census !

But here is Luther's house—or rather his lodgings—in the old University, where he was Professor of Theology, and which remains essentially unchanged, except that all its pu-

pils were transferred to Halle long ago. It is a grim, melancholy old place ; and this earthern stove, made after Luther's own designs, with a strange jumble of evangelists and hea-
• thenish goddesses—Matthew and geometry, John and trigonometry, etc., etc.—does not keep it warm ! Luther's ale-mug (very small for a German's draught) and a broken wineglass, which it is said was broken by Peter the Great when he visited these relics, are asserted and believed to be genuine. More interesting is the oak just outside the gate which marks the very spot where Luther burned the Pope's bull, Dee. 10, 1520.

Melanchthon's house is not many rods from Luther's, and is a fine house still. It was a gift to the great man from his appreciative townsmen. One room in it is of almost unequaled interest. Over the middle window is a Latin inscription to this effect : " With eyes looking to the North, here Melanchthon sat and wrote those works which the world now holds so dear;" and in the south-east corner another Latin inscription declares that, " Against this wall stood the little bed on which Melanchthon piously and placidly ended his blessed life."

There are many other things, especially pictures and portraits of Cranach, at Wittenberg, of lively interest. But Luther's and Melanchthon's traces absorb the attention wholly, and make other memorials unattractive. In the handsome church—so old without, so new within—the Stadt Kirche—is the pillar against which Luther's pulpit rested. The church is full of memorials of him, the font in which he and Melanchthon were wont to baptize children, pictures of his family, and old monuments of his friends. But the echoes of his voice are the best memorial, even here. That these walls have vibrated with that melodious thunder, is their best sanctification and protection !

This is a town of 23,000 inhabitants, situated on the little, and, for this flat region, picturesque stream of the Saale. It is an old, dull-looking town, but has some large manufactories—woolen, looking-glass frames, and iron foundries ; but is specially known for its salt-works and its University. The salt-works are small compared with those on the Salz-kammergut in the Tyrol, or with ours at Syracuse. But they are here worked by a special class of men, known as Halloren, and the works give the town its name. These Halloren have prescriptive rights, one of which is the right to attend and form a part of certain University processions. For instance, to-day the students and officers turned out in force to honor a student's funeral. The Halloren were present by a delegation of workmen. They are a thin, wiry-looking race, with all their thews and sinews distinctly visible. They work at a great heat in the rooms where the crystallization of the salt-water is going on, and are naked with the exception of a pair of loose breeches. They must sweat off all their fat in this constant parboiling atmosphere. They claimed that it was not an unwholesome life.

Halle has a noted orphan asylum, founded by a saintly Professor of the University, Francke, who begun it on Müller's principle of trusting divine Providence for the means of building and supporting it. It was carried on for many years very successfully under the pious inspiration which originated it, and attracted funds from religious people throughout Germany. There are about 400 orphans here, boys and girls, mostly between ten and fourteen years of age. The buildings occupy an immense space, and look as if designed to house thrice the number. We examined the school-rooms, eating-room and bedrooms. They were decently ordered, but there was no conspicuous neatness, meth-

od or wisdom in the external arrangements. **Various**
trades, especially printing, are carried on by the orphans.
There are day-schools connected with the "Waisen-haus"
which are largely attended by the children of the town.   A
beautiful statue of the founder, with two orphans at his feet,
made by Rauch, stands before the inner entrance in the
court.   I judge that the original spirit has somewhat fallen
off.   It being a holiday, we saw only few of the children, and
these did not strike us very favorably.   Music is a specialty
in the asylum, and the children are said to sing finely.   We
could get no special attention from the officers, who put us
in charge of an incompetent door-keeper, who could answer
none of our questions satisfactorily.   There was nothing in
the orphan-house that made it interesting beyond the interest that attaches to all such places, except a certain freedom
from routine and a habitual reliance on the good-will and
self-care of the children.   They were allowed, the porter
told us, to go into the town alone on holidays, which occurred
often.

The University here was in session, and the streets were
full of students in their club-caps, some of them of a very
tawdry and Oriental description, not two inches high, and
stuck on the top of the head, stiff with gold lace in a very
theatrical fashion.   There are 1200 students here—a very
rapid increase.   They appear to be their own masters, as is
common in German Universities.   They drink beer and fight
duels, spite of the energetic discouragement which Dr. Tholuck and other enlightened professors make to this barbarity.
The existence of a special administration of college laws,
exempting the students from the usual police laws of the
University towns, is the chief encouragement of this middle-
age folly.   A petition, very numerously signed, appealing
last year to the Government of Prussia to abolish the special

jurisdiction of the Universities in police laws, was vetoed, it is said, by the King, who, as a soldier, believes in duelling. He is not alone in this absurd prejudice. Very worthy men here are found justifying and upholding duelling as a means of keeping discourtesy and rude provincial manners from creeping into the Universities and the army. The theory of Prussia and most kingly states, that the army and the diplomatic service are the only highly honorable careers, and that commerce and the professions are occupations fit only for vulgar blood, is itself upheld by duelling, which is accounted a duty in the army and is enforced by a quasi-official authority. It is the high-born students who, in imitation of their knightly ancestors, keep it up in the Universities.

Halle, the old home of Gesenius (who died in 1840), and the present home of Dr. Tholuck, has between three and four hundred theological students. Julius Müller is here Professor of dogmatic Theology, and of the same school with Dorner. Erdmann, who has a European reputation, and Ulrici, who has lately written a valuable work, called " God and Nature," in which very positive theistic views are derived from a scientific examination of physical things, are among the professors.

Having but a very short time to spend here, I called on Professor Tholuck, at the afternoon hour when he daily receives visitors. I may mention, as an excellent Continental usage, that public men, subject to many calls, all have their hour or two, when alone they can be seen, *published in the town directory after their names.* Might it not be wisely copied in America? I found Tholuck, walking with a young man, in a covered way at the bottom of his garden, evidently the place where he gets his daily exercise. He looks a man of seventy years, of a slight figure, and with delicate and irregular features, of an unusual shrewdness and gentleness, an acute saint. He talks English admirably. He was evi-

dently not unpreoccupied, and my visit had clearly interrupted some serious conference with the young man, who looked
terribly disappointed at the sudden appearance of strangers.
This consciousness shortened our call, but in twenty minutes
I had enjoyed an interesting opportunity of tasting the quality of this extraordinary man, and of asking many questions
on which I desired his opinion. He showed his superiority
by the self-command with which he turned from his own interests to meet my inquiries, and his eminent courtesy and
kindness mixed with a self-centered fidelity to his own opinions. Tholuck seems to unite the largest measure of the
pietistic fervor, for which Halle has been marked, with a
spirit of open intelligence, a wide-minded charity for opinions,
and, what is better, for men holding opinions he deems erroneous in a truthful and reverent temper. Then he spoke
of Keim of Zurich—whose life of Jesus has of late awakened
much attention, and who has advocated strictly humanitarian
views of Christ—as a man for whose spirit and character he
had a lively respect. Tholuck is Orthodox, and sympathizes
with Orthodox men and Orthodox views ; but he is thoroughly liberal also, and understands the difficulties of Orthodox
theology, and the honesty and necessity which compels many
other earnest and true men to reject them. He evidently
had little sympathy with what he said was the rising school
in Germany, the school of Hengstenberg, the school of the
reactionnaires, whose first principle is " veneration for the opinions of their illustrious Protestant fathers," and who are striving to dam out liberalism and what they call atheism, infidelity and materialism, by heaping up all the opinions and
usages they can recover from the dogmatic faith and practice
of Luther and his fellow-reformers. This is the timid and
sacred work in which the German churchmen, the analogues
of the English Puseyites and High Churchmen, and the

American stiff-backed Episcopalians, are now engaged. And the aristocracy and wealth of the country are aiding their work. They wish to bring back the old principle of *authority*, so far as Luther spared it; and forgetting what an iconoclast of the ecclesiasticism of his day he was, they choose to remember only what assumptions and what exercise of priestly powers and rites he still left in Protestantism. To save the Church by denouncing examination, or any conclusions of examination other than the theology, pure and simple, which Luther taught, this is their policy. They are resolved to make Luther's theology true, by boldly declaring it so. Like the superstitious usage of those who make the Prayerbook more sacred than the Bible, and quote the Rubric as decisive of theological questions—these German Established Churchmen are boldly practicing the childish game—

> " Open your mouth, and shut your eyes,
>   And I'll give you something to make you wise."

In concert with the State authorities and the conservatives of existing wealth and station, they distribute places in the Church chiefly to those who will join them in this foolish, though just now successful, policy of carrying Protestantism forward on Roman Catholic principles. Tholuck was guarded in what he said, but it was clear enough that his heart was with Dorner and the school who, while fully accepting historical and supernatural Christianity, look to the inner consciousness and to spiritual experience for its everlasting basis and interpretation. I can not think these mild Orthodox men logical in their views, but they are so far in advance of the alarmists who have forgotten Melanchthon's motto, " Dare to know," and Luther's whole example, that it is most refreshing to get into their atmosphere. Tholuck said that since 1820 there had been a reaction in Germany upon the Rationalistic school, and that Rationalism might be consid-

ered as dead in its original character ; but that since 1848
there had been another tendency gathering force which was
more positively inimical to Christian faith. I suppose he
meant the materialistic school born in the chemical crucible,
or under the knife of the medical men. He said that in
spite of the general tendency of Physics to question or deny
revealed religion, the best and ablest physicists were now ex-
pressing other opinions and exerting another influence.
There was something very affecting to me in the evident
struggle in Tholuck's mind between a constitutional confidence in truth, a faith in the right to inquire and advance,
and a sympathy with liberal studies and liberal men on the
one hand, and on the other a foreboding of the possible results of these inquiries to opinions dear to his devout heart
and wrought in with his life-long habits. An old man, and
not likely to see the end of the present controversy, he seemed to feel himself and his party in Germany on the losing
side, and yet to be determined to live and die its advocate.
The moderate Orthodoxy of the noblest men in Germany is
not as strong as the positiveness and the organized diplomacy of the representatives of the by-gone dogmas of three
hundred years ago. There is no hope for the half-hearted,
illogical theology which is marrying together Trinitarian formulas and modern philosophy. Dorner and Tholuck and
Müller and the rest must have the courage of their principles,
if they do not wish to see such men as Keim and Schenkel
and Schweitzer taking the young mind of Germany, and
building up a thoroughly reformed faith upon rational foundations, without too much regard to foregone formulas. Dr.
Tholuck spoke with great affection of his old pupils, Rev.
Charles Lowe and Rev. Edward Young, and also of Rev. Mr.
Foote, whose acquaintance he had lately made. He hoped
such men would do something to convince the world that

Unitarianism was not exclusively a religion of the intellect. I told him that none who knew what it really was in the hearts and lives of its true disciples could feel that that testimony was any longer necessary.

LEIPSIC, October 31.

This is an important day in Leipsic. A new Rector is installed over the venerable University, one of the oldest in Europe, having been founded in 1420. The Rector of European Universities is elected either annually or for short periods, and for the time fulfills the duties of President. The professors and a crowd of students and guests assembled at 12 M. in the Aula, or Saloon of State in the Augusteum, the name of the chief University building. After singing Krummacher's Hymn, "Jehova's Wort kann nicht vergehn," a short speech of inauguration was made, and a mantle of office thrown over the new Rector. Then followed a festival song of Schiller, set to music by Mendelssohn. This concluded the in-door exercises, out-of-doors a procession in carriages, six-horse, four-horse, and two-horse vehicles, to the number of sixty, paraded through the city. This day falls upon the annual commemoration called the Reformation Festival, the 31st October, a day now very generally, with increasing fervor, celebrated throughout Protestant Germany. We found preparation for it making at Wittenberg, where Luther's house was garlanded with wreaths. Here it was celebrated by a general cessation from business, and by public religious exercises in all the churches. We attended the special service held in St. Thomas's school, where the celebrated choir of men and boys were expected to sing. Sebastian Bach was precentor to this school, and music has been one of its specialties for centuries. The choir of forty voices sang Luther's hymn, "Ein feste burg ist unser Gott," to very expressive fugue music, and in a manner beyond all praise. It was the perfection of chorus-singing, and excited the greatest enthusiasm. Then Professor ——, rector of the school, made an address in honor of the day, marked by earnestness, force, and nobleness of tone. He pictured the relations of Luther and Melanchthon, and distributed their honors with an impartial and most discriminating hand. It was clear that he loved Melanchthon, as scholars must, better than Luther. He called him repeatedly "our dear Philip," and said that he was the teacher of all Germany, and that his books had continued to be used in the schools of Germany for nearly four hundred years.

In the evening a concert was given at the Gewand-haus (I suppose the old Clothier's Hall), under the direction of the Conservatory of Music, doubtless the finest in Germany, and enjoying a reputation hardly second to Paris. These concerts are known to musicians everywhere as the most finished and classical performances anywhere to be heard. They are attended by subscribers only, who are so jealous of their places that it is only by the greatest favor that strangers can procure admission, and then only by buying through some broker tickets which the owners may through sickness or absence be unable to use. We were lucky enough to get three after twenty-four hours of seeking. The concert repaid our pains. The room holds only six hundred persons. The orchestra occupied a quarter of the space. Only instrumental music was given, comprising a glorious overture (to an unpublished opera) on the theme of "Luther's Hymn," in honor of the occasion, and some short pieces from Beethoven's "Fidelio." One of Schumann's piano concert pieces was performed, with full orchestra, by Fraulein. ——, of Hanover; Concert-master Deecke, from Munster, played admirably one of Spohr's pieces for the violin, and the concert concluded with Mozart's Symphony in D flat. Precision was the marked feature of the performance, which was as nearly faultless in time and tune as my senses could measure perfection. There was an extraordinary seriousness in the performers and in the audience. The orchestra seemed in the hands of men as grave and scholarly as if they had been professors in the university, and the people listened as if they had been at church. The applause, with the exception of a hearty tribute to the violinist at the close of the performance, was very measured. The Conservatory has a most thorough system of instruction running through three years. The pupils can only enter after examination as to character, attainments and fitness to make good musicians. It costs about sixty dollars a year in fees, and four or five hundred more in living expenses, according to the student's habits of economy. There are about one hundred and fifty pupils here from all countries. Leipsic is the centre of musical taste and studies in Germany and of the publication of music.

The city is a much more sightly and pleasant town than I expected to find it. It is open and airy, with fine promenades where its old walls used to stand. The university building, the museum, post-office, new theatre and other public edifices are all near each other, and make a very impressive collection of structures. There are many evidences of wealth and prosperity in the princely-looking private residences in the paved parts of the city. The gardens, the Johannen Park and the Rosenthal, joined by a charming forest drive, make the immediate suburbs very agreeable, flat as they are.

The great fairs, eight hundred years old they claim to be, occur three times a year and draw Oriental as well as Western merchants to their great sales. A hundred millions of francs is said to be the ordinary measure of the transactions of the year at these fairs, which last only three weeks each. Leipsic is, too, the centre of the German book-trade.   It has an exchange devoted wholly to book-sellers, who come here from all parts of the world.   It is open every day, and is devoted one day to Greek and Latin book sales, another to French, another to German, and so on.

The " Aula " of the University contains a few fine busts, especially one of Leibnitz, a native of Leipsic, and another of Goethe.   The History of Civilization just under the cornice, in a series of squares, is too high up to be seen to any advantage, but appears worthy of a better position.

The museum is rich in modern pictures, especially in four great landscapes of Calame, much the largest and finest, with one exception (at Basle), I have met with,   They exhibit his powerful pencil in all its various ways, and would hardly be supposed to proceed from one master.   The view of Monte Rosa at sunset is one of the boldest landscapes in the world. Spagnoletti never dared more vivid contrasts than Calame has triumphantly used in this master-piece.   Paul de la Roche's picture of Napoleon, at Fontainebleau, after the battles of 1813, which saved Leipsic and Europe, is very properly found in this museum.   Though familiar by so many copies, it has a new interest when seen here, where every foot of ground for miles around has been trampled by Napoleon's soldiers.   Leipsic is full of memorials of those days, and especially of monuments in which cannon-balls, saved from all the fields where the Allies succeeded, are piled up as memorials.   Few spots in the world are as blood-stained as Lutzen in its immediate neighborhood.

Bach's monument, erected here by Mendelssohn, is of special interest.   Hahnemann, too, sits upon his pedestal, in the midst of multitudes of followers.   Leipsic makes a large part of all the homœopathic medicine of the world. Germany has numerous physicians of that school, although they are more eclectic in their practice than our homœopathic doctors profess to be.

XXXI.

DRESDEN.

SAXONY, November 6, 1867.

SAXONY seems to be the New England of Germany. Protestant, industrial, stocked with an intelligent, order- ly, sober, moral and busy population, it is filled with facto- ries and workshops, and makes the whole world tributary to its skill in textures and in iron. It supplies America with a large portion of all its stockings, and produces an immense amount of linen and woolen fabrics. Its connection with the Customs-Union, of which Prussia is the leading and con- trolling member, has stimulated its production greatly, and laid the way for a final absorption in the great political union which is rapidly but cautiously forming all over Germany. The mild and liberal rule of its princes, under the unambi- tious, artistic or scholarly family of its ruling house, will not save it from falling into the arms of that great nationality which is fast rubbing out the little kingdoms and principali- ties that have so long spotted and speckled the map of the Father-land. Saxony made a sad mistake in the late German war. She sided with Austria, not because the sympathies of the people ran that way, although they were not positively inclined to the other side, but because her Catholic King leaned to the Catholic cause represented by Austria. With- out asking the consent of his Parliament, the King suddenly, almost furtively, sent 40,000 men to the aid of the Austrian Emperor. They left the city of Dresden on a Sunday morning, and before thirty-six hours a detachment of Prussian soldiers marched into Dresden, and occupied the city for nearly a whole year. Their conduct here was orderly, considerate and ingratiating, and won the sympathies of the best part of the people. They compared only too favorably their gentlemanly behavior with what they imagined would have been the conduct of the Austrian army, so largely recruited from Slavonic provinces, which produce, in their judgment, only a semi-barbaric population. Of the 40,000 Saxons who went to the late war, ten thousand never returned, a loss nearly equal to the whole destruction of Prussian soldiers, and a bereavement too heavy for this small kingdom not to be long remembered against the mistaken monarch who caused it. It is pretty certain that the Saxon kingdom will not long consider its fictitious independence worth the maintenance of a royal establishment. King John has less independence than the Governor of an American state. His Parliament is very much limited in its legislative functions by the veto which Prussia possesses in the Customs-Union. The sentiment of the people (the few nobles of course take a different view) is decidedly favorable to a complete union with the German Bund. The Crown Prince, who is a good soldier, and distinguished himself in the recent war, seems to count the succession so little attractive that he is reported to have made some overtures to the second son (his only brother) to exchange the political inheritance for the pecuniary heritage which by usage falls to him.

It is very unfortunate for Saxony that she possesses Roman Catholic sovereigns, a misfortune which is entailed most unnaturally on her in the bargain by which the crown of Poland was settled on one of her princes, on condition of his professing, against all the proud Protestant antecedents of the house, the Catholic faith. The descendants of this King of Poland have kept the bargain with superfluous fidelity. Losing the kingdom, they have held on to the faith that purchased it. It has produced no effect upon the people, who have not followed at all the lead set them. Dresden, the seat of a Bishop (who is hardly more than private chaplain of the King, and is nominated by him to his see), possesses only one Catholic church, and not over 5000 Catholics. The beautiful music for which this church is celebrated has not corrupted the Protestant faith of those living in its shadow. Protestantism flourishes, and possesses several beautiful churches, inherited from Catholic builders, which are fortresses of the faith of the old Saxon Electors, to whom the Reformation owed so much of its protection in the days it needed it most. Fortresses they are in every sense ; for some of their stone domes and towers have successfully resisted bombardments expressly aimed to destroy them. Black and resistful, they rear their smoked and grimy visors, battle-stained, against the sky, and seem to challenge the utmost malice of the Catholic power ; fit symbols of the enduring firmness and settled purpose of this sturdy Protestant stronghold. Not that Saxony, more than any other part of Germany, is marked by a very active religious life ; but it is characterized by an inflexible anti-Catholicism.

Even in respect of external religious observances, it is in advance of most other German states. Twenty years ago, the Rationalism which was nearly universal in Germany had inundated Saxony, and very much weakened the interest in any form of ecclesiastical life. It is attributed to Von Beust, the late vigorous Minister of Saxony—now transferred to Austria—that he brought to Dresden a Dr. Harless, an able and positively Orthodox pastor, who, by his earnestness and downright affirmativeness, changed the tenor of the preaching in all the pulpits, and the disposition of the people, and revived a very thorough-going, old-fashioned Lutheranism, which has since had power with the community. I do not find, on personal visits to the churches, any considerable verification of the statement that public worship engages the affections and the presence of the Saxon men. A fair attendance of women and children may be seen, but men are scarce in the churches. The pastors are exceedingly busy. In the chief Protestant churches service is held on Sundays four or five times through the day (never later than 4 P.M., when festivity is in order), beginning at $5\frac{1}{2}$ o'clock in the morning, for the accommodation of servants and other persons occupied through the midday hours. I attended two of these services on one Sunday, and counted in a range of pews near me forty-seven women and three men. I heard in one of the churches a most living sermon from an admirable pulpit orator, on the difference between Revolution and Reformation in Religious History—*apropos* to the three hundred and fiftieth anniversary of the Reformation. The two churches I visited were grand structures externally, and stately within, but were arranged too much like opera-houses for ecclesiastical seemliness. They had a parquette and a succession of tiers of boxes—which did not gain any thing in religious effect by being in the principal tier fitted with windows and thoroughly · enclosed and locked. These boxes are purchased in perpetuity by the more prosperous families, and handed down from generation to generation, like our pews. But they pay no annual tax, and what is worse, were almost wholly empty, though all disposed of. The Protestant churches are superintended by the government, but not supported by it. They have large funds which, it is said, amply support four or five pastors for each church. Two thousand dollars, with fees for special services amounting to a thousand more, is the utmost salary, and is considered a very ample support in this comparatively cheap town. The Lutheran service is formal ; the prayers are read with no pretension of devout absorption in the pastor's manner. The singing is excellent in Dresden, both in character and execution—thoroughly religious in style, being of the choral sort, and generally joined in by the people. I can think of no way of reforming our American church music more likely to succeed than that of sending a competent person to Leipsic or Dresden to study the methods used here, and carry back to America both the tunes and the training which are so satisfactory here. I believe it would reward any large city parish to educate abroad a chorister with special reference to its own wants.

Dresden is a dull-looking place — its squares gloomy, and unoccupied by a bustling population. Its streets are narrow, and its chief avenue is interrupted by a contracted archway under the heavy old palace, which admits the passage of only one vehicle at a time, and constitutes a nuisance of the first magnitude, which is borne with a humiliating patience by the people. The public buildings are chiefly due to Augustus the Strong, who plays the same great part in Saxon architecture that Louis XIV. did in French, or Maria Theresa in Austrian. To him, too, is due, with the aid of his great Minister, Von Bruhl, the foundation of the greatness of the Gallery which is the chief ornament of Dresden. The purchase of a collection in 1745, containing a hundred valuable pictures, from the Duke of Modena, when he was an exile from his kingdom and in sore pecuniary distress, was the first grand accession to the Gallery, which had already made a good beginning, and possessed, as early as 1722, the famous Venus of Titian, and the two celebrated landscapes of Claude. The history of the diplomacy by which the Madonna Sixtus, the Holbein Madonna, and Guido Reni's "Ninus

and Semiramis " were obtained, inclines one to say that kingdoms have been won and lost in a less painful and less skillful battle of wits than these pictures cost—where long residences abroad of the most adroit agents, maintaining a vo-
luminous correspondence with the Saxon Prime Minister,
often in cipher, were necessary to accomplish their objects,
and secure these prizes at a not too heavy cost of money.
Dresden possesses—when its variety is kept in view—an almost unequaled Gallery. It contains master-pieces of the
Roman, Lombardic, Venetian, Bolognese, Genoese and Nea-
politan schools; a few excellent examples of the Spanish
school, although Murillo is feebly represented. The French
school is well exhibited in numerous pictures of Nicolas and
Gaspar Poussin, Claude, Courtois, Watteau and Anthony
Pesne, as well as Vernet and Gerard. The Flemish school
is overwhelmingly rich is nearly four hundred pictures, where
Floris, the Breughels, Jordaens, Bril, the Franckens, Savery,
Rubens (in astonishing abundance, not less than thirty-five
pictures), Snyders, Teniers (also immensely abundant), and
Van Dyk, are to be studied and enjoyed to the greatest advantage. The Dutch school is still more fully represented
in about six hundred pictures—a full quarter of the whole
Gallery. Poelemburg, the landscapist, so great in small figures; Gerard Dow, with his pre-Raphaelite truth of interiors
and portraits; Brouwer, with his boors, always in row; Rem-
brandt, with his mastery of chiaroscuro and his richness of
color, and his profound insight into character and a certain
grandiose majesty in his treatment even of coarse subjects;
Bol, who renders Jacob's Dream so tenderly; Both; Ostade,
who must have lived in a Dutch inn, and spent his life
watching the smoking and drinking and card-playing of his
coarser countrymen; Ruysdael (Jacob), whose fine deep
greens and living water make him justly so great a favorite—

alone in the poetry of the landscapists among the Dutch ;
Metzu, a more refined Ostade ; Wouvermans, whose famous
white horse lights up at least fifty different landscapes, all
good, but each so like the others that one feels it would be
a mercy to the Dresden Gallery to burn or scatter nine-tenths
of all this master it possesses ; Berghem, who was capable
of landscape and figures, and shows a variety unusual in the
Dutch artists, as well as the finest technical excellency ;
Paul Potter, in three good but inconsiderable specimens ;
Mieris, who does so much better what a certain famous
French school are now making so popular—all that can be
done in rendering the texture and sheen and flow of silk and
satin draperies ; Mignon, fatiguingly successful in flowers
and fruits ; Netscher, full of elegance and exquisite finish in
his women, which are daintily grouped in fascinating interiors ; Schalken, whose candle-light effects are so widely
valued ; Weenix, famous for his game ; Adrian Van der Werff,
who possesses the softest and most ivory-like execution,
united to an aristocratic elegance, and a harmonious perfection not to be surpassed.

In the Flemish school, the Dresden Gallery contains valuable specimens of John Van Eyck, that originator of a new
school, especially a beautiful Virgin and Child, with St. Cath-
arine and St. Michael on either side ; of Quintin Messys, a
fine character piece ; of Albert Durer, three or four not superior specimens ; of Cranach, father and son, very rich and
various representatives.   A portrait of Luther in his shroud,
by an unknown artist, gives a finer idea of his noble character than any picture of the living man I have met with.   Holbein is represented by one of the two greatest and most
precious pictures of the Gallery ; the famous picture of the
Burgomaster Jacques Meyer and his family prostrate before
the Holy Virgin, who holds the infant Jesus in her arms.   A

great dispute exists as to the meaning of the puny and ailing child in the arms of the Madonna, many contending that she has put down the Christ-child (the vigorous and handsome child who stands in the foreground of the group on the *male* side of this picture) and taken up the sick child of the Meyer family, to indicate the truth of the Master's saying, "Whosoever does it unto the least of my disciples does it unto me." It is mentioned, on the other hand, that this idea is incompatible with the religious views of Holbein's time, and that no painter would have dared to insult the seated veneration of the day by putting any common mortal in the place of Jesus in the Madonna's bosom. It seems to me that there are other objections to this hypothesis. The attitude and expression of the healthy child has nothing spiritual in it. His face is rude and his arm outstretched in an unmeaning manner. Indeed, his figure and that of the boy behind him are both unsatisfactory, and form the only blemish in this magnificent picture. The expression, on the other hand, of the Christ-child is, in spite of the sickly aspect, intensely individual and spiritual; and evidently the real fact is that Holbein intended to represent the illness of the child, who, by supposition, is brought to be healed, as having been assumed by Jesus, according to the saying, "He bore our sicknesses." This idea, though doubtless refined beyond the time, is worthy of and not beyond Holbein's genius. He has made the health he transfers to the restored child bear too little trace of the source whence it came; but it is radiant health. The face of the Virgin is transcendently fine, considering its Flemish origin. It is too old and too queenly, and the figure lacks all the celestial drapery of blue that we so naturally associate with the Madonna—but it is full of meaning, and is wonderfully refreshing after the unideal softness in which the mother of our Lord is usually painted. The color is superb.

Was ever a detail more exquisitely rendered than the fold in the carpet at the bottom of the picture? Screta's portraits of the Evangelists and Saints are full of solid merit. Passing by Roos, special attention is due to the rare collection of Denner's portraits, which, for photographic rendering of the human visage, have never been equaled. Angelica Kaufman has three delicate works here, specially interesting to lovers of woman's genius. There is also an interesting collection of works of contemporary German artists.

The two alcoves devoted to pastels are unequaled in this class, which is too monotonous to interest any one very long. Raphael Mengs and Carriera are the chief artists in this line, although the most celebrated pictures are from Liotard, the painter of the famous "Vienna Chocolate Girl." I must confess that copies in oil of this picture, with which I was familiar, made the original in *pastel* quite disappointing. It seemed weak in color. Dietrick, the King's painter for thirty years, has filled the lower gallery with above fifty pictures, exhibiting a great versatility and a skillful and learned acquaintance with his art; but after all, no heart-piercing thrust in any one direction amid his many fair pushes in all quarters.

Canaletto is nowhere probably to be seen in such abundance and perfection as here, where more than thirty of his largest-sized pictures are found. His architectural rendering is certainly wonderful, and may easily be verified by his pictures of old Dresden, which might serve almost as a guide-book, so true and so expressive are they of buildings and streets still standing, almost wholly unchanged, in the old and the new town—the difference, as my guide humorously said, between new and old Dresden being that one was built in the ninth century and the other in the tenth! Ruskin says, in effect, that Canaletto, spite of his cognomen, did not know how to paint canals, and that his water is not worthy of the name, and would not be known as water if it were not in the place where water is usually found.   His reflections are admirably managed, but I must say that I do not differ from Ruskin in thinking his reputation as a water-painter very extravagant.

The Madonna of Raphael (known as the Madonna Sixtus) is so exalted in the world's praise that it is impossible to look at it with fresh and independent eyes.   Probably it has been more admired than any picture in the world, and I doubt not the admiration has usually been genuine.   It takes no culture and no taste to love and enjoy this picture.   A beautiful woman, serious and modest, holding a preternaturally lovely and spiritual child in her arms—with a saintly-looking old man gazing up into her face on one side, balanced by an exquisitely fair and holy girl looking down, oppressed by such sacred beauty, on the other side ; with two cherubs, just dropped from heaven, resting on the lower edge of the picture—with the celestial halo tangled in their hair and beaming from their upturned eyes — why every body must see and praise and bless such a picture, independent of any fame in its author, or any religious feeling on the subject!   It appeals to natural piety, to domestic affection, to veneration for age, to love of beauty and to reverence for maidenly purity and cherubic infancy.   How far Raphael has really conceived truly the Madonna, how far her innocent, gentle, serious face, without much past or much future in its look, expresses the Mary who had carried so many troubled thoughts in her breast, and who was the mother of such a glorious Son, may be well questioned.   That the child is more successful than the mother, considered from the point of character, is, I think, sure.   Certainly I had no disappointment in this picture, for I knew just what to expect, and

I disagree with those who think that very perfect copies of it do not exist. Indeed, it seems to me one of the easiest of all great pictures to render either by engraving or by color.

It is very different in this respect from Titian's "Christ Taking the Money"—to me far the richest and most valuable picture in this Gallery, and the only one I greatly coveted for my own. A very skillful copy from a capital artist on the opposite wall shows the hopelessness of transferring the subtle power of this great inspiration of Titian. The weight and majesty of the head of Christ, which positively communicates a feeling as if the contents of that solid brain were pressing upon your hand ; the intellectual dignity, combined with the utmost moral and spiritual elevation ; the exquisite refinement of self-contained sorrow in the mouth ; the holy sadness, free from the least tinge of sentimentality, in the eyes ; the unfeigned seriousness, as if smiles were no longer any expression of the joy of that deep heart ; the hair, not conspicuously parted, and yet thin and long, and almost as if each hair were instinct with life ; the brow, wide, full, but not the scholar's or the artist's brow, and not the saint's either, but a brow perfectly human and perfectly sound and pure ; and the hand, extending its back with two fingers open to take the money, so inimitably expressive of a natural distaste for details, and specially for money ; and a rapt and absorbed nature ! The contrast of the two faces is not more effective than the contrast of the two hands, which are exact symbols—the one, with its upward clutch and dark, knotty fist, of the spirit of the world ; the other, with its open and back-exposed form, with no tension to its muscles, and so fair and pure, of the spirit of Him who came asking nothing and receiving only stripes.

Correggio's Madonna, so celebrated, is not interesting to me. It is evidently only a study, although exquisitely finished.

His pictures fail in spirituality, and that celebrated diffusion of light in the "Notte" does not equal my expectations of it.

The elegance and refinement of Giordano has given me unfeigned pleasure. One picture of his, the meeting of Rachel and Jacob, is delightful.

The gallery of engravings and original sketches offers great attractions to students. The accessibleness and the warmth and hospitable fittings of the Gallery distinguish it from most others. It furnishes alone a sufficient reason for making Dresden a residence for one season at least.

The sculptures in the Japanese Palace are meritorious, and beautifully arranged; but the winter cold, not abated by any fires, makes this a poor season to visit this gallery.

The collection of armor in the Zwinger is, perhaps, the largest and finest anywhere to be found. A perfect regiment of wooden horses in armor, mounted by knights in every conceivable panoply of mail, are stalled in this endless gallery. Those who would understand the whole military equipment of the ages before gunpowder and cannon changed the whole character of war, have here their best opportunity. What human muscles were then, these ponderous suits of steel armor attest. One sees knights incrusted with such a weight of mail that to be unhorsed was certain death, by mere force of the short fall from their saddles to the ground, and yet the tremendous heaviness of the lances they bore was necessary to lift such a ballast as they carried from their seats. The exquisite finish and costliness of some of the few more precious suits of armor found here, wrought by great artists in silver and gold, inlaid in steel, must be seen to be credited. The endless amount of guns and pistols, decorated like imperial playthings, to be seen in this gallery, overpowers one with the sense of the wasted labor of past ages. The state of society when such multiplication of merely ostentatious industry was possible, it is hard to realize in our utilitarian days. A sample of a revolver, more than two hundred years old, proves that there is nothing new under the sun.

The life of Dresden is very attractive to English and Americans, and there is commonly a permanent population of many hundreds of both in the city. There is one part of the town known as the English and American quarter, and it is the pleasantest part of the city. These two nationalities fraternize very amiably. They unite in supporting the two English chapels—one very high, the other very low. There is no un-Episcopal service here in the English language, a deficiency very much deplored by those who love the simple forms of Protestantism. It seems strange that Dresden, so much more visited than Berlin by Americans, should be without an American chapel. By request of the active and popular American Consul, Mr. Campbell, who engaged the pleasant saloon in the Hotel de Pologne for the purpose, I preached yesterday to a congregation of two hundred Americans, gathered at short notice, and without the least drumming together. I had the pleasure of meeting a dozen of present or former parishioners in the assembly, and found as congenial a company of worshipers as I could desire to meet. As a sample of American enterprise and German facilities, I may state that the hymns, with the music to which they were sung, were struck off on a sheet of paper, and circulated through the hall, on a notice of only a few hours, and at a cost of only a few shillings. And this is a sample of the finish which belongs to the civilization of these old countries—where a dense population on an old territory compels an immense subdivision of labor and favors, nicety and cheapness in most things. Every thing not inspired by American enterprise is slow, but every thing that is done at all is well done, and things are done that could not be thought of in a country where time and labor are so valuable as in our own land. Housekeeping is rendered very easy where there are hundreds of experts waiting to do every thing for you at most moderate rates. The cheapness of servants and of labor frees the women of every social rank — corresponding to persons having a competency at home—from personal labor and housekeeping drudgery.

German ladies have abundant time here to share their husbands' occupations and pleasures. They direct the housekeeping and keep the accounts, but they do not cut and sew and make their own dresses, as so many women of twice their means would do at home. They knit and crochet, and that is about all. It is so cheap and so easy to get clothes made — that is, in the moderate style which with excellent sense they prefer—that it would be wasteful of opportunity, not to say unjust to the industrial class, not to employ them. They are poorly paid, but they know how to live comfortably on very little. There is no undue magnification of money above comfort, enjoyment, society and art; no impatient haste to get rich, and no grasping desire to exceed a fair competency. Merchants will not strain themselves beyond their safe and tranquil enjoyment of life to add to a moderate sufficiency if they possess it. They seem to throw away opportunities which Americans would account it madness to neglect, and this is explained by the worthlessness of money, beyond a fair competency, in a country based upon aristocratic ideas—where wealth secures no real importance and no social standing of itself alone. *Genius* is the only thing that conquers the settled obduracy of rank and title here. There is accordingly, amid great and sober industry, no enterprise.

Dresden is poorly drained and lighted; her public vehicles are shabby and rickety; her mechanics, thorough and excellent, are slow, and provoke great impatience. They can not

be driven, and have no conception of what we call hurry.
And the life of the people is all slow. They are quiet, tame,
unexcited, decorous people—with a great deal of inward culture and refinement—who live on music and in public gardens,
and in mild conversation, and seem never in haste, or under
any passionate impulses. A lady, living on a public square,
says that even the children in the streets don't run and quarrel
or play boisterous games. I breakfasted the other day, at
12 o'clock, at Mr. J. M. Drake's, one of my parishioners now
living in Dresden, with a delightful company of gentlemen,
among whom were Herr Von Weber, Privy Counselor of his
Majesty, and son of the great composer, whose genius he
inherits in the form of mathematics and engineering ; Dr.
Hirschel, a distinguished physician ; Dr. Hellwig, chief of an
important school ; Herr Lauterbach, the first violinist of Saxony, and second in authority in the Royal Opera ; Mr. Thode,
the well-known banker ; Mr. Campbell, our Consul ; Dr.
Humphreys and Mr. James Kent, American gentlemen. The
charm of the occasion was the perfectly unpreoccupied air of
these men, who, in our country, would each at that time of
day have been so inwardly vexed and haunted with their personal responsibilities that they could not have given more
than half their interest to the occasion. Another characteristic was the utter disappearance of their respective specialties
in their common humanity and general culture. The merchant was a musician, the musician a scholar, the man of
public affairs a social philosopher, the men of special pur-
suits men also of general interests, and all, busy as they
would have called themselves, were men of leisure, who could
sit three hours in the very heart of a short November day
and talk delightfully, and as if time had no better use, about
all matters of human concernment—ethics, art, music, statistics, American and European life, religion, politics.

The amusements (it is too light a word to describe so serious an occupation of Continental life) are of the best quality. The opera is superlatively fine, as to orchestra, scenery and chorus. All the persons connected with the institution of the Royal Theatre and Opera (one establishment) are government officials, engaged, on good behavior, for life, on small but comfortable salaries. This gives not only a domestic and fixed character to the players, singers and musicians, but also, by keeping them steadily together, secures an excellence, finish and unity in the musical performances, operas and plays of the rarest sort. The moral worth and personal standing of these artists is apparently as good as that of other citizens of their own grade. They look wholly unlike the meretricious, dissipated, smirking creatures you see so often on the French, English and American stage. Indeed, a German orchestra looks like a set of savans or ministers of religion, who have agreed to exhibit their *virtuoso* quality for a single evening. The soloists are not Italian in voice or in passionate *abandon*, but they are always thoroughly up in their parts, and thoroughly competent, so that they do not mar if they do not exalt the performance. The precision, serious attention to all details, and inability to be put out of time, are all marked. Every thing proceeds with oily smoothness, without hitch, and without painful intervals and delays. The opera begins at 6½ o'clock and is out commonly at 9, and you might set your watch by the beginning and ending of the acts, the time of which is often published in the bills of the night. The sudden explosion of a gas-chandelier the other night did not cause the orchestra to lose a note, and the accident was deliberately remedied without a person in the house leaving his seat, or without a moment's interruption of the performance! This is German phlegm with a vengeance.

Dresden is full of beer and music saloons and gardens, where men carry their pipes (and ladies their knitting), and with mild but long potations, sit out excellent concerts of four hours' duration, at a cost of sixpence a head. The Bavarian, it is said, can enjoy beer without music ; the Saxon, beer with music ; the Parisian, music without beer. The domestic and sociable character of these beer concerts is something indescribable. But it characterizes German life, and is really a substantial part of their existence.

Living is comparatively cheap and excellent in Dresden, although Americans are said to have greatly raised its price of late years. New buildings for the accommodation of strangers are always going up. Rent, according to the number of rooms, the story, and the position, is for an *etage* or set of apartments (all on one floor), from 50 to 175 thalers (80 cents each in gold) per month. A lady of my acquaintance, with three servants and three children, occupies furnished apartments with seven rooms, at 67 thalers per month. They are excellent, well-furnished, well-situated ; good as I should desire. Servants of excellent quality may be had at an average of five thalers per month. Food for this family and servants, of excellent and abundant quality, about six thalers per day. Dress is about a third less costly here. The environs of Dresden are charming ; the climate dark, sunless and rainy in winter ; and not very inviting in spring ; never very cold ; most agreeable in summer ; usually very healthy —changes, especially from rainy and cloudy to sunshiny— never *too sudden !* In most respects a very attractive place, and made so attractive to me by dear and numerous friends. that I could willingly pass the whole winter here. But we are off to-morrow, after ten days of inward sunshine and outward storm, for Prague and Vienna.

XXXII.

DRESDEN AND PRAGUE.

November 6, 1867.

IN company with some charming friends, we visited to-day the famous Dresden china works at Meissen. The celebrated collection of·china from all parts of the world in the Japanese Palace, in the new town of Dresden, had excited our lively interest concerning the processes of manufacture. That collection contains 90,000 pieces, and has been gathered by an industrious passion for old china, reaching back a hundred and fifty years. It is unique, I suppose, in its character and extent. Amid an immense quantity of bizarre and tasteless monstrosities, there is a very large amount of graceful and elegant form and of lovely color in the smaller articles, especially in cups and bowls and platters. It is rather mortifying to find semi-barbarous nations excelling all civilized people in such a delicate art—for I suppose that neither Sevres nor Dresden has yet made any china as light and strong, and at the same time as transparent, as some of the best made hundreds of years ago in China itself; nor are any of the modern colors as delicate and lustrous as some of theirs. Their yellows seemed specially tender and precious. The collection is kept in a cold, dark basement or half-cellar, where, contending with a freezing twilight, one is hurried through it by a showman who means to earn his extravagant fee of *two thalers* in as short a time as possible.

At the works at Meissen a different system prevails, a skillful workman, speaking English, being detailed to exhibit the processes of the manufacture in the most patient manner, and really executing his task admirably. Meissen is a dozen miles up the Elbe, and is reached by rail in three-quarters of an hour. It is a picturesque old place, and worth seeing on its own account. The works, which belong to the government, were only a few years back moved to this eligible spot. The clay to which the Dresden china owes its excellence is found in at least a dozen mines in the immediate neighborhood in inexhaustible abundance. It is composed of a degraded or rotten feldspar, and is nearly white in its native state. It requires only to be washed and then worked, very much as dough is kneaded, for a half-hour, to be ready for use. It contains veins of a greyish color, and also air-cells, which are worked out of it by a process of kneading in which the persistent cutting of the mass in two and packing it as dough is packed to secure shortness, effects at last a homogeneous color and texture. This clay is fashioned into ordinary vessels, bowls, plates, etc., by the potter's wheel. The more complex figures and shapes are made in moulds of plaster of Paris, the reverse of models formed in common clay, by the most skillful artisans. The number of these moulds is enormous. In moving them to the new establishment they were found to weigh some thousands of tons.

It may surprise those who have noticed the seamless unity of china figures, or *biscuit*, to learn that even the smallest figures are cast in many parts, and that sometimes every finger and thumb requires a different mould. The putting together of these parts in groups of *biscuit* requires a truly artistic knowledge and skill, and this is secured by a regular school of drawing and anatomy, through which the workmen are compelled to pass. The joints of the several parts are not

made until the parts have had their first baking. The parts
come from the moulds in a very unfinished state, requiring
minute handling with the chisel before they are fit for baking.
The baking is done in a hollow oven, round which five fur-
naces of coals (hard and soft) are burning. Each plate or
article is put into a separate vessel (covered) of coarse fire-
clay, and these fire-clay vessels are then arranged in tiers
upon each other in the large oven. A batch may contain
perhaps a thousand vessels. The oven is kept at a temperature of 2004° Reaumer, for twenty-four hours, when it
is allowed to cool slowly for three days. It is hermetically
sealed meanwhile. The greatest delicacy is required in the
arrangement of this baking process. When most prudently
conducted, at least one-sixth of the batch in the oven will be
ruined by some unevenness or excess in the heat. The clay,
either of the fire-brick holder or of the vessel inside, breaks
down under too severe a temperature. It is the boast of the
Dresden over the Sevres china that the Dresden clay bears a
heat 400° greater than the Sevres clay, and this secures a
harder and firmer china. Yet it is confessed that the Dresden china is not so light as the Sevres. There is no essential difference in other respects ; the external finish or painting depending on the excellence of the individual artists, who
are of course variable. The first baking produces only a
very brittle substance, hardly stronger than chalk. The once-
baked vessels are then dipped into a vitreous bath composed
of feldspar, mica and pounded glass, and absorb at one plunge
the necessary amount of flux partially to vitrify their substance, and, upon being subjected to a second baking, to
cover their surface with that peculiar enamel which is the
beauty and characteristic of china. Before this enamel is
applied, vessels which are destined to be painted and decorated are put into the hands of the artists, who, with the ordi-

nary paint-brush, and in metallic paints, picture the flowers, or arabesques or other ornaments of the pattern.

In the more common sorts of vessels they paint without pattern. In other cases the pattern is pricked in paper, and then transferred to the plate by rubbing charcoal over it; it is then filled in with the colors of the pattern. The colors are so changed in burning that it requires a very experienced knowledge to apply the proper shade to the unburnt surface. A dullish grey comes out a bright blue, perhaps, and so on. The gilding so common on china is a precipitate of pure gold, which looks more like made chocolate than any thing else, and is applied with a brush. The fire gives it only a dull brown aspect. The brilliancy is obtained by burnishing the surface with small tools of agate. Great delicacy in handling the finer points and edges of the china in this burnishing process, is required. It is done by women. In case of many colors, four or five burnings may be required, as some colors bear only a less heat. We saw plates valued at $50 each, and one set of twenty-four, in process, which had been ordered at $1200! The demand seemed greater for the more expensive kinds of work. About a quarter of the finest work is spoiled in baking. All the china shrinks at least one-third in the oven, and this shrinkage is likely to be just unequal enough to injure delicate proportion. This is perhaps the reason why accuracy of expression in copies of pictures can not be secured, and proves the unfitness of china to any real place among the fine arts. The work of the artists is always better on the unburnt surface. A truly-drawn eye may come out askew. The lustre of the burnt colors is very splendid, and the general effect of the Dresden china is certainly exceedingly elegant. After considering the number and delicacy of the processes, the amount of personal skill and individual handling to which every vessel is subjected, the length of training to which artists must submit, and the great risk and certain loss which attends the process of manufacture, Dresden china rises in one's estimation as a manufacture, and can not be considered dear for those who can afford it at the current prices. The manufacture is profitable in good years—having earned $25,000 last year for the Royal Treasury, and expecting to do more this year. Coals are cheap, coming only fifteen miles, and worth only twelve cents a bushel. They use about 160 bushels in one baking.

The green vaults at Dresden I had almost forgotten to speak of. They are so called merely because, being originally a suite of rooms opening upon the royal garden, they were painted green in harmony with the verdure they looked out upon. They contain a fabulous amount of objects of *virtu*, royal presents and works of ingenious artisans—vases, jeweled tankards, sets of plate, and china and glass, and table toys wrought with lavish and inconceivable toil and cost, to tickle the jaded taste and spoiled fancy of royal weariness and indolence. The Kings' goldsmiths, under different reigns, have vied with each other in producing all but impossible trinkets and representations, in minute model, of Oriental courts, in which gold and jewels, sometimes to the amount of a half-million of cost, have been expended on a single toy fit only for a baby-house. A necklace of diamonds, valued at $750,000, is among the curiosities of this collection, and a single green diamond worth a half-million more. A class of drinking-cups in the shape of griffins and fabulous animals, which, from the difficulty of drinking from them without spilling, were called "teasing-cups," is shown, with which the guests at royal tables amused themselves after dinner, under some penalty for any awkwardness in their use. It is a wearisome show, and provokes almost an angry disdain from its wasteful and tasteless magnificence. This collection belongs now not to the crown but the country, and it can not, by a compact with its old owners, be sold. It is hard to think how small a part of its cost it would now bring in any auction shop! The King of Saxony, whom we saw devoutly attending mass, and almost as seriously listening to the opera, is a grey-haired, thin-featured old gentleman, looking very tired of his life, and as if he would greatly enjoy being only a private gentleman. He has literary tastes, and has translated Dante.

The railroad from Dresden to Prague follows the valley of the Elbe, and runs through what is called Saxon Switzerland, a wild and singular country, in which the effect of very picturesque mountain scenery is produced at the smallest possible expenditure of means. Given, heights not to exceed 1200 feet, and rocks within this compass, *ad libitum*, with forests of a few miles square, and a muddy river of shallow depth—the problem being to produce a country in which violent contrasts of hill and plain, precipice and meadow, contorted strata and irregular sky-line should create in the beholder sensations not unlike those of the Alpine world, and the result could not be more successful than it is found in this surprising and effective Liliputian Switzerland. A kind of inland Giant's Causeway is presented in the architectural structure of the rocks. Sometimes Egyptian temples seem to have strayed into this region, so artificial and so Sphinx-like are the forms of the stones piled in monstrous order, and with great faces and heads jutting out over their square shoulders. Three or four isolated masses rising abruptly and with sharp sides a thousand feet high, and not much broader than high, offer commanding points of view, and form bold and sublime features in the landscape. On one of these the only fortress belonging to Saxony is placed, at a height so inaccessible that it has never been taken. Not unlike Ehrenbreitstein, it has the advantage of adding to the steep rocky mountain height of that great fastness a crown of noble woods (not visible from below) which gives an extraordinary beauty to the ærial loftiness of this commanding castle. There is room for thousands of men within the half-mile circuit of its walls. A beautiful stone terrace upon the casemates furnishes a walk from which all Saxon Switzerland may be viewed. A well, 625 feet deep, sunk in the solid rock, at least a dozen feet in diameter, is said to have cost years of drilling to sink it. Seventeen seconds we held our breath to hear water poured from the top strike the water at the bottom. Candles let down by a windlass, revolving as they descended, presented an image of falling stars, more striking than any I ever watched in the sky. It seemed almost as far to the place where they sunk at last as to the zenith of the sky above. The contents of the green vaults and the archives of Saxony have often found protection in this stronghold of Konigsberg.

PRAGUE, BOHEMIA, November 14.

It is a charming journey from Dresden to Prague, in constant view of the Elbe, until the Moldau is reached, a few miles from the old capital of this once independent kingdom. Bohemia is a kind of bowl, on all sides surrounded by mountains, while its own surface is comparatively smooth. Prague is nearly at its centre, and is itself a copy of the kingdom, being situated in the middle of a saucer of hills, up which the smaller and more interesting part of the city runs. Divided by the Moldau, a stream of shallow depth, but of dignified width, and to be seen from numerous points, Prague unites all the effects of hills and water, of bridges and towers, pinnacles and domes, to which must be added a middle-age architecture as well preserved as frequent bombardments have

S

permitted. The great importance of this place for centuries, when it was often an imperial, and still longer a royal capital, is fully attested by the grandeur of its palaces, the number and magnificence of its churches, the multitude of its statues, and the size and costliness of many of its private houses. The Alhambra itself can hardly exceed in distant effect the collection of buildings connected with the old palace of the Bohemian kings, known as the Hradschin. No palace in Europe yet seen by us holds so commanding a site, or occupies with such dignity so large and lofty a section of the horizon.

The old cathedral, which has suffered equally from foreign and from civil wars, from dynastic struggles and from Protestant violence, has saved enough of its delicate and beautiful Gothic architecture to remind one of the cathedral at Cologne, while it contains a vast store of undoubted curiosities, in the shape of costly pictures and carving, by Albert Durer and by Leonardo de Vinci and Cranach—with bronzes, one of which claims to be older than Christianity, and to have been brought by Titus from Jerusalem. The solid silver shrine of John of Nepomuck is gorgeous and beautiful, and occupies a large space in one of the aisles. The other churches are in florid Italian style, full of marbles and gilding, and of statues of gigantic size in the flaunting style of so much of the sculpture in wind-blown draperies in the Roman churches. The church in which John Huss preached, with the identical pulpit from which that glorious hero scattered his fiery protests, is still standing ; and the monument (a marble effigy) of Tyco Brahe, the Danish astronomer—the friend and co-worker of Kepler — occupies one side of a column near the altar. It is sad to see this cradle of Continental Protestantism, so boldly seized from the Catholic faith in its most absolute day, now reclaimed and quietly repossessed by the old Roman hierarchy. The Prince Cardinal of Prague is perhaps the most absolute and unqualified prelate in Europe, and he governs his Bohemian province with undisputed sway. His palace is regal and his dominion perfect. For here, in the morning-land of the Reformation, where Huss shone the glorious star of the new faith—the land that first made the greatest and bloodiest sacrifices for its fresh and ennobling convictions of religious freedom—a Catholicism more intense, more universal, more superstitious and more degrading than is to be found in any part of Europe, holds the entire Christian population of Prague and Bohemia in its smothering grasp. It is said that not two thousand of the one hundred and eighty thousand inhabitants of Prague are Protestants! There are, however, about thirty thousand Jews here, with over thirty synagogues. Among them is the oldest Jewish synagogue in Europe, which dates back to the eighth century, although in parts it is evidently as recent as the thirteenth. It is the only *Gothic* synagogue known. It was originally built under a hill, deep in the ground, and was covered up and buried for some centuries and forgotten. When found, the old parchment rolls of the Pentateuch were discovered hidden in the stone ark where they still lie. This small synagogue is begrimed with smoke and dirt, and is as repulsive a place as any spot so steeped in antiquity, and sodden in persecution, and glorified with stubborn adhesiveness to hereditary convictions, can be. The old cemetery near by, crowded with tombstones covered with Hebrew characters, is full of the dust of Israelites who never found rest out of its narrow walls. So sacred a spot has not failed to be contended for by pious Jews as a place of final repose, and four or five layers of graves are heaped upon each other, until the surface is raised ten or a dozen feet. The grave-stones are almost as thick together as paving-stones, fairly packed for room. But Judaism has had its revenge. Sternly holding its ground, it has flourished best where most persecuted, and Jews now hold the purse-strings and form the prosperous class in Prague and Bohemia. Curses upon them are carved in the monuments and wrought into the bridges they pass in their carriages every day.

The great bridge of Prague, the oldest and longest in Germany, is perhaps of all bridges in the world the most historic and the most worthy to be visited. It is the natural centre of the city, and is as sacred to the superstition and faith of the people as it is essential to their convenience and ornamental to their capital. Lined with gigantic groups of statuary—which show even from the neighboring hills—it is still more laden with associations. From its parapet the holy John of Nepomuck was thrown into the river, by order of the Emperor Wenceslaus, because he would not betray the secrets of the Empress confided to him at the confessional. Sainted for his priestly fidelity only two centuries after his death, he is the patron saint of bridges, and is visited by thousands every year when his day recurs in the calendar. The old palace of Wallenstein preserves the shell of its ancient magnificence, and makes Schiller's famous plays ring with a new reality, as one looks at the skin (stuffed and set up in his palace) of the very Arabian horse he rode at Lutzen, which was killed on the battle-field. His stern face looks down from the wall of the apartment. The hall where he kinged it over the monarchs of his time is still magnificent with marbles, and on the ceiling he appears in a chariot of triumph, with his star (which his astrologers had reported to him as troubled before the battle) shining in great splendor over his head after the victory was won. The picture at Munich of his assassination at Eger, which is so powerful, came back to my memory in redoubled force here in the presence of so many testimonies to his wonderful influence and transcendent powers.

The museum contains some manuscript writing of Huss, and a picture of his burning at Constance, which looks very ancient, and is very impressive, though small. Here too is shown a sword with the name of Gustavus Adolphus damasked into the blade ; and, still more interesting, a sword which belonged to Christopher Columbus.

Prague is as prosperous as a city ridden by a Catholic priesthood and population and managed as an Austrian province can be. It is divided between the rich and the poor— like Bohemia itself, which has no middle class. The land is owned by nobles, or rich proprietors, in immense sections, over which are scattered a set of miserable peasants, who are little better than the slaves of their employers. Sometimes a prince or count owns a territory of a hundred square miles, and all the population upon it are really his vassals. It is not strange that ten thousand Bohemians have emigrated to America this year. I see them on the streets in wagons, making their way to the depot, *en route* for America. Poor as they are, if they can only touch our shores with their last penny in their hands they are saved men ! Blessed haven to a population which all over Europe is landless and forlorn, and to whom their native soil offers no possible hope of relief from beggary and oppression. In Saxony I met not one beggar. Bohemia swarms with them. Catholicism and mendicity go hand in hand. Prague seems the refuge of ex-royalty. The old Austrian Emperor Ferdinand, who abdicated in 1848, lives in the old palace. I saw him to-day getting into his carriage—an old man of seventy-five, very infirm, with noble forehead and a mean face, and shrunken, decrepit figure. The Grand Duke of Tuscany has a palace near Wallenstein's old home, and another three miles out of town.

The Duke of Hesse has bought another palace, and is to be seen riding about in uniform in a state coach. Royalty in these days sees enough shadows in its path to line its secret pockets with the means of a wealthy retirement. The old Emperor, it is said, has many millions laid up in foreign funds. His wife gives much money to the Jesuits, and he is very generous to the poor. As I leave Northern Germany for Austria, I feel a great regret at quitting a soil that bears so interesting a population. The German seems to have an additional upper story to his brain. So intellectual a race, judging by the head alone, I have never seen. The German, by generations of culture and thought, has purged away his passions and impulses and become a kind of meditative intellect, walking round on somewhat thin legs and smallish feet, with no back to his head, but a great towering forehead full of perception and ideas. His chin is thinned away, and indicates feebleness of will, and his high head, narrow and long, topples for want of base. I do not see any evidence that the German will again rule the world, spite of Prussian success and expectation. I think the imperial day of the race is gone, and that the German brain is not likely to distinguish itself again in action. I hope it will not rashly insist on fighting France, which has just the impulse and genius for affairs that Germany lacks. But for companionship, courtesy, substantial and internal refinement, many-sidedness and knowledge how to enjoy life, and contentment, who can equal as a whole the Germans of our day?

The German *cuisine*, which at first was very repulsive, has grown upon us with experience, until we have come to think it about as good as the French. It is very various, and is specially good in the serving-up of vegetables and the preparation of gravies, free from grease and unwholesome condiments. A German dinner, at the *table d'hote* of a good hotel, is a capital institution. A light soup; a carp or an eel, with a cold sauce of salad-dressing; a piece of over-cooked beef (usually boiled), with a good gravy; and small potatoes cooked with butter; a fowl, with salad and some cooked fruit (plums or cherries or apples), served together; a roasted hare, larded; a pudding (mehl-speise) with a raspberry sauce; some ice-cream and a cup of coffee; this, or something very like it, is the usual dinner at a first-rate hotel. Every body drinks a half-bottle of Rhine or French wine with dinner, and many add a glass of light beer. The service is slow, an hour and a half being the usual length of the dinner. The Germans dine at one o'clock, but four or five is becoming not unusual. The waiters are attentive, respectful and intelligent, often speaking French and English as well as German. They are even polished in their manners, always carefully dressed, and wearing black dress-suits. They are fully equal in intellectual and social appearance to American clerks in retail stores. The hotels are almost uniformly good. In Austria bread is more uniformly good than in any other country. The flour seems whiter and the bread more skillfully made. This was recognized at the French Exposition, where Austrian bread was most commonly used in all the restaurants. There is one national dish in Austria which reminds us of the single platter, containing the whole dinner of the family, that in old times stood in the middle of the farmer's table in New England. It is a dish of meat garnished with five or six kinds of vegetables, each occupying its small section of the crowded dish, some small potatoes, some delicate baby carrots, spinach, choux de Bruxelles (little cabbages about as big as a walnut), some boiled rice, etc. Tomatoes are very little used, although well known. The American taste for raw tomatoes is regarded with a curious wonder.

The hotels furnish no common sitting-room, except the *salle-a-manger*, or dining-room, which usually contains a few newspapers, and is more or less used as a saloon, especially in cold weather. Travelers are isolated in their own apartments, and many dine apart in their own *salon*. As a rule, however, the *table d'hote* is visited. It is cheaper, better, and pleasanter. The old prejudice against meeting " Tom, Dick and Harry" at table is passing away. Either Tom, Dick and Harry have improved in their manners, or the social pride and exclusiveness has diminished. At any rate, the best people go to the *table d'hote*. At Dresden, the young Duke of Norfolk was for a week a regular diner at the common table. This is a great innovation on the customs of thirty years ago, when dignity made a private dinner in one's own *salon* almost a necessity for persons of any pretensions to fortune or station. American "*herding*," as it was contemptuously called, is becoming nearly universal in Europe. The introduction of common parlors, such as we have in America, will soon follow. Already, the general habit is now *not* to take a private *salon* with one's chambers. In Austria the *table d'hote* does not succeed, although it has been again and again tried in several of the hotels. The aristocratic basis of society is less disturbed here, and the old distinctions between classes make the people jealous of familiarity or intercourse with each other. But even here people dine in a common room, but at separate tables.

Nothing illustrates the essential diversity between European and American life better than the railroads. First, the European roads (on the Continent) are all slower than ours, and the trains have different prices for tickets, according as they are express trains, or mail trains, or accommodation trains. Their express trains do not make over twenty-five miles. The stops are long at the stations and very frequent on ordinary trains. The depots are uniformly large, commodious buildings, commonly the stateliest and most palatial edifices in town. And they need all their room ; for they divide and subdivide their business in an extraordinary way. There are always three and not rarely four classes of tickets and passengers, first, second, third and fourth class, with different waiting-rooms in graduated styles for each class. After buying your ticket, your baggage is carried by a porter (who must be fee'd) to the weighing-office near by, and a special ticket obtained for it, in which all above fifty pounds is charged at a high rate. With these two tickets in your pocket, you are prepared to be locked into your waiting-saloon and kept until five minutes before the train starts. Then you are let loose and must take such a place in the train as a uniformed official, of whom there are a dozen about, may assign you. The doors of the compartments are locked, so that you can neither enter nor get out without the conductor's leave. There are three compartments to each car. The first-class compartments hold only six, and are roomy and luxurious, but without fire in the coldest weather. Its want is supplied by a hot-water vessel for the feet, in some rare instances. The second-class cars are good enough in Germany and Austria, but not in France and Belgium. The third-class are rude and comfortless, although very much used by respectably-dressed people. The fourth-class are without seats. There is a difference of fare of at least one-quarter of the whole, in the four classes, *i.e.*, if the fourth class were twenty-five cents for five miles, the third would be fifty cents, the second seventy-five cents and the first one dollar. It is, then, a very real distinction. Americans are charged with a foolish pride in riding usually in the first-class cars. I have not seen a great deal of this extravagance.

There is one character in all hotels of the first importance to travelers, the *portier*—not the porter, or burden and er-rand-man, but the fixture who occupies the porter's lodge, and in his gay uniform opens the carriage door and welcomes travelers, ushering them to the presence of the landlord or head-waiter, and his suite. The more waiters on the stairs, the more honor! The *portier* is privy-counselor of all the guests! He knows every thing about money, letters, address-es, trains, carriages, theatres, shows, cigars, shops; talks usu-ally a little of three or four languages; is sweet-tempered and polite; never impatient; protects you from all frauds but his own little pickings, and expects nothing but a handsome fee when you leave, which every body pays cheerfully to so use-ful a person. We have nothing in America answering to this factotum and encyclopædia of travelers' information. I ad-mire unfeignedly the round, smooth, clean face and burly body of this cosmopolite, who seems to me to be the same man at all European inns, and I mentally shake hands with him at any new place, or with the excellent individual in the same laced cap (not hat) I left at my last inn. May his shadow never be less, and may he live forever!

XXXIII.

VIENNA.

AUSTRIA, November 20, 1867.

VIENNA, the third of the great capitals of the Continent, and one which has so often controlled the destinies of Europe, is a city of about 600,000 inhabitants within the limits of its Octroi, and with half as many more so closely united to it, in place or time, that it may be regarded as an aggregation of a million of people. The old town, whose walls and ditches were leveled only a few years ago, is a small, closely-packed district, built about the old palace, which has not room enough to show itself, and is a shapeless agglomeration of edifices. There is no plan, order or effectiveness about the old city. Its streets are narrow, tortuous, and mean. It is cut up with half-subterraneous passages, uniting its twisted streets by short cuts which it must take half a life to understand. It needs a weasel's wisdom to thread these dark and winding passages. I have been lost almost every time I have gone out without a guide, and only after beating about like a ship in a fog have found my way to my destination. And the walking in damp or rainy weather, which prevails for many months, and specially at this season, is as slippery, muddy, and dangerous as the streets are narrow, crowded, and irregular. " Culs-de-sac " are common. Then, alas, there are in the old town, and where they are most needed, no sidewalks. Old Vienna was made for an aristocracy who drove in carriages or rode

horseback. Its architects seemed to think the common
people had no rights in the streets, and were little better than
paving-stones. This notion is perpetuated in the habits of
the coachmen. They are all *Jehus*, and the people who
walk the slowest and have the most time to spare, drive furiously, as if on errands of life and death, and indeed they are,
for accidents of collision and from being run down are constant. Every stranger feels his life in peril in every shopping
expedition or lounge through the main street. Ladies can
not prudently go afoot about the best part of the old town.
On the other hand, the public carriages are excellent, clean
and handsome, cheap and abundant. The horses are commonly good, and the quality of the hacks reminds one con-
stantly of the private coupés used by ladies in New York.
They have but one fault, a great one—they are never high
enough to accommodate fully a gentleman and his hat. They
suit ladies and soldiers exactly! The old town still contains
the residences of the aristocracy, the chief hotels, the theatres and the public buildings of the court and government.
But it is now only a single *ward* out of eight—seven lying
beyond its limits. The old walls and the ditch and glacis
are now a circular promenade, the Viennese Boulevards, and
are fast taking on a Parisian appearance. Leaving wide,
and what in summer must be attractive walks and drives,
the government has encouraged the sale of the lands lying
between the old town and the former suburbs, by freeing the
ground from taxes for thirty years, which, considering that the
house-tax is about one-third of the rental, is an immense premium. The ground has sold at high rates, and is rapidly
becoming covered with lofty and elegant buildings. The
style is uniformly on the palatial order, each edifice containing many homes or offices. Indeed street *numbers*, as applied to buildings in Europe generally, but in Vienna special-

ly, are fearfully significant. No. 5 sometimes lies so far from No. 1 that you walk the distance of a whole American block to get from one to the other. In short, the buildings are all immense ; and when you find your number, you have still a serious task to find your destination, with a front, a middle and a rear staircase, opening each on four or five stories, and two or more suites of apartments, it may be, on each story. It is said that 2000 people live in one building in Vienna, and they do *not* live like the people in a New York tenant-house.

Beyond the Ring, or Boulevards, stretches out in streets not wide enough, and seldom commanding, but over a vast territory, the new city, which has overrun and absorbed the suburbs, and is said to be twelve miles in circuit. On one side, and running out three miles, spreading into a natural park very little adorned or regulated, is the *Prater*, a dull, uninviting place now, but the scene of much enjoyment and popular festivity in the warm season. Then and there Viennese character comes out in all its lightness and brilliancy, in music and dancing, and in garden-life, and here the Austrian taste for puppets and theatres and shows runs riot. Here, too, equipage emulates and even thinks it surpasses the gorgeous processions of the Champs Élysées and the Bois de Boulogne ; and it may well be, for when it comes to uniforms and horse-trappings, Austria is in the van. Her soldiers wear a white uniform which lights up every promenade and every public assembly. Her generals wear a light blue coat stiff with gold lace. The coachmen of the Princes, Counts and Barons are masses of gold, cocked hat, and laced coats coming down about their heels in such a way that I am not sure whether they have any legs or not. The porters at the gates of the nobility or the public edifices, at this season are so bedizened with fur and lace that a Russian bear

in regimentals could hardly present a more imposing appearance, especially when we add an official staff in hand that
looks like a sceptre. They are fully equal (could I say
more ?) to a drum-major ! Put these people, with gayly-
dressed ladies, in carriages of the most positive colors, and
behind horses housed in the heaviest harnesses overlaid with
plates of gilded metal, and set these gorgeous coachmen on
their thrones, and lackies to match on the foot-board, and the
dullest imagination may be left to fancy the effect ! The
Bohemian and the Hungarian nobility, who come to Vienna
to outshine the Austrian aristocracy, have a certain barbaric
splendor of costume and equipage, which is called up to most
minds by the mere name of Esterhazys and Lichtensteins.
Just now the hunting season is *in*, and the nobles are all out!
Vienna is dull with rain and fog, with the lull of business and
of social life.

Not that it has much social life in our sense, or in an English sense, at any time. The middle classes are sociable
outside their houses, in cafés and beer saloons. Public balls
for this class occupy the Sunday evenings. The people are
in general good-natured, witty, and devoted to amusement.
But above them, society appears hardly to exist in a Saxon
sense. The nobility associate exclusively with each other,
with a rigorous isolation. Nowhere has rank such rankness !
Title, family, blood, station are sacred realities. The Emperor, it is said, is not familiar even with his own brothers,
but stands a little apart, even in a hunting-field. There is
no want of domestic affection among the Austrian nobility,
but the circle is so close, and so inclusive and exclusive, that
it possesses a dull and stupid life, unenlivened and unre-
freshed by new blood or contact with men and things. Riding and hunting appear to be its chief solaces. The nobility, with vast estates but great entailments of expense from

old dependents, are usually in debt, and not seldom their affairs are in the hands of governmental commissioners who collect their incomes and pay them an allowance for expenses. They are not hospitable, and do little for the social life of Vienna. Almost all the elegant entertainments of the winter are due to the foreign embassadors. The aristocracy attend them with pleasure, and forget to return the civility. There are marked exceptions, but this seems to be the rule. The bankers or great merchants are beginning to have palaces of their own, and are likely enough to take the social lead. It is time ; for so exclusive is the noble circle here, that neither worth, distinction in letters, beauty, nor services (always provided they are not *military*) can pass its enchanted lines. A minister of state, who held a thousand offices in his gift, but who had married a beautiful, gifted, and every way presentable lady, not of noble blood, could not introduce her at court ! But a princess of bad personal reputation is still a leader in aristocratic fashion ! An advertisement appears in yesterday's paper, opening a vacant canonry (one of three founded by Prince Lichtenstein) to the competition of priests, but states that none need apply who have not six quarterings of nobility ! It is worth $700 a year, and will have fifty rival claimants ! There is clearly room, then, for a social life on a better plane, and the merchants and capitalists of Vienna might introduce it. But, alas ! they are all very much under the delusion that blood and title are the only things much worth having. We often regret in America that *money* has so much social power ! It is sadly to be deplored that it has not more here. Its inability to purchase admission into the noble circle makes it undervalued too much even for enterprise and success in its own proper sphere. Whether this false and feudal notion of the value of *blood* can be exorcised in Austria in our time is doubtful, but it is an incubus on a true national life, and keeps society here on an unimproving and a discouraging basis.

The next obstacle to a true participation on the part of Vienna in the life of other great capitals, London, Paris, Berlin, New York, is the shocking domination of the Catholic hierarchy. Austria proper is almost a purely Catholic country. Out of more than thirty millions it has only 300,000 Protestant subjects. Amid its myriad Roman Catholic churches stand scattered, here and there, 190 Protestant churches all told! And what Protestantism it has is essentially torpid and unprogressive, presenting nothing attractive or promising. Indeed, so far as I can learn, the Protestantism here, except so far as it has been invigorated by some twenty pastors educated in Prussian schools of theology, is a narrow, dogmatic, repulsive, and worse than that, a cold and apathetic thing, which supplies no real want and meets no heart-felt acceptance.

Vienna has three Protestant churches and a Protestant population of perhaps 30,000, an intelligent German, thrifty class, largely merchants. It has a Lutheran and a Reformed church, side by side, in one building (now a hundred years old), and these bodies, representing different confessions, are agreed in supporting one common school. It has another Lutheran church of costly character, capable of holding a thousand people. One of the elders told me that he never went to church, but was very attentive to the monetary affairs of the church. He said that none of the elders attended public worship! I met for a few moments, accidentally, a half-dozen of the pastors of the Reformed Church, gathered from a district reaching from Trieste to Prague. It was a very discouraging assembly! The Lutherans are stronger, but make no considerable headway. Their best hope lies in promoting schools of their own, which shall be legally protected, and in laboring to secure a law for which they are striving, to make all the public schools in Austria free from a religious test, either as to the teachers or the children. At present, Roman Catholic mass or prayers open the schools and gymnasiums. The Protestant children are allowed to come late, and to go out before the service. But the instruction is all in the interest of the Roman Church. You find, even in the medical schools, the universities, and all the most dignified places of instruction, the crucifix set up, with images of saints, and the whole hierarchical apparatus of appeal to the senses. I saw in a new hospital to-day, in Vienna, a half-gross of crucifixes in *biscuit*, set up on walnut pedestals (and worth each in New York ten dollars), all of one pattern, and lying in a heap like so many dolls on a counter, but which were destined to be set up in each room of the hospital.

With Protestantism thus dead and powerless in a country which it once might almost have called its own, Roman Catholicism is not (out of the Tyrol and a part of Bohemia) really alive, but its corpse encumbers the whole ground. The hierarchy (not the Church) is alive, and was never more powerful. The priests hold the royal family in their grasp, and, through the Emperor and the women of his house, largely control the policy of the government. The Catholic laity are not as a rule in sympathy with their hierarchy. They know that the generous counsels of Joseph II., and other liberal rulers and ministers, have often been repressed and defeated by these cardinals, bishops and priests. They believe that their present Emperor, when still uncertain of his life after the blow he received from the deluded Hungarian patriot, who nearly killed him with a blow at his neck in his own garden (in 1853), promised the archbishop who came to give him extreme unction, that, if he recovered, he would make the infamous "*Concordat*" with the Pope. This archbishop is

the only person who day or night has the privilege of entering unannounced the Emperor's presence; and the people
feel that this means only restraint and injustice for them.
They dread, too, a back-stairs influence, exerted under ecclesiastical inspiration by the ladies of the court, even more
than the influence on the Emperor.   They think measures.
often fail, after they have escaped all other opposition, from
a final blow in the dark, dealt by a priest through a woman's
sleeve !

But, more than all, and worse than all, Austria and Vienna are Catholic in all their usages, habits, expectations, tempers and sympathies, without having faith in their own creed
or their own priesthood!   Men and women, yes, and occasionally priests themselves, privately confess, it is affirmed
here, their unbelief in their religion; but a thousand more
have not interest enough to do even this.   A monstrous indifferentism is the true name for their condition.   And on
this stolid indifferentism the hierarchy builds.   It is almost
as firm a foundation as superstition itself.   Busy, skillful, patient and cautious, the priesthood preserves the powers and
sway of the Church and lets religion take care of itself.   It is
all they can do to protect and uphold the spectacle and keep
the solid income, and exercise the vast political and social
control they possess over education, marriage, hospitals and
asylums of all classes ; over the nobility and the women and
the children.   The men, so long as they are not noisy about
their indifference, may practice what negligence they will.
On one point, that of marriage, there is a general sensitive-
ness which promises some reform.   Every body knows that
if Protestants marry Catholics the children must be brought
up Catholics ; that divorce is not possible by any legal process.   This works in the present condition of things terrible
evils.   It drives thousands to matrimonial relations without

marriage. A frightful percentage of the children in Austria, and specially in Vienna, are born out of wedlock. There is an earnest effort, Catholics and Protestants uniting, to get marriage made a civil contract. Another vehement and well-nigh successful effort is making to free the teachers of schools and the character of schools from any confessional test. It would be the first great step in the emancipation of Austria from a Catholic paralysis.

But, after all, the character of the people themselves is the chief obstacle to the progress of religious or political liberty. Either they have so long been accustomed to a paternal government, and to an aristocratic or priestly hierarchy that they can not imagine the advantages of a state of society without it, or they are constitutionally torpid and inapt as respects economic, social and political life. For instance, they have in Vienna an excellent city charter and constitution—almost democratic in its character. There are at least 50,000 voters who, divided into three classes (according to the amount of taxes they pay), may elect and send to their Common Council—which has great powers—such representatives as they will. In one district, out of 1200 voters not a hundred used their privilege! Perhaps not 5000 votes could be got out for any election ! The offices of Mayor and Alderman go a begging. They are unpaid and laborious, it is true, but honorable and influential ; they can not find public interest enough among the citizens to take these offices.

The general government, in true Austrian style, continued one Common Council and its Mayor in office for twelve years, without calling on the people to elect new officers ; and they submitted as quietly as lambs to this atrocious infringement on their rights. What a paralysis of political life is here indicated ! The people have been so long accustomed to be superintended, interfered with, and protected, that they have lost the sense of freedom. Until recently they possessed no right of assemblage, and could not even meet together to hear the views of their candidate for an election. Joint-stock companies were all matters of special and exceptional privilege, and could not hold a business meeting without the presence of a government commissioner to watch their proceedings and forbid what he did not approve! Hedged and shackled in this painful way, is it strange that every form of large industry is behindhand? Two very important acts have this very week received the imperial assent, allowing the right of assembly, and the freedom of association in corporate bodies. But it is certain that the Austrians do not yet know how to use even the fresh liberties they so slowly acquire. The government may almost be said to be more willing to give than they are to receive liberal measures. Indeed so enlightened a minister as Von Beust must find his chief obstacle in the apathy of the people. The government sees more or less clearly that the Austrian people can not carry the necessary and fresh taxation which can alone relieve the national credit unless its spirit is quickened to more enterprise, activity and industry; and the only kind of food that will effect this enlivening is what was so long known as the wild oats of liberty! Thus more liberty for the people has become a government necessity. But, alas! the people who suppose they are very hungry for this food have hitherto shown very little appetite when it was set before them. They do not use a tenth part of the freedom they have. They take out their dissatisfaction with their Church and their aristocratic government in gibes and theatrical caricatures, or in pictures in their Austrian *Punch.* If they are only left free to laugh and joke at the expense of their superiors and privileged oppressors, they are content to leave them all their powers and privileges. There is a certain freedom in the press and on the stage here in Vienna larger than one meets in Prussia. The government seems so confident of the tameness of the people that it allows them (within wide boundaries) to say what they will. The editorial corps are witty Jews generally, who write with much *esprit*, but who neither lead nor intend to lead to any political action.

The theatre is an institution here of incredible importance. Many people seem to live on its breath. The performances are the most familiar topic of conversation, and in a banking-house, in the busiest hours, I was kept waiting to-day while the manager discussed the merits of Gounod and Wagner with a trio of earnest German visitors. The Court Theatre, a wretched place under the imperial roof, has a most refined and accomplished company, who act on the whole better than any company I have ever seen. The parquette is open to the public, but the boxes are all bought by the aristocracy, and they assemble as if at a family party, to meet always the same people and enjoy society without any domestic trouble or expense. There is no extravagance of costume and no excess of beauty in these boxes. It is very much the same with the Royal Opera, which has a shabby house, but an excellent company. A magnificent new opera-house, the rival of the one now building in Paris, is rapidly approaching completion. It will hold three or four thousand people, and is finely situated. But it is in the people's theatres that one sees how serious is the charm of dramatic entertainments for this community. Really, to see their democratic aspirations acted out in a play, seems almost better to them than to have the trouble of sustaining them in actual life! They enjoy a sharp satire on a brainless prince or a meddling bigot better than the abatement of aristocratic or ecclesiastical hindrances. The Viennese have lost the capacity for public life and ad-

ministrative and executive action, under the long reign of
military bureaucracy and that form of paternal government
which is an iron hand in a silken glove.

Soldiering is still more the bane of Austria than of Prussia.   From the monarch down, every Austrian is more or less
a soldier, on drill, under orders, and with a tendency to a hierarchical dependence.   Now there is no bigger *child* in the
world, in a political or social sense, than a soldier—if it be
not a sailor.   A soldier is one small part of a great human
machine, for whose general movements he has no responsibility.   His highest wisdom is to know nothing of reasons,
but to obey orders with the blindest punctiliousness.   He is
to love his flag and to adorn his uniform ; to know all the
etiquette of his rank, and to sink his personality in his regiment.   The Crown Prince is brought up between a soldier
and a priest.   He is first a soldier and then a Catholic, and
when he ascends the throne, soldiers and priests are his sole
idea of wisdom and influence, and this idea descends through
all the nobles and gentry and people.   The army is the only
possible way of rising socially.   All the finest young men go
into it.   It makes them essentially decorous idlers.   It helps
to keep labor of brain and hands under reproach.   There is
no proper emancipation yet from the notion that the professions and commerce and trade are ignoble occupations.
These dreadful standing armies are the curse of Europe.
They cost the people a hundred times more than the fearful
show they make in the budget !   Their worst influence is in
subtracting from industry such vast quantities of labor, in
making idleness respectable, and in substituting the drill-ser-
geant for the individual judgment and conscience of men.

Another sad blow at the prosperity of Austria and Vienna
is the number of saints' days and festivals.   About once a
week all labor ceases, and the people are given up to festivi-

ty and church-going. Twice in ten days it has occurred since we have been here. Once it was the day of St. Leopold, patron of the Austrian Church. The stores were universally closed, and all industry ceased. Even the theatres were shut—which they are not on Sundays. A few days later, the Empress's baptismal day was the signal for the closing of the schools. It is estimated that four hundred millions of industry is annually lost by the forty days of Church festival that occur in Austria. The worst is not the money lost, but the mental and social habits engendered. Religion and idleness move together. The saints give the people all their worldly pleasures, and take them away from their serious duties and disciplinary cares.

Austria is by no means overburdened with population, especially in her eastern provinces, which, under a proper land system, might support thrice their present numbers. But, alas! she is ridden to death with indigence and poverty, which she unconsciously increases by her false political economy. Beggary is rendered almost a necessity by the fewness of the hands in which the lands are found, and the habitual dependence of the people on a guidance and care which their masters seem ignorant how to afford. There is little dependence to be placed on agents and middle-men. The English system of letting lands for terms of years does not prevail. The proprietor deals directly with his tenants, who are little better than serfs. The people live meanly and without much possibility of saving. They are beggars almost by necessity—and beggary is even more common in the country than in the city. The priest is hardly more than a public almoner. The church-door is a place of alms. Beggary is made almost respectable by the public recognition it receives from Church and State. If a rich nobleman or a monarch visits the Austrian court at any point, he is sure to receive hundreds of begging letters! He must take it into account, as a part of his unavoidable expenses, to satisfy these starving cormorants. And so accepted is the poverty of the masses here that a vast system of almshouses, hospitals and asylums exists, which help to perpetuate the evil it seeks to relieve. I have visited at least a dozen of these institutions, for aged and indigent people of both sexes, for orphans and for the sick. And certainly Vienna has shown vast municipal liberality, and the government an immense zeal and charity in the erection of costly edifices, and in the internal ordering of them an un-stinted hand. •A new almshouse of a most imposing charac-ter, with stone pillars and galleries that would adorn a royal palace, with beds for twelve hundred, and accommodations of an almost luxurious character, may illustrate the subject. The furniture was all of oak, and every bed had an oaken wardrobe, which also opened as desk and table, connected with it. The chairs were handsome and costly. By paying a small sum, a room with only four, or even two beds, could be secured. Otherwise, the hospital was free. The ventila-tion was not satisfactory, even in this new house, which claimed to be a model. Water (of which a very poor supply is found in Vienna) was drawn from the Danube, and then carried by hand from the lower story to all the rooms. In a private house, a friend tells me that it takes the time of one man to supply wood and water to the three stories, a fact which illustrates the condition of mechanical ingenuity and of public enterprise here. This almshouse was not very su-perior to several others. But they were all of them far too good for any sound notions of philanthropy. They actually offered a kind of premium on thriftlessness and idleness. The unsuccessful, the unfortunate and the shiftless are better off under such management than those who by great exertions, constant forethought and self-control, keep their heads just above public charity. In all the Austrian charities I found neatness, abundant and good supplies, and a kind administration. The people, too, did not look cowed and wretched. But I felt terribly the injustice which these vast outlays and ministries was doing to the general spirit of independence and to the overtaxed work-people who saw the fortunate few among the wretched thus petted by a paternal government.

I should mention, in connection with the almshouses, one peculiarity which may be not unworthy of imitation at home. Instead of a certain allowance of food at a common table, each inmate has a daily allowance of twenty-two kreutzers (about ten cents) paid him in cash. A restaurant (the privileges of which are farmed out), with a tariff of very low-priced but wholesome dishes, is kept in a corner of the almshouse. And there the individual inmates go and buy their soup, their bit of meat, their stew or cooked vegetables at incredibly low prices. Enough soup for a man's dinner for three kreutzers, for instance. A man may spare three kreutzers a day for beer, out of this sum, and still feed himself sufficiently. The best effect of the system is some little spirit of independent choice preserved to the poor people, who have their own money to spend in their own way. It is worth thinking whether some similar plan might not be an improvement on present methods in America.

The orphan asylums of Vienna, both Protestant and Catholic, are excellent institutions, and managed at a cost of less than $100 per child. The children looked wanting in red blood, which is perhaps due to the climate of Vienna, in the valley of a river that carries malaria in its channel. Typhoid fevers seem the most common form of malady in this region.

The schools are as good as the want of eager appetite for knowledge and the absence of practical tendencies will allow. They spend a unconscionable time on drawing. They teach

T

writing before reading, by a process which merits the attention of teachers.   The children learn to read almost without
knowing it, by this method, which seemed to me both novel
and excellent.   There are three or four high schools, one a
Protestant school, another the commercial college, another
the gymnasium, which have sprung up in Vienna out of the
associated efforts and contributions of private citizens, which
interested me as much for their origin as their general character.   They uniformly make the casket finer than the jewel,
and expend absurd sums in the brick and mortar and decorations of their schools.   But they have learned teachers, and
no doubt education is as well carried on as it can be when
divorced from liberty.   But how is it possible to educate to
any real purpose, without the co-operation of that liberty
which secures an open career and stimulates with hope and
aspiration all the faculties of free peoples?

Only yesterday a great event in its symbolic import occurred in Vienna.   Parliament has just abolished *chains* as a
part of criminal punishment, and also *whipping*.   Yesterday
being the Empress's baptismal day, the new system was in-
augurated.   Two hundred criminals were carried in their
chains (which some had worn ten years) into the church connected with the prison, and there their chains were struck
off, and they were returned unbound to their cells and work-
yards.   It is a happy augury for Austrian liberty!

I visited with interest the abattoirs of Vienna.   This city
claims to have been the first to establish public butcheries,
and for a quarter of a century has enjoyed their advantages.
The cattle are driven in or brought by rail from Hungary,
Poland, and nearer parts of the empire, and seemed lean and
scraggy ; not in the least degree stall-fed.   It is not surprising
that beef in Austria is generally so poor, or that they find it
expedient to cook it so much and to serve it with a made

gravy, and never *à l'Anglaise,* i. e., rarely done, and with its own juice. Nor is it strange that veal should be considered as a greater luxury than beef, and should be sold at a higher price. Beef sells at from eighteen to twenty-three cents per pound, and is always rising. The butchers are obliged to bring all their beeves to the public abattoirs, where 2000 oxen per week are slaughtered. The carcass is cut up always in one way, and separated into its several qualities, weighed and parceled out to the butchers, not always from their own oxen, but according to a system by which they have their proportion of the whole lot slaughtered at one time. The various parts of the animal are almost completely used up, either by what is returned to the butchers as beef, or by various processes carried on in the abattoir itself. The entrails are used in blood baths, applied for the cure of various rheumatic and other diseases, in a cure-establishment carried on every slaughtering-day in the abattoir, and much resorted to. Extraordinary cures are boasted from this process. I saw no evidence of special success in keeping the premises sweet and inoffensive. Indeed, the want of abundant water in a running state is a great obtsacle to this result. Vienna is very far from being a sweet-smelling city. The air is loaded in parts of it with the odors arising from various manufactories. A large factory of the albumen from the blood of cattle is made profitable, and the smell of this valuable and necessary article taught me first what that peculiar odor that belongs to new cloth came from. It is extensively used in dressing woolens.

The currency in Austria has been for nearly twenty years of *paper.* About four hundred millions are afloat; all the country can bear. The national debt is about three thousand million florins. It runs behindhand a hundred millions a year, and borrowing has become almost impossible. The currency varies from 120 to 125 for 100 in gold. After the victory at Custozza, it went down to 107. But it has gone up again, and nobody sees any prospect of resuming specie payments. Prices, as with us, rise with the rise of gold, but do not fall with its decline, as we have seen in America. Vienna is thought a very dear city to live in ; but it is not dear compared with New York, although the people live much more closely. The Germans and Austrians are economical in their habits, but the Austrians are not thrifty. The women are poor accountants, and spend what they have on hand, and then live *small* until more comes in. There is a certain clumsiness in all their tools, methods and arrangements ; a want of practical adjustment and sense of proportion and fitness. Their public buildings are full of practical errors. They commit capital faults in architecture. They have placed their costly opera-house so low as to impair seriously its appearance and convenience. Their entrances and exits are strangely complicated, indirect and confused. It requires great skill and experience to get in and out of any of their most frequented buildings. Their chief houses are built with useless double doors to all the apartments, fitted with awkward and expensive door-handles, and most uneconomically divided up. Improvement in any of their usages is slow and difficult, and they have a strange inaptitude for taking hints from other countries. They excel, however, in small articles of leather, in optical instruments, and in working amber and ivory. There is little emulation in mechanical industry.

Austria is made up of so, many different peoples and original independencies, that its unity is always forced and difficult to maintain. There are at least twenty provinces, speaking as many different languages or dialects. Their Parliament, which invites all to representation, can not prevail on the Czecks of Bohemia to send any members ; and Hungary, half the whole empire, insists upon its independent parliament, which has been granted it under the new arrangement. A third body of representatives from the Austrian and the Hungarian parliaments is˜ now being constituted, which will have the regulation of their common interests. A more complex government than is thus projected it is difficult to conceive of. Wheels within wheels (some of them always on fire) fitly images this political machine, which it seems hardly possible can ever work. And yet Hungary, wildly independent in its temper, seems almost hopelessly incompetent to self-direction. The people are free in feeling, and yet with very little of the democratic practical instincts of self-government. The peasants are proud, idle, and as impatient as princes of any control. Deak, the popular leader, is often in Vienna, where he is called to counsel with the government. He is unmarried, and lives in the most democratic simplicity at home and when here. He will accept no office, but is greater than all the Hungarian Ministers in influence and power. He closes the debates at Pesth with unanswerable summings-up, and carries his points —which are all for moderation—with irresistible effect. He seems to be one of the purest and greatest of living statesmen. Pulsky, who was in America with Kossuth, is now in the Hungarian House of Deputies, and supports the Union. Kossuth stands aloof in Turin, and agitates still for the complete independence of Hungary. Judicious men here, who are republicans at heart, think Hungary must choose between falling under the control of Russia or adhere to Austria. It is a still uncertain problem.

The feeling of many here is that the dreadful blow of Sadowa was necessary to arouse Austria to a true sense of her situation. They speak of their defeat without bitterness.

Benedek is in disgrace, but most candid people seem to think his case misjudged, and that the fate of the Austrian army was not in his hands.   Its bravery is not disputed.   There are no great generals known to exist here, but few doubt that such will turn up if occasion again calls for them.   Military preparations go on as usual.

The new Minister, Von Beust, whom I saw in his seat in the Vienna Parliament, is an intellectual-looking man of fifty, with a very thoughtful, quiet air, a good German head, and bright hair and complexion.   He shows no impatience or heat, and is clearly sobered by his situation.   He is a Protestant and a North-German, and as such in a strange and somewhat unnatural position.   The Crown Prince of Saxony, who is a great friend of the Emperor, recommended him to the place he now holds.   He is evidently doing his best to bring Austria up to the times, but he will have hard driving, and continual opposition from the hierarchy.   He evidently hopes to break up the *Concordat,* the greatest obstacle to Austrian freedom.   The Emperor seems with him, and partially emancipated from Catholic bonds.   May it last!

There is a great deal to see in Vienna in the way of pictures.   The royal gallery is a rare and precious collection, specially rich in Italian pictures and in Rubens and Vandykes.   The Lichtenstein Gallery, for a private collection, is immense and most interesting and instructive, and so is the Ambras collection.   But I have no room to speak of them.

The public monuments are numerous; but almost uniformly bad, not to say disgraceful, in taste and execution.   There is not one really handsome statue in any public square in the old city.   Joseph II. seems gratefully and tenderly remembered as the largest and most liberal-minded of their sovereigns, always excepting his mother, Maria Theresa, whose fame certainly does not exceed her deserts.   Since Joseph, the sovereigns have been weak-minded. Ferdinand was proverbially feeble; Francis, his uncle, not much stronger. The present Emperor is a good-natured, reserved man, full of his prerogative, but of a shilly-shallying disposition; easily disheartened and easily recovering confidence. He is fickle and inconstant, and is said to often contradict himself flatly. Riding and hunting are his chief solaces. If he imitates the great sovereigns, it is in their follies—such as driving across his empire post-haste in a shorter time than any monarch had ever done before. His wife is the most beautiful woman in her court, but is somewhat masculine in her tastes for horses and dogs, and not of a serious turn except as it respects the authority of the priests. Maximilian had more sense and energy than his brother, but was selfish and ambitious, and has not as good a name at home as he enjoys abroad. The other brothers are commonplace and ill-looking. The Parliament is a dignified body in appearance, and seems to have a Greek priest and a Roman priest among its Deputies.

St. Stephen's Church, now under repairs, is a magnificent structure, with an exquisite tower of the most shapely proportions and delicate traceries. It is gloomy beyond expression within, and so obstructed with columns and stagings that it produces less effect than one anticipates. The other churches are not striking. There is a good deal of external gilding about some of the modern buildings, which gives a hint of the Orient. The Danube is here not impressive, and plays no important part in the aspect of the city. Several bridges —one with a set of new statues uncovered only yesterday— cross the canal, and give variety to the street views. But on the whole Vienna is not as impressive a capital as Berlin. I must leave a few paragraphs about the new city to my next letter.

XXXIV.

VIENNA AND TRIESTE.

AUSTRIA, November 24, 1867.

THE new city of Vienna promises to make up in due time for the deficiencies of the old town in sightliness, expanse and splendor. Already it is brilliant with ornamental buildings, and liberal in squares, which are adorned with fresh equestrian statues of a costly character. Prince Eugene, the Archduke Charles, and Schwarzenberg, are worthily commemorated in recent monuments of this kind, erected by the present Emperor. A few years will enable "The Ring" to rival the Boulevards of Paris with more success than any other city. The eight statues on the bridge, uncovered only day before yesterday, are exceedingly pleasing, especially one of a reigning Bishop, whose name slips my memory.

To-day a new store is opened at the most commanding business point in the city, which aims to be the "Stewart's" of Vienna. It has cost over a half-million of florins, and is built in a very showy style, on an irregular lot, where land was worth three hundred florins by the eight feet square. Yesterday the Emperor and Empress visited this establishment. I went over it to-day. It compares very poorly in extent or splendor, in stock of goods or in convenience of arrangement, with very many American "stores," but it is thought a miracle of enterprise here. Crowds hang about the windows, and policemen guard the doors. The house has six factories at work on carpets, upholstery and furniture; one in Bradford,

England. It deals almost exclusively in Austrian goods. It means to sell better goods at lower prices, and so command an extensive market. It gives six months' credit to substantial customers. It is a sign of progress of an encouraging kind in this slow community. May good success wait on " Philipp Hass & Sohne, Grabengasse, No. 32, Vienna !"

We visited the Ambras collection this morning, which is justly celebrated for its old armor; but it should be seen before the Dresden collection to be greatly enjoyed. The positive connection of the suits of armor with actual historical personages gives them a great additional interest. Philip II. and Alva are both brought vividly to mind by the very mail they cased their bigoted and cruel hearts in. A collection of portraits of apparent authenticity is of still greater interest. One of Mary Stuart and another of Queen Elizabeth hang side by side very harmoniously, which is perhaps accounted for by the diminished beauty the artist has given the Scottish Queen, and the diminished homeliness he has bestowed on the English. Some very rare Egyptian mummy-cases, of stone, are found in this collection ; and some curious relics of Montezuma, and of Turkish sultans. The ends of the earth have been most industriously compassed for the traces of all distinguished princes and warriors, who seem to be the only persons held worthy of commemoration in these Austrian museums.

One place in Vienna has a profound interest. It is the vault of the Capuchin monastery, in which are collected the ashes of a hundred and one imperial and princely persons— emperors and their wives and children, and brothers and sisters with their children, a few princely bishops and one plain countess—Maria Theresa's governess and friend. The oldest sarcophagus (they are all of bronze) is of the wife of King Matthias, the founder of the monastery; the newest contains

T 2

the remains of the King's sister, who was accidentally burned to death only last summer. It was still loaded with garlands. Maria Theresa, with her husband, lies here on a most costly but ugly tomb, near the very spot where, for so many years, she spent an allotted hour, once every week, with the ashes of her beloved Francis. Her sixteen children are gathered about her, and at her feet, in the plainest coffin in the vault, sleeps the son, Joseph II., who had so much of his mother's genius and nobleness, and who left orders to be thus unostentatiously buried at her feet. The great vault where all this imperial dust sleeps, is a simple, unadorned and almost unsafe place, approached by a narrow and unconspicuous passage through the monastery, and guarded by a little friar who, with a poor lantern, guides you through the extended circuit of brazen coffins. One half wonders that some unscrupulous adventurer has not profaned this sanctuary and stolen a handful of this precious dust! What would not Napoleon do to redeem the body of the young Duke of Reichstadt, who still lies by his mother's side in this family sepulchre?

The monument, by Canova, to the Archduchess Christina, is next in interest to his beautiful work in St. Peter's, the tomb of a Pope. But Murray describes it so well that I will not attempt to commemorate it. It is in the Church of the Augustines, where the "hearts" of the Austrian Emperors are buried. Their entrails are buried in still another church. I hope there is nothing ominously significant of Austrian policy and destiny in this strange partition of the imperial remains.

The city government erected, last year, a kursaal, or pump-room, in the small park on the Ring, which cost 360,000 florins—a mere place of morning resort for summer idlers not able to visit the watering-places. Mineral waters are sold here, freshly furnished from all the popular wells on the

Continent It is a costly bauble, and shows that it is not New York Common Councils alone that know how to squander the public money. The relative cost of building in Vienna and New York may be partly inferred from the following figures :

Cost of the Abattoir,	976,500 florins.	
Orphan House for Boys,	82,535 "	Without the
" " for Girls,	54,400 "	land.
Kursaal,	360,000 "	
New Almshouse,	570,000 "	

I can only say that at the present rate of labor and materials in New York, I do not believe any one of these buildings could have been erected for less than twice the amount they cost here.

The Emperor is building a beautiful Gothic church, which already shows that it will be among the finest modern ecclesiastical structures. Stone seems abundant, but brick and stucco are chiefly used, and brick is very skillfully and architecturally employed. No finer modern use of it is to be found than in the Gymnasium here. The stone galleries of the interior of this building are among the finest modern triumphs of architecture.

TRIESTE, ADRIATIC, November 27.

We left Vienna just as a glorious sunrise was ushering in what gave every promise of being a bright autumn day, such as that leaden sky seldom looks down upon! The Alps send a low spur of the Noric range almost to the gates of Vienna, and in its valleys are hid away many villas and shady hamlets, to which the citizens fly in the hot months to get out of the unwholesome breath of the city. The railroad over the Semmering rises after a few miles, by very sharp grades, and brings you in two hours from Vienna into the heart of a wild mountain district. You are surprised to find yourself,

sooner than from any other great capital, in the midst of Alpine scenery. But we were favored with another surprise !
The train took us from fair weather and bright sunshine
into the heart of a violent snow-storm, which had been raging
all night in the mountains, and three hours from Vienna we
found a foot of snow : trees bending under its weight, snow-
ploughs necessary to our progress, and the people out breaking the high-roads with heavy teams of oxen and sledges.
Winter in true New England severity was all around us, and
it seemed as if it had been there for months.   Five hours
more carried us over the summit—about three hundred feet
high — and down into the valley of the Fröschnitz, into Styria,
where, by noon, we left the storm and the snow behind
us, and through fields trying to smile and looking green in
warm spots, we came out into bright sunshine and clear cold
weather again, and found in the deep blue sky some evidence
that we were already on the southern side of the Alps.   The
scenery on this route is picturesque in the extreme, and it
never loses interest all the way to Trieste.   We looked for a
dull railroad ride of three hundred and sixty miles, such as
we had made between Frankfort and Hamburg, and Hamburg and Vienna, but every mile of the way was charming,
and wanted only summer greenness to be enchanting.   No
more wonderful engineering is to be seen in Europe than
that on the rail-track over the Alps at Semmering ; and between Gratz and Adelsberg, the Drave and Sau, or Save,
present a constant succession of picturesque gorges or openings upon which ruins and churches and castles look down.
Gratz is celebrated for its situation, and appears to be the
home of many retired families of wealth.   Liveried equipages
were waiting at the station for returning travelers.   Already
a certain tinge of the ostentatiousness of the Danubian states
of Europe is apparent in the dress of the people.   Bright

colors and heavy furs and sweeping cloaks, and extensive appurtenances for comfort appear, and the travelers seem to be almost exclusively (in the express trains) people of fortune.

We reached Adelsberg, sixty miles short of Trieste, after twelve hours' steady journeying in the cars, and were soon established in "The Golden Crown." The next morning we started off on foot, with seven guides and lighters, to visit the celebrated "Grotto of Adelsberg," generally considered the finest cave in Europe. The country is a porous limestone region, broken by abrupt hills and mountains, nearly bare of trees. It is swept by violent winds and badly watered, and the only lake in the neighborhood has the bad trick of disappearing wholly at capricious seasons, and then suddenly coming back before the peasants can get the small harvests they try to make in its bed safely out of the fields. It is now understood that the lake is drawn off under meteorological conditions into vast subterranean reservoirs beneath the mountains, and when the rains have filled them up, the waters overflow into the lake, through spouts that are visible and may be descended when the lake is empty.

The entrance to the cave is by a natural mouth in the side of a precipice about a mile from the village. The cave is state property, and is closed with an iron gate and protected by a government official who has an office in the village, where tickets of admission, with specifications of the number of guides and lighters and candles wanted, must be obtained, and paid for in advance. There is a regular tariff of charges, and you may order either a small, a moderate, or a grand illumination. Being four in company, we thought ourselves entitled to a grand illumination, although we had very little notion of what that meant. Paying down the re-

quired fee of seventeen florins and a half (about $10), we
started for the cave, accompanied by a man in shiny leather,
who looked as if he might have been used as a swab in a
cannon, by the smoke and grime and grease of his polished
skin.   After waiting fifteen minutes at the mouth of this in-
hospitable Hades (and a very cold one, too!) Pluto appeared at the other side of the gate and turned the lock to receive us.   Meanwhile, a short procession of amiable demons
with torches filed by, in the depths of the cavern, evidently
bent upon lighting our way; and, as we soon found, most
necessary and well-behaved spirits they were, who did an
amount of work for us in the next two hours which only incessant practice could have enabled them to perform so
adroitly and with so little show of trouble.   The road down
into the cave was as smooth and well made as if it had been
on the surface.   It was wide, free from mud or obstructions,
provided with stone steps wherever the descent was sudden,
bridged over chasms, railed in at points of danger, worked
into the sides of stone ledges when necessary, and so arranged as to make a circuit of all the points of interest without often retracing the steps.   A more considerate and judicious ordering of the whole show could not be desired.   Our
provision for lighting up consisted of 160 candles, with five
lighters, and two kept with us besides the chief showman, who
talked intelligible English.   The lighters preceded us, and,
in sconces ready fixed, placed the candles in the chief chambers, of which in turn six or seven were illuminated.   All
the lights were used in each chamber, the skillful hands
managing, while we were detained examining details in the
passages from one to the other, to hurry on and transfer the
candles from one hall to the next in order.   The Poik, a
river of ten rods width and a few feet in depth, enters the
cave, near where the visitor comes in, and is crossed sixty

feet below the surface, a few rods from the mouth of the grotto. It rushes across the floor of the "Great Dome," unseen but with a mysterious voice, and is crossed by a bridge, from which this grand chamber, duly illuminated, seventy-two feet high and one hundred and sixty feet broad, is finely commanded. Either our eyes had not become accustomed to the lamp-light effects, so that we did not discern the color of the walls, or else the external air had affected the freshness of the surface, for we saw here nothing but a brown cave, very grand and impressive, but with little to distinguish it from any other rocky cavern. But as we advanced the peculiar brightness of the limestone became more and more lustrous, the walls growing whiter and whiter every rod, and the crystallization more perfect.

It is impossible to exaggerate the grandeur and beauty of the effect that seemed ever multiplying and heightening about us as we advanced. The stalactites hung from the lofty walls, now in blunt masses ten feet in thickness and now in tender spikes, tapering twenty or thirty feet to a point. From the floor rose stalagmites of similar proportions and variety. Sometimes these met each other in hour-glass forms, and sometimes formed vast columns that seemed to support the roof. Here cathedral effects appeared as if the pillars of a hundred churches of all schools of architecture had been robbed to furnish one great temple. Sometimes I fancied I saw the roof of the Milan Duomo, with its three thousand statues turned upside down and hanging above us ; and here I looked down upon a city with a hundred spires and towers, seen from a distant height by torch-light ! Again, a vast grave-yard crowded with regal sepulchres broke upon the view. Here shrines and chapels, with sculptured images ; there great organs with pipes of the utmost regularity ; sleeping lions and fawns ; busts and uncouth mythological figures ; carved pulpits ; flowing draperies, as if a flight of Titanic angels were just disappearing, but trailed their sweeping garments as they rose into the gloom. The grace, elegance, artificial regularity and exquisite purity of these forms charmed us one moment ; the grotesqueness, novelty and grandeur the next. In one chamber Nature seemed in a rustic mood, and palms and firs and vegetable forms—the banyan and tropical or Norwegian plants—furnished her models ; in another she was in a Gothic humor, and piled up arches and windows and pillars, and hung them with a tracery no architect could have copied. The fluting of some of these columns was exquisite! Again, cushions on cushions of various sizes seemed heaped upon each other, like pillars of shining satin turned to stone. Over these forms the trickling moisture poured its ever fresh varnish, and the sparkling crystals twinkled and flashed like diamonds. The exquisite whiteness of some of the figures was beyond that of Parian marble. But this brightness was contrasted here and there with reddish tints and sometimes with yellow hues. Shawls and veils, wrought with fringes and borders through which the light of the torches came freely, hung in folds that a *modiste* could not have improved. Delicate curtains, thin as window-glass, drooped over our path. We walked for two hours through this palace, aching with wonder and delight, now awed by black shadows and Egyptian sphinxes, and vaulted darkness and solemn echoes, and the mysterious dripping of unseen rain ; and then ravished with the beauty and brilliancy and the convolutions of forms that were neither in the likeness of any thing in heaven or earth, but half of both. There was no gaudiness in the display, no prismatic colors and no bold crystallization ; but the total effect was lovely and perfect, or grand and subduing. When we reached the Calvarenberg, two miles from the mouth, we sang in quartette some familiar hymns, with the echoes for our orchestra, and with a solemn and worshipful feeling of which we shall never lose the grateful memory.

It may be added, for the encouragement of visitors, that there is nothing in the winter temperature of the cave to expose even a woman's health. The thermometer stood at about fifty, and it was a relief to come in and out of the external cold into this equable climate. We found the path nearly dry everywhere ; the dripping did not touch us, and there was no soil upon our garments when we came out. The changes in the cave, which are always going slowly forward, are so gentle that the showman remembered in thirty-five years none to be observed. In all that time not a stone had fallen. There is, therefore, no safer place to visit. It is wonderful to see what the simple law of gravitation, working with water and limestone, has effected in this palace of loveliness. No matter what exalted expectations the visitor may carry in, he will surely come out exclaiming, " One-half was not told me !"

Trieste, at the head of the gulf of the same name in the Adriatic, owes its present importance to the Emperor Charles VI., who made it a free port, and to Maria Theresa, who cherished it. It is now the only important port Austria possesses in the Mediterranean waters except Fiume, about seventy miles east, across the peninsula. The two places will ultimately be united by a railroad. Trieste has now about a hundred thousand inhabitants. Italian is the language most commonly spoken, although all tongues are heard here. A great variety of costumes is seen in the streets, the fez and the sash, the Turkish trowser and the gay frogged tunic with red waistcoat, with ornamental slippers or long boots ; and still more of the ordinary European dress. The women are coarse and weather-beaten, and without any special picturesqueness of costume. They carry all the waters from the public fountains, balanced in heavy tubs, upon their heads. Sailors sing and shout in the streets, and many bare-legged and half-clothed men are always at work on the piers. The wharves are of solid stone and great beauty, and exhibit a marked contrast with the rickety wooden structures that bear that name in New York. The streets of the new town are beautifully paved with stones of six or eight inches in thickness, and of the size of the flags on our sidewalks. They form the smoothest and clearest surface I have anywhere met in streets. Being of limestone, they do not appear to slip under the horses' feet, in spite of their nearly perfect smoothness. The buildings in the new town, which is built on a plain between the old city and the mountains that so steeply hem in Trieste, are modern and substantial; the new exchange and the theatre are even elegant. A canal runs up into the heart of the new town, permitting small vessels to come to the doors of the warehouses. Hundreds of vessels, generally small, lie within the inner or outer piers. They are somewhat crowded, and the accommodation is clearly insufficient. There is really no natural harbor here, only a fine roadstead—but art has furnished a tolerable harbor, which may be much farther improved. If Austria holds together, it will be worth her utmost pains to make Trieste a safe and large harbor as well as a free port. The trade of Hungary and of all Austria south of the Alps, not to say much Italian and German trade, may, by a judicious system of railroads, be concentrated on this port. Already a very large trade is carried on here with all parts of the Mediterranean, Great Britain, South America, and especially the Levant. Great quantities of wheat are sent to Buenos Ayres. Wheat, lumber, ship-timber, oil-cake, olive-oil, figs, raisins, currants, and other dried fruits, form the principal exports. The old town, built on the side of the hill, is a curious collec-

tion of stone streets, fifteen feet wide, and they creep up
toward the citadel and cathedral, walled on either side, so
that you might as well be in a tunnel so far as any view is
concerned.

The cathedral is a very ancient building, externally ugly,
but with an impressive interior on account of its simplicity
and its five-pillared aisles.   There are some curious old mo-
saics in the recesses that terminate the aisles, which date
from the fourteenth century.   Don Carlos, ex-king of Spain,
with his wife and son, are buried here in a very simple way.
The great antiquarian, Winckelmann, is buried in the adjoining cemetery, where a tomb erected by the subscriptions of
many kings and princes, and many citizens of Trieste, celebrates his genius and guards his memory.   On the face of it
his figure carrying a torch, the light of which falls on an
Egyptian enigma and some Roman or Greek mystery, is followed by the Muses and the Arts, whom he is conducting to
new triumphs.   Around the tomb are gathered fragments of
classical antiquity—slabs with inscriptions, bits of columns
and other very ancient remains, laid there from time to time,
as if waiting for the great antiquary's attention, or as tributes
to his taste and learning.   There are fine views to be had
from the citadel and the terrace before the cathedral.   Two
Greek churches (one of them a very costly one, which is slowly approaching completion) show the influence of Oriental
Christianity upon this community.   There are many Greek
merchants in town.   The funeral of a lady took place in the
Greek church the morning after our arrival.   At least fifty
persons, each with a burning candle of the size of a hoe-han-
dle, stood round her coffin.   It is astonishing what virtue is
attached in Catholic and Eastern Europe to wax and tallow!
So many pounds of it, burned at a festival or a funeral, are
indispensable to any proper expression of joy or grief!

No American merchants are here. I heard indeed of no American citizens excepting our accomplished Consul, Mr. A. W. Thayer, and two ladies, American born, wedded to English merchants. Mr. Thayer is still engaged upon his life-work, an exhaustive biography of Beethoven. The first volume has already appeared in German, and has been welcomed with enthusiasm by competent critics in Europe as the first reliable history of this wonderful genius. The two remaining volumes will follow just as fast as Mr. Thayer's scrupulous exactness will allow him to prepare them; and I fear that will not be under two or three years. Mr. Thayer's numerous friends of the press, and musical and literary companions, will be glad to hear that his health is improved since a very serious illness of some months ago, and that his duties here, which are not small, are fulfilled to the satisfaction of all his countrymen. His musical scholarship surprised and delighted me—but not more than his patriotism and his enthusiasm about his old Harvard College friends.

Three miles from Trieste, on the shore of the Adriatic which it overhangs, is the exquisite villa of the late unhappy Maximilian, styled Emperor of Mexico. Miramar is well named from its superb *sea-view*. The snowy summits of the coast-range of the western shore of the Adriatic are in distant sight. Behind the villa rise terraced slopes of wine-growing hills, half-tropical in their aspects; before the sea-wall spreads out the lovely gulf, its shallows purple, changing into blue as the waters deepen, while to-day white-caps and drifting sand, with a wind that sometimes smooths the sea in spots as with oil, diversify the prospect. At the left Trieste is in full view, with its piers glistening, its citadel and its hills sprinkled with villas, and above all its numerous masts. The villa is an elegant Italian mansion, large enough for dignity and not too large for domestic comfort. It is directly

over the sea, and has for a summer residence perfect fitness.
The grounds behind it, within thirty or forty acres, contain
more variety and elegance of arrangement than I have yet
seen combined within so small a space. There is hardly
any thing wanting in the way of winter or summer gardens,
sheltered retreats, shaded alleys, fountains and fish-ponds,
staircases mounting to new levels ; water-gates, reached by
broad stairs ; flights up successive terraces to Belvederes,
and surprises of caves and arbors, prepared against every
temperature of summer heats or winter colds. To these add
statues and ornamental trees, the choicest evergreens and
the richest flowers in hot-houses, and in the open gardens.
Even in this cold November day, roses are blooming in the
open air and the atmosphere is full of perfume. A most
delicate taste has presided over these grounds. The very
vines and plants seemed to us specially refined and lady-
like. No coarse creepers or large vines are seen, but only
the most exquisite and dainty ones. An inscription tells the
visitors that " The plants in this garden are committed to the
protection of the public." It is a fine feature of Austrian
hospitality that the gardens of the nobility are uniformly and
freely open to the people, who make a great use of them.
Maximilian, whose remains are weekly expected at this port,
was for a considerable time the commanding admiral in the
Austrian navy. He first went to sea in the Novara—the ship
that now bears home his ashes—and subsequently circumnav-
igated the globe in her and published some record of his
travels. He was popular and beloved in Trieste, for his
kindness to the people and his interest in the improvement
of the harbor and town. I notice a public subscription open
in the exchange, for a monument to his memory. It was
saddening to walk in the alleys and to sit in the summer-
houses where he and the Archduchess must so often have

been happy together, and to think that while he was wrecked in fortunes and she in reason—while the husband was floating in his coffin toward this beautiful shore, to find here a grave, and the wife was worse than dead, a widow without knowing it, a discrowned empress and a witless woman—Miramar smiles as if unconscious of its master's or mistress's fate! What a heaven on earth ambition has closed upon those hapless princes!

END OF VOL. I.

Lightning Source UK Ltd.
Milton Keynes UK
UKHW012206090622
404215UK00002B/45

9 783375 014216